LINGUS

A ROMANCE COMEDY NOVEL

NEW YORK TIMES AND
USA TODAY BESTSELLING AUTHOR

MARIANA ZAPATA

Editing: Hot Tree Editing

Cover Design: Letitia Hasser, Romantic Books Affairs

Formatting: Indie Formatting Services

To my bear—Chris,
the biggest pervert I will ever know.
Thank you for everything,
but mostly for being my favorite
pain in the ass.

Love you.

CHAPTER ONE

"I don't want to go in there," I snapped, trying to dig my heels into the concrete floor beneath me.

"You can't back out now!" Nicole, my best friend, hissed. She wrapped her fingers around my elbow and pulled me in the direction of the glass doors ahead of us. "Come on, bitch!"

This was a horrible idea. I had known it from the moment she brought it up, more than two months ago. When she mentioned coming to the convention, she had winked a sneaky eye at me and said, "We're going to the convention and you're *cumming*! Get it?" Yes, I did get it. Un-fucking-fortunately. Now there we were, right outside the convention hall with our passes around our necks, and I wanted to vomit and die, in no specific order.

"Nikki, I really don't want to go in there. Please," I begged.

She just rolled her eyes and sighed in annoyance. "I don't give a shit. I got you a pass, and we're going in. Do you know how hard it was to snag these bad boys?" she asked, pointing at the laminates around each of our necks. "It was a bitch. So, you and I are going in there whether you want to or not."

My eyes flickered left to right, watching the varied groups of people milling around the outside. There were men and women of every age, a few dressed in casual jeans and T-shirts, others not so much. Tiny skirts, platform heels, leather pants, and lingerie were also staples in the present fashion. I sucked in a breath and tried to ignore the bursting heat swallowing my cheeks whole. No one seemed to be paying any attention to us; we were both dressed pretty conservatively compared to the other people here.

For once, I felt out of place with my clothes. My skinny jeans, blue blouse, and flats seemed so conservative here I felt like I was starring in *Alice in Wonderland.* "Nikki..." I whined like a little kid.

"Shut up. You'll thank me for this later," she huffed and pulled at my elbow again.

I knew there was no point fighting with her. Nicole Jonasson always got her way. Always. It was one of the things I loved most about her; she was fearless and strong. Despite her current attitude and shit-talking, Nikki was one of the nicest people on the face of the planet. You just had to get to know her. When I met her for the first time in English Lit, she had just finished tearing a guy a new asshole for not holding the door open for a wheelchair bound student in our class. She was tall, sandy-haired, hazel-eyed, and just absolutely kick-ass.

I fell in love with her after she looked at the student with violence in her eyes, and muttered a frustrated, "I'm going to break into your room when you're sleeping at night and take a shit on your face if you ever forget to hold the door open for another person again." Needless to say, we ran into him a few years later and caught him holding the door open for at least a good minute for the person trailing behind him.

She was everything I wanted to be in life—strong and confident. There was nothing that Nicole, or Nikki as I usually called her, couldn't overcome.

Including me.

"Oh, my God," I moaned as she pulled me behind her through the glass doors.

The two security guards at the doors checked our credentials before allowing us into the convention. A banner loomed above the entrance, proclaiming to every person who entered that they were at the Adult Film Association's Expo. Just below it, a huge picture of a pretty redhead with jizz all over her face further welcomed convention goers, and I tried my best not to balk at her look of feigned pleasure. A big goop of it was stuck to her eyelashes, and I couldn't help but wonder to myself how much her eye stung after that.

"C'mon, Kat," Nicole called after me, making a beeline for the first booth.

I slowly walked after her, eyeing the really random people who were walking all over the place, crowding over and into booths like kids in a candy store. Well, I guess this was like a large candy and toy store—for adults. Ha.

"Kat! Look at this!" my best friend squealed, turning around, holding a huge glass dildo in her hand.

Oh, my God. How did I ever let her drag me to a fucking porn convention?

CHAPTER TWO

Nicole's warm, hazel eyes narrowed at the appalled look on my face. I couldn't help it, I swear. I liked dildos. They'd become some of my best friends over the last, let's say, three years, but who was counting? The idea of having everyone and their mamas know I liked them, though, kind of creeped me out.

Okay, well, it creeped me out a lot.

Nikki returned the massive, glass artifact to its place on the table. She was right in front of me, her pretty face pinched into a scowl. "Kat, you better wipe that look off your damn face before I slap it off."

My back stiffened instantly. The thing about Nicole was, she didn't make empty threats. If she said she'd run over your dog if it took a crap on her yard, she would. No kidding, and she loved dogs. She also *loved* me. So, I knew she'd slap me in the face.

"Fine," I grumbled, looking down at the floor like a scolded child. "I just feel so awkward..."

"Katherine Berger?" She grabbed my chin and pushed my face up to look her in the eye. "Repeat after me: My name is Kat Berger, and I love porn. There is nothing wrong with enjoying watching two people fuck."

"My name is Kat Berger," I groaned out, clenching my teeth after every syllable. "I like porn. There is nothing wrong with enjoying watching two people fuck."

Nicole dropped my chin and gave me one of her huge, perfect smiles. "Good job, baby. Now let's have some fun!" she cheered and dragged me back to the table where she'd been standing seconds ago.

I felt like everyone was looking at us, but really, no one was paying attention to Goldilocks and me. My nerves were getting the best of me, and my hands were sweating like crazy, and I knew my armpits weren't too far behind. God, I felt like an idiot here. Nicole cleared her throat in a way I recognized as a warning for me to snap out of it before she slapped me out of my funk.

A nice looking, older man stood behind the table, his arms behind his back and a big smile plastered on his face, while Nikki picked up pretty much every goddamn dildo and examined it like she's buying fruit. She was asking him things like, "Would it be okay if I froze it? How long will it last? Do I need to use any specific cleaning product for it?" This bitch was even crazier than I thought. I swear, my vagina clenched at the thought of sticking something frozen in it. Part of me hoped the man would tell her she could use Windex on it, but he didn't.

"You might as well put it in your mouth," I snickered when she held a clear one with a pretty pink swirl an inch away from her face, inspecting the design.

Nicole snorted in amusement and put it back down, telling the nice man she'd be back later on. Her arm slung through mine as we made our way down the first row of booths. There were so many people here that I didn't know what to think. I wasn't really sure what I was expecting from the porn convention, but so far, all the bystanders seemed like your average Joes. I even spotted a few Crocs along the way and shuddered, remembering that my doctor wore Crocs. I would really, really hate to see him here.

"Nikki, what should I do if I see someone I know?" I asked.

I knew I shouldn't care what people thought. I usually didn't, but there was something about the idea of being caught at a porn convention by, let's say, my neighbor, my mom's friend, my mailman, my boss, or just about freaking anyone I knew, that made me feel über uncomfortable. Nicole and I had this discussion at least once every six months. We blamed society for making sex seem so dirty and wrong.

There was nothing wrong with sex. There was nothing wrong with masturbation, blow jobs, anal, or whatever. There was nothing wrong with anything sex related, honestly, besides bestiality, which I refused to even think about. But I was still embarrassed to be seen here, and that made me feel shitty. I wanted to feel secure and nonchalant like Nicole.

"Well, there is something you could do. It's called, get this, saying hi. Have you heard of that before?"

I just laughed at her as we paused in front of another booth with a wide assortment of glittery, jelly-looking toys, and I knew I let out a tiny squeal of excitement. I looked from one side to the other to make sure my kindergarten teacher wasn't standing *right there* before leaning over the table to inspect the treasures laid out on the blue velvet.

After the saleswoman—another nice-looking, middle-aged lady in an 'I heart NY' T-shirt and denim shorts—showed me a particularly fantastic-looking red hummingbird and sold me on its finer attributes, my wallet was thirty dollars lighter. Luckily, I came prepared and stashed my new little friend in my gigantic purse while Nikki snickered and started shoveling out her own thirt dollars.

"Those are nice," a nasally voice said into my ear.

"Uh," I stuttered, turning around to look at the owner of such a creepy-ass voice. A short, stocky man with glasses, which rested precariously on the bridge of his nose, stood there with a weird smirk on his face.

"When you put it on the fourth level of vibration, it's unbelievable," he practically groaned out, eyes rolling and everything, like he was reliving some fond memory in his head.

How the hell did this man know what the fourth level of vibration felt like?

I grabbed Nicole's forearm and dragged her away from the booth as quickly as I fucking could before the man came back to his senses. *That* was the kind of person I was expecting at a porn convention. An uncomfortable feeling of ick crawled across my skin as I tried to mentally bleach out the roll of his eyes.

"Hold on," Nikki hissed as she thrust her little package into her purse. "What the hell was that about?"

"Level four vibration," I said simply, and she grimaced, nodding.

"Disgusting," she agreed and started thumbing through what looked like a pamphlet of some sort. She nodded solemnly, finding the page she was looking for, and winked. "Okay, here's what we're going to do. We need to take advantage of our time. I want to see that fucking sex beast, Calum Burro," she said in a sultry, Spanish accent. She could never say his name with a straight face, and I couldn't hear it with a straight face either. Calum Burro was her absolute favorite porn star. Yes, we had favorites. What's funny was that, obviously, Burro wasn't his last name, you know, but I was fluent in Spanish. I knew *burro* meant donkey. Seriously though, I could see why he chose Burro as his porn stage name. That man was hung like a horse. Yes, I knew a donkey wasn't a horse, but I got his drift.

"He has an autograph signing in an hour, so we should head over there, and then do whatever," she continued.

I snatched the pamphlet out of her hand and started looking through it quickly. If I was here, and I was, I was going to take advantage of this shit, I guessed. I wanted to screech in excitement when I saw the name I'd been looking for on the list of people signing autographs. *Thank you, Lord Jesus,* I said in my head. I really didn't feel comfortable being here, and if this was the one and only time I came to a porn convention in my life, well damn it, I was going to tap into my inner Nicole and take advantage of it, even if it was only for a minute.

"I don't give a shit what we do. We're going to Andrew Wood's booth if I have to get through my old minister to get there," I stated with as much conviction as I could muster.

CHAPTER THREE

I had never seen Nicole this excited before.

I've seen her excited, but never *this* excited. She got excited about the little things in life: sales at Macy's, getting the perfect seat at the movie theater, when I'd buy her a white chocolate mocha from Starbucks, firing employees when they messed up—things of that nature. However, her reaction right then was unheard of. I had always doubted that shaking in excitement was a part of her DNA. I had no idea her eyes could glitter like a kid's at Disney World. I also, sure as hell, didn't know she started yapping a mile a minute when she got really ecstatic.

Jeez, *why*?

Any other person would assume she was on crack by the way she was acting in line. Her big, blonde mane was flapping from side to side as she looked down the walkway between the booths trying to spy "the love of her life." Nikki was the most amazing-looking girl I had ever seen in my entire life; paired up with a loyalty to her loved ones, which rivaled a German Shepherd's, and her passion for standing up for others, she was a force of nature. She was the real deal inside and out. She also knew exactly what she wanted from life, which only heightened her larger-than-life personality. Right then, what she wanted was to get on Calum Burro's radar. There was no doubt in my mind that the half-man half-horse wasn't going to have any idea what hit him.

"Kat, is my makeup okay? I don't have runny eyeliner or anything, right? Do my boobs look good?" she ranted.

I tried my best not to roll my eyes, because really, this was pretty freaking cute, despite the fact that her giddiness was borderline annoying. I loved it when Nikki was happy, though. "Your face is perfect as always, my dear, and your gigantic boobs look motorboat-able." I winked at her and she grinned.

Meaning, she wanted Calum to motorboat her tits. I laughed my ass off for a solid thirty minutes when she admitted that to me a few months before. He could totally do it. I'd seen those 36Ds in person more times than I could count, and those puppies were immaculate.

"Shit, I need to go pee. Will you hold my spot for me?" she asked. I nodded.

He wasn't scheduled to come out and do

autographs for another ten or fifteen minutes, but there were already eight people ahead of us and at least another ten behind. The eight bitches in front were all dressed up like trashy versions of country girls in microscopic cut-off jean shorts. If that wasn't bad enough, the old geezers behind us were wearing enough makeup to stock Sephora for at least six months. It was pretty weird to think that all of these people around me had masturbated to Calum Burro at one point or another. The mental image of the woman behind me, who was old enough to be my great-grandmother and wore something renaissance slash gothic inspired, enjoying some solo time made me want to gag a little.

I was trying to keep my head down as much as possible. The nervousness that bubbled through my veins at getting caught seeing someone I knew was absolutely overwhelming. I would more than likely crap my pants if I recognized someone.

Oh, lord.

"I'm back, biatch." Nicole greeted me a couple minutes later, saddling up next to me.

Suddenly, I realized Nikki wasn't holding a video or a magazine for him to sign when it was her turn like all the other women in line. "What is he signing?" I asked her suspiciously.

"My ass, Kat. What else?" she replied, like I was an idiot who should have known the answer. Out of nowhere, she tugged down one side of her jeans to a patch of tan skin right to the side of her butt crack.

"Classy."

Vivaciously, a guy with frosted tips and a ton of gel appeared behind the signing table, waving his hands. "Ladies! Calum will be here in one minute to begin his autograph session! Thank you for being patient!" he yelled into the crowd.

Nikki squealed like a pig and started hopping around like a cracked-out rabbit. She was acting more like our friend Zoey than herself, but it was too funny to ruin my entertainment by laughing at her and making her self-conscious. I made a mental note to do things like this in order to get the same reaction out of her more often.

She spotted the tall, blond mop of curly hair coming down the walkway first. The man was easily six four, if not taller, and built like a linebacker. Personally, I was more of a fan of soccer players' bodies, with their lean muscles, but who the hell gave a crap when hotness incarnate was *right there*. He was wearing a T-shirt that was a size too small, accentuating the broad, thick muscles of his chest, arms, and back. What surprised me was the big, goofy smile on his face while he made his way up to the booth.

"I'm gonna go over there, okay?" I told Nikki, but by the glazed-over look in her eye, I knew I could tell her I was born a hermaphrodite and she wouldn't bat an eyelash. I stepped out of line and went to stand closer to the empty booth on the opposite side. The girls in line were going insane. Who knew Calum

Burro was the heartthrob of older, horny women?

He sat down, started signing autographs, and talked to his fans, all with a big smile plastered on his dimpled face. Nicole's eyes were frozen to his body. I laughed at the intensity of her glare. I was leaning my butt against the empty table behind me, my ankle crossed over my other foot, when I felt that familiar creep of fabric going up my ass. My eyes were still glued to the pure happiness radiating from my best friend that I didn't even feel my traitorous hand reaching behind me to pull out my wedgie until it was too late.

"Digging for gold?" the person, who I didn't see standing next to me, asked.

In a perfect world, I would have turned around and come face-to-face with a snot-nosed, middle-aged man in desperate need of Proactiv. Oh, how I wished then that my life was based in a perfect world, so my embarrassment would have been apparent, but ultimately, who cared? My ideal Peeping Tom would have been notorious for digging for gold in his nose *and* ass. I could live with that.

Unfortunately, this wasn't a perfect world. In the real world, I peed on myself sometimes when I sneezed or got tickled, I usually farted when I first woke up, and I'd also heard my dad and mom doing the dirty tango in third grade. I swung my head around to look at the witness to my wedgie pulling, when I came face to chest with a very tall guy. I had to look up, and then farther up, up, and up to find the prettiest emerald eyes I'd ever seen looking right at me. They were so bright, they reminded me of the Lite-Brite toy I had as a kid that lit up the colored pegs magically. Those eyes were set into the most perfectly created face of all time, all high cheekbones, chiseled jaw, and full, pink lips.

That pouty mouth morphed into an amused smirk. "Did you find a golden nugget?" the rich, velvet voice asked me.

"Uh..." My fingers were still pinching the material of my godforsaken panties out of my butt crack, and my face felt like there was a wildfire going on beneath my cheeks. And cue the word vomit. "I wish."

Oh, my God. What was wrong with me? The words slipped out of my mouth at the same time that I finished pulling out my wedgie, because I had already gotten caught, so why stop? I was firmly aware that a normal person would have denied picking at their underwear, but there I was, going along with it.

The guy laughed, a deep, throaty sound that should be illegal in fifty states, and his eyes sparkled from underneath the rim of a worn-in, green baseball cap that hid his hair. His face was really way too pretty, so it was weird how disarming his smile made me feel. He eyed my flaming blush, and then gave me a convincingly bashful smile. "I'm sorry, that was rude of me," he apologized. "I tend to say stupid shit all the time."

"It's okay. I say and do stupid shit all the time, too," I tried to say as evenly as I could, but I was a humiliated mess. It was one thing to pull out a wedgie in front of Nikki, Zoey, or Josh, my other closest friend, but a hot stranger? There was no doubt in my mind that God was laughing at me right then.

His entire frame, which seemed to be around six foot two or six foot three, turned toward me. He had a narrow waist and broad shoulders that blocked any view from his other side. I could tell he was muscular underneath the black hoodie he had on, but his gaze was so intense that I forgot for a second where we were. "Are you here for an autograph?" he asked, with a raise of a dark eyebrow.

"What? *No!* I'm waiting for my friend," I said, pointing at the five-foot-ten blonde in line. I felt embarrassed for some reason that he assumed I was standing in line for an autograph from a porn star, but really, we were both at a porn convention, so neither one of us had room to judge the other. "Are you here for an autograph?"

What the fuck is wrong with me? I wondered. I wished there was a version of Pepto-Bismol for verbal diarrhea, because I'd invest in it. My awkward social skills weren't a problem when I was around people I knew. They were well aware of the fact I quite often spouted shit out of my mouth without thinking.

He laughed again, this time a little louder, but

quieted down after a second, looking at the growing line in front of us like he was worried about someone catching him laughing. "No, I'm waiting for my friend, too," he said, with a big smile, displaying perfect white teeth.

I wanted to ask him which whore in line was his friend, but I didn't. I also silently wondered why such a good-looking male specimen was at a porn convention. This guy didn't need porn to get off; he could easily just flash that perfect face at any girl. I was sure they'd flock to him like a bitch in heat looking to get mounted. We just looked at each other for a moment, not saying a word, before I nodded and turned back to look for Nicole, who was next in line to get an autograph from the inspiration of the majority of her masturbatory dreams. Grinning, she looked slightly like a lunatic. The girl talking to Calum started walking away, and I saw Nikki's face transform from a crazed expression into the confident, assured Nicole who I knew and loved. *Oh, shit.*

She leaned over the table to talk to him, voluptuous ass on display for everyone in line to see. A second later, Calum stood up and walked around the table while Nikki started tugging down the back of her jeans.

"What is she doing?" the stranger whispered, leaning to the right, so he was closer to me.

"She wants him to sign her ass," I snorted, watching Calum drop to a knee so her butt was in his face. The girls in line were going ballistic, and I had a sudden fear there was going to be a riot.

He was up a minute later, grinning like a goof, and Nicole looked up at him, saying who knows what, until his face turned bright red. She then slipped something into his back pocket, her hand lingering on his ass longer than necessary. She turned and sauntered toward me, her hazel eyes locking on each of the women in line, like she dared them to say something to her. Fortunately, none of them had a death wish, so no one said anything.

The guy next to me chuckled. "Well, I'll be damned, she made Calum blush."

I wanted to ask him why he thought that was funny, but Nikki was in my face a split second later, smirking. "What did you tell him?" I asked her.

"I told him I wanted to look for his g-spot with my tongue."

Even the guy standing next to me laughed at Nicole's admission.

"I bet he's never heard that one before," she scoffed, a big smile on her face while her eyes flickered between looking at me and the perfect face just to my left. "Ready to go?"

I nodded at her, taking a step forward to walk around the line, but I stopped and turned back around. The big green orbs were burning a hole into me, but his face was so calm it seemed like an oxymoron, so I didn't know what to think. I settled for just giving him a little wave. He gave me a crooked, soft grin and waved at me, too, before I filed out behind Nikki.

"Who was that?" she asked me when we were a couple of booths down.

"Some guy who caught me pulling my underwear out of my crack."

She made a little humming noise in her throat like she was thinking, completely disregarding my wedgie pulling. "He looked familiar..."

Nikki was an attorney who practiced family law. She had the memory of an elephant and could remember each and every one of her clients' names along with their faces and could recite the most obscure things from memory. For example, when we went to Washington D.C. a few years back, she randomly began reciting the Gettysburg Address in its entirety. I wouldn't be surprised if he did look familiar to her. She remembered absolutely everything.

"He was pretty cute," she offered, elbowing me in the rib.

I snickered, elbowing her back. "Cuter than—"

"Are you blind? Hell no! That guy isn't my type. You know what kind of men I like."

"Men with dicks, I know!" I snorted, and she laughed in response.

"You're such a bitch, Kat," she said between laughs. We both knew she tended to like the huge muscular-type build. Frankly, I'd be afraid to get squished by the weight, but she was pretty much a giant of a woman and lean, like an Amazon, so I guessed her body build could handle that much man.

Our conversation was forgotten when she spotted the booth that Zoey was at a few feet away. There were so many people crowded around the corner where the tables were stationed that a tiny feeling of claustrophobia filled my senses for a second before Nikki pulled on my arm and dragged me around the mass of people.

A girl with long, black hair stood at a pole, wearing clear platform shoes on steroids, tossing her hair one way and shaking her ass the other. I wanted to ask her if she stole her skirt from her six-year-old niece, because it wasn't covering up anything. The hot pink scrap of nylon called a shirt had less fabric than my bathing suit tops.

I guessed I could safely assume this was another porn star.

"That's Dakota Amber," Nicole confirmed in my ear. "She wants to be the new anal queen of porn."

Well, hello there. That would explain the huge mass of men crowded around her, all chattering like excited little frogs.

"NIKKI! KATHERINE ALBA BERGER!" a shrill voice screamed out from the edge of the crowd, and sure enough, people turned to look at the source of the voice.

Fuck me.

Of course, the one person in existence who insisted on calling me by my entire name every time she saw me, would continue to do so at the convention where I was trying my best to be as inconspicuous as possible. After eight years of screaming out my full name when we first saw each other, this was the first time I'd dreaded it. Thin arms wrapped around my neck as she clung to me, all ninety something pounds wrapped around me like a spider monkey.

The crowd of people, who were following the trail of the loud voice, locked their gazes on the three of us, and then nodded in appreciation at our spectacle.

Zoey Quinn, or Zoey Star as she was known as by her fans, was one of the most popular porn stars in the world.

She was famous because she only did girl-on-girl scenes.

She jumped up and down while also giving me kisses on both cheeks, like she always did, but usually in private, not in front of a ton of fucking people at a porn convention.

I asked the sweet Lord Jesus to bless me with the power of invisibility, at least for a few minutes.

CHAPTER FOUR

"I've missed you both so much!" Zoey gushed against my neck before dropping her hold and giving Nicole the same treatment. Her appearance at the convention had been a last minute deal. She'd just gotten back to Florida from a filming session California that morning.

The men closest to us were staring, their eyes glazed over much like I imagined a brain-eating zombie's gaze to be when it caught sight of a living, breathing human. I could only imagine what in the hell was going through their minds, and it made me feel really fucking uncomfortable. All they needed to do was go a little slack-jawed and start making droning noises from deep inside their cavities to complete their *Dawn of the Dead* impersonations.

"Did you get to see your future husband?" she asked Nikki, who had an arm draped around our much shorter friend. Where Nicole was freakishly tall, I was freakishly average, and Zoey freakishly small. My brown hair and brown eyes only added to my average status in comparison to my blonde and raven-haired friends.

I once told Zoey she could pass for a middle-school-aged boy, and she laughed her ass off. I really wasn't joking, but I think she thought I was. Zoey was the epitome of petite. Everything about her was doll-like, with her short, vibrant black hair, almond-shaped eyes, tiny boobies, and delicate facial features all packed into a small frame courtesy of her half-Japanese ancestry.

I wanted to put her in my pocket and take her everywhere with me.

Nicole told Zoey all about our escapade at Calum's booth, but my attention span was practically nonexistent. I found myself glancing at the mass of people who were creating a half-circle surrounding the booth where the future anal queen was blowing kisses as she dropped her ass to the floor like a seasoned stripper.

"I'm gonna go pee." I poked Nikki in the back, and she just waved me off.

"I'll wait for you here," she said.

Shouldering my way through the crowd, I tried to venture in the direction where I thought the restrooms were. It amazed me how many people were here. Miami had some major pervs, I had to say. Myself included, of course. A couple of minutes later, I took a sharp left down a row of booths only to find that I was back right where I started.

"Need a tour guide?" a familiar, silky voice asked from behind me.

I turned around to find the same green eyes from earlier peering at me in amusement. "I'm looking for the restroom."

He tilted his head in the direction I had gone earlier, a soft smile crowding the corner of his full lips. "C'mon, I'll show you where it's at before you pee on yourself."

"Thanks," I told him, giving him a smile.

My new friend shoved his hands deep into the pockets of his slim-fitting, worn in jeans. I noticed he'd put his hoodie up and over his baseball cap, so only his face was exposed beneath the black cotton. He smirked. "Are you having fun?"

An unladylike scoff escaped my throat. I blushed furiously, keeping my eyes glued to the floor while I followed him around a left turn. "Well, it's an experience, you know?"

He just laughed as he nodded, as if he completely understood what I was talking about. "That's a polite way of putting it. Did you come out of curiosity or...?"

"You can put it like that," I said, with another smile, looking far up at him. His pretty, sparkly eyes flitted between the floor and me. "I keep expecting to see my grandma here, or something though. It's weird."

I really didn't know why I told him that. It might have been because he seemed to be trying to blend in, like me, by wearing that cap and hoodie, or maybe not. It was his smile, probably, that did it. I was normally pretty quiet by nature. It took me six classes to talk to Josh for the first time, and he was the second most outgoing person I knew besides Zoey.

"I saw my aunt at one of these once a couple of years ago. I think we both wanted the ground to swallow us whole," he admitted.

"I heard my parents having sex once. I was traumatized for life," I offered him like a moron. If I could have punched myself right then without looking like a demented fool, I would have.

He grimaced, but chuckled. "Did you say anything to them afterward?"

"Are you insane?" I snorted.

"Well," he shrugged his broad shoulders, "if you're stuck being traumatized forever, they should be too. Don't you think?"

As stupid as it sounded, I realized he had a point. "I guess," I said before my bastard brain made me relive the memory of that fateful night. *Hurl.* I had just come down the stairs to get a glass of water when I happened to walk by their room and heard noises that would haunt me for the rest of my life. The shudder that made its way through my body was ridiculous, but he chuckled.

After taking another left turn, I realized we were

actually just two booths away from where we'd started our walk, and I looked back and forth down the row before settling my gaze on his face. He gave me that cute bashful smile again, knowing he'd been caught. "The restroom is right here. I'll wait for you so you don't get lost on your way back, okay?"

He was too cute for his own good, and I wanted to know why he was being so nice. "Okay, Magellan."

He held his hand out to me for me to shake. I found myself grasping his large, warm hand without a second thought. "It's Tristan actually, you little gold digger," he said, with a wink.

I laughed like a crazy person the entire time I was in the restroom. The lady who came out of the stall next to mine, wearing a dominatrix outfit, looked at me like I had two heads. I was so thoroughly amused, I didn't give a shit.

A gold digger.

I snorted while I rinsed off my hands, then dried them. This guy, Tristan, was too adorable for his own good. It didn't help that he seemed to feel comfortable enough around me to crack jokes about me. It took Nicole months to start whipping out lines about my bladder control or hair when it resembled a rat's nest. Should I have been offended? Probably, but if Andrew Wood, my all-time favorite porn star, made fun of me, I would laugh and smile. If he said I was a man, I'd go with it. Tristan felt like an old friend, and I liked it. I felt more comfortable around him than I probably should have, but oh well.

He stood right outside the door when I made my way out, his back facing the crowd behind him, but he looked up the moment he heard the door swing. Bright eyes looked me over so quickly I almost missed it, but didn't. "I was starting to worry you fell in the toilet."

I rolled my eyes at him, but smiled. "I didn't even take that long."

"I know," he said, and we started walking toward where he found me. "So... I didn't catch your name..."

"It's Kat, well, Katherine, but everyone calls me Kat," I said, and his face snapped up to peer at mine. He even stopped walking.

"You do porn?" he asked really low, like he didn't want anyone to hear the question. Tristan had a confused expression on his face. He looked at me up and down again, like he was assessing me.

"No!" I huffed and almost said something that I definitely shouldn't and could never bring up. "I mean, *no*, I don't. Why?"

His eyes narrowed. "Kat sounds like a porn stage name. Next thing I know, you'll tell me your last name is Lips or something."

My face blanched because for the first time in my life, I really thought about my God-given name. Suddenly, my lady bits reminded me of two hamburger buns for some stupid reason. I felt like I was giving in to my childhood nickname: Cheeseburger. To your average eight-year-old, Berger was as good as burger.

Holy shit. My name could pass for a porn name.

"It's Berger," I croaked out, mortified. Seriously? Kat fucking Burger, I could see it now on the cover of a DVD at the XXX Super Video down the street from my apartment. It was bad enough that I'd grown up getting called a cheeseburger, hamburger, and a kitty burger. As an adult, Josh called me Booger after our professor butchered my last name for an entire semester, calling me Katherine Booger for three and a half long months. But this was in a league of its own. I could already imagine Nicole telling me I needed to get my burger eaten.

The smile on his face started out small as my words sunk in, then it grew and grew until it was so big and bright, there was no need to have any lights on in our near vicinity. He was amused beyond belief, and then he started laughing. "That's rich," he spit out between laughs. "I'm sure your parents never intended to give you such a usable name."

We started walking again, but he kept chuckling.

"You aren't a stalker or anything? I guess I probably should have thought about that before telling you my last name."

"Nah, I gave up my stalker days after the last time I got a restraining order against me." He gave me a crooked grin when he slightly turned his head to look at me. "My last name is King, if it makes you feel any better. You aren't a stalker either, right?"

I couldn't help but shrug at him, playing along. I kept telling myself not to think about how cute he was inside and out because he already admitted to me he was here with a friend. What kind of friend, I didn't know, but there was one thing I did know— I was not a homewrecker. I pushed the thought out of my head, because if he had a girlfriend and she was here, there would be no way in hell he would be walking around by himself.

"No, I'm not," I said to him.

There was a ringing sound that I recognized as robot noises coming from the front pocket of his hoodie. Tristan pulled his phone out and looked at the screen, frowning. He looked back up at me, but the light in the spot we were in was so dark, I could only see one side of his face. "I need to go meet up with someone," he sighed. It almost seemed like he was disappointed to get the phone call, but I didn't allow myself to dwell on his body language.

"Okay." I forced a smile.

Tristan took a step back. Standing back under the light, and despite the fact that the brim of his hat covered a good portion of him, I could tell he was grinning. "Put the bat signal up in case you get lost trying to find the restroom again, and I'll come to the rescue, okay?"

"Okay," I repeated, a very real smile now taking the place of the one I forced out a split second before.

He took another step back, still facing me. "Bye, Kat," he practically purred, before turning and heading in a different direction.

Who knew how long I stood in the middle of the aisle, looking in the direction he walked. I couldn't even process my thoughts until a stinging sensation at the back of my head pulled me out of the parallel universe I was just visiting. This parallel universe consisted exclusively of Tristan and me, not an entire convention dedicated to porn.

"What the hell took so long? You get diarrhea again?" Nicole's all-too-familiar voice asked from behind while the she-demon tugged at my ponytail again.

"Oooh, I hate it when I get the runs in public places," Zoey winced as she stepped in front of me.

"I don't have diarrhea," I whispered loudly, so much so that it really couldn't be considered a whisper.

Nicole rolled her eyes as she grabbed my wrist. "C'mon then, we still have a few more hours left here, and Zoey is done being a porn star for the day."

I looked down at my watch to see what time it was, and realized we hadn't even been there for two hours yet.

Something told me this was going to be the longest day of my life.

CHAPTER FIVE

I almost crapped my pants when I spotted Sarah Love, an old friend from high school, signing autographs at a booth we had passed.

When we were in school, Sarah was one of those girls who really kept to herself. While I certainly hadn't been one of the popular kids, back then I had a handful of friends that I hung out with regularly, while Sarah's shyness and quiet nature had kept her circle of acquaintances much smaller than mine. She was a sweet girl, and the last time I'd seen her at graduation, she had told me she was heading to UCLA for college.

Interesting.

"Close your mouth before someone shoves a dildo in there," Nicole laughed from my side.

Instinctively, I shut my trap, noticing my mouth was, indeed, hanging wide open while I looked at my old classmate. "We went to high school together," I whispered to her, and she nodded.

"She's probably making more money now than we do," Nikki waggled her eyebrows and Zoey, who was on the other side of Nikki, snorted.

It was a well-known fact in our small square of friends, which consisted of us three and Josh, that Zoey made a killing in her 'profession,' as she called it. Our Zoey was a modest little thing who never bragged about how much money she made, or even mentioned when she got a new job. In fact, the first time she got paid more than twelve hundred dollars for a scene, you would have figured she won the lottery by her screams.

It was her agent's idea to keep her solely with the girl-on-girl scenes, and it's for that reason Zoey was so popular. I figured it had something to do with men wanting what they can't have, but aren't all people like that? Even though she was only paid to be with other women, she didn't consider herself a lesbian or straight, she was just Zoey. That was enough for me.

When I first met her, it was the summer before I started college while we worked at a bookstore together. I was a refrigerator, she was a magnet, and we just clicked together over our love of reading. Every other friendship I'd had before ours seemed shallow in comparison after only a few short weeks. We seemed to understand and respect each other at a cellular level, and the fact that she happened to be the sweetest and happiest person I'd ever met only added to my nearly instantaneous love for her. After my dad met her, he told me she reminded him of my mom, endearing her to me that much more.

She had always dreamed of becoming a star, and for years, I followed her from audition to audition for moral support. Zoey never got any roles she really wanted, unfortunately. So, when one of her other actor friends mentioned how much money he was making "fucking girls," an imaginary light bulb lit up in her head. She wasn't involved in any serious relationships and didn't have any issues with her body, so it was an easy choice for her. Based on the look on her face while she signed an autograph for a fan who approached her while we walked around, I didn't think she regretted her decision at all. She loved attention, so this career was perfect.

"What time is your boyfriend signing autographs?" Nicole asked, referring to my own personal version of Calum Burro.

An image of short brown hair and a perfect penis floated around in my head for a second before I snapped out of it and flipped through the pamphlet for information. "At five, by the food vendors."

Nikki smirked and stopped at a booth with more glass dildos like the ones she had looked at when we first got to the convention. I swore she was a dildo connoisseur. "Are you going to cream your panties when you see him?"

"Probably. Did you have to change your

underwear after you saw Calum?"

She shook her head, this time leaning closer to the dildos instead of holding them up to her face. "Nah. I didn't bother wearing any," the blonde hussy cackled, while Zoey and I laughed.

"I was wondering what that stain on the back of your pants was," I said.

"That would explain why those people were pointing and laughing at you a second ago," Zoey chimed in.

"Fuck you both," Nicole hissed, but the smile on her face gave her away.

Zoey leaned into me, but kept her eye on Nikki, completely disregarding the masterpieces on the table. "I've always told you, you could make some extra money..."

Nikki shrugged like usual when Zoey started mentioning doing porn. For all the shit-talking she did, along with the amount of casual sex she's had, Nikki was extremely private and closed off around people she doesn't know. You got to know the bitch first; I thought it was her test to see whom she let into her life. Hence, the reason why she only had three friends.

"Miss Star?" a small voice asked from behind.

Zoey spun around slowly on the balls of her feet, a big smile painted on her mouth, to see a young, Asian guy standing there with his face flushed. "Hi, darling," she cooed, going from the Zoey Quinn I knew, who talked about her bowel movements like it was every one's business, to Zoey Star.

"Do you mind taking a picture with me?" he asked. I noticed that even the tips of his ears turned red, and I had to smile at the guy. "Please?"

"Of course!" she answered him in a huskier voice than her natural one.

I really tried my best not to laugh at her because I knew this was a part of her persona. The real Zoey, the one I had been friends with for years before she got that star tattooed on her hip, ate children's vitamins and farted in front of me on a regular basis.

Oh, the wonders of appearances.

CHAPTER SIX

"I'm going to punch that bitch in the cunt," Nicole attempted to mumble, but her naturally loud voice was anything but subtle. Part of me also knew she really didn't give a shit who heard what she said.

Nikki was infamous for messing with people. She'd made an old woman cry at a Black Friday sale a couple years back. Not to mention the countless other people she'd reduced to puddles of piss in the courtroom. Her middle name should have been Ruthless.

Her hazel eyes were locked on a petite Hispanic girl lying across a table signing autographs. Her inky hair was pulled back into pigtails — her trademark — and she was dressed in a slutty Catholic schoolgirl outfit.

"Want me to remind her she's too old to be dressed like that?" I asked my best friend, elbowing her side.

She just smirked, never taking her eyes off the cute girl, reminding me of a pit bull ready to attack. "Do it right before I punch her."

"Don't do it, Nicole!" Zoey squealed, slipping her small body between Nikki's and mine. "You'll get kicked out of here, if you do it."

"It'd be worth it," Nikki said through gritted teeth.

I was actually a little scared for the girl's safety. If my memory served me correctly, I was pretty sure her name was Maya. The reason why Nicole wanted to rip out her uterus was because the love of her life did some pretty dirty things to Maya a couple months back. I'd told Nikki not to watch the video, but she had done it anyway.

A hole appeared in her wall shortly afterward, so you could imagine how that had gone.

I think Nikki had secretly dreamed of being the first recipient of Calum's tongue doing those freaky things and Maya had ruined that dream.

Zoey managed to distract our resident serial killer wannabe by leading her toward a booth with all kinds of books. Well, all kinds of sexual books. The three of us squeezed in together, butts pressed up against hips and stomachs while we browsed the collection on the table.

"Anything I can help you beautiful ladies out with?" a soft voice asked.

I looked up to see a pair of clear, gray eyes

looking at us inquisitively. "No, we're just looking, thank you," I answered. The guy was young, maybe in his mid-to-late twenties and pretty cute with a mess of light brown hair and a sweet smile. He looked like someone I knew, but I couldn't figure out who.

Zoey picked up a small, pocket sized Kama Sutra book and held it in front of Nikki's face. "Hey, didn't you want this?"

I browsed the different titles splayed out, touching each spine carefully until I felt a warm gaze on me. I looked up to see gray orbs watching me. The guy smiled, looking embarrassed. "I'm sorry, I'm just trying to figure out if I know you from anywhere. You look really familiar."

Oh, my God.

It hit me.

He was one of my student's brothers.

Well, technically, an old student.

Dylan's fourth grade class, the one I taught throughout the fall and spring semester, let out for summer a little more than a month before.

Growing up, I had wanted to be an astronaut. My plan had been to study aeronautical engineering and go work at NASA. All it took to kill my childhood dream was an advanced Calculus class my senior year in high school, and that dream went down the drain like dishwater. According to some bullshit requirement for majoring in engineering, you had to be really good at math. *Huh*. Calculus, or just math in general, was a sworn enemy to the Berger family. Who would have known? My dad told me about his failure at everything besides basic arithmetic when he consoled me after my broken career dreams.

It was my dad, Frank, who brought up the idea of going into teaching; he egged me on by reminding me how much I liked kids and how much kids liked me. With that in mind, along with the added bonus of getting summers off, my fate was sealed. I loved my kids even though they were a bunch of little dingleberries at times, but I reminded myself daily that some adults were full-blown shit-heads all the time. I figured I was doing the world a favor by shaping the young minds of potential little butt-heads and, hopefully, steering them toward a less asshole-ish existence in the future.

In that moment, when the gray eyes relaxed and his face flushed, I seriously doubted I had made the right choice in switching careers. I could tell he remembered where he knew me from. He had come to pick up Dylan enough times to recognize me.

I steeled my back, deciding to be the adult here; he was at the convention too, so who was he to say anything? "Dylan's brother, right?" I verified, trying to keep my voice even.

"Yeah. Ms. Berger?" he asked, scratching absently at the side of his face.

I laughed, but it sounded really awkward. It didn't help that Zoey made a stupid noise in response to the tension radiating off of us. "It's

Katherine," I told him, ignoring the moron next to me.

We stared at each other for a moment, which felt as if it lasted forever, before Nicole started cackling at the tension. "Well, that was awkward," she said to Zoey, who nodded all too eagerly in response.

My face was so hot it felt like my cheeks were going to melt off. "Yeah, well, uh, it was nice seeing you?" It came out of my mouth more like a question than a statement. "I'll see you later." I almost told him to say hi to Dylan for me, but that would be really fucking awkward. I could only imagine the explanation he'd have to come up with if Dylan asked where he'd seen me. Either way, I didn't even know why I said I'd see him later. The last thing I wanted to do was see him again.

Zoey gasped for air between laughs as she followed me away from the table while Nikki was probably buying her travel-sized book. "Oh, KAB, you crack me up."

I shot her the dirtiest look I could muster, which really wasn't that dirty at all. I probably looked more constipated than angry. "Thank you for enjoying my agony."

"It happens," she shrugged, smiling. "Remember when my brother called me after he found out what I was doing?"

Ryan, Zoey's older brother, found out about his sister's pornographic occupation the worst way possible. By witnessing it. I was there when Zoey was listening through her voicemails one morning and the sound of his ear-splitting screams filled the line. I didn't think a man could reach that octave, but Ryan proved the impossible. Every other phrase on the recording was punctuated by "*What the fuck!*" and then followed by a pained scream. It took months, several conversations with me, and then another dozen with Zoey herself, to calm him down. He may have even gone to therapy, because no one should see his or her sibling in that way—ever.

I was well aware she was trying to make me feel better about being embarrassed by bringing up something that I knew had been really hard and very personal for her to overcome. The situation with Ryan was harder than it had been when she finally came out to her mom. Mrs. Quinn simply shrugged, and then asked Zoey what she wanted for dinner.

I caught Nikki making a beeline toward us as we casually strolled past some booths. Her hazel eyes were sparkling like the Saharan sand under the sun on a perfect day, while the grin on her face was borderline demented. "Guess who just texted me?" she gushed.

Nicole had never gushed in her life, so I knew it was a momentous occasion.

It hit me and I gasped. "No!"

"Uh— yes!"

Zoey gasped then, putting a small hand against her negative 32AAA boobies. "No!"

"Yes, bitches!" Nicole clenched her fist right in

front of the mini circle we'd formed.

Holy shit.

Holy shit.

Calum Burro had texted Nikki.

She thrust her brand new phone in my face. My eyes caught the unknown number with a Miami area code before seeing the message.

I want 2 talk about ur offer, sweet <3

I wanted to laugh at the fact that he put a heart instead of actually writing it out, but I didn't. Instead, I put my hand up for Nicole to give me a high-five because her dream had come true.

She started galloping in place with Zoey air-spanking her ass, exclaiming, "I'm gonna ride that dick raw!"

CHAPTER SEVEN

"I'm starving," I whined to the two hookers for the millionth time.

Zoey, Nicole, and I had been walking around for almost two hours going from booth to booth, looking at everything under the moon. In those few hours, I'd learned there was a ton of variation in floggers, women liked porn just as much as men did, and what sounding was— although that little ditty I wish I wouldn't have found out about. A couple years ago, Josh asked me to go with him to get tested for STDs. I, like the idiot I am, went with him, and even stayed in the room at his insistence.

What I saw that day in the doctor's office would haunt me for the rest of my life. I firmly believed that the only thing that should be coming out of a guy's penis was pee and semen. Nothing, and I mean nothing, should ever go in there. I think I screamed louder than Josh did when I saw what the doctor did to him. Sweet baby Jesus, I cried for the both of us, and my vagina clenched up like a steel trap for weeks afterward. The only positive thing about the whole experience was the fact that Josh, as well as I, learned a very valuable lesson: wrap that pecker up. Every. Single. Time.

I had picked up the sound, wondering what in the hell a thin steel rod was doing on the table, until Zoey whispered its purpose in my ear. I dropped that shit like a hot potato. Whatever makes a person happy is their business, and really, I couldn't care less as long as it didn't affect me, but that... ughhh.

I was still shuddering hours later.

It took me a good half an hour after picking up that little toy to get over reliving the horror that was Josh's STD exam. After all that, I was ridiculously hungry, and neither one of my friends was paying attention to my cries.

"I'm going to start eating your ass fat if I don't get food in me soon," I moaned. Nicole didn't even bother turning around to look at me while she shot me the finger.

After getting the text from Calum, she'd been on cloud nine. We stood in our little circle rallying together for a few minutes before she got all serious and said she was going to make him wait. So she ignored his text message along with the one he sent an hour later. Something told me that stud muffin wasn't used to not getting what he wanted.

I could only imagine what a future with Nicole Jonasson would be like for him.

Had I mentioned she was a praying mantis? A Venus flytrap? She wasn't just a man-eater— she was a human-eater. But I loved her more than words.

My poor stomach grumbled so loudly that the pretty girl standing next to me laughed at the noise.

"Screw you, guys, I'm going to get some food. You know where to find me, Whoricole and Bitchey." They just waved me off while they finished looking at whatever corset crap they were interested in buying.

It took me a few minutes to find my way around the booths and the huge masses of people milling about. There were a lot more visitors at that point than when we first arrived, but I tried to ignore the flutter of nervousness in my heart by focusing on the churning of my stomach eating my fat to survive. I was used to eating pretty regularly, and if I skipped a meal, I turned into Nikki—a bitch.

Finally making it to the small semicircle of food vendors and rows of seating and tables, I sighed in contentment. There was a lady on the end selling what looked like dick-shaped cookies and little cakes that were probably supposed to be imitation vaginas. The man right next to her was selling pretzels and nachos, which I considered. The next booth had hot dogs and more hot dogs, and the last booth sold something in a cup that smelled disgusting.

Hot dogs at a porn convention. *Oh yeah.*

I laughed at myself a little at the idea of eating a phallic-shaped object, but oh, well. I bought two and doused them with mayonnaise and ketchup before I went and sat down in one of the two chairs at the table furthest away from the crowd.

"I'm starting to think you were lying to me about being a stalker," a familiar low voice suggested from right behind me.

The dark hoodie caught my peripheral vision first, before the long figure pulled out the chair across from mine and plopped down into it. Those spectacular green gems called his eyes focused in on my wide, open mouth mid-bite. I snorted, and bit into my hot dog anyway, ketchup staining the corner of my lips. "Hey," I said between swallows, covering my mouth with my hand.

Tristan smirked at me as he tugged the hood portion of his hoodie down to his shoulders, so only his cap covered his head. "Hungry?" he asked, eyeing my other hot dog on the table.

"Starving," I replied, taking another big bite. "You have no idea," I practically moaned out between chews. "These hot dogs could probably be made out of roach poop and I wouldn't care."

He laughed, the corner of his mouth tipping into the same crooked smile he'd given me earlier. God, even his skin was perfect and clear, I noted. "They probably are made out of roach poop."

I frowned and took another bite out of the hot dog while he eyed the other one longingly. "You hungry?"

"Yeah," he sighed. "I left my wallet in my car and my friend won't let me borrow money."

What kind of a friend wouldn't buy someone lunch at least? I knew for a fact Nikki would buy me half of Whole Foods if I asked her to. I nudged the remaining hot dog in his direction while chewing. "Have it."

His eyes went from the beef frank to mine and back again. "No, I couldn't do that, Kat. You don't even know me," Tristan said quietly.

"Your name is Tristan... King?" I asked, and he nodded in response. "You caught me pulling my wedgie, so consider this your blackmail money and we'll never speak of it again." I covered my mouth while I finished chewing.

"You really don't need to..." he started saying again as he eyed the hot dog for the fifth time.

I rolled my eyes and nudged the wrapped food closer to him. "Eat the freaking thing already."

He smiled that perfect, blindingly white smile before tearing the hot dog out of its package, practically shoving half of it in his mouth. He groaned for all that is holy in the universe. A groan that was all man and rich, and I knew my eyes probably glazed over in appreciation at the sound. Luckily, he was so preoccupied with having a beef sausage in his mouth that he didn't notice the crazy look I had in my eye.

There was a small possibility that Tristan had a

big bald spot hidden underneath his cap. He might also have an extremely hairy chest, or maybe even a third nipple for all I knew. Or, and I gasped internally at the idea, a crooked dick. Those things creeped me the hell out.

Based on that groan and the pure pleasure that rang up my spine, I just knew there was no way this man was here alone...

And damn it, I was going to find out for sure.

CHAPTER EIGHT

"So, Tristan," I started to say as he shoved the last bit of food in his pretty mouth. I hoped I wasn't overstepping my boundaries by asking him what was about to pop out of my mouth. "What kind of friend doesn't give you any lunch money?"

He smirked while chewing. "The same friend who's waiting for *your* friend to text him back."

"Wait. What?" *What the hell was he talking about*? I wondered for a split second before his words sunk in. "Calum Burro is your friend?" I couldn't begin to grasp the idea that the universe was incredibly small and this was my luck. I mean, seriously? Of all the people here, I started talking to the one person who personally knew my best friend's infatuation? My brain screamed at my instincts that I should freeze up and stutter. Then again, I would think it was super fucking weird if someone was a fan of Zoey and thought it was awesome to meet me just because I was friends with her.

Tristan frowned like he smelled something bad, but chuckled. "I told you I was waiting for my friend during the autograph session."

I wanted to be a smartass and ask him how I was supposed to know he was talking about the only other guy nearby instead of one of the psychos in line, but I didn't. "Well, that's awkward."

"Can you keep a secret?" he asked me, leaning forward in his seat. I nodded a little too quickly, causing him to smirk again. "Why is that hard for me to believe?"

Pulling my finger across my lips like I was zipping them closed, I tossed my hand back to make it seem like I threw away an imaginary key. "My lips are sealed, I promise."

"I think Calum's in love. He's been babbling about your friend for the last three hours." He tugged at the brim of his hat, smiling. "He said he wouldn't let me borrow any money until she texted him back."

The snort that erupted out of my nose made us both laugh. "Well, he's out of luck because Nikki is playing hard to get right now," I told him, wiggling my eyebrows. Thinking better of what I just said, I added, "But don't tell him that." Nicole would have my ass on a platter if he found out. Besides, as Zoey always said, "Hos before bros."

Tristan shrugged as he leaned back against his chair. "Why are you eating all by yourself?"

"My friends didn't want to eat with me."

He frowned again, a wrinkle creasing his flawless forehead. "I'm glad I found you then."

"Better you crashing my lunch than the other guy who caught me pulling my wedgie." I smirked at the perfect male specimen in front of me and he grinned.

"Your boyfriend won't get mad, right?"

My eyes narrowed in his direction, wondering if he was trying to fish for information like I had been earlier. It seemed really strange to me that out of the hundreds of women here, with prettier faces, sexier bodies, and wearing a lot less clothes, he'd chosen me to harass. Pushing the thought to the back of my head, I decided I'd rather focus on the fact that he did, instead of why he had.

"Nah, but my husband will," I said, with a straight look on my face.

Green eyes immediately drifted to my left hand, which was resting on the table. He shook his head as he let his eyes drift back to my face slowly. "You got me, little gold digger." Tristan leaned forward in his seat again, casting a quick glance around.

"Are you... hiding from someone?" I pointed at his head, and then his hoodie.

"Not really."

My eyebrow rose on its own. "Are you balding?"

I realized Tristan smiled more than I did, and I was known for constantly grinning, especially when I did something stupid or when it was frowned upon.

"No."

"You have a really bad haircut, don't you?"

"No, I have great hair, thank you."

I rolled my eyes and smiled at him. "I've got it, your head is as big as your ego, and your cap is hiding your Jack in the Box sized noggin."

He sighed and looked from side to side again. "I do not," he said with an annoyed and exasperated tone, but the crooked smile on his face said otherwise. Long fingers went up to trace the seam of his cap before he yanked it off his head, his grass-colored eyes looking right at me.

The oddest mixture of auburn, brown, and gold colored his hair. Tristan ran a hand through the strands, the ends went everywhere automatically, like he'd been zapped by an electrical current. Of course, he couldn't have normal colored hair like every other human being on planet Earth.

"My hair's really..." he started to say quietly, his voice laced with indecisiveness.

"Cool," I added with a laugh. I couldn't remember the last time I'd used the word *cool*.

"I was going to say recognizable, but I like cool more."

His eyebrows were almost the same color as his hair, I noticed, which just made him cuter. "So you're trying to be anonymous then?"

"Exactly."

"Pussy," came out of my mouth before my brain even registered the word. My verbal filter had officially left the building once again.

Tristan burst out laughing, and then right in the middle of it, snorted like a pig. I was sure my eyes went wide at the sound that came out of such a seemingly perfect being, so human and unexpected. I started laughing like an idiot and then snorted too, like a full-blown hog for freak's sake. We both laughed so hard at each other for our mirrored noises that he snorted again even louder and I followed as well.

The porn con had officially become a farm.

I'd always kind of hated the fact that I snorted when I laughed. When I was little, kids would call me Miss Piggy and even though I liked her because she was kind of a bitch, it still hurt. My mom used to hold me in her lap when I'd come home from school and whisper, "*Be who you are and say what you feel, because those who mind don't matter and those who matter don't mind.*" Even as an adult, Dr. Seuss always seemed to connect with me on a level that no one else ever could. It took me a long time to fully understand what she meant by the words, but by the time I finally got it, it was so deeply ingrained in my being I could never forget. So yeah, I hated that I snorted like a pig, but oh, well. It could have been worse— I could be one of those people who farted when they laughed really hard.

Not that it had ever happened to me, you know, but I'd heard of it.

Tristan's perfect face was thrown back, his hands

covered the upper part of his face while he cracked up so fully his chest heaved, and he might have possibly been crying. My stomach started hurting from laughing, and my cheeks kind of ached, but I still giggled like a fool.

Then, Tristan snorted one more time, and I was dying.

To die laughing would have been the best way to go. I hurt in a wonderful way and I couldn't breathe either, but I couldn't have cared less. There were people at the tables surrounding us, staring like the men who had stared at the anal queen earlier. The last thing I wanted to do was bring attention to myself, but I was doing the opposite by laughing my ass off with my new friend. I buried my face into my arms to control the nonstop laughs that erupted out of me like a geyser.

"Holy shit," he started huffing moments later, eyes glazed over with the tip of his nose tinged pink. Tristan was out of breath, and he mirrored me by holding his stomach. "I don't think I've ever laughed that hard."

"You save those snorts for special occasions, or what?" I asked, trying to conceal the grin that covered the lower half of my face, but another laugh escaped anyway.

Tristan pinched his nose, his chest shaking again with the effort to control himself. "Please," he begged. "Please don't ever tell anyone I snort."

I raised a wary eyebrow at him because I hadn't

gotten rid of the giggles completely. "Why does it matter? I snort too, and yeah, it's pretty embarrassing, but..." I just shrugged to end my sentence.

His bright green eyes searched my face while the corners of his mouth turned up. Whatever he found, he must have liked because his pearly whites came out as he leaned forward in his chair. "I'm not a cute girl. I can't pull off a snort like you can. I look like an idiot when I do it."

It didn't escape me that he called me cute, and of course, my face got warm all of a sudden at his compliment. It wasn't like I thought I was unattractive, but it somehow meant more coming from his mouth. He didn't resemble an idiot at all, like he claimed, but I was definitely not going to disagree with him. Luckily, part of my brain still functioned because I made an effort not to graze my eyes over his torso, or over his sharp jawline and face. I nodded at him instead. "Yeah, you're right. You do look like an idiot when you snort."

"Well, shit," he laughed for what seemed like the hundredth time.

I suddenly felt a little bad because that was mean of me to say, even if I was joking. I barely knew the guy, but then again, he'd been merciless with his teasing of me, so screw it. Regardless, I still felt just a little bad because I didn't like to insult people I didn't know well. Once we were on even ground, it was a different story. "I'm kidding," I mumbled out sheepishly.

Tristan was really quiet while he got himself put back together, tugging the hood up and over his faded green cap. He still had a silly smile on his face as he leaned back against the chair. "What are you doing the rest of the time you're here?"

"Nikki, my friend you met earlier, drove, so I have to wait for her to get tired until we can leave." Suddenly, I remembered the fact I'd been planning on going to Andrew Wood's booth. I looked at my watch to see that the signing would start in thirty minutes. "Actually, I just remembered I'm going to Andrew Wood's booth," I said, raising my eyebrows at him. "That's the only thing I wanted to do today."

Tristan's brown eyebrows went up, questioningly. "Andrew Wood?" he practically spat out.

"Yeah. Why? What's wrong with him?"

"Nothing," he said, but frowned. "Andrew Wood? Why?"

My eyes widened in an effort to say, *hello*. "Because he's my favorite porn star of all time. He's like... in the porn hall of fame."

"He's... old."

I'd never guffawed in my life, but I was pretty sure I guffawed then, and said the first thing that popped into my head. "Wine gets better with age, so do some men. Specifically him."

Tristan rolled those bright green eyes, but smirked. "I don't get it. Why is he your favorite?"

I realized then that I was talking about my favorite porn star to someone I barely knew, and that was pretty strange. However, logic evaded me and my mind settled onto the fact that Tristan looked disapproving at my choice. "You want me to tell you why he's my favorite?"

"Yeah."

I sighed and didn't even need to think about the reasons why I favored Andrew Wood porn. "Okay, well, have you seen his movies?"

Tristan just shrugged, giving a half-assed nod. Mr. Wood was a legend in the porn industry. He'd been around for nearly two decades and was still considered to be one of the most sought after porn stars in the business. In his early forties, I thought he looked to be in better shape than pretty much any other man. With dark hair, piercing blue eyes, and an olive complexion, the man was a looker. Nikki and I had joked around for years about agreeing to do porn if we could do it with him. I had compiled a list one drunken night of the things I'd do to him if I had the chance. Weird? Maybe.

"He's just so... passionate in his movies," I emphasized the word by widening my eyes. "He likes what he's doing, obviously, but he's not like these guys nowadays who just want to fuck a girl like they're a machine or something. You know? He's not a bam, bam, bam, sort of guy. He puts a little something into it. I think it's hot," I finished. How in the world I managed to say that without giggling, I had no idea. Who the hell talked about porn with a stranger? I guess I did.

He gave me a really funny look that I couldn't even begin to decipher. "He's old."

"You're going to be old someday too, Magellan," I responded with a wink.

He huffed, crossing those arms, which I was pretty positive were packing some serious muscle, over his chest. "I got awhile." He looked up at the ceiling and sighed, whispering, "Andrew Wood."

"Oh, whatever, Mr. I'm-Hiding-Under-My-Cap-and-Hoodie-Because-I'm-A-Pussy-and-Don't-Want-Anyone-To-See-Me."

"I don't!" he answered with a big smile on his face. I swear he smiled so much it was impossible not to smile back at him. I think he could have told me I looked like Gollum in *Lord of the Rings* and I'd still smile back at him.

"Pussy," I called out one more time and laughed.

Tristan shook his head as he pushed back from his chair, gathering up all of our trash. "C'mon, little gold digger, I'll walk you to Grandpa's booth. It's on my way."

"I barely know you, yet, somehow, I already know you're full of shit," I said while getting out of my chair, waiting for him to come back around after throwing away our mess.

"Oh, Kat," he sighed, shaking his head again.

He looked down while we started walking, carefully sidestepping a lot of people who were still looking at us curiously, remembering our earlier snorts and laughter. I couldn't help but take inventory of the fact that he was so good-looking it was unreal, and his personality was just... I didn't know how to describe it. Knowing he was walking me over to the booth and it might be the last time I saw him, made my chest clench up a bit. It was probably because he was unbelievably hot that I craved his attention like a teenage girl with uncontrollable hormones. So I asked myself, *what should I do?*

Nicole's face flickered in my head, and I knew what I needed to do. Grow a damn backbone.

"You okay?" Tristan asked me, like he could sense I was deep in thought.

"Yeah," I answered back. "I was just thinking about what you asked earlier." I wanted to vomit, but that would be terrible. Beyond terrible. "I think Andrew Wood has a perfect dick."

The noise that came out of his throat, not his mouth, sounded like a backed up dishwasher.

He opened and closed his mouth a few times. Those pretty pink lips moved silently up and down for no apparent reason. The movement of his mouth made it seem like he was having a silent conversation with me. He looked flustered as he glanced at me out of the corner of his eye, making another funny noise deep in his throat.

"Well, um..." he said with a gravelly voice, looking down at the concrete floor beneath us. The sound of robots chiming from his pocket broke the awkward silence we were in as Tristan fished into the front of his jeans for his cell. "I'm sorry, I need to take this. Hold on a second, okay?" he asked, already pressing what I could only assume was the answer button. In less than a second, he slipped the phone into the space between his ear and the cotton of his hoodie.

We walked slowly through the crowd while he talked quietly into the phone. The only thing I heard him say was "Five minutes... yes... I understand..." Tristan's eyes stayed glued to the floor as he made his way through the throngs of people.

I eased my step to follow his trail because his much larger frame moved through the crowd easier than my average-sized one. He was so tall that the top of my head only grazed his broad shoulder. He turned around to make sure I was still following him, even though he was on the phone.

Having memorized the map of where Andrew Wood's signing booth would be, I knew we were close. I spotted a small line just a few feet ahead. A giddy feeling spread through my body all of a sudden, knowing I was just minutes away from meeting the man who had kept me company for so many nights via the internet.

We were right in front of the booth at the same time that Tristan ended his call with a long, drawn out sigh. The line was already about ten people deep, facing a large poster of a girl with a Texas-sized amount of jizz spread all over her face. "ANDREW WOOD" was printed across the bottom of the poster in huge, block font.

Like the perv I was, my eyes stayed glued to the pearl necklace made of bodily fluids decorating the girl.

I eased my way into the short line while my new acquaintance pocketed his phone and cast a wary glance at the line of females ahead of me. He ducked his head a little more before facing me again.

Tristan gave me a soft smile. "I'm sorry about that. Someone is waiting for me. I need to get going."

I wanted to ask him why he'd been so vague every time I had seen him, but that would have been kind of uncalled for. We barely knew each other, so I just nodded and forced a smile. "Okay."

My auburn-haired companion shoved his hands deep into the front pockets of his low-slung jeans, and I caught sight of the sliver of creamy skin where his hoodie failed to meet denim. "I'm," he whispered, as he took a step closer to me when the woman in front of me turned to give us a curious look. "I'm glad I found you digging in your butt."

"Oh, God, I was only picking my undies out," I murmured, trying to keep my voice low enough that the nosey woman didn't hear us.

He smiled a big, toothy grin only a foot away from my face since he was ducking to talk to me. "Whatever you say," he teased. "Thank you for lunch, Kat."

"You're welcome."

"I really need to go," he said, straightening up. "I'm glad I met you."

I couldn't help but smile a little weakly, disappointed that he was in such a rush to leave. "Me too."

Tristan stepped back, but smirked a split second later. He then took two steps closer, his shoulder hovering only a couple inches away from my face. I caught a whiff of his clean, soapy scent. His warm breath tickled my ear as he leaned in and made a sound like he'd inhaled my scent too, but I was so focused on how close he was that I really couldn't know for sure. A fire ran up my spine at his proximity.

"I think you should find a younger porn star to watch from now on," he said in a husky voice before brushing his hand down the length of my ponytail and stepping away. "Bye, Kat."

My ponytail whispered to me that she would never be the same again.

I felt like I'd been put under a spell from the moment he started breathing right against my ear until he was out of sight. Was I in a trance? My ear felt warm and tingly even in the long moments after he'd left.

My brain was in such a daze I didn't hear the nosey woman in front of me talking.

"Hmm?" I asked, trying to focus in on the heated words coming out of her mouth.

The woman, who looked to be in her late twenties, rolled her eyes in exasperation. "Was that Robby Lingus?"

"Who?" I asked her again.

"Robby Lingus." she whined, her pale eyes looking in the direction Tristan had walked.

"No," I snapped back at her, annoyed by her sharp tone.

Her eyes narrowed in my direction like she didn't believe my answer, but she turned back to face forward again, completely ignoring me. I busied myself with sending Zoey a text to let her know I was in line at the Wood booth, and then started looking around, trying my best not to think about Tristan again. I knew I'd probably never see him again, so it was pointless to get caught up thinking about him. I mean, he could have asked for my number if he was really interested, right?

"There you are!" Zoey's sweet voice rang out through the masses as she slid through the people in line to stand next to me. Linking her arm through mine like she usually did, the nosey woman in front of us turned to look back again.

Her eyes narrowed at Zoey and me with a sneer on her face.

People had given us that look before, and just like every other time, it managed to piss me off instantaneously.

My sweet Zoey was extremely affectionate. Even before all of this madness of porn and girls, she'd always been very touchy-feely, and I liked it. I didn't care. Being an only child, and then on top of that, losing my mom at such a young age, had left me the tiniest bit starved for attention. My dad loved me, I never had any doubt of that, but he wasn't much for outward displays of affection. As the years rolled by, Zoey had started getting recognized more often, but every once in a while, the appreciative looks she usually received were replaced by ugly, mean sneers courtesy of people who didn't understand.

They didn't know her the way I did. If they wanted to think something bad about her, or about the both of us, so be it. But, *really*? If someone recognized her, they weren't exactly in a position to judge anyone else. So the look on nosey-ass' face made me mad. Fortunately, Zoey was oblivious as she looked everywhere but ahead.

"I'm really good at spitting across long distances," Nicole barked at the woman staring at us as she made her way over with one eyebrow drawn up in a challenge.

"Don't be mean, Nikki," Zoey sighed.

Nicole stalked over, but her vision was locked on the nosey woman's face. She was really scary for being so pretty, and luckily, the woman has some survival instincts, because she turned her body to completely face away from Nikki.

I could only snicker in response to Zoey's words. "That would be like asking the world not to turn."

Our blonde friend just shrugged as she planted

herself right next to us. "You wouldn't want me any other way."

Zoey and I just looked at each other, like we'd done a hundred times in the past, and shrugged. "Meh."

"Bitches," Nicole hissed at us while digging through her purse. "Here I was, buying my favorite asshole a present..." She'd been referring to me as an asshole for as long as I could remember. She loved me, I had no doubt about it. Nikki pulled a shrink-wrapped DVD out of her impressively sized, fancy purse and thrust it in my face. "You're welcome."

A picture of Andrew Wood from the mid-nineties was plastered on the front of the cover with psychedelic neon colors highlighting his name. "Nikki..." I started to say, but she waved her hand around, looking away from me.

"Yeah, yeah. I love you, too," she muttered like the act of buying me a DVD of my favorite porn star wasn't awesome.

I lived on a teacher's salary as well as royalties from my e-books. While I wasn't poor, I had to limit myself to what luxuries I spent my money on. I bought generic brand everything, cut out really good coupons, and relegated myself to free porn websites. On the other hand, Nikki shelled out the big bucks for the good porn sites and splurged on whatever she wanted. She was a good friend though— she shared her passwords for the good sites, so I could enjoy them too, and bought me little things randomly. Like me, she was an only child, so over the years our friendship bridged the gap that we missed out on as kids.

I slung my arm around her shoulder, which was pretty awkward. I had to stand on the tips of my toes because she was a giant. "Thank you, Nikki," I said, quietly squeezing her to my side.

She rewarded me with a small smile out of the corner of her mouth. That was good enough for me.

"LADIES! Andrew Wood will be out in just a few minutes. He appreciates your patience and looks forward to meeting you all!" a tiny woman with very short hair hollered at the line.

Nicole's phone chimed the instant the woman started talking. She quickly pulled it out of her purse like her life depended on it. She grinned at the screen in a creepy way and nodded. "That was Calum again," she cackled to herself before typing away on the touch screen.

"Are you finally texting him back?" Zoey asked.

She nodded in response, tapping away on her phone with a smirk on her face. "Yeah, I'm tired of playing games. I just want to sit on his face, the sooner the better."

The nosey woman in front of us did something that sounded like a half-choke, half-cough sound, but Nicole just ignored her.

I suddenly remembered all about my lunch with Tristan and let out a little gasp. "I met his friend, Nikki."

"What friend?" she asked before I even finished saying her name.

"The guy earlier? The one who caught me pulling out my wedgie?" I reminded her and she nodded, her face serious. I decided to skip the part about having lunch, well, more like a snack I guessed, with him for some reason. "He said he was friends with Calum."

She looked pensive for a moment, almost looking like the lawyer she was if it wasn't for the tight clothing she wore. "Huh," she muttered in response.

The women ahead of me started shifting around, extending the line as they prepared to assault Andrew Wood himself. There weren't as many people as there had been with Calum Burro earlier, but whatever. I busied myself ripping the shrink wrap off of my new DVD, so I could get him to sign it when it was my turn. I missed the brown-haired sex god make his way into the booth followed by a small entourage. The women in line started going insane.

I saw a bra go flying in his direction and hit him square in the jaw. He picked it up and grinned before tossing it onto the other side of the table. The lady behind me, who looked old enough to be my mom, screamed at the top of her lungs, "I finger my pussy to your movies!" Unfortunately for the lady, everyone went silent.

I wanted to die for her.

The line began moving forward as the autograph

and picture taking began. Soon enough, everyone was making noise again, probably laughing at what the lady behind me said. Zoey and Nikki stepped out of the line, shoving me forward, while giving me their own versions of a smile. Zoey looked like a cute little angel, while Nikki looked like she was thinking of a way to murder Maya.

My feet moved on their own; I clutched the DVD to my chest as the line kept getting shorter. In no time, the small woman handling the line earlier gently pushed me toward the table.

I took the eight shortest steps ever walked in existence, and yes, I included baby steps, to stand in front of the forty-something-year-old man who was looking at me with big brown eyes. "Hi."

Like an idiot, I just shoved the DVD case in his direction, whispering a squeak of a "Hi" in response.

"What's your name, sweetheart?" he asked in a voice that was slightly higher than what I remembered in each of his videos.

"Katherine with a K," I said with my best *Stuart Little* impersonation. I wanted to kick my own ass for being such a puss.

Andrew Wood signed my DVD, handing it back to me with a big smile before there was another fan pushing me over to get her own signature. Scurrying over to where Nicole and Zoey stood, while Zoey beamed at me in excitement, seemed surreal. I'd been thinking about getting his autograph for so long, and now it was over and I'd frozen up.

"Let me see," Zoey hummed in excitement, reaching for the case in my hand.

"To Beautiful Katherine," Nicole read out loud slowly before snapping her line of sight back over to the table and observing it for a moment. "You should have given him your card too, Kat. We both could have been getting lucky tonight."

Zoey let out what sounded like a squeak. "You're going to try to have sex with Calum tonight?"

"Not tonight. I have a date with Jason, Jesus Christ. What do you think I am? Easy?" Nikki asked, like we were stupid.

I gave her a smug little smile as I nodded. "Well, yeah."

CHAPTER NINE

I felt like I was on cloud nine as we continued walking through the convention hall with my DVD in my purse. 'Beautiful Katherine' kept going through my head like the best broken record ever. *Beautiful Katherine. Beautiful Katherine.* A girl could get used to that. We hung around by the booth for a few minutes after I got my signature, checking out what the other people in line got signed. From what we saw, I was the only one who got anything besides just a name written out. My self-esteem went up about a hundred million points, if not more.

Growing up, I was really insecure with myself, just like most other kids. Thanks to my dad, I had been a tomboy with a really bad haircut for the majority of my childhood and teens. We didn't have a ton of money when I was younger, especially after my mom died. Dad and Mom were only children too, so I didn't have too many female influences in my life outside of teachers; with that being the case, he took it upon himself to cut my hair for me every few months. Let me tell you one thing— there is a reason why stylists go to cosmetology school. Even back then, I knew my uneven bangs were horrific and my so-called 'layers' looked like a blind man on opium had gotten hold of them, but I never complained once. I knew my dad tried his best with me. If the disaster that was my thick, uneven, brown hair wasn't bad enough, I'd inherited my mom's worst genes: gaps between my two front teeth and weight problems until I hit puberty. I'd always been kind of awkward and clumsy, but fortunately, I grew into my body, and a good hairstylist and braces solved the rest.

I grew out of my ugly duckling stage right around the end of high school, thank God. Dad called me a late bloomer. I called it one of God's jokes.

"Calum wants to meet up with me before we leave," Nicole said, while she typed away on her phone.

Zoey started grumbling, "I'm tired of walking around in these shoes, Nik."

"No one told you to wear them," she replied, pointing at the 4-inch rhinestone, red platforms Zoey teetered on. Her shoes probably weighed half as much as she did.

"You know it's part of my job," Zoey mumbled as

she squeezed through a small group of people walking in the opposite direction. A couple of men turned around to look at her curiously, probably recognizing her short mess of inky hair.

"To look like a stripper?" I teased her.

She just scowled at me in return. "You're buying me a steak when we're done then, Nikki."

"Deal."

The three of us weaved our way through the people. Nicole led the way since she was the one on a mission and we were her meager minions. It seemed crazy to me just how many people there were at the convention center; there was so much diversity it was overwhelming. I passed by a couple dressed in clothing I'd seen at a Renaissance festival. A man wearing only short pleather shorts and a ball gag in his mouth walked by me, as he trailed behind a pretty blonde in a pleather strapless dress. I was more into the people watching than looking at what was in each booth, until I saw it.

I think my mouth fell open, and I stopped so abruptly that Zoey ran into me.

"Oh, Mylanta," she gasped, staring at the same thing I was.

The booth specialized in blow up dolls. Life-sized male blow up dolls. I didn't think they even existed.

"We have to get one for Josh," I said to Zoey, scanning the different dolls tacked to the curtains that separated each booth. She nodded at me in response as she took a step closer to the booth.

I turned to look for Nikki only to see that she was already making her way down the row, completely oblivious to having left us. I stepped toward Zoey to check out the different dolls available. There was a policeman, an American Indian chief, a sailor, a cowboy, a construction worker, and a biker. All men. Josh's birthday was coming up next weekend, and neither one of us had bought the picky bitch anything yet. This was perfect.

"Which one should we get him?" she asked me at the same time our eyes landed on the same blow up doll.

"That one," I said, pointing at the policeman. As long as I could remember, he'd always had a thing for men in uniform. There was even a time when he'd sped on purpose to get pulled over by a cop on a motorcycle who he said had a cute butt. I wouldn't even get started on how he jogged past the fire station on a regular basis to try and catch some poor fireman's attention. He denied those claims with a sly smile.

"Yes!" she squealed.

A guy with a long ponytail appeared in front of us with eager eyes. "Can I help you, ladies?"

"We want to buy the 5-0," I told him, pointing at the blow up doll we wanted.

He turned to look at where I was pointing and nodded. "Officer Spanksalot is one of our best sellers. Let me get him for you."

Zoey turned to look at me with an amused

expression. She mouthed "Officer Spanksalot?" I smirked, but just shrugged.

The guy appeared with a big white box that had 'Spanksalot' written across the side and held it up at us. "Who's the lucky one taking him home?"

"It's for our friend," Zoey answered. "How much is it? I mean, how much is *he*?"

I should have been glad I wasn't drinking anything when the guy gave us the total, because I would have spit it out all over Zoey and myself. Two hundred and twenty dollars. We each shelled out our debit cards and asked him to split the bill in half. He handed me the box in a bag, which was a lot freaking heavier than I expected, and after a round of him thanking us, we took off looking for Nicole, who was just a couple booths away.

"Officer Spanksalot better have a butt-hole for Josh to wank off into for two hundred dollars," I groaned, hoisting the heavy bag over my shoulder.

"They should make one with a hole in his mouth too," she giggled.

I was so focused on getting to Nicole while also trying to avoid hitting anyone with the gigantic bag over my shoulder that I almost missed looking at the booth directly across from where Nikki was standing talking to Calum. A big guy pushed past me, knocking me off balance to where my body turned to face the booth surrounded by a bunch of half-naked broads.

The sharp jaw was the first thing I recognized

about the man standing in a wave of women. I managed to catch a glimpse of high cheekbones and pink, bow-shaped lips.

I felt my stomach drop to the floor, or maybe even all the way to hell.

The guy's hair color was all wrong. It wasn't the light, multicolored brown that I had seen less than an hour before; it was jet black. The eyebrow color was wrong, too. The guy had trendy black-framed glasses perched on his nose, and he was wearing a button-up plaid shirt instead of a hoodie.

I felt like Moses then, because the sea of people spread apart in front of me at the same time the guy looked up, right at me. He froze.

I knew that face, maybe not the hair color or the glasses, but I knew that perfect face.

It was Tristan.

CHAPTER TEN

It all snapped into place then.

The cap he had on, the hoodie he wore on top of that, why he constantly looked around, and the reason he kept his voice low.

Tristan didn't want anyone to recognize him. His hair color was so unique it was a dead giveaway, even in a large group of people.

He was a porn star.

He was a fucking porn star.

Fuck my life.

My stomach hurt, and I couldn't pinpoint the reason why. I knew he hadn't lied to me at any point. I didn't ask and he didn't offer up any information. He was so funny and cute... I felt stupid because I'd seen the warning bells. Someone that good-looking wouldn't be watching porn and roaming around this place by himself just for the hell of it.

He was making porn.

Ugh.

Tristan stared straight at me from behind the table, ignoring the swarm of women surrounding him as they yapped like Chihuahuas. I swear his face even blanched a little. I'm not sure how much time we spent standing there staring at each other in shock, but it wasn't long; it just felt like a lifetime of seconds.

One tentative hand came up and gestured for me to come over to him. The women around him finally caught onto his movements and followed the path of his eyesight to me. *Me*. I had fifteen women looking at me like they wanted to rip me to shreds, and I couldn't have cared less.

My stomach hurt.

He was a porn star.

This perfect looking person who caught me pulling my underwear out of my ass, called me a gold digger, walked me to the bathroom, referred to the bat signal for assistance, ate a hot dog with me, and said he enjoyed meeting me was a freaking porn star.

Tristan motioned for me to come over again, his mouth set into a grim, hard line.

I felt a shove from behind, and turned to see it was Zoey who was looking at me with big, gray eyes. "Robby Lingus wants you to go to his booth!" She ripped the heavy bag from my hand as she pushed me again, tipping her head in his direction.

"Go!"

Robby fucking Lingus.

I walked slowly toward him, keeping my eyes steady on his face because he hadn't lost eye contact with me at all. A sudden urge to flee in the other direction, away from him, charged through my system. *Run*! My brain screamed at me, but my traitorous legs continued their sluggish path to Tristan.

One of his fans moved over while I approached, leaving a big poster of a black-haired Tristan visible. A topless girl stood in front of him, with big, fake E cups jutting out in the air while one of his arms wrapped tightly across her chest between her breasts, his beautiful face cheek to cheek with hers. His other hand was clutching her shoulder, seemingly to press her against him even tighter.

Under different circumstances, I might have thought the picture was incredibly erotic, not to mention hot. I probably would've run home and started looking up Robby Lingus on my favorite websites, but I wasn't going to. I couldn't. I felt like shitting out my organs. I had just spent some funny and embarrassing moments with him, and I felt a little betrayed.

My mind was racing so fast, hollering at me to run, yelling at me that I had no right to feel anything about his obvious occupation. My brain told me he wasn't mine and he hadn't expressed any real interest in me. I couldn't get upset. I had no right. But my poor heart felt otherwise. My heart felt a strange connection to him.

I'm so stupid.

I found myself directly in front of his table, the line of women staring at me like hyenas ready to make me their dinner. Tristan's stunning eyes stared at me as if he was trying to convey some message to me without words.

"Hey," he said softly, so I could barely hear him over the chatter of his fans.

"Hi," I croaked out, my throat feeling parched.

"Robby!" a sharply dressed man standing behind Tristan called out, his face impassive. Tristan just waved him off, not bothering to look behind.

"Kat," he said, before leaning across the table as far as possible.

I stood there, not moving an inch, looking back and forth between the poster and the real thing. I wasn't mad at him. I knew that. My feelings were just haywire because I felt dumb.

"Kat," he repeated, pleading at me with his eyes.

I took another step toward the booth, brown eyes locked on to green ones before I leaned across the table and sucked in a strangled breath. "Yes?"

His lips brushed against the shell of my ear, his warm breath lingered like fog over my skin. "I'm done in ten minutes, will you wait for me?"

No.

Yes.

No.

"Yes."

The tip of his perfect nose brushed against the skin right by my ear. "Okay," he whispered, before stepping away and giving me a soft smile.

I looked at him, and then back at the poster again before turning on my heel and marching away from the table of hookers as quickly as I could. I figured I'd be able to hear when he was done, and then just walk back. All I knew was there was no way I'd want to stand there like a moron and stare at the parade of women embarrassing themselves.

Nicole, Zoey, and the big hunk of a man I recognized as Calum stood in the same spot they'd been in when I'd last seen them. The booth closest to them had a huge assortment of different lubes. In the middle of the table was an eight-by-ten-inch frame of Calum holding up a small blue bottle.

He was a spokesperson for DrizzLube. Go figure.

Zoey grabbed my hands, pulling me toward her with a strength I didn't know she possessed. Then again, I guess she was used to having her way with women on a regular basis. *Ha*. "What did he want?"

"That was Calum's friend," I tried explaining, but she gave me a confused expression. "The one I told you guys about that I met earlier?" She nodded at me in understanding. "He asked me to wait for him until he's done with his signing."

Zoey squeezed my hands between her two smaller ones as she looked deeply into my eyes. "What did you tell him?"

"Yes."

She let out a shaky breath and squeezed my hands again. "You know he's in the industry right?"

"I do now," I said, biting my lip subconsciously.

Zoey gave me a sad smile, and I knew she was aware of the way I was feeling right then. It was perfectly fine for me to like watching porn, but besides Zoey, who I'd known for so long that she was Zoey Quinn to me instead of Zoey Star, I never bothered to realize that porn stars were more than just that. "You'd still be my friend even if I didn't do this," she stated, not even opening up the conversation for me to interpret her words as a question.

Zoey would be my friend regardless of what she did with her life because I liked who she was, not what she did when I wasn't with her. Unless she was a serial killer, I'd take her friendship in any way possible. "Of course I would."

She threw her arms around my neck as she pulled me to her so tight my boobs pressed against her throat. Zoey stepped away from me, smiling. "Just remember that when you talk to him. He's a nice guy."

The severity of her words sank into my brain for me to mull over. Yes, he did porn. Yes, I liked to watch porn. Yes, he'd more than likely been with a lot of women. Yes, that idea made my stomach hurt, but it wasn't like he expressed an interest in me other than possibly friendship. Could I deny him friendship if he asked it from me? We got along so well it was strange.

I pushed away a tiny fraction of a thought that entertained the idea of seeing what he'd learned in his profession. I was jumping ahead of myself.

Maybe he didn't even want to be friends? He might just want to ask me not to tell anyone his real name.

"Kat, where is Josh's party?" Nicole's loud voice tore me from my thoughts.

I looked over to see her standing really close to Calum's massive, muscular form. He looked like a professional wrestler from how large he was, but his face was very open. He smiled in my direction, a sweet grin. "It's at Breeze," I told her, referring to the lounge Josh preferred going to.

"I'm inviting Calum and his friend," she said to me before shaking her head. "Oh, shit, Calum, this is Kat. Kat, this is Calum," she introduced us.

I reached out to shake the gigantic hand he held out toward me. We each said, "Nice to meet you," to the other, and then just stood there awkwardly.

Calum looked from Nicole back to me, and then again. I cleared my throat and scratched my cheek. "So, uh..."

A sharp, bony elbow stabbed me right in the spine. "He's done, KAB," Zoey informed me.

I took a sharp breath, and turned to look at Nikki and Calum who were standing there staring at each other in silence. It was kind of creepy. "Nik, just call me when you're ready. I'm gonna go... do something."

Like usual, she didn't respond, so I looked at Zoey, who had dropped Officer Spanksalot's box on the floor and had her hands on her hips, looking as serious as she could possibly ever seem. "You remember this, Katherine Alba Berger, you are beautiful, smart, funny, and just plain awesome even when you say the wrong thing half the time."

"Thanks, I guess," I laughed at her form of a compliment, and held up my hand for her to give me a high-five.

I'd taken maybe two steps away from her when I heard her yell out after me, "You need some cock in your life, and he knows what he's doing!"

Unfortunately, even though I was two steps away from Zoey, Tristan was two steps away from me.

He heard her rant, as well as everyone else nearby.

CHAPTER ELEVEN

If my life were a commercial, that would have been the instant where time stopped and a man with a deep voice asked, "Need a moment?"

I'd eat a Twix and my life would rewind just enough so that I could tell Zoey to zip her lips, and I could meet up with Tristan with my dignity still intact.

Regrettably, none of that happened. My face heated up enough to melt wax. I'm sure it was the exact same shade of red as a fire truck. I ground my teeth as I looked down to compose myself for a second, only to see Tristan looking at me with a gigantic smile on his face. At least someone thought this was funny.

I turned around to look at Zoey, who had a hand slapped over her mouth like she realized too late that the shit that came out of it was *that* loud. I raised my hands up to my sides and mouthed, 'What the fuck?' She mouthed back, 'I'm sorry!' and at least had the decency to look apologetic. If it were Nicole who had done it, I knew that bitch would have repeated it again, if not louder.

"C'mon," Tristan called out to me, heading in the direction I'd walked from.

The nicely dressed man who had screamed at him while he had been talking to me before was in front of Tristan, talking on his cell, and leading the way through the crowd. I trailed a little behind my newly discovered porn acquaintance. He kept glancing back every few steps, shooting me little smiles each time. It was strange how people turned to look at him every once in a while. Recognizing the looks of pure lust in many women's eyes when they spotted him was pretty unsettling as well.

The only other thing that was more uncomfortable was how I felt right then. If it wasn't bad enough that I found out he did porn, now he knew I "needed some dick in my life." I liked what I knew about Tristan so far; he was funny and so hot my eyeballs ran the potential of sizzling just by looking at him, but I just felt strange. I was probably being a hypocrite, and maybe a little sexist by allowing myself to feel weird since I couldn't care less what Zoey did. Was it because I knew she was just with women, and Tristan was using his dick to have sex with girls?

My stomach churned at the thought again.

Once we were out of the majority of the crowds and heading toward a row of doors that lead somewhere else, the man in the business suit turned around to look at Tristan with a shake of his head, and then looked me up and down. "This is a terrible idea for your image, Tristan. I mean, she's really lovely, but—"

"Shut up, Walter," Tristan groaned, holding the door open for me to follow the man through the new hallway we were in.

"You know how bad of an idea it would be to—" the man I assumed was named Walter continued. There were more doors down the hallway with a lot of people coming in and out of them. He stopped abruptly in front of a door to the right that said Covert Entertainment on a taped-on piece of paper.

"That's all for today, Walt. I'm leaving once I get cleaned up." Tristan cut him off again before ducking into the room we had stopped in front of. He motioned for me to follow before he shut the door in front of Walter's face with a loud sigh. He gave me a cheeky grin, but his face looked resigned and a bit weary. "Sorry about that. Walter is my manager."

"Okay." I nodded before glancing away.

The room was pretty sparse with a vanity mirror, a chair on one side, couch on the opposite corner with a pile of clothes draped across it, and a small wardrobe. There was also another door to the right, probably leading to another dimension, knowing my luck.

Tristan cleared his throat as he slid one of his slender hands up to his hair only to yank at the short strands. He pulled his hand away from his head, staring down at his palm. He frowned, before flipping it over to show me the black smudges trailing across it. "I hate this crap."

"It's washable?" I asked him, referring to the black color in his hair. I felt so nervous for some reason. It was like my senior class salutatorian speech all over again, with sweaty palms and pits.

"Yeah, it gets out after one or two rinses," he answered, looking down at his palm again. "Do you mind helping me wash it out in the sink?"

I should have wanted to tell him no when I realized why he invited me here. Hopefully, he wasn't stupid enough to think we were going to *get to know each other better*. I knew deep within me he wasn't like that. At least with me, he wasn't. He'd been nothing but kind and silly. Once again, another reason to deny he wanted anything besides friendship with me. If he really wanted to, he'd have me pushed up against the wall, but he hadn't. Instead, I simply nodded as I followed him through the door I'd seen earlier to find it was a small restroom with a sink and a toilet. There was barely enough room for both of us to be in there together, so I had to squeeze into the area between the sink and the toilet. I saw him turn on the left knob for the hot water and spotted two white towels hanging on his right side.

He was staring at me through his black-framed glasses when I looked back at him. "Is there something on my face?" I asked.

He smiled and shook his head. "No." Tristan looked at me for another heartbeat or two before taking off his glasses and placing them in the front pocket of his jeans.

"Are those prescription glasses?" I blurted out another awkward question.

He nodded slowly. "I'm farsighted." Tristan ran a hand through his jet-black hair again, grimacing when he was halfway done with the action, probably remembering it stained his skin. "Kat, I—" He sighed. "The water should be ready now."

Tristan dipped his head closer to the sink. He was so tall that he had to bend over at the waist to get parallel with it. I had to scoop my hand under the tap to get a steady stream of water over his scalp. A faint swirl of charcoal tainted the vivid white color of the sink as the hair color washed off easily with the help of his fingers pulling at the strands. Within a couple of minutes, the auburn color started peeking out from under the black. It took about ten minutes of running water, using one hand to scoop water onto his hair while using the other to help him rub and scratch at the temporary hair dye to get about 95 percent of the color off.

"Thank you," he said softly once we were done. I put a towel over the back of his head for him to dry off. "Did you get your autograph?"

"I did," I replied. "His voice was a little squeakier in person."

He chuckled, still facing down while he ran the towel through his damp hair. It was still a bit darker than it had been earlier when he'd taken his cap off, but nowhere near the shade it was at when he was in Lingus mode. "Most of us are a lot different in person," he said simply, but I felt like he was trying to convey more into his words. It didn't escape me that he said *us*, like he acknowledged the fact that he really was a porn star despite the fact he didn't tell me about it earlier. It suddenly hit me why Nikki thought he looked familiar when I first saw him at Calum's booth. She'd seen his work before. My stomach clenched at the mental picture of the poster he had by his booth with the big-busted bitch.

"I see," I mumbled out. "I won't tell anyone your real name, if that's what you're worried about."

Tristan's bright green eyes looked right at me like he was trying to look through me. "I'm not. I know you wouldn't tell anyone."

It was so awkward in the tiny restroom; the tension felt suffocating. I didn't like this weirdness. Whether it was with him or with someone else, I'd hate it. Tristan dropped the towel, which was then more black than white, on the floor and waved for me to follow him out of the bathroom almost as if he read my mind. *Don't check him out. Don't check him out. Don't check him out,* I repeated to myself to no avail.

I didn't want to look at him, but really, who wouldn't eye-molest the shit out of him? I bet if my grandma were still alive, she'd probably fondle his perfectly round ass. It looked like he'd cut a soccer ball in half and then stuffed the two ends under his snug-fitting jeans.

Ugh. *Why? Why?*

Why couldn't he have a flat ass? A butt chin? At least a really crappy personality? I could live with that. I could use that as a reason to leave, but I knew he didn't. Even if he was a porn star, I knew he wasn’t a bad person. My bullshit-meter had become finely tuned after teaching pathologically lying fourth graders. I'd be able to tell if he was full of shit, but he wasn't.

"This is really making you feel weird, isn't it?" he asked me all of a sudden, stopping in front of the couch to pick up the black hoodie he had on earlier.

I wanted to tell him no, but I couldn't. "Yeah, a little. I just... I don't know. I just thought you were some bored guy who was really friendly, and now... you have fans who probably think... I don't know. I don't know what I'm saying." It was a struggle to express what I was feeling because I really didn't know what I thought or felt exactly.

"I am some bored guy who was friendly to you." He gazed up at me through those long eyelashes without saying anything. He shrugged more to himself than to me, I thought. "Can I tell you something and you won't laugh?" he asked, but I was nodding before he even finished the question. He shook his head in amusement just a little. "It's hard —"

My phone started ringing obnoxiously loud right then. "Hold on," I told him, digging through my purse for my phone. Yanking it out, I saw the picture I had for Nicole, which was actually of her ass crack, displayed across the screen, so I knew I needed to answer the call. "Yes, Madame?"

"Let's go, Slut McGee. If I hear Zoey cry one more time about how hungry she is, I'm going to kill someone. Meet me in the parking lot. Or do you want us to wait inside so you don't get lost?"

"I'll meet you by your car." We each said a quick bye before I hung up the call and tossed my phone back into my purse.

"You need to go?" Tristan asked, zipping up his hoodie.

I nodded at him. "My friend, Nicole, is ready to leave," I told him, starting to make my way over to the door. "Umm, I think she invited Calum to our friend's birthday party next week, so you're welcome to come too, if you want," I blabbered like a moron.

"Okay," he said, standing there, hands shoved into the pockets of his hoodie.

"Well, I guess, hopefully, I'll see you... there." My hand was on the knob, and I felt bad for just storming out of there. "Bye, Magellan," I added, not bothering to make any eye contact before throwing the door open and hustling down the hallway to leave.

I was about halfway out the door when I realized he never got the chance to tell me what was on his mind.

CHAPTER TWELVE

Fifteen minutes and eight wrong turns later, I found Nicole's silver Mercedes in the parking lot.

The closer I got to the car, the more I realized I was going to be facing the Spanish Inquisition as soon as I got in.

Zoey was already sitting in the front passenger seat, offering me a quick wave through the window as I slipped into the backseat. I looked up to find Nikki adjusting the rearview mirror to face where I was sitting while Zoey moved the mirror on the visor to see me as well. They stayed quiet, staring at me through the reflection.

"What?" I asked, because their silence was stifling.

"Oh, you know what," Nicole responded with an inquisitive purr.

Zoey raised a perfect, dark eyebrow at me. "Spill the deets."

Nicole snorted as she cocked an eyebrow at Zoey. "Deets, Zo? Are you watching ABC Family again?"

"No," she answered quietly, looking away before sighing in resignation. She was a terrible liar. "Yes! Okay, I have been. They have entertaining programming! Leave me alone."

About a year and a half ago, Zoey had broken up with her long-time boyfriend, Blake, because he said he "had it" with her profession, and then continued on tearing her a new one. Our little ray of sunshine and love became depressed in the aftermath of her split, and somehow ended up spending two straight weeks watching anything and everything on ABC Family. I tried to explain to her that real teenagers didn't say things like "L.O.L" and "L.M.A.O" when they talked in person, but it took us months to break her out of the lingo she picked up.

Secretly, I watched a couple of shows on there every once in a while, but I would take that to the grave with me.

"Oh, lord," I huffed to myself, because I knew they wouldn't give a shit whether I wanted to share or not. "I just helped Tristan wash the hair color out. That's it."

"Wait. Tristan?" Zoey asked.

Only the top half of Nicole's face could be seen in the mirror, but I knew her expressions well enough to know she was confused. "I thought he was Robby Lingus?"

"Tristan is Robby Lingus, dumb-dumbs," I said

with a roll of my eyes.

"Huh," Nikki whispered to herself. "And Tristan is the guy who caught you pulling out your wedgie?"

Zoey started giggling as she turned in the seat to look at me face to face. "I can't believe you did that in front of Robby Lingus."

I snapped the seatbelt in. "Why are both of you calling him by his entire name anyway? That's stupid."

"You never call Andrew Wood just Andrew, asshole," Nicole said, and she was right, I didn't. I mean, I could just call him Andrew, but he wasn't just any Andrew; he was Andrew Wood. Nikki began reversing out of the parking spot, making funny noises from the front seat. "I knew black wasn't his natural hair color," she mumbled. "You really didn't know who he was?"

"Nope. I just thought he was some guy." The more I said and thought that, the more it genuinely bothered me. It seemed to be that everyone knew who Robby Lingus was except me. It wasn't like I watched porn every minute of the day, but still. This was exactly like the time everyone else knew not to drink from the punch bowl except me, and I ended up drunk off my ass.

"He's really nice, Kat. I've met him a couple of times in passing," Zoey said in a cheerful voice, her gray eyes still peering at me through the visor mirror. "Did he ask you for your phone number or anything?"

Part of me felt like such a fucking loser, while the other half was relieved. The loser half was disappointed he didn't make an effort to at least try to build a friendship with me, because I thought maybe he sensed that we got along really well, but maybe he was just that nice and funny to everyone? He probably was. The other part of me was relieved that he hadn't asked for my number, or even made an effort to give me that idea.

I was an only child; I didn't know how to share, and I wasn't willing to learn. What was I going to do if I started developing feelings for a porn star? I already felt mopey about the situation after just three talks.

"Nope."

Zoey frowned, flipping the visor up. "Well, whatever. You don't need any real dick as long as you have batteries."

"Oh, yeah, thanks for that by the way, Zo. Real smooth," I groaned, reminding her of the embarrassing outburst over by the booths.

She gasped, and I saw her throw a hand over the left side of her face. "I'm sorry, Kat!"

"It's fine," I grumbled back, knowing I couldn't stay mad at her even if I tried.

Nikki had been surprisingly quiet for too long, which I knew from experience was never a good thing. Her intense hazel eyes were locked on me through the rearview mirror. "You wouldn't do a porn star?"

"The jealousy would eat me alive," I said with a sigh. "I don't want to set myself up for heartache being with someone who was with other girls on the side, Nik. No offense, Zo," I finished, knowing that even though Zoey's situation was different, her job had still cost her a pretty good relationship, but we all knew now that a pretty good relationship wasn't a great relationship.

"So, what you're trying to say is you wouldn't let him fertilize your flower?" Nikki snorted.

Zoey made a stupid noise that sounded like a cough and a choke. "You wouldn't let him hide his salami?"

"Pump gas into your tank?"

"Hibernate in your cave?"

"Catch a ride on the Kitty Kat Express?"

"Tenderize your meat?"

I groaned between laughs. "And I wonder why none of us have steady relationships."

CHAPTER THIRTEEN

I tugged at the bottom of my dress for the fifth time in the last thirty minutes, earning a scowl from Josh.

"Quit fidgeting with your hem!" he hissed before tossing back a shot of whatever the bartender had supplied him with. Josh used his thumb to wipe at the corner of his lips. "You look great, Kat, so quit that shit."

"I don't mind showing off some leg, but I don't want everyone to see my ass," I tried to explain to him.

I wasn't shy with my body for the most part. I'd inherited my dad, Frank's, excellent metabolism later in life, exercised regularly, and ate pretty well. Obviously, I was no size zero like Zoey, but I was content and comfortable with my size four. Well, usually more like a five or a six, depending on how often I went to the gym.

Josh cocked an eyebrow at me, shifting on the stool he was occupying at the bar as he raked his dark blue eyes up and down my frame. I'd feel uncomfortable if any another man looked at me like he would some prized sports car, but this was Josh. Josh who I had caught wearing my underwear multiple times when we were roommates in college. Josh who liked DP, and I wasn't talking about Dr. Pepper or double penetration in the form of vag and ass.

Zoey and I were more excited about giving him Officer Spanky, as we'd started calling him, than we were about his birthday party. Unfortunately, the birthday boy and I were the first ones at Breeze. Zoey was coming with some 'friend' named Eva as well as bringing along Ryan, her brother. Nicole was going to pick up Calum. That idea made me laugh a little because it was typical Nikki behavior. She always picked up the guy on their first date. I think she was trying to send a message of dominance, but who really knew. I was surprised she managed to wait more than an entire week to meet up with Calum instead of caving in and meeting him up for some "P and V time," as she deemed it.

It had already been seven days since the porn convention. Time went by so fast it felt like only a couple of days instead. Now that school was out of session, I was busy working on my newest book and hitting up the gym with Zoey. Unfortunately, the stud muffin I'd created for my newest novel shared pretty much every trait with Tristan King. Go fucking figure. The one person I tried not to think about was also the one person I couldn't stop thinking of. I didn't go as far as to name him Tristan too, but I settled for Christian the moment I came across the name randomly one night.

"I like your dress," Josh said, running a manicured finger down the strap of my polka dot black dress. It had tiny spaghetti straps, a sweetheart neckline, reached me at a respectable knee-length, but the best part of it was that I found it on sale.

I squeezed Josh's nose between the knuckles of my index and middle finger because I knew how much he hated it. "Thank you. You look nice too." He grimaced as he pulled away, adjusting the dark gray suit he was wearing over a crisp white shirt, and looked around to make sure any potential suitors didn't interpret my action as a romantic advance.

"So, is Robby Lingus coming or what?" he asked, picking up the mojito, which he ordered at the same time as his shot.

The bad thing about having three friends who were all really nosey, as well as really closely-knit, was that if one knew something that the others didn't, it was only a matter of hours before everyone knew. It was a blessing and a curse. I'd have to give Zoey and Nicole credit though, Josh didn't find out about the Tristan and Robby situation until the day after the AFA Expo. Being the good friend that he was, he spent an hour going into details on how much prettier, smarter, and sexier I was than any of the other girls he'd ever seen Tristan with in his pornos. My boobs, ass, legs, face, and intelligence had never been more complimented in my life before that conversation.

It was a testament to my ignorance that my gay best friend knew who Robby Lingus was and I didn't. I didn't even know Josh watched anything other than male-on-male porn.

"No clue. Nikki didn't say anything, so I wouldn't put my money on it."

Josh frowned, raising his hand to touch his rock-hard hair. I swear he used half a bottle of gel on his blond hair every day. Where Zoey, Nikki, and I didn't bother highlighting or coloring our hair, Josh didn't hold back. His white-blond highlights were redone every three weeks, religiously.

He frowned and shrugged. "You think he might be at least a little gay?"

I snorted before I picked up my glass of vodka and cranberry juice. "I don't think you can be a little gay," I laughed, but secretly asked God not to let him swing both ways.

"You never know, Booger. Maybe he secretly likes a pink pickle," Josh said with a straight face. I couldn't help but wince at his use of my nickname.

"Is that what you're going to wish for tonight?"

Josh crossed his fingers on both hands and closed his eyes. "All I want for my birthday is for Robby Lingus to be gay," he chanted before we both burst out laughing.

A manly snort interrupted us, followed by a velvety voice that sounded amused. "I'm flattered, but I think you'd have better luck wishing Calum was gay. He likes crossing swords."

Josh and I spun around in our stools to face the source of the milky, smooth voice, but I already knew who it was. Tristan was, of course, standing just two feet behind us, his hands as always, buried into the front pockets of his charcoal-colored, slim-fitting pants. The black button down shirt he had on was neatly tucked into his pants and the sleeves were rolled up to his elbows.

Good golly, Molly. I was worried Josh would try to bite him if I didn't get to it first.

Tristan grinned at both of us, when we noticed that Calum stood right behind him with Nikki in tow. "It happens. It's just... life. When you have two shafts that close together, you just can't help it," Calum explained with a shake of his head.

Josh snickered from beside me. "Don't I know it, baby. You wanna sword fight?" he purred at Calum with a wink.

I started laughing, looking up at Calum and Tristan just standing there for a moment, completely silent and looking at Josh with blank expressions before they both burst out with loud laughs too. The three exchanged introductions while Nicole squeezed through them, smoothing down the strapless cream dress she was wearing and tossing her straight, long sandy locks over her shoulder.

She leaned down to wrap me in a hug. "You look pretty," she said, tugging on a few strands of my wavy hair.

"Thanks, Nik. You do, too," I told her.

A second later, Josh let out a squeal, before darting past Calum and Tristan, saying something about having spotted his birthday present. Josh had a special gift for being able to spot a gay man in a crowd. It was like gay-radar, but more along the lines of a male dog catching a female dog's scent in heat.

"Calum, you want to dance?" Nicole asked him like he really had a choice.

The massive man just nodded and shot her a big smile. "My pleasure," he purred, and Nikki snorted, but didn't say anything as they headed off.

"Hey," Tristan said in a smooth, deep voice while rooted to his spot a couple feet away. I could see his eyes move from my face down to the exposed skin of my chest for a very brief second before he looked at my eyes again.

"Hey," I said really low before clearing my throat. "I didn't think you'd come."

He smiled at me as he planted himself onto the stool Josh left unoccupied. He twisted it around to face my direction. "I don't really have a life outside of school and work," he said with a shrug of a broad shoulder. "I wanted to see you, anyway."

I snorted, rolling my eyes in his direction. "You're

full of it," I told him, trying to wave down the bartender. I'd mentally prepped myself for his charm; there wasn't a doubt in my mind that he was a professional at luring and seducing females on a regular basis.

"I'm serious. I wouldn't lie to you."

"Okay," I agreed unwillingly, with a smile and sip of my drink.

"What are you drinking?" he asked and took my glass to smell it.

"Vodka cranberry," I answered while he tipped it back, finishing off the little bit that was left. His pink tongue peeked out to lick his bottom lip. "Do you drink out of every random person's glass?"

Tristan snorted and looked at me under eyelashes. "No, just my mom and now you."

"I guess now would probably be a bad time to tell you I have the flu then."

He laughed, a full throaty chuckle. The space between us was so narrow, his warm knee pressed against my thigh. "I'll take my chances," he said with a smile. "Your friend Josh seems like a nice guy. How old is he?"

"He's twenty-seven," I told him.

"How'd you meet?" Tristan asked, his clear green eyes locked on mine.

I start telling him about how we were in the same Spanish class, and it took me half the semester to finally talk to him. Then I went off into a rant about being roommates our junior year, and how I caught him walking around naked one too many times until I had to set up a mandatory clothing rule when outside of the bedrooms. He kept asking me questions about when we lived together, and then bought me another vodka cranberry while he sipped some kind of beer I'd never heard of.

"What do you do?" he asked. We were both a little more relaxed than we had been at first, and somehow we'd shifted our stools so that the inside of his right thigh was pressed against my outer left thigh creating a pleasant heat on my bare skin.

"I teach fourth graders."

His smile reminded me of the sun after I'd been in the dark for too long; it'd be so bright you had to squint. "That's neat. Where do you teach?"

I sipped my drink and waved at Josh, who was talking to some guy behind Tristan. "Tucker Elementary."

"Really? The law office I work at is right down the street."

Law office? I was a lightweight when I drank and my tummy had already been feeling a little fuzzy. I remembered he mentioned working and going to school. "Hammond and Associates?" I asked, because their office building was one of those modern masterpieces I liked to look at on my way home.

He nodded with a smile on his face, swallowing his beer. "Yeah, I have an internship there until I pass the bar."

"You're studying law?" It seemed so weird to me

that he did something else besides his porn crap. Did he not get paid enough? Zoey just did her scenes for a living, but I could faintly remember hearing her mention that women got paid a lot more than guys did.

"Family law. I have one more semester left until I'm done," he answered me.

I felt a bump on the back of my stool as I was opening my mouth to tell him how great that was when I felt cold liquid spill down the front of my dress. I was pretty sure I yelped and pulled the front of my dress away from my body as the stream of cold flowed down my chest.

"Oh, shit! I'm so sorry!" a masculine voice said from behind and started passing me napkins from the bar.

I patted down my skin with the napkins to soak up whatever crap was in his drink. "It's okay," I said between drying myself and looking up at the guy who held a half empty glass of something brown. "I'm fine."

The guy finally walked away once I was done, but I caught Tristan's eyes running over my chest again. He reached out and swept his finger over my collarbone, wiping off a spot I'd missed. His finger was warm and callused on my skin. I couldn't control the goose bumps that spread out over my arms in reaction.

He gave me a soft smile, taking his sweet time to pull his hand back. "I really did want to see you."

I really wanted to believe him, but it was hard.

CHAPTER FOURTEEN

"HAPPY BIRTHDAY TO YOUUUUUUUU!" Half of the lounge sang along; it was more screaming than singing, which was followed by deafening cheers as Josh blew out the candles on his cake. We had kept it to two sparkling candles at his insistence; he claimed he didn't want anyone to know his real age.

I stood between Zoey and Tristan as we watched the birthday boy try to drunkenly cut his cake into squares, but instead made the slices come out like sloppy looking geometric shapes. The guy he had started talking to earlier helped pass out slices, which I thought was sweet. A sharp elbow jabbed into my rib cage out of nowhere.

"Kitty Kaaaaaat..." Zoey moaned in a singsong voice. Her gray eyes were wide and glazed over, hinting at the fact she was hammered. "Kaaaaaat..."

"Yes?" I asked, trying my best not to snort.

Her bird-like arm wrapped around my waist as she snuggled into my side, resting her head against the top of my chest; her date, Eva, looked at us with an amused smile. "My little kitty cat goes meow, meow, meow. Allllll over town!"

I could see Eva start cracking up, and heard Tristan snicker from his spot right next to me. "I think it's time for you to get home," I told her, stroking her back while trying not to laugh.

She was a silly drunk, my Zoey, like I was, but I'd stopped drinking hours ago when she had just gotten started. I knew she was going to be disappointed tomorrow when she couldn't remember the facial expression on Josh's face when he opened up his box. Ryan had been taking pictures randomly, so I made a mental note to ask him if he took one of the presents. Nicole got him anal beads as well as tickets to see his idol, Adam Lambert. I couldn't remember what Ryan got him, but the big surprise was that Calum and Tristan got him something too. Zoey had been trying to climb on top of the bar then, and Eva and I were too busy trying to get her down to see what it was.

"I'm gonna go find Ryan and see if he'll take us home," Eva said, before heading to look for Zoey's brother.

"Heading home after this?" Tristan asked, coming to stand in front of a drunk Zoey and me.

I nodded at him before shifting my arm to rest against my best friend's shoulders. "Yeah, I'm pooped. You?"

"Definitely, it's past my bedtime. I'm usually asleep by midnight," he said with a grin. I made a really unladylike noise from my nose, which sounded like a mutated snort that made his green eyes go wide. "How many times do I have to tell you that I won't lie to you?"

I watched his face to see if he looked amused, but he didn't. I was starting to believe he was being serious. "Okay, okay," I said, my voice much softer than before.

Zoey started making some sort of grumbling noise from her face plant between my boobs that sounded like, "Buhday to jew."

"Hear that? She's still singing happy birthday to Josh," he chuckled, looking down at the baby koala I had wrapped around me.

"I'd rather her do this than when she starts trying to stick her hands up my and Nikki's skirts, making really loud honking noises," I told him, remembering the many times Zoey had gotten piss drunk and molested our asses and breasts.

"Kaaaaaat...." Zoey started moaning again, but squeezed her arms tighter around me. "Member that video? Jou kissed me..." and I knew the road she was going down when she started bringing up a video. Sober Zoey would never, ever bring up the video, but Drunk Zoey had less of a verbal filter than normal, so I slapped a hand over her mouth and coughed.

Tristan raised an eyebrow. "What was she talking

about?"

"No clue," I told him, and knew I needed to change the subject so he'd forget anything he had heard. "So, uh, Robby Lingus? Huh? Who came up with that one?"

He made a face that lasted for two split seconds before he smiled, looking very forced. I was starting to think he didn't really feel comfortable talking about that side of his life with me for some reason. "Robert is my middle name, so I got Robby from that, and Calum actually came up with Lingus. He thought it was the funniest thing he'd ever heard."

I wanted to ask him if he was good at cunnilingus, but I didn't. If I were at least a little tipsy, there would have been a huge risk of actually asking, but Ryan and Eva appeared a moment later. Ryan huffed about Zoey's inebriated state as he tucked his little sister close to him.

"Remind her she owes me tomorrow," he moaned with a shake of his wavy, black hair. His beauty equaled that of Zoey, his build thin, tall, and extremely attractive. "You need a ride, beautiful?"

"No, I'm good. From the looks of it, I'm driving Josh's car home," I said, and pointed to where Josh stood with his new friend while getting fed cake.

He simply nodded and gave me a tender kiss to the cheek, said bye to Tristan, and left.

"Your husband doesn't mind you getting kisses from guy friends?" he asked with a bit of a smile.

"Nah," I told him, but refrained from winking like

my inner whore suggested. I wanted to ask him if he had a girlfriend. I doubted he did. I was sure Nikki would have mentioned it if she knew, but you could never be too sure. There was no really suave way of asking that question indifferently, so I just jumped for it. I'd look like more an idiot if I tried to be slick and ask. "Do you have a girlfriend?"

The words sounded harsh against the air, but he just smiled, shaking his head. "No. It's hard enough to have friends," he almost sounded a little sad saying that. "I've tried having a girlfriend, but I just can't. It's not... a good idea to be attached to someone and then go and have sex with other people, you know?"

I got it. I'd seen what it did to Zoey and her past relationship. When they first got together, he thought having a porn star for a girlfriend was the hottest thing ever. He bragged to anyone who would listen that he was dating Zoey Star, vag-eating champion of the world. Then slowly, it stopped being so awesome for him. He started getting jealous as well as frustrated with the idea of Zoey being with other women. Imagine if she was with men? I couldn't bear the thought of it.

I knew what he was trying to tell me, even though my disappointment reached a level that hadn't been seen since I was ten and I didn't get that pony I wanted for Christmas. He didn't want a girlfriend. He was not interested in me in that way because he did porn. I gave myself an internal cheer, screaming at my self-esteem to get up, because if I really wanted to be in a relationship, or have sex with someone, I wouldn't have a problem finding a person to do that with. I was pretty, smart, and funny, I reminded myself.

I nodded, forcing a smile because I knew I wouldn't gain anything but loser points by letting him see how his words had bothered me. The awful thing was, I knew I was a terrible actress. Nikki and Josh had drilled that reality in my head forever, but I couldn't care less. "That makes a ton of sense," I said with an even voice.

By the look on his face, I could tell he sensed my discomfort, because his smile was a mix of sweet and sad. He started pulling at his wild brown hair and sighed. "Kat, I don't have any friends besides Calum, but he's more like a brother to me."

Josh decided in that moment to start hollering my name across the bar where he stood with his newest friend. I put my index finger up to let him know he needed to give me a second. My stomach didn't know whether to drop or do flip-flops, because obviously, he wasn't going to be asking me out with this speech, but the anticipation was quickly killing me.

Tristan continued pulling at his hair, rocking back and forth on his heels like a nervous kid. "Back at the convention, I was just trying to tell you that I hope we could try to be friends?"

I wanted to give him the finger.

But I also wanted to hug him and tell him I'd take whatever he was willing to give me, like a fool.

But fuck.

Shit.

"Yeah," I told him with as much enthusiasm as I could muster.

Should I tell him that my three friends had all seen me naked multiple times and vice-versa? Probably not.

He gave me a happy smile, nodding at my acceptance of our possible friendship. "Okay."

I still wanted to give him the finger.

Twice.

A deeper urge made me want to yell in frustration because *really*? I had three great friends already, and I was more about quality than quantity, but my heart was weak and unable to say no to Tristan's request. He was too hot and that was what was terrible about it. He was the most beautiful person I'd ever seen, more so than any movie star or model, and I really couldn't put my finger on what set him apart. I think it was because I had a suspicion he may have been a reformed nerd, or something along those lines. He was too goofy to have been a well-adjusted person his entire life.

"I'm gonna go get Josh's keys so I can drive home. It looks like he's spending the night with his new buddy," I told him, not really knowing whether or not I was asking him to stay and wait for me.

Tristan nodded. "I'll wait for you here then," he

answered, tucking those big hands into his front pockets.

Josh hung off the bar, standing way too close to his new blond buddy. As soon as he saw me approaching, he stepped away from his friend, holding his arms out to wrap me in a hug. "Thank you so much for everything," he said, squeezing me so tightly against him I ran the risk of letting out gas.

"You're welcome. I hope you had a good party," I mumbled against his neck while he clung to me. "Are you gonna butter your roll tonight?" I asked, poking him in the belly.

Josh laughed against my hair. "Hell yeah. Have you seen his ass? Those buns were baked to perfection."

"Oh, Lord," I snorted.

Pulling me away just a bit, he dipped his head to look me in the eye. "You're fine to drive my car home, right?"

I used to roll my eyes at him when he'd assume the role of an over-protective parent, but now I indulged the lad. I asked Nikki and Zoey to call me when they got home whenever they'd leave my apartment, so I wasn't much better than Josh. "Yeah, I'm good."

"All right, Booger Bear," he said, pulling even further away from me before dropping his car keys into my up-turned palm. "Want me to walk you out?"

I tried to hook my thumb in Tristan's direction as

discreetly as possible, and I guessed Josh took the hint because his heavy-lidded eyes went wide. "I'm covered."

"Are you two...?" Josh started saying before making awful noises. I knew him well enough to get that he was trying to replicate music from porn movies made in the 70s.

The sigh that slipped out of my lips was heavy and dramatic; I even grimaced at my best friend. "He just asked me if we could be friends. He says he doesn't have girlfriends," I spat out, like the words were venomous.

"At least he's being honest with you," he started to say before pausing, and then wiggling his ash blond eyebrows. "I think,"—he leaned down toward me with a devilish look in his eye—"I think you should be the best fucking friend he's ever had."

"I think you're drunk."

Josh rolled his eyes at me as he pushed me toward Tristan. "Think about it, okay? Remember what I told you on the phone, too. I love you!"

"Love you, too," I told him as I tried to let the confusing words sink in. What could he mean by being his best friend? All he conveyed over the phone were compliments. I clenched Josh's electronic key fob in my hand while I made the trek back to Tristan, who looked at me warily with his hands down the front pockets of his pants. I knew I probably looked like a mess after a night in a hot club. My eyeliner had to be runny, and I was sure my hair was frizzier than a lion's mane, but I was really too tired to care. "Will you walk me to the car?"

"Yeah, I wouldn't want you to get lost on your way over there," he joked with a smile as he followed me out of the lounge. He was only a few steps behind as we made our way out, and I secretly hoped he was checking out my ass.

"Yeah, yeah," I muttered with a grin when he caught up to me. Josh and I had found a really good parking spot about two blocks down the street, so the walk wasn't too far. Tristan was so tall next to me I had to look up to talk to him. "So I guess you should tell me what's with the Clark Kent get-up, Magellan."

He snickered, "Clark Kent?"

"You know... Superman," I teased.

"I know who Clark Kent is, thank you." He chuckled, while his eyes were steadfast on another couple walking the opposite direction on the sidewalk. I felt the pressure of his fingers ghosting across my lower back as I walked a little bit closer to him to avoid running into the couple. "Well, do you think people take employees in the adult video industry seriously?"

Was that a trick question? I wondered. As much as I loved Zoey, I'd seen the way people looked at her like she was the spawn of Satan, and it was hurtful. She was one of the best people I'd ever met, but strangers didn't know that. "No, I guess."

"If Andrew Wood ran for President, would you

vote for him? Even if he had all the experience in the world?"

I knew what my answer was, and it made me feel bad because I was just as bad as those people who looked at Zoey weird. "Probably not," I answered softly.

His fingers brushed against my lower back again. "Don't feel bad. I wouldn't either," he admitted with a sigh. "It took me a long time to decide I wanted to go into law, Kat, and by that time, I'd already done a couple of scenes. If people found out I was Robby Lingus, my chances of finding a firm willing to hire me and take me seriously would be pretty slim. So, I changed my hair color, and with the glasses, I've never had anyone recognize me in public."

I wanted to ask him why he just didn't quit if he was so worried about finding a job after he finished his JD program, but I didn't. Maybe another day. I saw his point though, and it made a lot of sense why he'd go to such extremes to keep his identity a secret. I looked up at Tristan and saw him looking down the street with a furrowed brow. "The only people who know my real name and know Robby are Calum, Walter, and you. Everyone else just knows me as Tristan."

"Nikki and my other friends won't say anything," I promised him.

He looked down at me and smiled. "I trust you. As long as my parents never find out, then it's fine. I think my dad might give me a high-five, but my mom would probably cry and blame herself for raising me wrong," he said and we both started laughing. I could easily remember Zoey coming out to her mom; Mrs. Quinn had handled it a lot better than that.

I spotted Josh's Subaru less than ten feet away before pointing at it. "Are you parked nearby?"

"Yeah, I'm a block down." He gestured down the direction we were walking in. He shuffled his feet again on the sidewalk, like he'd done earlier. "Can I see your phone?"

"Yeah." I handed him my phone and watched him press numbers on the screen. After a moment, his robot ringtone started ringing within his pocket.

"I saved my name under Magellan in your contacts," he told me, handing me back my phone. "I may or may not save yours as Little Gold Digger," he chuckled.

"Oh, God," I groaned. A girl in a white strapless dress was getting out of a cab across the street when it hit me. I'd said bye to Zoey, Ryan, and Josh, but—"When did Nikki and Calum leave?"

CHAPTER FIFTEEN

"Have you heard from Nicole today?" I asked.

Josh was looking down at the screen in front of him, typing in names for our monthly round of competitive bowling. In reality, our 'competitive bowling' was an excuse for the winners to talk shit to the losers for three weeks. "No, and I bet we don't hear from her until tomorrow."

I snickered and kept on tying my damp bowling shoes, silently praying they were wet from disinfectant spray and not sweaty feet. "You're right. She'll probably be walking funny for a week."

According to Tristan, he'd seen Nicole and Calum sneak out of the club about an hour after they'd gotten to Breeze. He also thought he might have seen Nikki stick her hands down Calum's pants, and I, unfortunately, had to assure him that he probably did witness exactly that. I'd tried calling and texting her, but the call went straight to voicemail. If it were any other person missing, I'd be worried, but this was Nikki. If anyone could take care of themselves, it was her.

I also had a feeling that if she were ever kidnapped, they'd give her back after a couple of hours.

A big figure settled down onto the seat next to mine, and I knew without looking up that it was Tristan. When Zoey had called with news that she was nursing "a hangover worse than kidney stones" and couldn't come bowling, I texted the only other person I'd want to go bowling with— Tristan. Friends went bowling with each other, and he was all too excited to tag along. Josh enlisted his buddy from the night before, Leo, and we were set.

I looked over to see Tristan tying his laces with a big grimace on his face. "Are your shoes wet, too?" I asked.

He nodded, tying the other set of laces before sitting back against the chair. Josh was busy finally putting on his shoes, and Leo was ready and waiting across from us, looking at the screens where our scores would show up. Tristan snorted while squinting as he looked at the monitor above our lane. "Does that say Mack Truck and Anaconda up there?"

I opened my mouth with the intention of explaining that it did, in fact, say Mack Truck up there, but not Anaconda, when the words died on my lips. Anaconda was listed on the screen right below Mack Truck.

"Kat is Mack because she has a big front end and a big bumper." Josh motioned toward his non-existent pectoral muscles, where my breasts would be. "You're Anaconda because we all know that's what you have in your pants," he said matter-of-factly. He gestured toward his crotch then, but the look on his face made it seem like he thought we lacked the common sense to understand his reasoning.

Tristan laughed, not seeming to be bothered in the least bit by Josh's explanation, but I was dying. Heat crossed my face, giving away my blush. It wasn't because he was talking about my boobs and ass, but because I, in fact, did not know he had a beast hidden in his pants. The wink Josh gave me when I looked away from Tristan to gain my composure told me he did it on purpose. The bastard winked and mouthed 'BFF' to me like it was supposed to make sense.

Josh and I went up to start our first game, and he owned my ass on the first frame when I knocked down six pins total against his pickup of spares. Tristan gave me a high-five on my walk back and leaned in close to my ear. "I used to play in a league."

He'd told me he wouldn't lie to me a couple of times by that point, but after the first and second ball both made it to the gutter with gusto, it was obvious he had.

On his walk back, he held his hand up for me to

give him a high-five and I did, but I was laughing. "I thought you said you played in a league!" I smirked. "You were talking about little league, weren't you?"

Tristan scowled at me, amusement written all over his face before pushing me in the direction of the lane. "Shut up. I'm warming up."

By the end of the first game, Tristan ended up with a whopping score of 35, and I was at 130. Josh and Leo were whooping from their side as they claimed how our asses got handed to us, and things of that nature. I sat in my chair with my arms crossed over my chest, staring at the two lovers while they did a horrific chest bump.

"Suck it, Josh!" I yelled at him.

My blond friend pointed at Leo with wide eyes. "That's what he said!"

According to Josh, a gay guy couldn't say, "That's what she said!" So, he put his own gay-appropriate spin on it. I swear, all of my friends were their own form of idiot, but I loved them anyway.

One game turned into four, one beer turned into three, and our two lanes made more noise than the rest of the bowling alley put together. When I started going up to bowl, Josh would run up and slap my ass as hard as he could, which wasn't very hard at all, but it still scared the shit out of me each time and caused me to drop the ball. Leo showed us that he could do the moonwalk when he got a strike. Tristan finally warmed up enough to the point in which he was actually knocking down pins, and then making these really horrible R2D2 noises afterward to celebrate.

Two hours later, we were on our last frame. By some miracle, we'd tied, and I could have thanked the beers, which made Josh giggly, because they made him play crappy. He did horribly, only knocking down about six pins, while I got nine. All we needed to win was for Tristan to not suck completely. *Ha*.

He leaned his head toward me when I tugged at his shirt, so he could hear me over the loud music. The smile he'd had on his face over the last two hours was tremendous; I was sure he could have lit up a city with it. He stood so close to me I could taste his soapy scent down the back of my throat. "Don't blow it, okay? I want to win at least one game."

"If my little gold digger wants to win a game, we'll win a game," he promised with a crooked, wicked smile.

Mary Magdalene.

Could friends have benefits?

Tristan brushed a hand down the length of my ponytail and walked backward to the lane. Of course, he got a gutter ball on the first turn while Leo managed to knock down four.

"Don't blow it!" I screamed before laughing at him.

He gave me another crooked smile when he went for his ball again, while Josh threw his ball, managing to only knock down three pins. I was squirming from foot to foot like the outcome of the game decided the fate of humanity, but I really, really didn't want Josh to walk around talking about how he'd won every game for the next month.

Tristan then did the unthinkable by somehow knocking down nine pins.

By the way we both screamed, it was like we'd won the World Series. My tall, new friend, who wore a tight, soft, blue shirt that accented the perfectly flat abs and pillow-like pecs underneath, beelined toward me with his arms stretched out in front of him. I didn't even think twice about jumping into them and wrapping my own around his neck. He was warm and hard against me. His chest was like a solid wall of muscle and it was... ugh, amazing.

At some point, I became aware that my feet weren't touching the floor anymore, but two more sets of arms wrapped around me about the same time.

Tristan stiffened before I felt his chest, which my face was pressed against, start rumbling in laughter.

"Which one of you just grabbed my ass?"

It was Josh, of course.

After saying goodbye to each other in the parking lot, we headed in separate directions toward our cars. Tristan followed me to my car, laughing and retelling me his favorite moments in the game; like when Leo stepped over the line and then slid five feet across the lane. He had to crawl back to avoid busting his ass.

"Thanks for inviting me," he said with a big smile when we were standing right in front of my car door. Covered in a thin layer of sweat, his face glistened just a little by his temples. "I don't think I've had that much fun since high school," he said, and I could tell he was being truthful.

His words made me burst at the seams. A majority of what he told me hinted at a lonely life, and I felt good that, if that was the truth, my loved ones and I could change that for him even if it was only for a few hours. "I'll remind you when we play next month," spilled out of me.

Tristan nodded as he stepped toward me, wrapping a single arm around my shoulder to pull me in close for a hug. I wasn't sure where his other arm was, because I was so distracted by the fact that I was eye level with where his nipple should be; then I felt his other hand rest on the small of my back. He was warm and smelled so good; my brain shut down for the ten seconds I was wrapped up in his hug, completely aware of the fact his entire frame casually brushed against mine.

Was this how Josh hugged me? No, it was not.

He pulled away from me a second later. "I'll call you tomorrow," he said, before turning around to walk where he'd parked. Like 'calling me tomorrow' was something he did every day.

"Drive safe!" I hollered at him in a squeaky voice.

Those green eyes looked back at me one last time. "You too, gold digger!"

Once in my car, I let out a huge sigh. This friend thing was going to be a lot harder than it seemed.

CHAPTER SIXTEEN

I'd been sitting on my couch eating pita chips and staring at my computer screen for an hour. As if they had a mind of their own, my fingers had typed *Robby Lingus* into Google on at least three different occasions, and then erased the search each time. Both my brain and heart were having a debate on whether or not I should go through with the search. Did I want to see videos of him?

I tended to weigh the pros and cons of everything, especially when I needed to make a decision, and right then, I just couldn't. Luckily, my phone started ringing when I typed in the R again.

I groaned, realizing it was all the way on the other side of my couch, so I grumbled my way over to see Nicole's ass crack splayed across the screen. The picture had been taken six months before; the dirty whore had been bent over tying her shoelaces when I'd taken it. Just like Josh had called it, I hadn't heard from her for almost two days. It was only two in the afternoon, making it a little strange that she'd be calling since she was normally at work at that time of day.

"Hey, I was worried you overdosed on dick," I told her first thing.

Nikki snorted. "I came close to it," she said with a hoarse voice.

"Are you sick?" Nicole never got sick. Ever. She'd caught a minor cold once about three years ago, and it lasted all of twelve hours before she was back to normal. Personally, I thought even germs were scared of her.

"No," she said with a deep, throaty laugh before making a pained noise. "It hurts to talk, so don't make me laugh."

"Why do you sound like crap if you aren't sick?"

Nikki sighed dramatically. "I've had a salami down the back of my throat on and off for the last thirty-six hours," she replied, frankly.

My face instantly grimaced. I'd seen Calum's peen a few times in the past when Nicole had shoved her laptop in my face, and that thing was... gargantuan. Colossal. Ginormous. I thought it was fake the first time I saw it. And Nicole tried to deep throat that thing? I was surprised she didn't have permanent damage to her vocal chords, larynx, pharynx, and freaking esophagus.

"Well... as long as it was worth it, then don't

complain."

She giggled softly. "Oh, it was worth it. It was definitely, definitely worth it. That man is a machine. Maybe even a god. It was un-fucking-believable, Kat. I've slept about four hours since Saturday."

"You're such a slut," I told her with a laugh, rolling up the bag of remaining chips.

"Fuck yeah," she tried to purr, but sounded more like a chain smoker with her gravelly voice. "I'm seeing him again later tonight."

"Jesus, Nik. Don't your petals need some rest?" I asked her this despite already knowing the answer. No. For Calum Burro, she'd probably take cocaine to stay awake for the vaginal slaughter that would surely take place.

"Yeah, but I'll ice myself later," she explained. "I'm gonna go make some tea now to soothe my throat. Hopefully, I'll be able to go to work tomorrow."

"Okay then, text me if you need me," I told her.

She made a funny noise on her end of the line before saying, "I will."

I got a flashback of the porn convention and the little thing she said to catch his attention. "Oh! Did you find his g-spot?" I spit out, laughing.

She snickered roughly. "I sure as hell did. He was calling me God, Jesus, Allah, Ghandi, and every other divine being all night. "

CHAPTER SEVENTEEN

R

O

B

B

Y

I hit the delete button.

After a minute, I pressed the delete button again.

The frustrated groan that pushed its way out of my chest was exhausting. I started typing in Tristan's porn name only to stop, delete some letters, type in a few more, and then delete all of them. I knew if I went through with looking up Robby Lingus on Google or any other search engine, there wasn't any going back.

Do it.

Don't do it.

Don't do it.

It really wouldn't be a good idea to see his videos, I repeated to myself at least six times.

Not a good idea.

Not a good idea.

His words from yesterday tumbled through my head. He said he'd call me. It was ten, and I hadn't heard from him. It was hard to beat back the disappointment creeping over me. I hated it when people said they would do something and then didn't. It ate away at me little by little until I was just a measly crumb.

What else could I have expected? Guys seemed to lack manners because they worried so much about what other people thought, and obviously, Tristan wasn't an exception to that. It was ridiculous of me to expect him to be any different from what seemed to be every other guy on the planet. In fact, he was one of the worst.

He fucked girls on video.

I thought if I said it enough, I might become desensitized to the words and general idea.

As soon as the idea echoed through my thought

process, I felt like vomiting. *He just wants a friend.* Tristan told me he wanted to be friends, and most friends didn't talk to each other every day. Right? I had no reason to be jealous or upset. My cat's loud purring distracted me from my man-hating. Matlock, named after my favorite old TV lawyer, was a big, white, Siamese-mix that had shown up on my doorstep last Christmas. He was a hermit and kind of a bastard at times, but I'd grown to love him.

Said bastard was walking over my keyboard like he owned both the computer and me. I had to push him off my laptop; otherwise he'd try to sit on it or lick the screen like he'd done so many times in the past. He hissed at me for kicking him off before sauntering over to the other side of the couch and flicking his tail back and forth.

He reminded me of Josh in cat-form.

I had to force myself to open up my Christian files to work on my newest book. I'd been publishing my own murder-mysteries for about a year and a half. I sold them under my penname, Sophia Nylund, after two of my favorite Golden Girls. My dad used to blame my lack of grandparents as the reason why I liked to watch shows with seniors through middle school and most of high school. I wasn't making enough money to quit my day job, but even if I would have been, I didn't think I could go through with it. I liked my kids. Maybe in a few years I'd think differently, probably when children became the spawn of Satan in general, and I hated them all.

The sound of my phone beeping unexpectedly made Matlock hiss at it.

New Message

Magellan

Showed up on the blank screen of my phone, and even though I should have taken my sweet-ass time unlocking the phone and reading his message, I didn't. The little white box just said:

Please tell me you aren't busy.

Hmm. I wrote back a simple: **No**, when I should have written 'yes' so he didn't think I was sitting around waiting for his call, which I was.

Less than thirty seconds later, his name was across the screen again.

Please take me to urgent care?

CHAPTER EIGHTEEN

I officially hated the navigation feature on my phone.

I should have known better than to trust it to get me to Tristan's house as quickly as possible. For some reason, the navigation always took me somewhere completely random that was most definitely not the location I wanted to go to. It had been close to an hour since I'd gotten his last text message that included his address and informed me his front door was unlocked. After driving across town, several wrong turns, braking at every street sign with hopes that I could see the reflective lettering in the night, I finally parked in front of a Craftsman-style house that matched the address in the text message.

Did he live here by himself?

The house was close to twice as large as the home I'd grown up in, and the neighborhood was a nice, upper-middle-class subdivision. Thinking better of just standing on the street and gawking at the gray house with white trim, I made a beeline for the door and raised my fist to knock, before remembering I could just walk right in. He was really vague after the initial text message, insisting he was sick and needed to go to the hospital.

"Tristan?" I called out, closing the door as quietly as possible behind me.

The hallway was pitch black until I felt around the wall for the light switch. Flicking it on, the hallway and stairs ahead of me were engulfed in bright, pure, white light when my phone vibrated from my pocket. Magellan's name showed up on the front screen before I unlocked it and saw that he wrote **Upstairs on left**. I toed off my tennis shoes before noticing the pile of shoes right by the door and ascended the stairs. I wondered what exactly was wrong with him, because we'd just seen each other the day before, and he seemed perfectly fine.

The upper floor of the house was painted in a neutral tan, and there was only one door on the left of the staircase that was slightly cracked open. "Tristan?"

A pathetic sounding moan came from the other side after I slipped in. I really didn't know what to expect in his room. It took me a second to absorb how large the bedroom was, considering it was only lit by the bedside lamp. A repeat of the same moan came from underneath a lump of comforter on the left side of the bed. I dropped my purse on the floor and walked over to the large pile that I was assuming Tristan was laying under.

"Hey," I called out softly to the human-sized lump.

A few seconds later, there was movement underneath the covers as the portion closest to the head of the bed began shifting around. Tristan's head peeked out from the top of the crisp, white sheets he was rolled in. His poor, beautiful face looked unnaturally pale and clammy. His eyes opened, and then he blinked until I could see the green in them was dull and heavy, completely unlike the vibrant emerald that I'd seen the handful of times before. A deep, painful sounding cough shook its way out of his chest.

"I'm sick, Kat," he groaned out, looking more ashen than he had a moment before. "I'm hot, but I have the chills and everything hurts."

I wasn't a doctor, but I knew those symptoms all too well. It sounded like the flu. I put my hand against his forehead, only to wince at the extreme heat pulsing under his skin. "Do you have a thermometer?" I asked him.

He closed his eyes and nodded, wiggling a hand out of the wrap of sheets he was in to point at the nightstand. Sure enough, there was a white oral thermometer resting on the edge. I asked him to open up his mouth before setting the timer and putting it under his tongue. I knew even without the little contraption that he was much too warm for it to be safe. I brushed my hand over his forehead and hair, only to touch sweat across the span of his face. "I feel horrible," he rasped out with a shiver.

The thermometer beeped a few moments later, and after slipping it out of his mouth, I frowned. It read 103.1. Not good at all. "Tristan, how long have you had a fever?"

"A while."

I sighed. My mom died when I was eleven, and even though my dad did his absolute best with me, I had to learn to take care of myself. There were dozens of times that I'd gotten sick and had to stay home alone so he wouldn't miss work. We needed the money, and his job didn't count staying home with his sick kid eligible for paid sick time. Fortunately, I paid enough attention when my mom was still alive to know, for the most part, how to take care of myself and get over most illnesses without having to visit the doctor. "Does your throat hurt?"

Tristan closed his eyes and swallowed a few times. "No, I'm just thirsty."

"Let me see your throat," I demanded, just to make sure he didn't have crappy, white dots that would mean he had strep. Tristan made another grumbling noise before opening up his mouth. There was enough light from the lamp to see straight down the back of his mouth, which looked well enough. I couldn't help but notice that he didn't even have any fillings. I tapped his chin so he could close his mouth.

"I think you might have the flu, okay? I can take you to the doctor if you want, or else I can probably help you feel better here. Whatever you want."

One dull green eye opened, squinting at me in a haze. "You gave me the flu?" he asked hoarsely.

"How the hell did I give you the flu?"

He let out a short, dry chuckle. "Josh's party," he reminded me. I snorted because he remembered drinking from my cranberry vodka and how I had joked around about giving him the flu. One of his fuck buddies probably gave it to him, I decided. I rolled my eyes at him and started pulling the covers away from his body. The heavy, white comforter was knotted around him in a twist, so I tugged it away as well, only to have him groan. "Be gentle. My body hurts."

"You're too hot to be wrapped up," I told him. I wrestled the comforter away, leaving him in only a white sheet that was tucked closely around him. I tugged it off, and then stood there like a frozen idiot.

I'd seen plenty of nice bodies; all three of my past boyfriends had all been athletic and fit. My movie collection consisted of every film that starred hot, half-naked actors. I saw *300* five times in the theater with Nicole and at least another twenty times on DVD. Josh and I had seen *Thor* six times and drooled during each view. You could consider me a seasoned gawker.

Nothing could have prepared me for that moment.

Tristan lay across his bed in just his boxer briefs. Little, black boxer briefs that did nothing to hide big, muscular thighs. His chest was perfect, pillowy, and hard with just a sprinkle of dark hair across it, but his abs were the Holy Grail of all abs. They formed the kind of eight-pack you could only see on Abercrombie ads. The v-cut of muscle on his hips disappeared beneath the band of his underwear, and then my eyes instinctively froze on the soft bulge the black cotton was covering. Holy shit. Josh's words flitted through my brain. *You're an anaconda because we all know that's what you have in your pants.*

"Like what you see?" Tristan teased softly.

I snapped my eyes up to his smirking face and scowled. Why didn't I expect him to be just as observant as always? "Shut up and get up."

He chuckled wearily and braced his hands on either side of his perfect body to push himself up; my eyes immediately went back to his abs and the rippling muscles that contracted as he sat up. I had more fat around my hips than he did on his entire body. With a few grunts, he was up, his legs swung over the side of the bed. "You don't think I need to go to the doctor?"

"Only if you want to," I told him, but really, I was staring at the lines of sinewy muscles on his biceps and triceps like a person on the verge of dehydration seeing water for the first time.

Tristan ran a hand through his mess of auburn hair and sighed. "I feel like shit, Kat."

"You feel like shit, but I bet you haven't taken anything, right?" I knew he hadn't. When my dad would get sick, he refused to take medicine. He didn't even like to take Tylenol, and every other man I'd ever encountered had been the same way.

"No," he said with a tired grimace.

"Get up then. Your fever is too high, and we need to get it down. You need to take a cold shower at least."

Tristan got up and slowly made his way over to the opened door across from his bed. The bathroom was large, brightly lit, and modern in comparison to the older style of the house. A walk-in shower with clear glass doors and double vanity sink dominated the room. I pretended to look around the bathroom, but stole glances at Tristan's reflection in the large mirror every chance I got. Opening up the doors, he messed with the taps in the shower. "How cold?"

"Cold."

He dug the palms of his hands into his eyes and grunted. "I feel so weak," he moaned. "I tried calling Calum, but he won't answer, and my parents are in New York this week. Otherwise, I wouldn't have asked you to come."

It was hard for me to believe he didn't have anyone beside his parents and Calum in his life who he could turn to. I had my three bitches, Ryan, who I could always rely on, and my dad was only a few hours away. I felt bad for Tristan, but I also wondered why he didn't have anyone else to turn to.

I figured he'd met enough people in his life to find someone worthy enough to let in. "Don't worry about it, Mag."

Tristan tried to give me a smile, but he was feeling so crappy it didn't reach his eyes. "Thanks, Kat." I saw his hands rest on the elastic of his underwear before he hooked his thumbs into it, and then began dragging the material down toward the floor.

Oh, my God.

I didn't know whether to look at him or away, so I hissed. "What are you doing?"

"Taking a shower," he said casually, but his eyes were playful and intense as they fixed on mine in the reflection of the mirror. It almost seemed like he was challenging me to look down. I was tempted, because it seemed like everyone else had seen him except me. He didn't wait for me and turned around to step into the shower. His perfect, globe-like ass teased me. I could still see him through the doors, and since he was taking a cold shower, there was no heat to steam up the doors to create a hazy barrier.

"Do you, uh, have a set of clean sheets?" I stammered out, distracted by the lean figure angled away from me as it stood like a statue under the spray of water. It was almost as if he knew my inner dilemma with seeing his peen. What if I saw it and it ruined me for others?

"In the top drawer of my dresser," he called out, weakly.

I wanted to stay and watch him, but I knew better. He was sick, and I needed to do what I could to make him feel better. Clean sheets always did wonders for me. I knew with the temperature his fever was at, as well as with the amount of sheets and covers he'd been wrapped in, they had to be soaked in sweat. I walked out of the bathroom, heading toward the big dresser parallel to his bed. There were two top drawers, so I opened up the one on the left first and froze. There were piles of extra-large and extra-extra-large condoms practically filling the entire drawer.

Oh. My. Fuck.

CHAPTER NINETEEN

The sheets were in the *other* drawer.

Somehow, I managed to correctly change the sheets in my condom-induced stupor. The water from the shower had shut off a couple of minutes ago, and by then I was fluffing his pillows and trying not to think about the massive amounts of condoms stocked in his dresser.

Who did that?

I didn't know if I was scared of the fact that he had so many, or if I was kind of excited by the prospect that he had to buy the plus-sized ones.

I tried my best not to think about why he had so many condoms; otherwise, I may have been tempted to put on some gloves before touching anything else in his bedroom. Hell, his entire house might have been contaminated with dried bodily fluids. Yuck. Maybe he bought them in mass quantities when they were on sale?

Tristan stepped into the bedroom with only a towel wrapped around his slim waist, his wet hair going in a million different directions. Despite the fact that his body was immaculate in proportions, his shoulders were slightly hunched, and his face was droopy.

Then, I thought about those Durex XXLs sitting in his drawer again, and my face broke out in a wild blush.

He stopped at the foot of the bed, looking at me intently before a knowing, tired grin spread across his pale face. "You opened up the wrong drawer, didn't you?"

I hated him.

"Did you raid a Trojan factory and steal their yearly supply?" I sputtered out instead of denying it.

Tristan snickered, but it was a weary noise, and he just shook his head before turning his back to rifle through the second row of drawers. "Calum buys me at least ten boxes for my birthday and Christmas each year, because he likes the looks on people's faces when he checks out. They're for... you know, *work* even though I have more than enough to last me a lifetime right now."

Wait. *What?*

"You wear condoms in your scenes?" I should have been more nonchalant about asking, but I wasn't. My verbal filter needed a serious replacement because who asks that? But then again, there were men who still wore condoms in pornos? According to Zoey, STD testing had become so standardized in the industry that most men didn't wear them anymore, because the chances of catching a disease was very slim.

I still thought it was kind of fucking gross, but whatever. Yet another reason why I was not in porn. I couldn't imagine a guy dipping his bucket into more than one well before mine.

What I lacked in a verbal filter, Tristan lacked in modesty. His towel fell to the floor when he stepped into a clean pair of boxer briefs, and I got fifteen seconds worth of smooth butt-cheeks to appreciate. "I do. It's a stipulation in every contract I sign. It's harder to get work because of it, but I'm not willing to compromise, you know?"

Suddenly, I gained a whole lot of respect for Tristan.

I wanted to ask him how much work he did during the month, during the year, over the course of his career, but I didn't. I knew he wasn't feeling well, and I doubted we were at that point in our friendship where we could ask each other anything, like I could with Nikki, Zoey, and Josh. Zoey liked to send me pictures of her turds when they were "special ones," as she called it. I guessed that was part of what made our friendship special, because I laughed when I saw the pictures instead of being grossed out by it.

"That's good, Tristan," I told him, but my face was

still flushed. Those were a ton of fucking condoms, and that fact was not easily forgotten. "So does that mean I don't have to rinse my hands off with bleach since I touched your bed?"

He was facing me then with an indescribable expression. "No, you don't need to scrub the skin off your arms either. I'm not a whore." I knew he wasn't feeling well, but I opened my mouth to make a smart-ass comment about his whore status when he recognized the look in my eyes and gently slapped a hand over my mouth. "My mattress is the epitome of cleanliness, Kat. Trust me."

I snorted while his warm fingers lingered over my lips. "Fine, fine," I mumbled beneath him until he pulled them away. I caught his eyes flickering to the bed. "You should lie down and rest. I'm gonna guess that you don't have any medicine in the house or food, so I'll be back in a little bit. I'm just going to run to the drugstore and come right back."

"Okay." He nodded, stepping around me to lie down on his bed. "You'll be back though?"

He pulled the sheets up to his neck, leaving the comforter thrown off to the side. He looked so cute with his sad face and pouty mouth. I stepped toward him without thinking and ran a hand through his hair to brush it off his forehead. "I will. If I'm not back in an hour, take another shower, okay?"

"Okay," he mumbled with a drawn out sigh.

I was out of the house and in my car heading to the grocery store I saw on my way over at almost midnight, hoping it was open late. Since I didn't exactly check his cupboards to see what he had, I figured I was better off assuming he didn't have anything sick-appropriate in the house. Luck was on my side, because the grocery store was open. I roamed the aisles looking for Gatorade, bottled water, saltine crackers, whole grain bread, canned soup, tea, the generic kind of Tylenol, and two different kinds of over-the-counter flu medicine.

It took me a little over an hour to make it back to Tristan's house. I made sure to lock the front door, toe off my shoes, and grab the Theraflu bottle, leaving the other stuff in the bags on the stairs. I snuck into his room to find his bare back peeking out from under the covers again.

"I'm back," I said softly, watching the muscles in his back tense up.

"Shit, Kat. I didn't hear you come in," he said, flipping over to rest against the headboard. His brown hair was all wet again, the telltale sign that he'd taken another shower, and his abs looked just as nice as they had before.

"I bought you some Theraflu," I told him, peeling off the plastic that covered the top before pouring some of the thick, red liquid into the tiny measuring cup. "Drink it."

Tristan made a face at my outstretched offering before plucking it from my fingers. "I hate this crap." He kept his disgusted face as he tipped the cup back and gulped down the contents. Tristan shivered once he was done and stuck his tongue out. "That's gross."

"You're fine." I snorted and took the measuring cup away from him. "I'm going to go put up the stuff I bought for you. You don't mind if I put it away, do you?"

He shook his head and even waved his hand a little. "Do whatever you want downstairs. *Mi casa es tu casa,*" he said in a perfect accent.

"I'll be back then," I told him before walking out. I took my time to look around the second floor of his house on the way downstairs. There were three other doors on the other side of the hall. A simple, metal chandelier illuminated enough to see that he only had a few things hung on the walls. I decided to maybe snoop later on when Tristan was asleep... if I was there long enough.

I jogged down the stairs, grabbed the two bags of groceries, and took inventory of the bare walls of the staircase. There was an opening on the right side of the room, and I peeked in to see that it was a not-so-formal dining room. I turned the opposite direction, spotting a living room that opened up to his kitchen. After flicking on the nearest light switch, I made my way into the kitchen, which was all stainless steel appliances, sparkly, black granite countertops, and mahogany cabinets. It was my dream kitchen come true.

Finding things in the spacious kitchen took some time because even though it looked like Tristan was neat, he didn't have anything organized intelligently.

I finally put a pot of water on to boil so I could make him some Echinacea tea like the kind my mom used to make me when I was sick. She claimed it helped make me get better faster. Years later, I learned it was known to help boost a person's immune system.

I headed back upstairs with a bottle of orange Gatorade under one armpit, his tea in one hand, and a packet of saltine crackers in the other hand. When I walked in, Tristan was resting with his eyes closed but opened them as soon as he heard my footsteps. I moved his stereo over on his nightstand to set down the crackers and Gatorade.

"Drink this," I ordered, handing him the cup.

He winced as he tried to sit up. He peered inside the cup, but frowned at the discomfort in his body. Flu muscle pains were the worst. "What is it?"

"Tea." I pushed the cup closer to him. "Don't be a pussy, just drink it."

"I should be offended that you call me a pussy, but I'm not," he said softly with a tired smile on his face. He looked at the cup again before taking it from me, sniffing it, and then he gagged.

"You're the worst, you know that?" I laughed at his bullshit. "Just drink it. It's good for your immune system."

Tristan made another face before sipping the hot liquid. "I'm really not picky, but this tastes like ass."

I raised my eyebrow at him. "You know what ass tastes like?"

Even though he was tired and sickly, he

snickered in amusement. "No, I haven't had the pleasure of tasting ass, thank you. What I should've said is it tastes like shit," he murmured, before thinking about what he'd said and snorted. "Don't even say anything. It tastes horrible, and I've definitely never tasted shit," he said, taking another drink and keeping an eye on me. "Can you stay for a little bit?"

"Sure," I answered and went to sit on the end of the bed around the same time he started patting the empty spot next to him. The mattress was king-sized, so I nodded and climbed over to sit to where I was only a couple feet away from him.

In the middle of a sip, he stopped and turned to look at me sharply. "I'm going to get you sick, Kat."

"Don't worry about it. I get my flu shot every year, so if I do catch anything, it won't be too bad. My immune system blows, so I drink that," I pointed at his cup, "all the time."

He tipped the cup back to drink the last bit and shivered again, setting the cup down on the nightstand. "Gross," he muttered, licking his lips. Tristan closed his eyes and wiggled his way down the bed to lay flat against the mattress. "I don't have a TV in here, so you're going to have to tell me all of your secrets to entertain me."

"In that case—" I started to say, but laughed. "I don't have any secrets."

"I don't either besides Robby. Just tell me about your family... or anything, I don't care. Just talking makes me feel terrible," he groaned.

So, I told him. I told him about my dad, Frank Berger, and how he was the hardest working electrician in Gainesville, Florida. I told him about my mom, and how she worked odd-end jobs until she died from a brain aneurysm right before her thirtieth birthday. Tristan learned about my bad haircuts, which made him laugh even though his eyes were closed. He found out about the time I went to a Marlins game with my dad and was dumb enough to wear a skirt, which I ended up tucking into my underwear after a restroom break, so I practically mooned hundreds of people with my white cotton panties. He had tears in his eyes after he asked me how old I was when it happened, and I answered with a whopping sixteen. How he managed to stay awake and pay attention to me while I rambled, I didn't know, but he did, because he constantly chuckled quietly despite the fact that his eyes were closed.

I wiggled my way off the bed and headed over to his side to take his temperature one last time. Once the reading was over, the digital numbers showed that his fever was down to 101.8. "Can you take another cold shower?" I asked him, and he nodded, rolling out of bed sluggishly before heading toward the bathroom.

Exhaustion hit me while I paced around his room, waiting for him to finish his shower. He was fast; in and out, dressed, undressed, and dressed again in less than five minutes. He looked tired and half-asleep despite the freezing shower. Tristan dragged his feet across the floor, making moaning and grunting noises as he settled into bed. The noises were so distracting that later on I realized I didn't get a chance to ogle his abs or the little trail of dark hair from his belly button down the front of his boxers.

"Thank you for coming, Kat," he whispered, his silhouette illuminated by the side lamp.

"Don't mention it," I said softly. My watch showed that it was past two in the morning and more than an hour after he took the Theraflu. I let out a big yawn and rubbed at my face. "Will you be okay alone the rest of the night?"

He opened a single eye, but didn't focus it on me. Instead, he settled that piercing gaze on the ceiling. "I think so," he said, but I could hear the hesitation in his voice. "Can you come back tomorrow and make sure I'm not dead?"

"Of course," I said. I'd stay if he'd asked me to, but he didn't.

Tristan rolled onto his side and started digging through his nightstand drawer, moving all kinds of things over before pulling out a shiny new key and holding it out for me. "Can you lock the door for me, and this way you can let yourself back in? I think my neighbor might try to sneak in and molest me if the door is unlocked all night."

"Oh! The old guy next door?" I joked, even though I didn't see anyone outside.

He groaned and pulled the sheet up to his neck again. "Wait until I feel better," he threatened in the worst ominous voice I'd ever heard.

After a brush of my fingers over his forehead, I slipped his house key into my pocket, and gave him instructions to set an alarm so he could take the Theraflu again in a few hours. I was in my car and heading back home while trying to fight back the fatigue that overwhelmed me. It was so damn hard to keep my eyes open, and I immediately regretted not asking him if I could sleep on the couch. I was so tired that I barely made it up the stairs before kicking and yanking off all of my clothes as I fell onto the bed in a tired heap. Tristan's house key lay discarded on the floor inside of my jeans.

Right before I fell asleep, I remembered randomly that the last guy I'd gone on a couple of dates with wouldn't even tell me the security code for the gate to his apartment.

CHAPTER TWENTY

Four hours after I had passed out on my bed, I woke up to my phone ringing and felt utterly exhausted. I should have gone back to sleep for at least another hour or two, but my mind was already racing between the events of the previous night and wondering who the hell was calling me so early. Frustrated and annoyed, I grabbed my phone like it was the phone's fault why it was ringing at the crack of dawn and stared at the screen to see Zoey's picture from last year's Halloween party. She was dressed up like a member of KISS.

"Hello?" I asked, my voice thick with sleep.

"Katherine Alba Berger, I'm so, so sorry to call you this early, but have you talked to Nicole? I'm worried," she spilled out as quickly as possible. Zoey knew I'd never been a morning person, whether it was back when I was a student or now that I was a real adult with a full-time job. I hated the morning time.

My yawn sounded like something out of *The Lion King*. "Yesterday. She's fine. She's having a sex marathon with Calum."

I think Zoey chuckled, but I was so out of it, she could have been braying like a donkey for all I knew. "Oh, okay. Go back to sleep then."

"Okay, bye, Zo," I tried to say, but yawned instead.

"Bye!" she chirped out before ending the call.

I had a headache, which could only be blamed on how exhausted I was, but all I could think about was the sick man I left across town. It wasn't even eight in the morning, and I was wondering if he was conscious enough to call into work to say he was sick. There were times I really hated how stubborn I was, because once the idea that I should call in for him popped into my head, I had to do it or else it would bother me the rest of the day. I wouldn't want him to get fired, I reasoned with myself. After doing a quick search on my browser with one eye open, I called the law office he worked at and left a voicemail explaining that Tristan King was very sick and couldn't make it in.

I shot a quick message to Tristan. There was no use in coming over if he was dead.

Are you alive?

About two minutes later, I saw 'Magellan' pop up on the screen while I was still in a half-dream, barely awake stage.

I wish I wasn't.

I snorted at his dumb antics and gradually crawled out of bed, showering, and getting dressed to go visit quite possibly the most annoying sick person on the planet. He whined more than I did even as a kid, which hadn't escaped me, but how could I avoid that handsome face? The handsome face that also needed to use the largest kinds of condoms made.

I waged an internal battle from the Starbucks drive-thru window all the way to his house, debating whether I should have tried to sneak a peek at his mighty scepter or not.

My phone chimed when I was only a few minutes away from getting to Tristan's house, and sure enough, 'Magellan' appeared on the screen again.

Are you pro assisted euthanasia?

Oh, lord.

I waited to reply until I was parked in front of his house. It was one of the nicest and well-kept homes in the neighborhood with a really nice front lawn and lots of pretty flowers. I wondered if Tristan mowed his own lawn. He probably did, and then there was the possibility that if he did, he didn't wear a shirt. That would explain the neighbor he was worried about yesterday. I was a little surprised that he lived in a house and not a condo or an apartment. Maybe I'd ask him about it later, but by the text messages he sent me, he wasn't feeling any better than yesterday.

I whipped out my phone and sent him a reply with a snort.

No, puss, but I am pro involuntary euthanasia.

Tristan's key was now attached to the rest of my keychain, so I unlocked the door and then kicked my shoes off to run upstairs and check on the whiney, too-hot baby with the flu. The door was cracked and all I could see were long, bare legs and the smooth, creamy flesh of his back sprawled over the bed. His head was buried beneath the pillow and only the long strands of hair at the nape of his neck escaped the cover.

"Hey," I said softly.

He let out a muffled noise, but didn't move an inch.

"Tristan."

Another muffled noise.

"Tristan," I said again, in a singsong voice.

I finally stepped closer to the bed and took in every inch of his pale skin. He had muscles I didn't even think existed; there was a ripple on his back when he breathed, and there were these two small dimples right above the elastic of his dark boxer briefs. That ass...

"Get up. Have you taken your temperature and your Theraflu?" I asked, tearing my thoughts away from the round curves of his butt.

He made another strange noise against the mattress in response, but didn't move.

"C'mon, Tristan." This time I poked him in the ribs and he tensed at the contact. "I need you to get up."

Finally, he rolled over lazily and pulled the pillow away from his face. He was so pale and sickly looking; his green eyes looked even duller than they did the day before. A pitiful whimper slipped out of his dry, chapped lips. "Kill me now," he moaned.

I pressed my hand against his forehead, noticing how ridiculously hot it was. Measuring his temperature with the thermometer, I noticed that he managed to drink all of the Gatorade I'd left on the nightstand while I waited for the small tool to beep. It read 102.5 across the small display. Fifteen minutes later, he'd managed to shower, brush his teeth, and take more Theraflu. He put on some lounge pants and an undershirt before following me downstairs, where I forced him to eat two slices of toast while he made a big fuss because he was, "not hungry."

"Calum hasn't called me back," he said in a voice laced with exhaustion, before sipping the glass of water I left out.

"I think he's still with Nicole," I explained, and he nodded with a weary smirk.

"I hope she doesn't break him."

I snorted and took a bite out of the toast I made for myself. After all, I paid for the bread, right? "His career might be over after Nikki."

Tristan smiled, but it wasn't the same as his usual smiles because he was sick. His right hand moved up to reach for his head, but dropped to the side after a second with a sigh. "I hate being sick."

"Why don't you go lay down?"

"No energy," he mumbled.

I put up a finger for him to give me a second while I ran upstairs for his comforter, sheet, and pillow. Folding the huge comforter in thirds, I made him a couch palate on the big sofa he had in the living room. It was wider than any normal sofa I'd ever seen, but something told me we probably didn't shop in the same places. "Tristan!" I called out.

He shuffled out of the kitchen, wide shoulders slumped and body tense with discomfort. He stopped behind the couch and looked at the way the couch had been set up, giving me a tiny, crooked smile. "Can I put my head on your lap?" he asked so sweetly that I couldn't find it in me to make a smart-ass comment.

"If you want," I told him, taking the pillow off the couch to set on my lap.

In a speed that was much faster than it should have been, he shuffled around the couch and plopped down, facing up with his head on the pillow that rested on my thighs. "Thanks, Kat," he cooed, looking straight up at me. "Will you rub my head for me?"

I couldn't help but snicker. "Are you serious?"

He nodded, looking sheepish. "My mom would always do that for me."

I rolled my eyes like I was annoyed, but it was

pretty cute. I started running my left hand through the wet locks of hair slowly and brushed my fingertips against his scalp. "Your parents live in Miami?" I asked. He nodded in response before his eyes screwed shut. "Are you from here?" I asked another question. He shook his head.

"We lived in Houston until I was about fourteen, then my dad got a job transfer," he explained, quietly. "Are you from here?"

I knew he was probably not exactly crazy about wanting to talk, so I did most of the talking myself, like the night before. I explained how my family lived in Gainesville. We talked quietly for minutes, asking each other questions about our families. I learned he was an only child just like I was. He also had an imaginary friend named Mickey until he was nine. I didn't bother asking where he got the name Mickey from, even though I really wanted to laugh. Soon enough, he'd fallen asleep with a relaxed look on his face. Exhausted and so warm with body heat, I felt myself nodding off and fighting the urge to close my eyes.

A quiet chuckle pulled me out of my dream state; my neck hurt from how I'd been positioned and my legs were asleep. I opened my eyes and looked down to see two green orbs looking at me in amusement.

"What?"

He chuckled again. "You snore."

"You're a liar," I snorted.

"I don't lie. You snore like a tiny, baby chainsaw.

It's cute," he told me with a straight face.

"Shut up."

He cracked a tired smile. "You should look into voice-over work. If someone ever makes a movie with a little chainsaw, you could cover it, hands down."

I snorted again. "I'm going to hock up phlegm into your Theraflu."

"I could use the protein," the smart-ass said with a wink.

CHAPTER TWENTY-ONE

"You," Zoey emphasized by pointing at me with her fork. "Spent three days at Tristan's house taking care of him because he had the flu?"

I pointed my fork tines in her direction. "Yes."

It'd been four days since Tristan had come down with the flu. After three days, he finally began to feel better, despite still being weak. I had to explain that he'd probably be fatigued for a while since he'd hardly eaten anything besides soup, toast, and crackers at my insistence. He was really sweet and thanked me every couple of hours when I stayed with him. We watched TV and talked in the few hours when he was feeling about a six out of ten on the sick scale.

Not wanting to overstay my welcome, I told him I had plans and wouldn't be coming over. I did have plans; Zoey and I had a set date every Thursday morning for hot yoga class. Then we'd eat lunch afterward — and by lunch, I meant we stuffed our faces with the most fattening thing we could find — because that damned yoga class made us nearly pass out each time. I'd tried convincing her to just stick to a regular yoga class in the past, but she would start going on long rants about how the heat cleaned out our systems and a million other benefits you could get out of being in a one hundred and fifteen degree room for over an hour.

"Hmm," she mumbled, spearing her fries with a fork and shoving about five of them into her mouth at once. "You still want to get up close and personal with his joystick?"

"I never said I wanted to," I tried to explain, knowing it was futile. "He's already told me about a million times that he wants to be friends, how he doesn't want a girlfriend because of the porn, how I'm such a good friend, blah blah blah. We're friends. There won't be any test drives going on for this old clunker," I said, pointing at myself.

Zoey scowled, chewing a huge bite of cheeseburger. "That's stupid," she literally spit out. Bits of hamburger bun splattered across the table, and I grimaced. "I mean, I get why he wouldn't want a girlfriend, and it's admirable that he's honest with you, but still. Maybe he's trying to convince himself that you are friends by saying it so much?"

"Doubt it." I shrugged. He seemed to treat me the way I always imagined an older brother would treat a younger sibling. With my luck, the next thing he'd tell me would be that I was endearing. Ugh. "I don't know, Zo. I like him a lot, but what am I going to do? Seduce him and then get him to have sex with me? Then a week later he goes and fucks five other girls? I couldn't do that. Maybe if I didn't like him, it'd be possible, but I do like him."

"If he wants to be friends, then you be the best freaking friend he's ever had."

Another Josh. Oh, lord.

"What does that even mean?" I asked her before cutting up the last bit of my chicken fried steak.

She rolled her eyes while chewing. "That means just be you. You're beautiful on the inside and the outside, Kat. Just don't wear those fugly clothes I hate around him."

"Does that mean I can't wear my—"

"Yes! I've been telling you for years to burn those awful jeans. They look like something you stole from your pregnant mom twenty-six years ago."

I faked a gasp in horror; I loved those jeans. The material was super worn-in and more comfortable than cashmere, but they were pretty hideous. I wore them at home mostly.

Sometimes on grocery store runs.

I even wore them to go run other errands every once in a while.

Okay, I wore them pretty much every chance I got. "I'm not burning them. I'll just... avoid wearing them more than usual."

Zoey frowned at me over the bun of her burger. "Fine. Look, all I'm saying is this: I think you've gotten so comfortable having me, Nicole, and Josh in your life that you've quit allowing other people in because you're fine. Now, Tristan walks into your life, and I'm beyond happy that you're letting him in, but I don't want you to just give up and let him join the ranks with me and the other sluts, Kat. You want him? Get him. The Kat I know is no wuss. He chose to talk to you out of a thousand other people at the convention for some reason, and I'm going to guess it wasn't because you have nice hair, bitch."

Well, when she put it like that it made a whole lot of sense. I'd asked myself plenty of times why Tristan chose me to talk to, follow, and try to befriend out of everyone he came across. Especially when he told me that very few people knew his two identities, I questioned it. I felt better about myself and started being optimistic about the situation, but the problem was still the same.

"Zo, what am I going to do though, even if he does like me? I don't want a boyfriend who does porn, and he practically refuses to talk to me about that."

She looked pensive for a moment and then nodded. "I think it's a good sign he doesn't want to talk to you about boning other chicks," she said with all the eloquence that was Zoey Quinn. "I don't know, Booger. What do you do when you get the porn star?" I knew that out of everyone, Zoey would be the only one to truly understand the situation I was in. She knew the pros and cons of being in the adult film industry, but most importantly, she loved me. Zoey would never put me in a situation that would hurt me physically or emotionally. "I'd punch him in the gut if I found out he was with other girls at the same time he was with you. I guess you're, *not literally*, screwed."

"I am screwed." The harsh reality of it was beyond disappointing. I knew I was already the tiniest bit attached to Tristan, and if we were to get together, it wouldn't be casual and meaningless. At least not for me. While I didn't consider myself a prude, I was not one for one-night stands unlike my friends. I guessed I'd just have to weigh what was more important to me— a giant cock or a friendship that seemed as easy as breathing minus the sexual tension on my behalf. Fuck.

I think she recognized the look on my face as a positive, because Zoey smiled and winked. "You might not be very tall—"

"Zoey you're practically a midget," I threw back at her.

She chose to ignore me. "Your abs might not be ripped—"

"That's rude." Sure, I didn't look like a bodybuilder, but I mean, I was fit. My stomach was flat... unless you counted the two days before my period and the four days during it.

"You definitely don't have the biggest boobs or

ass—"

I had to snort that time because she was getting downright insulting. "Uh—"

"But what you have is perfect, Kat. Your personality is second only to mine."

I snorted even louder.

She kept going. "Any guy would be lucky to have you, and you know that. So just be his friend like he wants, but show him those perky little Cs." She pointed at my boobs, and then palmed her own tiny, little mosquito-bite boobies, pushing up against the sports bra she had on— more for looks than support. "They're better than any of those rock-hard, fake titties he's had in his mouth before. You hear me? I don't want you to change for anyone, regardless of how good his oral skills are."

I knew she wasn't telling me to go for anything with Tristan, but I felt like she was supporting me on my journey to be a good friend to him. Maybe he'd fall madly in love with me and then quit porn. *Ha.* Well, whatever. I'd been asked out on dates, though I always just said no, because I had no interest in dating since my last boyfriend. I was happy with the way my life was going; between my dad, my friends, work, and my drawer of toys, I couldn't ask for more.

"You're the best, Zo. "

She looked at me with wide eyes. "Of course I am." Snapping her fingers all of a sudden, she continued, "I forgot to say that you don't really have a nice tan, but I mean, tans are kind of overrated. I like your shade of peachy colored skin."

"Zoey?"

"Yeah?"

"I'm going to punch you in the vag when we walk out of the restaurant."

CHAPTER TWENTY-TWO

I'd just finished showering when my phone chimed from its spot on the counter. My first guess was it was Josh, because I hadn't heard from him in a couple of days. When I went to reach for my phone, 'Magellan' showed up on the screen instead.

Come over. I'm bored.

I finished drying off before responding.

Then you'll just be bored with me there.

Less than a minute later, my phone chimed again.

I'm never bored with you. Come over. I'll order a pizza and think about letting you choose a movie.

I really didn't have anything planned for the rest of the day, besides vegging out in front of the television and trying to get some writing done.

Meat lover's pizza and I choose the movie. Deal?

Deal

I got dressed, opting for a stretchy pair of shorts and a tank top before feeding my cat, Matlock, and heading out. My lower back was hurting just a little, but I figured it was from overdoing it at yoga. After so much driving to his house, the trip across town didn't seem as long as it did the first three times. The now familiar gray house stood out from its neighbors, and when I pulled over to park in front of it like I'd done each other time, I spied a middle-aged woman standing on the porch next door. She wore shorts that were just as short as mine, but her top was cut lower than the one I had on. She stood there and stared while I jogged up to Tristan's front door.

The last three times, I'd let myself in because he was too sick to get up and open it himself, but now, I didn't know what to do. I was standing there, debating whether to knock or unlock it with my key when the door swung open to reveal Tristan in plaid sleep pants and a T-shirt that was a size too large. He still looked a little pale, thinner, and his eyes were a bit heavy.

"Why are you standing out here?" he asked, raising an eyebrow.

"Why are you standing right by the door?" I replied, not wanting to have to explain why I was out there.

"I thought you were the pizza person," he said, stepping to the side after waving me into the house. "C'mon, I don't want Mrs. Goldberg taking the open door as an invitation to come over."

I came in and toed off my shoes, earning a big smile from Tristan before following him into the living room. He had taken his comforter back upstairs from the look of it and maybe even cleaned a little. "Is she the cougar next door? She was staring at me when I walked over here."

He groaned before plopping down on one end of the couch. "She's crazy. I'm pretty sure she has cameras outside, because every time I mow the lawn, she always just happens to drive up. Even if it's at three in the afternoon during the week, she's there. It's creepy."

"Do you mow the lawn with your shirt off?" I asked, sitting down on the other end of the big sofa with my short legs dangling off the edge. Tristan nodded at me in response and I shrugged. "Well, there you go. She just wants to check out the goods. Don't be upset with the lady. I have a neighbor who sits on the stairs to check out girls in their running outfits."

He gave me a lazy smirk. "Do you let him look at you?"

"No way. I've told him before that if he checks out my ass when I'm going up, I'll kick him in the face. Once, he did it to Nicole, and she got right up in his face and told him she'd knee his balls back into his stomach. Now, he just ignores me and runs to hide when Nikki comes to visit," I told him with a grin.

He shook his head and positioned himself so that his back rested against the end of the couch. "I think

Calum has his work cut out for him with your friend. Don't tell her anything, okay?" he asked, waiting until I nodded in acceptance. "Calum usually calls me at least four times a day, every day. Since last weekend, I think I've heard from him a total of five times this entire week. He said he's *smitten* with Nikki. Smitten! How the hell does he even know what that means?"

I had to smile because Nicole had been the same way. "I talk to Nikki every day, and she's only called me about three times, too. Once was a couple of days after Josh's party when she could barely talk, and the other two times were just short conversations to tell me she's alive."

The doorbell rang right then, and Tristan hopped off the couch to get the door. I heard him talk to the pizza guy before coming back carrying a familiar cardboard box. "You have no idea how glad I am that you wanted a meat lover's," he said, as he set the pizza box on the coffee table and headed into the kitchen. My eyes followed his plump ass cheeks as he walked around. The faint pain in my lower back was starting to get really distracting, so I got up to look at the various things set up on the bookcase and shelves surrounding the big screen television that was mounted above his fireplace.

There were pictures of a pretty woman with blonde hair and a really, *really* attractive, older, auburn-haired man standing together in front of a church. Another picture was of a much younger

Tristan and Calum at Disney World, each wearing Mickey Mouse ears. Then, there were several in various ages of a light brown haired little boy with bright green eyes, with the same man and woman in the first picture. I had to guess that these were his parents. "Tristan! Are these pictures of your mom and dad?"

"Yes!" he yelled back from the kitchen. The opening and closing of cabinets muffled his voice before he reappeared holding two plates, napkins, a glass of water, and a can of soda. He gave me that cute, crooked smile as he set the things down on the coffee table before coming around to stand very close next to me, looking at the same pictures I had just finished inspecting. He pointed at the first picture. "They renewed their wedding vows about five years ago." The more I looked at the picture, the more resemblance I noticed between Tristan and his father; they had the same jaw, mouth, and the same wild disarray of hair.

"If you look like your dad when you're his age, your wife is going to be a lucky, lucky woman," I laughed.

He scowled at me as he grasped my forearm to pull me toward the couch again. "I'm going to pretend like you didn't just imply that my fifty-year-old father is attractive."

"He is!" I giggled, sitting in the middle of the couch in front of one of the plates he'd set down.

Tristan waved me off, frowning, before opening

up the pizza box and extracting a slice of pizza with just his hands and setting it onto my plate before putting another one on his. "Just eat. I don't want to lose my appetite thinking about you finding my dad..." he trailed off before faking a gag.

I elbowed him in the ribs, and then started eating the slice of meaty goodness. We each polished off two slices in silence before he pressed a hand against his stomach, moaning about how he hadn't gotten his appetite completely back yet. The pain in my lower back had gotten worse, and when I stood up to help him clean our mess, I felt it.

That familiar throb between my legs and lower stomach.

Suddenly, I felt wet.

Not the good kind of wet either, so I didn't think twice about shoving my hand between my legs to feel the proof of my body's doing.

Oh God, please, no.

Tristan, who was still sitting on the couch, leaned back against the cushion and burst into laughter. "Please tell me you peed your pants," he gasped.

CHAPTER TWENTY-THREE

I wanted to die a quick death.

"Do you have a bathroom downstairs?" I asked him in a voice laced with dread and panic, fucking horrified that I started my period two days early.

He nodded and pointed to where the stairs were, still laughing. If he were Josh, I'd kick him in the leg and then run, but since he wasn't, I settled for speed-walking in the direction he pointed. My shorts and panties were on the floor the instant the door closed, and sure enough, all I could see was red. Everywhere. It looked like I'd slaughtered a small animal in my underwear. *Shit!* I used the bathroom and cleaned myself off as best as I could, when I heard a knock on the door.

"Kat? I can go buy you some panties and tampons from Target if you want," he said, quietly and evenly.

I wanted to die again. I wanted to die not because

the situation was embarrassing, but because he'd just offered to go buy me undies and tampons. Josh would have done the same, but only after he rolled his eyes and huffed to make it seem like it was a big inconvenience. Then, he'd probably buy me extra-large pads that looked more like diapers than anything, just to spite me.

"I have undies in the glove compartment of my car and a pad in my purse. Can you get it for me, please? My keys are in my purse."

"Okay, I'll be right back," he said in the same voice.

I grabbed my underwear and shoved them under the tap in the sink to rinse them off, but when I picked them up, I noticed there was a stain on my shorts, too. *Jesus.* I grunted in frustration, standing there in Tristan's half-bath with no bottoms on. This wasn't exactly the way I'd envisioned myself having my panties off in his house, but this was my luck. I shouldn't have been surprised.

There was another knock on the bathroom door a few minutes later. Tristan's soft voice spoke up from the other side of the door. "I have your stuff. Do you need anything else?" There wasn't a remote sense of laughter in his tone, which made me feel a little better, but casting a look at my soaked underwear and stained shorts, I knew there wasn't any way for me to get out of the bathroom with my dignity intact.

"I stained my shorts," I muttered, my face flaming red in embarrassment.

I swear he snorted, but then it was silent. "Just come upstairs, shower, and I'll let you borrow some shorts or something."

My shorts were back on an instant later and my wet undies stowed in my pocket, when I opened the door very slowly to find Tristan leaning against the opposite wall biting his lip. He wanted to laugh; I knew he was fighting the urge. His eyes were wide and the sides of his mouth were pulled up, but he just looked at me. "Thanks, Tristan."

"Don't worry about it, it happens," he said, but his voice broke at the last syllable, and he snorted. "I'm sorry!" He pinched the bridge of his nose to stop the noise before making his way up the stairs. I was glad he'd gone up first and on his own, because there was no way in hell I would have let him walk behind me with the gigantic stain on my clothes. It was bad enough he was holding my emergency underwear in his hands; they were yellow cotton things with more stains on them than a motel room's sheets, but I didn't want to make it worse by flaunting my period disaster.

Making my way through his bedroom, I found him in his bathroom, messing with the taps to the shower a few moments later. I crowded against the wall to keep my ass from view. Green eyes peered over at me from their spot across the room, but they looked a little too amused. "Are you going to get naked, or what?"

"Excuse me?" I let out what sounded like a

hysterical giggle. *Did he just...?*

"Take a shower. I'm sure you have... some stickiness going on down there," Tristan tried to say with a straight face, but the corners of his mouth lifted up a little.

"I will, when you get out the bathroom." I was sure my voice was higher than normal; I could feel it. Was he seriously telling me to get naked in front of him? No way.

He left the stall door open and folded his arms across his chest. "Kat, you don't have anything I haven't seen a million times before."

His words cut me. Oh, my God. They cut me, but they were true, even if I hadn't seen proof of it yet. I knew he was only speaking the truth. I was stuck trying to understand what he was telling me. Who in the hell tries to see another person naked with so much nonchalance? I couldn't help but stare at him, stare at those lines of muscle that outlined his forearms, stare at the sharp jawline with a bit of dark scruff. It was his words that drove me to nod at him like a lunatic.

Fuck it.

Zoey, Nikki, and Josh had all seen me naked. It wasn't like I had anything not to be proud of.

As I peeled off my T-shirt to reveal the plain beige bra underneath, my eyes staying locked on Tristan's throat. I didn't have the balls to look him in the eye while I did this. A huge part of me couldn't even comprehend what I was actually doing until I was walking toward the stall, right next to where he stood, and then I was undoing the clasp on the back of my bra. It was strange that I blushed for the dumbest things, but my body seemed to be on my side because there wasn't a hint of red or pink anywhere on me. I was perpendicular to him, facing the shower while he leaned against the wall, but this time, I looked at him over my shoulder.

"You haven't seen anything of mine before, Mag," I said calmly, slowly pulling one strap over my shoulder and arm, while the beige material bunched in front of my chest.

He didn't say anything, but I could see his eyes flickering from my face, to my throat, and then to the side of my chest; back and forth, back and forth, while I pulled the last strap over my arm and dropped the bra to the floor. My heart pounded so fast in my chest it felt like it was going to explode out of its cage of bones with a vengeance. I didn't know the first thing about trying to be sexy, but I felt empowered by Zoey's speech earlier. I valued myself, and nothing could change that. She'd be shitting her pants in excitement that I was being so bold, but ultimately, I didn't think she'd be surprised. I had balls— I just didn't use them very often.

I smirked at Tristan's silence before shoving my shorts down my legs while also thanking the Holy Spirit that I decided to shave earlier. I hoped I didn't have a big red smudge on my ass. He stood as still as a statue. I didn't think he was even breathing, but I stepped into the shower regardless and closed the door behind me. By the angle I'd been in before, I knew all he got a look at was me from the side, and now he only had a plain view of my ass, back, and legs. I pushed out any self-conscious thoughts from my head. In less than two minutes, I'd lathered up my lower body with the bar of soap he had in the shower, the scent I'd become familiar with was clean and simple, and rinsed off.

When I opened the door to the stall, I realized Tristan wasn't in the bathroom anymore, but there was a towel hanging off the rack and the underwear and shorts I'd left on the floor were now missing. My clean period panties were sitting on the vanity sink along with a pad and what looked to be an old pair of boxers. Once dressed with his boxers grazing my knees, I made my way downstairs to find him sitting on the couch with his feet propped up on the coffee table and his arms folded behind his head.

He gave me a lazy smile and looked me over. It confused me. I wasn't expecting him to do anything after seeing me buck naked, but by the look on his face, it was like nothing happened.

"Better?" he asked me when I walked over to sit on the other end of the couch.

"Much," I responded as evenly as possible. I didn't want to make it seem like I felt any differently after that little ordeal, but it was hard to keep my face from giving me away.

"I put your clothes in the washer," he said, picking up the remote to turn on the television.

"Thanks for everything."

He smiled at me and then pointed behind him in the direction of the kitchen. "I have soda, juice, and cookies in the kitchen."

"Okay..." I trailed off, wondering about his random thought.

"That's what they usually give me when I go donate blood," he teased with a snort. "I wouldn't want you to pass out from blood loss."

"Tristan?"

"Yes?"

"Shut up."

CHAPTER TWENTY-FOUR

I was slowly aware of three things:

One, I could not feel my hand.

Two, I was unusually warm.

Three, I was not on my bed.

Very slowly, I slipped from dream state into consciousness, but my brain was running, trying to remember the details that led up to my three realizations. I slept in the same position every night; I was one of those heavy sleepers who hardly moved, and right then, my body was positioned in a way that it normally didn't sleep in. Also, this unfamiliar clean scent lingered in my nostrils. The last thing I remembered was going to the pharmacy to buy more pads, then sitting on Tristan's couch with my legs tucked underneath me while watching a movie and laughing my ass off. Tristan had the entire movie memorized, which only added to the fun.

I couldn't remember anything after about halfway through it.

"You chose the last one, so now we get to watch what I want," he exclaimed, already on his feet and heading to the shelves filled with DVDs.

I groaned loudly. "You're going to choose something terrible, aren't you?"

Tristan let out an audible, mock gasp. "You shall never speak those words in my house again." He faked a hiss. "My taste in movies is unparalleled."

So continued our evening and night, watching funny movies with the green-eyed jackass, who recited all of his favorite lines.

My saliva was thick and gross tasting. There was a thin layer of tartar on my teeth from failing to brush them the night before, which was fucking disgusting. Blinking, I had to squint at the amount of light filtering into the room, only to face a wall of white. The white was moving closer to me, and then back away with each breath. I became faintly aware of something heavy and warm draped over my hip and back. What the hell was going on? I moved my head slightly up, only to come in contact with something very hard. I could also see a sliver of skin. My face was practically buried against his chest, and I had to assume the hard thing over my head was his chin.

I couldn't move my head down to see what was over me, but it had to be his arm. My right hand was wedged under his ribs, and I couldn't feel it at all. To top it off, my feet were burrowed in between hair and bones. Maybe his feet? We were pressed together; my chest was against his stomach because of his height advantage, and it felt nice. It'd been close to a year since the last time I slept with anyone besides Zoey, and this only made me realize how much I enjoyed and missed having someone to snuggle with.

I'd had three boyfriends in my life after high school; the first was a snuggler, the second I unfortunately had no idea, and the third was not. The two I'd gotten well acquainted with complained of my body heat, claiming I was too warm, but really, I got cold easily at night so that never made any sense. Even though they didn't like to spoon or anything, I missed the butt cheeks that would at least keep me company. My dear Zoey was one of those people who moved around a lot all night. Nine times out of ten, I got slapped in the face or kicked in the stomach when we happened to sleep in the same bed together.

"Kat?" Tristan's hoarse voice asked from above my head. His body stirred before arching against me in a stretch.

"Hey," I said, my voice still thick with sleep. "I don't remember falling asleep."

The arm thrown across me was now moving up and down my back, his palm smoothing over the material covering the area from my shoulders to my spine. "I remember you started falling asleep. Your head was bobbing back and forth, so I moved to put your head on my shoulder, but that's pretty much it. You snored again, but it seemed like a dream," he groaned against my hair.

His hand continued sliding up and down my back, detouring to glide upward to touch the crown of my head before smoothing down my hair. I knew I had a ponytail up last night; my hair wasn't down like it should have been, which was strange. "Oh," I mumbled, only an inch away from his chest. My hand was still asleep, but I could not have cared any less.

"You're warm," he said in a soft voice. "You're like my own personal electric blanket."

I wanted to ask him if he slept on couches with girls regularly, but something told me I already knew the answer. He mentioned to me last night that I was the third female to ever come over to his house; the first and second being his mom and aunt. His words from a few nights before when he assured me his bed was clean and he wasn't a whore rang through my brain as a reminder. Maybe I should have been less trusting because he could have been lying, but I highly doubted it. If it really was hard for him to not only have friends but girlfriends too because of the porn, there would be no way he'd invite someone over who only knew him as Robby Lingus.

"What are you thinking?" he asked after my silence.

"I was thinking about you and your house," I answered him honestly. "You never bring people over?"

"Only Calum, some people from school, my family, and you," he answered. "Why?"

I wanted to ask him, but should I? "Just wondering," I mumbled against him as I pressed my forehead to the hard muscle of his chest. "Do you mind if I ask you some personal stuff?" I paused. "You don't have to answer if you don't want to."

He freaking laughed. "I've seen you dig in your ass, I've washed the PMS off your clothes, and seen you…" he hesitated, "in the bathroom. I really don't think you can ask me anything that's so personal I wouldn't answer, Goldie."

I registered the fact that he avoided saying he'd seen me naked; I'd mull over that later on. "You've really never brought a girlfriend over here?"

"Kat," he sighed. "My last two girlfriends didn't even know my real name. They thought my name was Robby."

I had a feeling I was starting to go into territory I didn't want to get into, but I knew for the sake of our friendship, I should know some things. I could tell anyone everything and anything about Nicole, Zoey, and Josh. So, wouldn't the same be expected for Tristan at some point? Maybe I didn't want to know the answers, but I should. "They were in the, *err*, adult film industry too?"

His heavy hand started doing laps on my back

again. "Yeah," he answered. "One of them was the reason I got into it. It was her idea, actually. She came up to me at a bar and asked me if I was interested... Lexy was... I mean, she was hot as shit, so how was I going to tell her no? She didn't even ask me for my name that night, and by the time she did, Calum had already come up with Robby. We only stayed together a few months before she got all psycho on me for getting offers to be with other girls. Then, there was Ashley a few months after Lexy, and that lasted maybe a month or two. I met her on a scene, too."

I couldn't help the jealousy that spiked through my spine and nervous system. Two porn star girlfriends? I wasn't sure how I didn't projectile vomit at the thought. I wanted to push him away from me and climb off the couch, but I didn't. It was like he could sense my unease because he started stroking my hair from the crown down, his fingers brushing through the strangely untangled locks.

"I guess I knew there wasn't anything serious going on with either one of them since I never told them my real name, huh? It's hard to lie about what you do and what your life is like when you're away from L.A.," he continued. "Ashley was almost two years ago now, I guess. I started in the industry a year before that, right before I started law school."

"Hmm," I managed to mumble out, half in a daze with his hands and half in thought at his words. How could he have gone through having a relationship with someone who didn't really even know him? Did that even count as a relationship when so much was fabricated, I wondered. "Zoey has been doing it for four years."

"I can't believe you know Zoey," he said, and I felt hot breath against the top of my head. "Is she the reason you went to the convention?"

I snorted at his question, wishing I could blame sweet Zoey for my visit to the porn convention. "No. Nikki and I are just curious pervs." The tingling in my hand started to get worse when it felt like needles bit into my skin. In an effort to pull my hand out from under his ribs, my shoulder fell back, and I expected it to land against the couch cushion, but of course, no such luck.

I was flat on my back, sucking in a breath at the impact of falling off the fucking couch. I could hear Tristan laughing from his spot above me; the asshole didn't even bother to make sure I was okay before he was laughing his ass off. Two ragged breaths later, a semi-composed Tristan hung off the side of the couch while looking at me through wide, amused eyes. "Are you okay?"

"I will be," I mumbled, trying to push myself up to a sitting position. Even though the couch seemed pretty wide originally, between the back cushions, Tristan's lean frame, and my body, we took up the entire width of it.

He sat up with his legs thrown over the side, and two hands extended to help me up. "C'mon, I'll let you make me some pancakes to make up for having to hear you snore all night."

As I was getting up, I noticed my ponytail holder on top of the coffee table.

CHAPTER TWENTY-FIVE

Zoey and Nicole were in tears and gasping for air in response to my humiliation.

Bitches. That was exactly what they were. Two bitches.

"I don't even know why I'm friends with either one of you," I grumbled in their direction.

We were over at Nicole's loft on Saturday night, getting ready to head out and see an outdoor concert that Eva, Zoey's friend, was dancing at. I'd decided to tell them about my period incident at Tristan's house two days before, and in response, they were making noises that could have signaled they were either crying or dying. I couldn't have cared less which one by that point. I mean, a girl can only handle so much laughter at her own expense. I did have to give them credit though, they managed to hold themselves together until I got to the part about falling off the couch at least. I had left his house hours later, after making pancakes and sitting on his porch for a good hour until his neighbor Mrs. Goldberg came out and scared Tristan away.

Three minutes later, Nicole was pawing at her face and gasping for air. "Only you, Kat," she managed to sigh out.

"Shut up," was the only response I could think of. Yes, it was embarrassing to freaking bleed all over myself in front of Tristan, but oh, well. It was done, right?

Zoey leaned over the couch to pinch my cheek. "You are too much."

I rolled my eyes and got up, noticing that it was five minutes past when we needed to leave. "Let's go or we won't make it in time."

My blonde and black-haired friends hustled out of the door after me, loading into Zoey's little Volkswagen to head over to the venue. I was in the front seat while Nikki took the back; Zoey was a notoriously absentminded and reckless driver. A couple of years back, after a particularly horrifying cutoff, Nikki swore to never ride in the front seat with her again. Despite all the exercises that I learned in yoga to control my breathing, I'd find myself panting and pressing the toes on my right foot down like I could brake the car myself each time Zoey was behind the wheel.

"How's it going with Calum, Nikki?" I asked to distract myself from the trip.

We'd kept our conversations to an absolute minimum over the week, so I really had no clue how things were going. "A-fucking-mazing. He's so delicious, and he's really sweet too. I'm so used to dating pricks that it's weird for me to accept that he isn't a dick like every other dick before him. He told me that I'm special." She snorted out the last word like she wasn't sure whether to accept it or not.

I wanted to tell her what Tristan said, but I promised him I wouldn't. "Maybe you are, Nik."

"Ehh," she said softly from the back, but I could hear the hesitation in her voice. "He's leaving next week to go film a couple of movies so..." She trailed off. "Tristan is going with him, too."

I'd just spent more than twenty-four hours with Tristan less than two days ago, and he never mentioned going to film, but I could only blame myself. What did I expect? For his scenes or movies to get filmed using CGI? Luckily, it was Zoey who voiced the question that was floating around in my head. "Are you going to keep seeing him once he comes back?"

"I think so. I like him and not just for his gigantic dick. He's nice, and he's funny," she said. I knew Nicole. I knew she wanted to say more, but she'd always been very private about a lot of things. Whatever internal battle was raging under her skin right then was only for her to take on. I wanted to tell her I had an idea what she was feeling and going through, but I wouldn't. Nikki had always needed to figure things out on her own.

My phone vibrated from its spot in my purse; the chime was muffled. 'Magellan' showed up on the screen.

I think I want a dog.

Well, that was random.

Get one then.

Go with me to the shelter?

Sure.

I have to go back to work on Monday, so maybe after I get off?

I have plans.

Total lie. I had nothing to do.

Bullshit. Monday after work. I'll pick you up.

"What's that smile on your face for?" Zoey teased.

Did I have a dumb look on my face that gave me away? Probably. "Just making plans, Slutey."

She looked at me out of the corner of her eye as a sad smile crossed her features. "Still no progress?"

I only had the heart to shake my head. There was no progress on the romantic front. He treated me like a sister except for the whole-sleeping-on-the-couch-while-pressed-up-against-each-other thing. The ponytail holder incident still bothered me. Using deductive reasoning, I was pretty positive he took the elastic out of my hair, because I knew I wouldn't have done it in my sleep, but why would he do that? I wasn't naïve; I noticed that he flirted with me sometimes, and I had caught him looking at me in a way that was definitely more than friendly, but that was it.

"He's probably confused, Booger. Give him some time... but not too much time," Nicole piped up from the backseat. "You can't wait around for him forever."

I wanted to tell them I wasn't waiting for him, but I guessed I kind of was. I was just settling for taking what I could get from him. "Yeah," was my lame reply.

Zoey decided to be merciful and blast the radio a moment later. It was a pop music extravaganza with her singing at the top of her lungs for the next twenty minutes until we made it to the venue. Eva was dancing with a modern company, and we sat out in the humid warmth, enjoying the hour and a half of performances. Zoey beamed every time her friend appeared onstage, which was too cute. I made a note to ask her later about Eva, because something told me she really liked her.

The three of us were shuffling down our aisle when a voice from behind stopped us. "Zoey?"

Zoey turned around first, and then Nikki and I followed. A gorgeous girl with chestnut hair and striking blue eyes was standing two rows behind. She had gigantic fake boobs, which were barely holding themselves back from popping out of her shirt. I could hear Zoey snicker before she talked. "Hi, Ashley... What a surprise."

Ashley.

You've got to be kidding me. She better not be the

same Ashley who Tristan had just told me about. What were the fucking chances?

"—Visiting my cousins for the weekend before I go back to the Valley." I caught the end of what enormo-boobs said. Her voice was sickeningly sweet. I hated it. I also wanted to punch her in the face for some reason.

"Nice. I'm not going back for another two weeks," my inky-haired friend said. I could see the tension in her shoulders as she shot me a look out of the corner of her eye. The look told me she knew about Ashley and Tristan.

"Well, it was nice seeing you, Zoey! I should really go find my cousins before they forget about me. Toodles!" Ashley said with a curl of her fingers, which I guessed could have been considered a wave.

Nicole growled right next to me. "Who the hell says toodles?"

"That cunt-wagon," I said with a point in the direction Ashley walked off in. I considered for a moment that it might have been incredibly childish of me to be so hateful, but *screw that*.

"You two are some hateful asses," Zoey laughed before pushing me forward. "It's her job, you know?" She tried to defend Ashley, but I had a feeling she was trying to tone down our bitchiness. She'd probably been with Calum, too. I had to remember to tell Tristan I'd seen her.

"She's still a bitch," Nikki and I said at the same time.

Zoey just rolled her eyes and laughed. "You two kiss your daddies with those mouths?"

"I do more than kiss your daddy with this mouth," Nicole added with a snort before we all laughed.

CHAPTER TWENTY-SIX

I had barely closed the apartment door before I was whipping out my phone to call Tristan.

"Hey," he answered, two rings later.

"Hey! Are you busy?" I asked, knowing he was probably at home doing a big, whopping nothing.

The goofy man snorted. "Not at all. I'm watching a movie and trying to read. How was the show?"

"Good. It was fun, and Zoey dropped me off with all of my limbs intact," I told him. He'd already been warned about Zoey's awful driving skills and the fear she put into my heart each time she was behind the wheel. Then again, I guess I could have offered to drive instead, but I didn't.

"Nice."

I hesitated for a single moment, trying to decide whether I really wanted to tell him about Ashley or not. I mean, what if he decided he wanted to go see her since she was in town? That thought alone made me want to projectile vomit. *Friends. You're friends,* I reminded myself. If he saw my ex, I'd want him to tell me. I'd be curious to know whether the guy had gained weight. *Ha.*

"So, we were at the venue and this girl screamed at Zoey. Her name was Ashley," I started to explain. His response was a low grunting noise, signaling me to continue. "I think it might have been your ex-girlfriend. She was really pretty with huge boobs. Reddish-brown hair and blue eyes."

Tristan stayed quiet for a moment. "Did she have an annoying voice?"

"Is that a trick question?" I asked.

He chuckled. "Why would it be a trick question?"

I made a low noise in my throat that sounded amused. "Because she's your ex? Maybe you guys are still friends, I don't know. I don't want to talk shit about someone you're still fond of!" I laughed.

"Kaaaaat," he grumbled, but I could hear amusement in his tone. "We weren't friends. Ever."

I know he didn't mean for his statement to be a verbal punch to my ovaries, but it was. They'd never been friends. Ugh.

CHAPTER TWENTY-SEVEN

"Have you ever had a dog before?" I asked the man also known as Robby Lingus.

We sat in his Audi, heading to the shelter closest to my apartment. Since Saturday night, every other text message he'd sent me had been regarding our trip to look for a dog. Not once did he ever bring up Ashley again, but the damage had been done. My stomach had hurt for hours after we'd hung up, and I'd decided right then that I wasn't going to let it bother me any longer.

So, when the dog-related text messages kept coming, I went with it. He had admitted to me the day before that he thought of getting one because he was tired of being lonely at his house. I was excited for him. I loved dogs, even though I could never admit that to Matlock. The only reason why I didn't have one was because the deposit for a dog at my apartment complex was way too expensive. I managed to get some writing done and was waiting for him on the steps to my building when he pulled up after work.

"Yeah, I had a dog growing up. Old Gozer was my best friend," he said wistfully.

I raised my eyebrow at him, recognizing the name. "Please tell me you named him Gozer after the *Ghostbusters* character." Gozer was the demon-woman at the end of the movie; my dad and I had been obsessed with *Ghostbusters* when I was little. I think he secretly had a man-crush on Dan Aykroyd, but he never officially fessed up to it.

Tristan's face flamed pink as he gave me a sheepish smile, looking at me out of the corner of his eye. "I did," he snorted, embarrassed. "I had a crazy crush on her until I found out about Spanish-language soap operas."

Immediately, I imagined a teenage Tristan masturbating to stunning Hispanic women on the Spanish channels and it made me laugh. "Your soap operas were my *Men's Health* magazine!"

"What's with you and older men?" he teased, throwing an empty water bottle from the console at me.

"They're just like fine wine!" I laughed, hitting his forearm with the bottom of the plastic bottle. I couldn't help but take note of the fact that his nice, blue dress shirt was rolled up at the sleeves and unbuttoned at the top. God, he was so handsome it was unreal.

"There are men in that magazine old enough to be your dad!" He turned to face me when we stopped at a red light. His eyes narrowed in my direction. "Please tell me you haven't dated an older man before."

"Well..." I trailed off, trying to keep the expression on my face straight, but I couldn't. I had a horrible poker face, and then a snort blew out of my nose when he gave me a horrified expression. "I haven't, I promise. The oldest guy I've dated was six years older than me."

"How old *are* you, Goldie?"

I was not ashamed of my age at all, and I didn't think I ever would be. My mom still looked like a teenager right before she died, and the father of one of my students thought I was joking when I told him I was the teacher. *Heh.* "I'm twenty-five, Mag. How old are you?"

His eyes widened at my admission. "You are not twenty-five."

"Yes, I am." I told him, perking up expectantly. He was going to tell me I didn't look a day older than sixteen, I could feel it.

"No way. You've got to be at least thirty," he laughed.

"Fuck you," I laughed in response, whacking him with the plastic bottle again.

He winked at me before turning his attention forward. "I'm kidding! You look like you're eighteen max. I just turned twenty-nine."

I did the math in my head; if he was twenty-nine and almost done with law school, what did he do after finishing his undergrad? He'd never mentioned taking time off between schools. Before I could think any more about it, he'd parked the car in front of a drab looking little building. "Mag, what did you do between your bachelor's and law school?"

The sigh he let out was long and drawn out while we walked up to the building. He held the door open for me, ushering me in. "Remember I told you it took me some time to figure out that I wanted to go into law? I was pre-med in college and went to medical school for two years. Then, I figured out that the last thing I wanted to do was medicine, so I dropped out."

There was a sweet looking lady with hair that resembled white cotton candy sitting on the other side of a table, who cleared her throat to gain our attention. "Hello, darlings. Can you sign in for me, please?" she asked in a sweet voice.

We made our way over to the table, where Tristan started signing in for the both of us. The lady was looking at me with a smile. "You two are precious together," she mused. "Come to find a new addition to your beautiful family?"

I saw Tristan's head shoot up. Not missing a beat, he nodded at the old lady. "We sure are. We want to get a dog."

Her cute little face pruned up in a smile. "I am

sure you two will find a perfect companion back there. You can go through those doors. All the animals are in separate rooms," she said, indicating toward the heavy metal door behind her with the sweep of a hand. "Have fun, sweethearts."

Tristan's arm slung over my shoulder a moment later, his side pressing into mine as he led me in the direction of the door. He opened it up for me, and then threw his heavy arm over my shoulder again. "Well, precious, let's find us a dog."

We made a plan to start on one end of the building and make our way over.

"So, you went through two years of medical school, and then quit?" I asked, thinking of the amount of money that four years of pre-med and two years of medical school must have cost, only to get flushed down the drain at the end of the day. *Shit.* I still owed a good amount of student loans and couldn't imagine how much more he could have possibly owed before starting law school.

"Yeah," he mumbled as we walked down the aisles still pressed together. There were so many dogs of all colors and sizes that it made my heart hurt looking at them. "I had to go back and take more classes before I applied to law school," he explained.

Each cage had a dog in it, and I pulled away from Tristan to crouch by the gates separating me from the friendlier dogs. Some of the dogs barked when we walked by, others growled, but a good portion of them were all too excited to have visitors. We made our way out of the first room and into the next one, where I saw about ten dogs that I wanted to adopt for myself.

"I want to take all of you home," I whispered to a particularly sweet pit bull that licked my palm through the holes in the fencing.

"Choose one," Tristan said, squatting down next to me before pressing his hand against the gate to also get a lick.

When we started to get up, the honey-colored pit bull whimpered, and I had to bite my lip not to cry. She was so sweet it broke my heart, but I just didn't feel like she was the right dog for Tristan. My dad and I had two dogs after mom died, and he let me choose each one of them. I just had this feeling when I found each of them, it was a type of connection telling me the dog was destined to be mine. Even though I wanted to feel it, the cute pit bull baby didn't feel that way to me. Tristan sensed my emotional turmoil because I felt his hand on my shoulder as we went through to another room. It was getting harder and harder for me to go from room to room, looking at the countless dogs that deserved to be adopted.

"Hey," he whispered right next to my ear. His hand trailed down from my shoulder, over my arm until it slipped right against my own, before interlocking his fingers with mine. "Don't be sad. Just find one you like and we'll take him or her." He squeezed my hand.

There were so many sad faces looking at us while we walked by that tears pooled in my eyes. I wanted them all, even the mean ones, but I hadn't found the right one yet. His hand was warm and reassuring in mine, long fingers wrapping my shorter ones in a meeting of long and slim. We were getting close to the end of the row of dogs when I heard something that sounded like a whisper coming from up ahead. There was another whisper again a minute later. I pulled Tristan toward the cage where the whispering came from, only for me to let out some sort of squeak.

He was there. A massive looking puppy laid out on his back with four huge paws that waved in the air. He had a huge, square head with oversized, floppy ears resting against the floor. Best of all— his legs were spread wide and his gigantic balls were pressed against the fence. The puppy had a dark fawn coat. He was all puppy fat and rolls, and as soon as I dropped to my knees I heard another whisper... and realized it was coming out of his ass. The smell was so awful I had to pull my shirt up over my nose as Tristan started gagging.

"What the hell is that smell?"

I pointed at the puppy's crotch. "He farted!"

Tristan made a face and started reading the information listed on the outside of his crate. "He's eight months, a mastiff-Great Dane mix, and it says he weighs... holy shit, he weighs a hundred and forty pounds, Kat."

The oversized puppy rolled over onto his tummy with one ear cocked back and the other flopped over his face. He was looking at me with big brown eyes and a slowly wagging tail. "This one," I said softly to Tristan, but kept my eyes on the big boy sitting up across from me.

"This one? You're sure? I was thinking more about a small one. You know, maybe like a terrier or a Yorkie."

I had to snort at the idiot behind me. "You want me to buy you a carrying bag for your Yorkie, Miss?"

The dog started licking the fence when I put my hand against it. "Whatever." Tristan laughed before dropping to balance on the balls of his feet next to me. The giant puppy looked at him and wagged his tail even more. "Fine, get him if you want, but if my mom doesn't want to watch him for me, then you're stuck on babysitting duty."

Nicole's words from a few days before reminded me that he was leaving without telling me. "Oh, yeah... Nikki told me you're leaving next weekend for work."

"Just a weekend," he replied in a low voice. He was up on his feet again, holding a hand out to help me up. "Let's go start the paperwork to take him home," he said, effectively cutting off any talk about him leaving to do his porn stuff. The puppy started crying when we walked away, so I pushed Tristan, taking a split second to enjoy the press of my fingers against his back like a deprived hussy, to hustle him out of the room faster.

Over an hour and one hundred and twenty-five dollars later, I was dragged through the parking lot while holding the big baby's leash. Tristan was walking fast and the puppy was trailing right behind him. You could tell he was enamored with his new owner, like he realized and appreciated the gift Tristan had given him. When we got to the car, he muttered an "Oh, fuck," when he looked at the leather covering his backseat and shrugged. "Oh, well."

"I think you should try to let him pee before we take him anywhere," I warned him.

"We're just going down the street," he protested, waving the unnamed puppy in. While we waited for the adoption paperwork, I helped him make a list of the things he'd need to go buy his son before going home.

The giant child just stood there looking at Tristan like he was an idiot for a good five minutes. After five more minutes of careful weight distribution, Tristan finally hauled him into his arms and shoved him into the backseat as gently as possible. As soon as we were both inside, the dog's large, square head popped into the space between the two seats with his long, pink tongue dangling.

"We need to come up with a name for him," he said, putting the car into drive.

"Nuh-uh, you need to come up with a name for him. I'll just approve it," I told him, rubbing the big boy's head.

Since the radio wasn't on, the short blow of air that sounded like a whisper filled the car. A second later, I was pulling my shirt up to block the godforsaken smell of garbage coming from the backseat.

"Oh, my fuck! You had to get the farting one, didn't you?" Tristan half-laughed and half-groaned, throwing an arm over his face.

The dog pulled away from me to hop up completely onto the backseat before I saw him start to squat while the top of his back grazed the ceiling of the car.

"Pull over! He's peeing on your seat!"

CHAPTER TWENTY-EIGHT

"T-Rex?"

"No."

"Hercules?"

"No."

"Fat Boy?"

"Definitely not."

"Stewart?"

"Are you out of your mind?"

"No." He sighed. "Okay, what about Chuck?"

I had to think about that one for a second. "Maybe."

"Romulus?"

"Isn't that from *Star Trek*?"

"I think you're a closet nerd."

"I think you should shut up. I had a thing for the guy who played Kirk."

He laughed, but I couldn't see his expression. "At

least he's in your age range. I was worried you were going to say you had a thing for old Spock."

"Leave me alone." I laughed in return.

"Skittles?"

"No."

"Midas?"

"Maybe."

"Bruno?"

"No."

"Gomer?"

"Maybe."

"Jigsaw?"

"You are not naming him after a character in that movie."

Another sigh. "Fine. Yoda?"

"Ooh, I kind of like that one. He looks like a Yoda, doesn't he?" I asked, propping myself onto my elbows to look at the unnamed puppy. He was busy taking a nap on the grass five feet away from us.

His big face was all scrunched up in a deep sleep, and he totally looked like freaking Yoda. Tristan snorted, and I saw him prop himself up on his hands to look at his new buddy. "He does look like a Yoda."

It had been five days since Tristan adopted the mastiff-mix from the shelter, and the poor dog had been called everything from Sugarpop to Spot to Wesley. I finally had to tell Tristan he needed to decide on a name before the poor baby had an identity crisis. Every day, Tristan had dropped by my apartment to pick me up and take me over to his house after work so we could spend time with his son. After the pee-incident in the Audi, I sensed the hesitation in Tristan's body language when he first walked into his house. I think he expected to see the worst, but the gigantic baby was an angel in his crate. We'd taken him for walks around the block, but mainly, we hung out in the spacious backyard and lay around. Every once in awhile, we tried to teach Sugarpop/Spot/Wesley how to play fetch. It wasn't going so well.

At that moment, we were plastered on the grass with the late afternoon sun warming our skin. It was kind of wonderful out there. Two huge trees loomed over the backyard, the grass was cut short, and Tristan had been training the future Yoda to poop in the same section of backyard, so we could pretty much lay down anywhere and be safe from his huge shits.

Tristan made a funny noise from his spot a couple of feet away. "I think Yoda it is," he paused, before turning to look in the puppy's direction. "Yoda!"

Big brown eyes looked up in Tristan's direction when the name was called out. His huge head tilted in a way that looked like he was asking what was going on. I'd grown to really, really like the big boy in the time I'd been around; he was the sweetest thing. Even though he farted every ten minutes, I thought he was awesome. It was even more awesome that he followed me around everywhere instead of Tristan. When we sat on the couch, Tristan on one side and me on the other, he'd go and stick his big head right in front of one of our faces to get our attention. Matlock, on the other hand, was not so fond of the dog smell when I got home every night.

"Kat?" Tristan's voice was softer than usual.

"Hmm?"

"I'm really glad we're friends," he said, and it was enough to make me tear my eyes away from Yoda licking his butthole in order to look at him.

I was sure the smile on my face was so big and goofy that it looked like my face might get stuck like that, but his words seemed so sincere and sweet that I couldn't help it. "Me too, Mag."

CHAPTER TWENTY-NINE

"Do you think she has a bun in the oven?"

I made a noise of disbelief in my throat while simultaneously keeping my eyes on the road— I also didn't trust Zoey to multitask safely. Driving and talking was much harder for her than talking on the phone and ironing, which she had failed at spectacularly on several occasions. "No way, they've only been seeing each other for how long? Two weeks?"

Nicole had called earlier in the day demanding that we meet at a pub down the street from her place. Zoey and I were at the gym when I answered, and as soon as I told her I wasn't in the mood to go out, she threatened to change the password to her online porn subscriptions. That bitch. She claimed she had something very important to tell us. Which was exactly why Zoey and I were brainstorming ideas as to what could be that important.

"Maybe she got a promotion at work?" Zoey chirped up, taking a sharp right turn that made my toes curl.

Nicole worked at the same law firm that her dad owned, so that could have been a big possibility. "Yeah, maybe, or knowing Nikki, she probably managed to deep-throat Calum and wants to celebrate."

Zoey snickered and nodded, while steering her Beetle into a small spot on the street. "Maybe she's getting a sex change?"

We'd joked around about Nicole being more of a man than a woman because of the sheer size of her imaginary balls. People at work called her Nicole "The Ballbuster" Jonasson because of her take-no-shit attitude. Men cowered in fright from her like they rightfully should. Last Christmas, Josh bought her a set of those metal balls that guys hung off the back bumpers of their trucks as a joke.

We were out of the car and through the door of the pub a few minutes later, still thinking up ideas as to what Nicole could have been planning on announcing. It wasn't too packed considering there was a baseball game on the large screens mounted over the bar. I spotted Nikki's tall frame in a back corner and pointed in her direction before Zoey poked my side, gesturing toward the bar.

"I'm going to get a drink first. What do you want me to get you?" she asked.

I was glad it wasn't so loud that I couldn't hear her. "Whatever you get, Zo." I shrugged. She tended to stick to really girly drinks, which I was all for, so I knew her choice would be good. She nodded and headed to the bar while I weaved through the people milling about, spying both Nicole and Calum sitting on stools at a table.

She shot me a big smile and wrapped me in a tight hug. "I've missed you," she admitted, and I had to nod in agreement. I didn't think I'd ever gone three consecutive days without seeing her in all the years since we'd met. Even though I had Tristan's company to distract me from her absence, my heart still recognized that I hadn't spent any time with someone I loved and valued. My mom has been dead for almost fifteen years, and I still missed her in a way that words could never explain properly. I'd learned over the years that when you genuinely loved something, it left an impression on you forever.

"Hi Kat," Calum piped up from his spot next to Nikki.

"Hey," I said, holding my hand up for a high-five, which he slapped with vigor. I liked him. A good high-five said a lot about a person; just like a handshake did. I hated limp fish handshakes like you couldn't imagine.

I felt my ass being grabbed roughly, and although I should have been alarmed by the intimate gesture, with Zoey and Josh possibly in the picture, I had no doubts that it was one of their perverted asses. Sure enough, I turned around slowly to spy two blond heads behind me. One head had short hair, while the other had much longer and darker blond hair. Josh and Leo, of course.

"Booger Bear!" Josh exclaimed in his loudest shriek. He only did that when he had already started drinking, so I was a little scared.

"What's up, homolofagous?" I laughed and gave my friend a hug. I hadn't seen him since we'd gone bowling, and we had only been texting intermittently since he began seeing Leo the day of his party. That sort of absence with my closest friends seemed to be going on much more frequently now than ever before, leaving me a little unsettled.

He rolled his eyes and shot me the middle finger. He hated it when I called him that, but seriously, I thought he got a kick out of it secretly. Josh busied himself saying hi to Nicole and Calum while I tried to high-five Leo, who played hand-tag with me until he awkwardly landed his palm against mine. I'd forgiven him for the weak high-five since he could moonwalk. In no time, Zoey was back with what looked like two margaritas before shoving one in my direction. Nicole made us rally around the table, her hazel eyes wide and a little maniacal.

I sat between Zoey and Josh, smashed in close to their thin bodies when I felt two big hands land on my shoulders. Looking over one, I spotted the familiar reddish-brown hair towering over me.

"Hey," he said, very close to my ear. I raised a hand to squeeze his fingers. I wanted to lean back against him, but I didn't; he was warm enough to feel through the thin material of my blouse.

"Now that all of you bitches are here," Nicole began. She stood right next to Calum, holding hands like cutie-pies. "We have something very important to tell you."

Oh, my God.

Then it hit me, *she's going to start doing porn, too.*

"What? No!" Nicole blurted out, her pretty face screwed into a grimace. Oh, shit, I guessed I said that aloud. I blushed all over. "Calum asked me to marry him, and I said yes!"

I gasped.

Tristan's hands squeezed the hell out of my shoulders.

Zoey tensed up.

Josh made a noise that could only be described as a snicker and a snort mixed together.

Then there was silence.

"Seriously?" Zoey's small voice squeaked.

Nicole rolled her eyes and held up her hand to show a mighty nice-looking solitaire diamond resting on her ring finger. "Yes, dumbasses."

What. The. Fuck.

My brain raced, and I was sure everyone else's did the same. Calum and Nicole had only known each other for three weeks. Three weeks! They'd only been seeing each other for two of those.

I had fish that didn't survive longer than that same amount of time, and Calum and Nikki were deciding to get married. I was dumbstruck. As my brain continued trying to process all of it, I only thought of Nicole and the person she was. She was the most self-assured and confident individual I had ever met; she knew what she wanted and always got it. Nikki didn't wear her heart on her sleeve, and never made decisions without seriously considering all of her options. She knew what she was doing.

This was the Nikki who always catered to all of my whims, regardless of how stupid she might think them to be. Who stood in line for four hours to watch the last Transformers movie with me at midnight on opening night? Nicole. Who went with me to a book signing the day before her bar exam? Nicole. Who had always been there for me no matter what? Nikki. I loved her, and the fact that she was excited as hell while the rest of us just stared dumbly forward snapped me out of my haze.

"I'm so happy for you!" I gushed out while my head spun with information and acceptance.

She lit up like a firecracker and smiled so brilliantly I felt terrible that I hadn't been immediately excited for her. The only time I'd ever seen her so excited was when we'd been at the AFA Expo waiting to meet Calum. Go figure.

"I can't believe it!" Zoey finally snapped out of her mind-trip, hopping out of her seat to jump into Nikki's arms.

Very quickly after that, the other two idiots, not including Leo—who hadn't given me enough reason to consider him one — were offering their congratulations to the newly engaged couple. I was sure we were all wondering the same things, but none of us wanted to ruin their happy moment with difficult questions. Technically, it shouldn't be any of our business how they decided to work out their relationship, but I was so attached and protective of Nikki that I needed to have answers at some point.

"I'm going to need another drink," Zoey whispered into my ear once our circle had dispersed a bit. She was sucking her margarita down like it was water on a hot day.

It turned out that everyone needed another drink after the announcement. We chugged down drink after drink at the table before deciding to move to a different side of the pub.

"Honk!" Zoey exclaimed, palming my boob roughly as we walked over to the pool tables located on the opposite corner of the bar. She was plastered after two margaritas and paid the bathroom about eight visits since we'd gotten there. I was the one stuck going with her each time, and she fondled my ass or boob on every run.

I swatted her hand away, carefully maneuvering my way over the step that led up to the pool tables. I'd only drank two margaritas and was now on a strawberry daiquiri. I wasn't drunk, but I was slightly more than buzzed. I was pretty relaxed, and

I couldn't really judge distances very well by that point. I had been laughing at everything back at the table a moment before.

"Nicole! Play a game with me!" Zoey yelled, while simultaneously pointing at Nikki who shrugged her acceptance.

Josh pushed Leo toward the other open table with a thrust of his hips and a wink in my direction. "Gross," I murmured.

A moment later, Leo was bent over the pool table while holding a pool stick like he had absolutely no experience holding phallic-shaped objects in his hand. Josh was hunched over him, pressing his hips way too closely to him. For the record, Josh sucked ass at pool and had no business trying to teach anyone how to play, but I guess he just wanted an excuse to publicly rub his junk against his man-mate, so who cared.

"Hey, good-looking," a voice purred from my left.

I looked to see a guy with jet black hair standing on the other side of the railing that separated the pool table area from the rest of the pub. "Hi," I replied dumbly and borderline drunk.

"You wanna play pool?" he asked me. His eyes were so dark they reminded me of those belonging to a seal; it was creepy.

"Uhh," I mumbled out, because yes, I did want to play, but I doubted I could hit a ball if I tried my best.

"I have a pool table at my house," the stranger

offered, leaning over the railing with a smug look on his face.

"Kat!" a silky, strained voice yelled from over by the pool table Nicole and Zoey were playing at. I looked back to see Tristan and Calum waving me over.

The strange man frowned in their direction before shrugging. "Maybe another time."

All I wanted to do was sit down to gain my bearings, but there were only two chairs on the side of the pool table closest to my best friends, and Calum and Tristan were already sitting in them. I frowned and made my way over. They were in the middle of a conversation, but after the amount I'd drank, my verbal filter had left the building.

"Can I sit there?" I asked slowly.

Their conversation ceased. Tristan raised an eyebrow as a crooked smile splayed across his lips. "I'm sitting here."

"I know, but I want to sit there. Can I sit there?"

Calum snorted, and I thought Tristan gave him a look, but my brain felt like slush so I couldn't be sure. "But then where am I going to sit?" he asked.

I shrugged and pointed down. "On the floor."

"I'm not sitting on that dirty-ass floor," he replied. "Do you need some water?"

"Yeah." I nodded, taking notice of the dryness in my throat. "But I also need to sit."

Tristan laughed and uncrossed his arms from over his chest. "Come here," he said, and I took a step forward because I trusted and listened to him more than I should. When I was standing right in front of him, he reached out to grab my hips and pull me down so I was sitting sideways across his lap. My left side was resting against his chest, while my bottom was planted on his muscular thighs.

"I promise I won't fart on you," I mumbled while squirming on his lap to situate myself a little better.

He chuckled against my ear as his hot breath fanned out and gave me goose bumps. "Thanks."

"I'll go get you some water," Calum announced before standing up and walking off.

I thought about getting up for maybe a nanosecond, but when Tristan didn't say anything about taking Calum's seat, I didn't either. It was so easy to rest my head against the crook of his neck, so I did. "You smell nice," I told him with a deep whiff of his natural, clean scent. He smelled like something manly. My nose brushed against the vein in his throat when I smelled him again.

"You do too," he said so softly I almost didn't hear him. I felt one arm wrap around my lower back and the other one rest on top of my knees. "You smell like oranges."

I sniffed him again, wishing I wasn't so out of it so I could recognize whether he shivered a little or not. "You smell like a man."

"I'd hope so," he chuckled. I couldn't help but notice how close he was to me; I thought his lips brushed the skin right by my tragus. "What was that guy telling you?"

I shrugged against him, letting my weight come to rest against his sturdy frame. Usually, I'd feel uncomfortable lying against or on top of someone, but with Tristan I couldn't care less. I knew that if it bothered him or if I weighed too much, he wouldn't have a problem telling me. "I don't know. He said he had a pool table at his house or something."

"What—" he started to say before Zoey's shrill voice cut through the air, effectively ending our night out.

"I think I'm going to throw up," she groaned.

CHAPTER THIRTY

Tristan was many things.

He was smoking hot, but also beautiful. He was also funny, smart, a jackass, and compassionate, among many other things.

Two traits he was not: organized and neat.

I'd been watching him fold his laundry for nearly twenty minutes, and I didn't know how I managed not scream in frustration or yank his clothes away from him to do it myself. I shouldn't have been surprised, considering the haphazard way his kitchen was set up, but nevertheless, his folding skills were some of the worst I'd ever seen. Right then, he was folding his T-shirts into something that looked like a geometric anomaly. Yoda and I were sitting on his king-sized bed staring at him. I was pretty sure even Yoda was wondering what the fuck he was doing.

"Why are you looking at me like that?" he finally asked, a couple minutes later. He shifted his eyes from me, to the pile of folded clothes teetering in a tower.

"You're really shitty at folding laundry," I admitted.

He scoffed. "You think you can do better?"

"Tristan, a blind man with no hands could do better." I gestured toward the big lug next to me with my head. "Yoda can probably do better than you," I laughed.

He sighed before dropping to his knees, disappearing from view. "I'm not that bad," he argued from underneath the bed. A moment and some scraping sounds later, he was dumping a black duffel bag on top of the mattress, and I realized the time had come. He'd only mentioned in passing a few times that he was leaving the next day to film over the weekend. Each and every time he said it, I got this sickening feeling deep in the pit of my stomach. It was the same kind of pain I used to get when I had to do some form of public speaking.

"How long are you going for? A couple weeks?" I tried to joke when he shoved about ten shirts into his bag.

"I always need to be prepared," he said with a chuckle. He was leaving the next afternoon, Friday, and coming back sometime Sunday evening. Zoey usually flew to Los Angeles for an entire week each month for her scenes. I'd asked her before why she didn't just move there. All she did was roll her eyes and ask me, "Who do I have in L.A.? No one. No thanks." It also helped that the cost of living was cheaper here than there.

A couple of piles of underwear, jeans, dress pants, socks, three containers of his temporary hair dye, little reusable bottles filled with shampoo, and a razor went into his duffel bag, but he didn't zip it.

He walked over to his dresser and opened the drawer, specifically the top one I became familiar with the night he got sick. I saw him reach in, and I had to look away. Yoda was lying down next to me with his massive head resting on the bed, so I scooted down and lay down alongside him before throwing an arm over his muscular frame to bury my nose into the rolls of skin on his neck.

Tristan was grabbing condoms. Dozens of condoms for all I knew. Dozens of condoms to use on other girls.

What was wrong with me? I'd known since the beginning of this friendship that Robby Lingus was a part of who he was. Regardless of how rarely he brought up this side of his life, it was still there. What did I expect? The feeling in the pit of my gut was getting worse. It spread from my stomach to my heart, and now made its way up my spine to the back of my head. Why did I feel like he was cheating on me? Why was I doing this to myself?

I squeezed my arm around Yoda, holding him tighter to me when I felt my eyes start to get watery.

Fuck. I couldn't remember the last time I'd gotten so emotional. I heard him close the drawer, and then start moving around the bedroom while humming the main theme song for *Star Wars*. The zipping of his duffel bag and the soft thump of its weight hitting the floor played background music to his humming. I closed my eyes before starting to blink away whatever remaining tears were still traitorously squatting in the corners of my eyes. I didn't want to cry in front of him. I didn't want to cry, or feel like this. Period.

After last Friday, I'd had hopes that he'd act differently around me, but he hadn't. Wouldn't a normal guy put the moves on me, or something after I'd sat on his lap? The last time I sat on Ryan's lap, I'd had his massive erection pressed against my ass for fifteen minutes, right before he tried to make out with me. Sure, we were a little drunk, but still. Ryan made me feel *something*.

"Are you asleep?" his milky voice asked at the same time the bed dipped right next to me.

"No," I mumbled against Yoga's brown coat. The big lug smelled like maple syrup.

"Want to go downstairs and play rummy?" he asked sweetly. It was my favorite game and he knew that. I'd brought it over one day and just left it. Zoey and Josh didn't get how to play, and Nicole was a good opponent, but only when she was in the mood to play, which was never.

"Okay," I responded, but didn't loosen my death

grip on Yoda. I didn't trust myself to not be upset in front of Tristan. I didn't want him to be able to tell that the situation was bothering me, because I had no right to feel emotional and disappointed. We were just friends. That's all he'd ever promised me and continued to reassure me of on a regular basis. I sucked in a deep breath to help steady my emotions. Once I felt like my breathing wasn't ragged and tears wouldn't spontaneously spill out of my eyes and down my cheeks, I rolled onto my back and sat up.

I made an effort to keep my eyes on Yoda's bulky form as he got up and jumped off the bed to follow us out of the room. I wanted to avoid looking at those intense green eyes as long as possible. "So, your mom is keeping him for the weekend?" I asked to keep him busy so he didn't notice the change in my mood. He was too perceptive for his own good.

"Yeah. She hasn't seen him yet, so I'm a little worried. I warned her he's really big, and she said it was fine, but I don't think she realizes just how huge he is," he told me on the walk down his steps.

I looked to the side, seeing the three other doors upstairs, which I still hadn't gone into, before following him down with Yoda trailing behind me. "He's a good boy. I'm sure he'll be fine."

Once we were in his kitchen with the tile pieces spread out on his breakfast table, he snuck to the fridge and brought us both Cokes. "What are you doing this weekend?"

What he meant to ask me was, *what are you doing*

this weekend since I'll be gone? The urge to punch him in his porn-star face was overwhelming; I'd seen him so much over the last few weeks that it was starting to make me feel pathetic. Before he came into the picture, I was perfectly content sitting at home with Matlock or hanging out with Zoey, Nicole, or Josh when they had time, but now... Nicole was busy with Calum, Josh busy with Leo, Zoey with Eva, and me with my *friendship* with Tristan. God, I was seriously fucking pathetic. I knew Tristan wasn't an asshole, so it was unfair for me to bitch when I knew he'd never promised me anything.

"Hanging out with the sluts, going over wedding stuff with Nikki. You know, fun stuff," I said.

"Hmm," Tristan crooned while moving tiles across the table. "I don't get why Nicole and Cal don't elope if they're planning on getting married in Vegas."

I had to laugh at him; this poor sucker didn't know Zoey Quinn. He had no idea of the damage she was capable of. "Zoey would kill Nikki if she did that. She's been planning her bridesmaid speech for the last two years. We all pulled names out of a hat to see who would be whose maid of honor, and Nikki got Zoey for hers. I don't think anyone expected her to get married before forty, honestly, much less the first one out of all of us to do so. We thought that bitch would get hitched after one of our first-borns."

Tristan snorted as he sipped his coke. "Who did

you get as your maid of honor?"

"Nikki," I said with a laugh, imagining her bossing everyone around. "I'm going to be Josh's best woman."

"Who did you guys think would be the first one to get married?" He was looking down at the pieces I'd just moved, and even though I felt like I should lie to him, I didn't.

"Me."

CHAPTER THIRTY-ONE

"I can't believe you're getting married." My words were slurred as they slipped out of my mouth.

Nicole raised a lazy eyebrow in my direction, cradling her chocolate martini close to her huge jugs. "Who would've guessed, huh?" She smiled as she nudged me with her big toe. We were sitting around her sectional; the two of us sprawled out and halfway to our destination— Hangover City, with an estimated arrival time around tomorrow morning.

I whacked Nikki's foot away from me and let out a deep sigh. "I thought your bitchy ass would be the last one."

"Me too," she agreed.

Nikki looked so different than what I was used to. She'd always been a happy person in her own way. She wasn't all shits and giggles like Zoey. She was the calm and collected type underneath her tough layer. Nicole was very serious and determined on whatever task she had ahead of her, but recently things had changed. Her facial expressions, energy, and just everything about her now radiated light, love, and all that other great corny stuff she'd never believed in. I couldn't count how many short relationships she'd been in over the last seven years, but it'd been a lot, and she had never, ever been like this. Not even close.

If she were any other person, I'd be bitter with resentment at the level of happiness she'd obtained, but this was my Nicole. She deserved all of this and more. I wouldn't belittle her into asking for reassurance with her decision, because I knew her. When the entire world might be crumbling in chaos, Nikki was the epitome of solid and steady. She knew exactly what the hell she was doing.

Hence, why we were both desperately trying to get drunk as quickly as possible and stay drunk.

Calum and Tristan had left a couple hours before, and I thought we were both feeling it in our own ways, but I could only begin to imagine how Nikki must have been feeling. She was marrying someone who was going off to "bone bitches," as she'd eloquently put it earlier. She gave him her blessing because she understood that he kind of had to go since he'd already made his commitments. She was not one to break her promises, but by the glazed over look in her eye, that knowledge and acceptance was eating away at her.

My friendship was eating away at me.

I cried last night for at least half an hour after Tristan dropped me off. It wasn't pretty *at all*. I was a sloppy mess when I cried. Big gasps, snot everywhere, body heaving—the works. Matlock freaked out and hid under my bed until I got myself under control. Almost as if she knew what I was doing, Nikki sent me a text message a little while afterward demanding that I spend the weekend with her.

"Let's go get haircuts and blow some money on cupcakes tomorrow. What do you say?" she suggested with a slow waggle of her eyebrows.

"Deal," I accepted without a second thought. The key to our hearts was through cupcakes. Stuffing our faces was a tried and true method in healing our souls. There was also something about getting a haircut, regardless of whether you cut off an inch or six that just made you feel better about yourself.

Nikki smiled at me sadly, before plopping her foot way too close to my face. "I hate feeling like this," she moaned in misery.

"I know, Nik. I can't even imagine," I told her simply, knowing she'd understand what I was trying to express. I couldn't imagine how she felt. I could barely contain my own emotions, but somehow voicing them made them seem so much more painful and harsh.

"And you, you asshole. What's going on with Tristan? I saw you all snuggled up at the bar."

I snorted because I figured it was the only reasonable noise to express. "There is nothing going on, trust me. He just wants to be friends, and I'm not going to try to force anyone to be with me, you know?"

"Of course I do." She rolled her clear, blue eyes. "You're better than that. I better not ever hear you trying to make anyone be with you, K. Any guy would be lucky to have you. It kills me enough to know that you're pining away for Robby, I mean Tristan—"

"I'm not pining away for him!" I said a little too loudly and indignantly.

"Is that why you're always hanging out with him?" she asked, smiling smugly when I didn't bother responding. "K, don't you waste your time on him when he doesn't want the same thing you do. At least, don't waste all of your time on him hoping that something will come out of it. You need to live your life, too. Okay?"

I saw the reasoning in her words because they made a lot of sense. What was I going to do? Waste away years of my life on a guy I liked, hoping that he'd see me as more than a friend at some point? Is that the life I wanted to live? A part of me screamed, *yes!* Tristan was worth it. The other half yelled back, *no!* Life was too short to wait around.

"Okay," I agreed with her. There wasn't a point in disagreeing; she was completely right.

She gulped down the last bit of her martini in a

way that was anything but feminine. "I love you, and I want you to be happy, Kat. I know he makes you happy, but I just don't want you to get your heart broken. It isn't fair he gets to go off and bang other girls while you sit around and wait for him to pull his head out of his ass. You need to get laid," she enunciated in a singsong voice. I knew she was well on her way to being drunk. She didn't singsong. Ever.

"I love you, too, Nikki. So much." I grinned, flicking her big toe. "You're fucking right, too. Who does he think I am? His girlfriend? I can do whatever I please."

"Hell yeah, you can!" she cheered on from the other side of the sofa. "I'm going to need to live through you from now on, Kitty!"

I made my face relax and go blank. I wanted to lay it on her when she was least expecting it. "I'm not planning on sleeping with any gay guys though, Nik."

"Bitch! One time! It happened one time! I didn't know he was gay!"

CHAPTER THIRTY-TWO

I should have known that something was terribly wrong when I woke up to Nicole singing along to Alanis Morissette at ten in the morning while showering.

It was the Jagged Little Pill album and I groaned. If there was ever an anthem for pissed-off females, it would be that one.

Then she played it again in the car. Over and over again.

The last time she went on an Alanis binge was four years ago when she found out her boyfriend at the time was cheating on her. One day of "You Oughta Know" on repeat later, she'd slept with his best friend. On her ex's bed. Even my heart hurt after that. So, I knew enough to be a little worried about her emotions. Where Zoey and I would cry in frustration and sadness when something bothered us, Nikki didn't. I didn't even think she had tear ducts, honestly.

We made it through our haircuts without a hitch, bought our cupcakes without anyone getting murdered, and then we blew money shopping. I really tried my best not to spend a lot of money randomly, but with the hangover I was nursing and the way my poor heart felt constricted, I deserved the little bit of happiness I got from buying clothes. It didn't help that Tristan had been sending me sporadic text messages throughout the day with jokes. By the time I'd woken up to Nicole's rendition of "Ironic," I had two texts sitting in my inbox for over two hours from him.

Kat, when did Anakin's Jedi teachers know he was going bad?

In the Sith grade.

I thought about just ignoring him, but I didn't want to be petty. I also lacked a backbone, so I sent him the only Star Wars joke I knew off the top of my head.

Why does Leia wear buns on her head?

In case she gets hungry in a Senate meeting!

I didn't get a response from him until a few hours later, which made my stomach groan, but every time I picked up my phone to check it, Nikki would start slapping the screen obnoxiously to get me off it. By the time I got another message from him, he had sent me three in a row.

Which star wars character works at a restaurant?

Darth waiter ha ha ha!

Am I annoying?

The last message had been sent over an hour before while we were at Macy's. Nikki had slipped into the fitting room to try on a dress that looked more like a shirt, so I took advantage of her absence to make myself more miserable by responding.

Only on days that end in a y, Mag.

Hours passed and I didn't hear from him. I tried not to wonder what he was doing, or better yet, who he was doing, but it was impossible. Everything reminded me of him, and it was horrible. It was worse than my obsession with my first boyfriend in high school, and it was so far off from the person I was now that it bothered me a great deal. I really wished Zoey would have been around because she always brightened my day. Now it was just Nicole and me doing our best to fight off the constant urge to vomit. We were pathetic bitches. This was a fact.

I wasn't much of drinker. I only did it socially and very rarely enough to get me halfway drunk, but that night, just like the night before with our endless supply of chocolate martinis, Nikki dragged me out of her loft to some trendy, new gay club downtown to meet up with Josh while she blasted more Alanis through her speakers. I was a little scared. I hadn't seen her reach for her phone very often, and I was a little worried of the repercussions. She kept playing with the ring on her hand absently while she drove, or sat, or just breathed in general.

"Is it cheating if I dance with someone?" she asked once we were seated at a table as far away from the speakers as possible.

"No way!" I had to yell back at her. For the record, under normal circumstances, I would probably tell her *yes* because I'd seen Nikki dance. She gave strippers a run for their money, but taking into consideration how miserable she was and what exactly her future husband was doing, she definitely had some leeway on the things that could be considered appropriate. Honestly, I was glad she hadn't called up some guy to have vengeful sex, but I guessed her self-control was a sign as to how serious she really was about Calum. It made me tear up a little, but I would never tell her that. Also, she was going to dance with gay guys, which was probably safer than dancing with a woman, at least at this club.

"Ladies!" Josh whooped out later on as he sauntered over to our table. He frowned at us as he got closer. "Why do both of you look like hell?"

Nicole didn't miss a beat and rolled her eyes. "Why do you look like you've gained weight?"

"Rude!" he exclaimed, patting his soft but flat stomach through the thin material of his lavender button-up shirt. "Who wants to get jiggy with me?"

I groaned at his words before he grabbed my hand and dragged me toward the dance floor with Nikki trailing behind me. Somehow, we ended up in a sandwich with Josh as the sandwich meat. It was hot, and at some point, I got pushed into the middle of the two, ricocheting off their gyrating bodies. It also didn't help that the cheap bastards who owned the club kept the temperature up high so we were sweating our asses off after only a couple of songs. I felt like I was there with them in spirit, but my mind felt a million miles away, like I was a balloon tethered to a fence by a mile-long string.

Later on, Josh kept turning around to talk to a big guy standing behind him. His expression went from pleasant to annoyed, and then pissed off.

"What's wrong?" I leaned into his ear to ask.

"This queen won't take no for an answer," he explained, pointing at the guy who was still standing behind him looking like a complete creep.

As I was leaning in again to talk into his ear, Josh's eyes went wide like saucers, and he spun around faster than I thought physically possible to shove the man back. I was an idiot — let's get this straight — so I didn't move an inch as I watched the big guy shove Josh back toward me. A split second later, my blond friend threw up his hand and reared his arm back to throw a fist in his stalker's direction.

The unfortunate part?

My head was in the same spot his elbow needed to be.

CHAPTER THIRTY-THREE

"Quit touching my face!" I spat out, swatting Josh's trembling hand away.

"I'm so sorry, Booger!" the poor guy cried out while reaching for my face with his fingertips again.

I wasn't mad at him, but I was mad at the fact that I got elbowed right smack under my eye. My cheekbone was throbbing and tender, so the touching wasn't helping any. The one thing I was glad about: even though he got me in the face, Josh didn't stop. He went ahead and punched the guy right in the jaw before turning around to make sure I was okay. Thank God. I would've been pissed to not only be collateral damage, but to also be collateral damage in something that wasn't worth it. The-Day-that-Josh-Wheeler-Punched-A-Guy-While-Also-Elbowing-Kat-In-The-Face would go down in the record books as monumental.

"Do you want to go to the hospital?" Nicole asked from my other side, bending at the knee to get a closer look at my damaged face.

Going to the hospital was the last thing I wanted to do. Besides being an unnecessary expense, how dumb would I look going into the emergency room with a black eye I got from my gay best friend at a gay bar? Yeah, no.

"No way," I told her, covering my cheekbone with my hand while we made our way to her car. Right after the punch/elbow, we hustled out of the club to avoid Nikki going to jail for getting into a fight with the big guy who had been harassing Josh.

"You might have a concussion," Josh piped up.

I snickered. "There is no way in hell you hit me hard enough to give me a concussion."

"I hit you hard enough to bust up your face!" he interjected, a scandalous look crossing his features like he couldn't believe I doubted his physical power.

"Don't sound so proud of yourself!" I hissed back at him, shoving my elbow in the direction of his ribs.

His face blanched as he remembered that it wasn't cool he hit me. "It was an accident!"

Nicole groaned while spinning her keys around her index finger. "I get that you don't want to go to the hospital, but I don't want you to fall asleep and never wake up again. How about we call Ryan and see if he can check you out at least?"

I knew there wasn't going to be a way for me to get out of it when they were both worried about me.

I'd be exactly the same if it were one of them. Ryan, Zoey's brother, was the lesser of two evils when it came down to seeing him or getting hauled to the emergency room where there were people who actually had a legitimate reason for being there—you know, gunshot wounds, broken appendages, stab wounds, that sort of stuff. Ryan was a medical student in his third year of residency; we'd been calling him Doctor Quinn since before he'd even gotten into medical school.

"Fine," I grumbled as we made it to Nicole's Mercedes.

Fifteen minutes later, Nikki and I pulled into Ryan's apartment building. We'd sent Josh home, knowing there was no reason for him to come, too. Ryan opened the door wearing only sleeping pants and a thin undershirt. It was only a little after midnight, but I knew he was busy working at the hospital at all hours of the day. So, when he yawned lazily and waved us in, I felt bad.

"What happened to your face?" he asked quietly, standing just inches away from me.

I sighed as he reached up to lightly graze the pained skin on my cheek. "Josh elbowed her in the face," Nicole explained as she walked through his living room to plop down on his couch. She had called him on our way over, simply telling him that he had a very important patient that needed his care. Ryan, being the sweet soul that he was, didn't think twice about inviting us over when he was clearly on his way to bed. "I'm going to take a nap. Wake me up when you're done making sure she's going to live."

Ryan shook his head and leaned even closer to me, his clear gray eyes peering into mine. "Are you dizzy? Nauseous?" he asked, and I shook my head. I felt fine except for the on and off again throbbing from my face. "No headache?"

"No, I'm fine. My face just hurts," I admitted.

He sighed and smiled. "I think you're fine, but if your head starts to feel funny, you need to go to the doctor immediately, okay? Let me go grab you some ice." It was hard not to look at Ryan's perfectly round ass as he walked toward the refrigerator to rifle through the freezer for an ice pack. I'd grabbed that ass before, and my hands were well aware that it was a good one. I'd always liked Ryan in a very subtle way, but he was always busy with school and always had a parade of women after him. He was smart, sweet, and very handsome, so it was inevitable that he was a magnet for women.

"Thanks," I said to him after he handed me the soft, blue ice pack.

"You're going to have a hell of a shiner tomorrow," he teased, leaning against the kitchen counter behind him. "Can I take a picture?"

"Why?"

He grinned before grabbing his cell phone from the counter. Holding it up, I pulled the ice pack away from my face and winced. "So I have something to look at when I have a bad day and need to laugh."

"Fine," I sighed and gave him a small smile as the shutter in his phone chimed.

He pressed a few buttons on the screen before sliding his phone back onto the counter with a wink. "At least school isn't in session, huh?"

I groaned, thinking of how awkward it would be if I did in fact have to teach on Monday with what I imagined would be a hell of a bruise and partial black eye. What would I tell my students? *My best friend hit me in the face by accident, kids*. Then they would ask, *why?* I'd have to make up some ridiculous lie, and that was one thing I tried to teach my students— lying wasn't acceptable at all. I didn't lie to them, and I expected them not to lie to me. "I guess it could be worse if I was teaching." I smirked then winced at the pain with the movement of my facial muscles.

Ryan nodded, distractedly running a hand through the curling hair at the nape of his neck. "This probably isn't the right time to ask, but I was planning on calling you sometime this week. One of my friends is getting married in two weeks and my original date can't go. Would you mind going with me?" His forehead wrinkled as he asked. "I can always ask Zoey if you can't..."

"Of course I will, Ry. How could I ever tell you no?" He had done countless things for me over the course of my friendship with his sister. We might not be "best friends forever," as Zoey always said, but he was my friend too.

"I wasn't sure if you were dating that guy at Josh's party," he explained, smiling sheepishly

Tristan. *Of course*. I had spent most of the night talking to him, so I couldn't really blame Ryan for being under that assumption. If motor-mouth Zoey had talked to her brother over the last few weeks, I was sure she'd probably spilled the beans on how often I was doing things with him. "Nah, we're just friends," I told him, noticing the pain in my stomach wasn't as horrible as it had been the last time I'd referred to us as friends.

"That's great, Kat. Thanks. I'll call you next week and tell you what time I'll pick you up," he said.

Nicole started grumbling, dragging herself away from the couch she'd been sitting on. "Is she going to live?"

"Yes, ma'am," he drawled.

"Thank God, I thought I was going to have to find another bridesmaid."

CHAPTER THIRTY-FOUR

The next day, Nikki and I went looking for bridesmaid dresses to try and narrow our choices down to two different styles that we liked in a plum color. I kept my eye on her to make sure she was doing fine, and fortunately, she seemed really happy looking at different things for her wedding throughout the day. We laughed on and off about the reality that she was going to tie the knot with someone she had an insane crush on for years *and* the serious bruise on my face. My cheekbone was purple and the outer half of my eye was red. The more we talked about the wedding, the more insane it seemed that life worked out in this way for her. Nikki's story was something out an adult fairy tale; she was marrying her charming porn star prince, who was giving it all up for her. It was perfect.

Tristan texted me in the evening, telling me he

was getting on his flight to come back home. I didn't hear from him again that day.

The day after, he texted me around one, asking if I wanted to come over, but I'd already made plans with Josh to go look at suits in the evening. He sent me a sad face in response, and then texted me goodnight around eleven.

On Tuesday, Tristan called me on his lunch break to invite me over because Yoda missed me. In all honesty, I missed the big lug, too.

My cell started ringing around three in the afternoon when I was right in the middle of showering. Reaching out of the tub to check the screen, I read 'Magellan' off the display.

"You're early, Mag," I said as loudly as I could into the speaker. I balanced the phone on the tips of my fingers as far away from the shower as I could, because I knew my luck. I'd probably electrocute myself if it were possible.

"I got off early, Goldie. Ready to go?"

"No, I'm in the shower. Just come up. I'm in 214. There's a key on top of the doorframe, so just let yourself in."

The other end of the line was silent for a few heartbeats. "Please tell me you don't have a key on your doorframe." His voice sounded desperate.

"I don't have a key on my doorframe," I laughed.

"Kat."

"Just come up. I need to finish showering. 214." I hung up, not bothering to wait for a goodbye. A couple of minutes later, I finished my shower and got dressed, shimmying into my leggings and blouse. Opening up the bathroom door, I walked into the living room of my small apartment to find him sitting on the couch with Matlock curled up on his lap, purring.

The little shit.

I could count on two hands the number of times the furry asshole had sat on my lap.

"Hey," he said softly, petting the big white ball of poof on top him. His eyes narrowed and he leaned forward, causing Matlock to jump off his lap and scurry into my bedroom. "What in the world is wrong with your face?"

I snorted and stepped closer to him, watching his eyes widen. "Josh hit me in the face," I told him bluntly, squeezing into the spot open between him and the armrest.

Tristan shifted forward more, his green eyes scanning the bruised skin. He didn't say a thing as he got closer to me. I knew without his glasses he couldn't see very well. "What happened?"

"We went to a gay club on Saturday, and this guy was harassing Josh. One thing led to another, and when he went to punch the guy, he elbowed me," I said, trying to repress the smile creeping up on my face. I'd kept the number of people I'd seen since Saturday to a minimum, but each time I had to retell my story, it sounded more and more funny. Sometimes I felt like someone up in heaven was laughing his or her ass off at the crazy stuff that happened to me.

My lovely friend on the other hand, gave me a small smile that just kept growing second by second until it covered the lower half of his face. He was so close to me his breath washed over my cheek, his teeth were even more strikingly white than usual it seemed. I saw his hand reach up in my peripheral vision, and I expected him to touch my bruise like everyone else had, but instead his fingertips pressed into the underside of my chin to tilt my face up. His smile was all encompassing; it warmed me up from the inside out. "Does it hurt?" he murmured.

"Only if you touch it." I managed a dry swallow.

He raised a single dark eyebrow. "So, can I touch it?"

His words sunk in and I had to snort, shoving him away lightly. "No, ass."

Tristan laughed and reached both large hands up to hold my face between them with mischief written all over his features. "I'm kidding!" His fingers cupped my cheeks tighter as he leaned forward again, scanning his eyes over the discolored skin. "I thought I was going to have to murder someone," he sighed dramatically, the sweet scent of peppermint wafting into my nose from his closeness. "I think you look pretty badass."

"Why thank you," I said, pulling away from his grasp to get off the couch. My throat seemed really dry all of a sudden. "Want something to drink?"

"Freshly squeezed orange juice would be nice," he suggested.

I snorted and fought the urge to flick him on the ear as I looped around the couch to go into the kitchen. "Water it is, then."

"Do you mind if I check my fantasy baseball on your MacBook?"

"Go for it," I answered him, pulling two cups from the cupboard before filling them with ice and water from the refrigerator. "How was your weekend?"

"Shit," he said simply, making a humming noise from his throat. "I didn't know you had a Facebook account."

I remembered that I'd left my account window open before I'd shut the screen, but there was nothing embarrassing on there besides some posts courtesy of Zoey. "Everyone has one. My *dad* has a Facebook."

"My mom has one, too. She'll call me and tell me if she doesn't like something I posted, so I don't even bother getting on there more than once a month anymore," he chuckled. "We're about to be friends."

Walking back around the couch with the glasses in hand, I set one down in front of him and cupped the other one in my palm, peering at the screen to see what he was doing. My profile was up on the screen and he was clicking around, looking at my random posts and other ones left by my "friends," who were really more acquaintances than anything, but whatever. "When was this?" he asked, pointing at a picture in my profile album of Josh and I dressed as members of KISS last Halloween.

"Last year for Halloween," I laughed. "Zoey and Nicole dressed up, too."

He snorted and shook his head, looking through more of my pictures, which pretty much only included my three closest friends with a few of others who had come and gone in our lives. "You and Zoey went to Disney?" he asked, pointing at another picture that Zoey had posted right after I graduated with my bachelor's. We were sandwiching Mickey Mouse between the two of us, kissing him on the cheek. Normally, I'd cringe taking pictures like that, but with Zoey, I'd do just about anything she asked me to without a sour face.

"Yeah, it was my graduation present. My dad was supposed to go with us, but he tore his meniscus right before we left," I explained.

Tristan smiled to himself, and then started browsing a different album. The first picture that showed was one I hadn't seen before, but immediately recognized by the gigantic red spot on my face. "Who's Ryan Quinn?" he asked, enlarging the picture to see the name of the person who had tagged me.

"Zoey's brother, remember? From Josh's party?" I reminded him, and he nodded solemnly with his eyes locked on the screen. "Nikki drove me over to his apartment so he could make sure I didn't have a concussion. He's a doctor." I thought about telling him I was going with Ryan to a wedding in two weeks, but why should I? It wasn't a big deal, and even if it was, it wasn't like I was calling Josh to tell him what I did constantly.

He nodded and exited out of the picture, heading back to check his stats or whatever fantasy baseball required on the browser. I caught him glancing at me out of the corner of his eye a few times before he logged out of the website he was on, and then shut my laptop. "Ready to go?"

"Ready," I told him, getting off the couch to slip on my flats. He brushed off some of Matlock's hair from his jeans and followed me toward the front door, looking around at the random things I had laying around. I hardly had anything on the walls, but I did have a lot of picture frames and curiosities I'd collected over the years on my bookshelf and side tables. We both walked out, and when I turned around to lock the door, I froze. "Did you put my key back up there?"

Tristan was walking backward as he made his way toward the stairs slowly. "Nope."

I raised an eyebrow while turning the lock. "Where is it then?"

"On my keychain," he answered slowly, like I should have known that.

"Oh, okay then," I said sarcastically with a roll of my eyes. "Don't come letting yourself in randomly. I walk around in my underwear, and I use my hummingbird religiously."

"What's a hummingbird?" he asked me once I'd caught up to him.

We started walking down the stairs together despite the fact that they weren't built to fit two adults at the same time. "Oh, Magellan, Magellan, Magellan..."

CHAPTER THIRTY-FIVE

A few nights later, Tristan was driving me home, and it was almost two o'clock in the morning. He'd been yawning for the last hour, but insisted he was fine to drive after we finished watching a documentary. I'd started dozing off toward the end of the movie, but he kept reaching over and digging the pads of his fingers into my ribs each time he caught me snoozing.

"Stop yawning," he whined, finishing his words with his own long and drawn out yawn.

"You started it," I told him with a lazy smile. I'd been making an effort to spend more time with my other friends since he'd come home, limiting the amount of time we had spent together. He called me and texted me every day to invite me over, but with Nicole's wedding coming up in less than two months, she seemed to have an endless list of things to do. Secretly, I was relieved she was doing it in Vegas because I could only imagine what it would be like if she had a big affair.

The interesting part of the time Tristan and I had spent together since he'd gotten back six days before was that he'd been acting normal, but *not really*. His smiles were the same, his jokes too, but there was a different look in his eye. His fingers lingered on me when he touched me, lasting a second or two longer than normal, and I felt like Texas grass getting a rain shower after a drought. I was soaking it all up, but I couldn't help but be a little wary. Tristan made me laugh, and made me feel so much more differently than my other three friends that it seemed foreign. I wondered if ten years from this point, if we were still friends, if he'd make me feel the same way. Would it ever get easier to look at him and not wonder what his mouth was like? It had gotten easier to not be so hung up on my expectations. Our friendship seemed even easier than before, if that was possible. Tristan accepted me for me, and I relished it.

When Zoey and I first became friends, she used to go on and on about how we were meant to be; how she and I were long lost souls destined for each other. Then, as Nikki and Josh came into our lives, she kept reiterating that idea. It wasn't difficult to accept her ideas because I had friends before them, but it was never anything half as meaningful as the relationships I shared with them. With Nicole, I could just look at her and, without moving a single muscle, we could read each other's minds. With Zoey, I felt like my happiness was tied to hers, and when I was with Josh, he just knew what I was feeling or what I needed to hear. These friendships were effortless. I loved them. We didn't have to work at them, and I couldn't remember a time when any of us had gotten so mad at one another that we didn't speak out of anger for more than a day.

Tristan was this way to me, as well. I didn't have to censor my words to make sure I wasn't being crude, and I didn't have to pretend to like things I hated. I could just be me. I could stuff my face, cry during a movie, scream when he held dead crickets and threw them in my direction, and it was all fine. I just wished he was ugly. Or gay. Either one of those would have been a nice balance to the perfect mess that I found him to be.

"You better not fall asleep," I heard him chuckle over from the driver's seat when I felt my eyelids start to droop again.

I made a weird grumble in my throat in response before leaning my head back against the leather of his headrest, letting myself rest on the long ride home. We'd been outside with Yoda most of the afternoon and well into the early evening, trying to teach him how to sit and stay. The sun wore me out more than usual. Yoda was such a rebel that he refused to do anything unless he got a damn treat. Personally, I thought that showed how intelligent he was, but Tristan thought it just demonstrated his epic level of stubbornness.

It seemed like my eyes had only closed for a second when I felt a cool draft of air from my right, replacing the previous heat. "C'mon, Sleeping Beauty," that velvet voice I'd grown so fond of murmured into my ear.

"I'm so sleepy," I moaned out as he pulled at my hand, leading me out of the car. I squinted against the bright floodlight that illuminated the walkway and stairs leading up to my apartment. Tristan held my wrist as he pulled me up the stairs toward my home.

"We're almost there," he said in a husky tone before stopping in front of my door. I was awake enough to notice he used the key he'd taken from me earlier in the week to unlock my door. He hadn't come upstairs since Tuesday, and it was only the slightest bit surreal that he was the one unlocking the door. The only other person to have a key to my apartment was Josh because I didn't trust Zoey or Nikki to have enough manners to come over announced. Tristan's warm hand brushed up and down my forearm as he led me through my apartment.

I made a drowsy beeline to my bedroom, pushing him aside. The heat of his presence behind me singed my skin as he followed me through my small apartment. Pushing open the bedroom door, I went into my bathroom first to brush my teeth before I passed out with a dirty mouth. Tristan stood in my bedroom, and from what I could see in the reflection of my mirror, he was yawning these huge gulps of air. "You...okay...to...dwive?" I meant to say *drive,* but with the toothbrush in my mouth, it sounded like something else completely.

He shrugged, looking away from where I was at to pick up some photos I had stuffed into the crevices of my vanity mirror. "Do you care if I look through your stuff?" he had the decency to ask.

"Go fow it," I said, spitting into the sink, and then rinsing my mouth. I didn't own anything that I was ashamed of besides the small array of dildos I had stashed in the top drawer of my nightstand, and even then, this was Tristan. I wanted him to think of me as more than a sister or friend. *Hmm.* For the briefest second, I contemplated asking him to look in my drawer for something. That would be the ultimate test. If he flinched, I was screwed, but if he didn't... I shut down that train of thought. I wasn't doing it. Once I was done washing my face, I headed into the bedroom to see what he was doing. I hadn't seen him in the reflection of the mirror in a couple minutes, and it was making me a little nervous.

"You look just like your mom," Tristan said quietly from his spot on my side of the bed. He sat, holding a picture frame of my dad, mom, and me at Disneyland when I was eight. It was the last vacation we ever took together and one of the dearest things I owned. We all looked so happy that it pulled at my heartstrings each time I saw it.

"It reminds me every day that life is really short," I said while trying to kick off my boots. They were fake, brown suede and went up to my knee, which meant they were a bitch to take off.

Tristan patted his knee after tearing his eyes away from the frame and setting it back in its rightful spot. I set my foot on his leg as he tugged the boot off from the heel. "I'm sorry you lost your mom so young, Kat." His voice was soft like melted butter. "But I think she probably would have wanted you to appreciate life for the both of you." His big hands squeezed my calf as he yanked the boot off and threw it in the direction of the open closet door. He patted his knee again, and I put my other foot on there. "Has your dad dated anyone since she passed?"

My snort was almost too low to be heard. Dad dating anyone? *Ha.* "No way. He loved my mom like crazy. Now that I'm older, he's a lot more open with me about his feelings," I began explaining. "He told me not too long ago that he could never love anyone else if he tried." The last few words came out as a whine, because I was tearing up while thinking of my mom and dad and the love they lost.

My other boot was off a second later as Tristan began pulling me onto the bed next to him and draped an arm across my shoulder. "Don't cry," he said, pushing my hair out of my face.

The tears were right there, some teasing me while others fell to their demise after making the long trek down my cheeks. I hated death, especially when I thought of losing someone I loved. "It makes me so sad that my dad is alone now." I attempted to wipe at my face with my fingers, but Tristan beat me to it. "I only see him like twice a month now, and it makes me feel like a terrible daughter."

"I'm sure he's okay with knowing that you're happy and well," he said gently against my temple, and a few more tears sprung out of my eyes. "C'mon, don't cry."

I sniffled, trying to control my emotions while he yawned again, blowing hot breath all over my face. "Gross," I grimaced, wiping at the cheek he'd just blown steam over. He smiled smugly like he did it on purpose, or at least enjoyed making my face feel nasty. "Are you okay to drive?" I asked, and before my question was even complete, he yawned for the millionth time. "I guess not."

I was stuck between telling him to stay the night and... who was I kidding... telling him to stay the night. Letting a sleepy friend drive home was just as bad as letting a drunk friend drive home in my book. Both were tragedies waiting to happen, and I'd feel devastated if something happened to any of my friends if they fell asleep driving and I could've prevented it. The only thing was though, I felt awkward suggesting that he to stay over. What I meant by feeling weird was that I wanted him to stay over, sure, but I really wanted him to stay over on my bed. Naked. Maybe spooning if it wasn't too much to ask for.

God, my life was a joke.

"Just sleep here. Yoda will be fine at home." I finally snapped out of my mental battle long enough to suggest.

Tristan looked at me through heavy-lidded eyes. He was so tired an astronaut could have seen the signs from outer space. "You don't mind?"

I rolled my eyes and got off the bed, wiping at my face one last time before toeing off my socks. "I wouldn't be suggesting it if I did." I started unbuttoning my jeans just a couple feet away from him, ignoring the silent alarm in my head that told me this was inappropriate. Seriously? The guy had just slept with who knows how many girls the past weekend. If anything, I should have been embarrassed taking off my clothes in front of him because there was no way my body was up to par with what he was used to. But I wasn't. Zoey and Nikki's words swam through my brain, reassuring me of my assets. Fuck him and his friendship.

His eyes went back and forth between the clumsy fingers on my buttons and my face. "Thanks, Goldie," he said in a voice so low it could have been considered sleepy, but I'd like to think that was not the case.

My hands quickly pushed my jeans down my legs then tugging at the hem to get them off because they were so tight. "There's an extra toothbrush under my sink," I told him, throwing my pants into the closet. He just sat on the bed, hands on his lap, looking back and forth between my black boy shorts and my face.

"Okay," he said, not moving an inch off the bed to look for the toothbrush.

"All right..." I turned around to face my big dresser when I peeled off my T-shirt. I knew for a fact my ass cheeks were hanging out of my underwear, but fuck it, with the amount of exercise I did, I knew you could bounce a roll of quarters off it. Plus, my bathing suit bottom was a lot skimpier than some underwear I owned, so it wasn't like I was really being indecent. After taking off my bra and slipping on a sports bra, I turned around to catch those piercing eyes dart away from me quickly, he was up and in the bathroom a second later.

Flicking off the overhead light, I turned on my side lamp before crawling under the covers. A few minutes later, Tristan's sinewy frame stood in the doorway as he took off his T-shirt. I couldn't lie, I squinted in the darkness to try and catch the masterpiece that was his upper body in the dim lighting. He walked around to the other side of the bed before unzipping his jeans. "I can't sleep with pants on," he admitted, almost apologetically.

"Me neither."

His eyes flickered up to mine for a brief moment as he shoved his jeans down his long legs, and then climbed onto my bed.

Oh, my God.

I blessed the seven angels as I watched the muscles in his arms, back, and abs ripple.

A man that hot should have a squeaky voice. Be dumb. Have a tiny wiener. Even have chicken legs. A third nipple! Or big nipples!

Anything to balance out the perfection that he was overall, but fucking — and I didn't mean literally — Tristan was just perfect, and I kind of hated him for it.

He smiled at me smugly, and then wiggled between the covers. I had to wonder whether or not I'd just said any of my thoughts aloud, but I didn't think so. "Read me a bedtime story?" he tried to ask, but laughed instead.

"Shut up." I groaned, tearing my eyes away from his pillowy pecs to turn off the side lamp. My bed was big enough for me. It was queen-sized, but with both of us on it, I couldn't move my hand more than a couple of inches without risking the chance of grazing bare skin that didn't belong to me. Damn it. "Goodnight."

"Night, Kat," he replied. I sensed the movement of his hand before the heat of it. He brushed his fingertips across my palm, squeezing lightly for just a moment.

I laid there, clenching my eyes closed so I was not tempted to roll over and stare at him in his sleep.

"Kat?"

"Yes?"

He let out another yawn. "You're my favorite

person in the world. Goodnight."

I was trying to just manage to breathe, and then think after his words. By the time I realized I should have responded, his breathing was low and even. He'd fallen asleep, and I felt like I'd just cured cancer. How the hell I managed to fall asleep after that, I wasn't sure. I was aware that at some point, I woke up after dreaming I peed in the middle of a grocery store. I was secretly paranoid I may have actually peed on myself for the first time in twenty years, not including the little pees I'd experienced laughing. I squeezed my thighs together and thanked Morpheus, the god of dreams, for not being a cruel jokester.

As I came to my senses, I realized I wasn't on my side of the bed anymore. I was still facing the bathroom door, but in the middle of the bed, and there were lips on the back of my neck. Dry lips with warm breath trailed down the length of my neck while a big hand with calloused fingers grazed my bare stomach and hip, pressing my bladder just the slightest bit. There was a chest so close to my back that I thought if I were to lean back just an inch or two, I'd be pressed against it.

I couldn't help the shiver that rolled through my spine or the goose bumps that prickled up along my arms at the feeling of lips and hands.

Was he awake?

I wanted to know, but I didn't move.

Lips touched the crook of my neck and shoulder,

but this time they were wet. Then, a second later the mouth disappeared. The hand stayed on my hip and only warm breathing washed over my neck. This was so inappropriate...

I didn't move an inch.

CHAPTER THIRTY-SIX

With a heavy heart, I picked up the phone to call my dad the next afternoon. The previous night's conversation with Tristan had shaken me deeply. Dad and I had always had a great relationship. We became each other's best friends after my mom died. He'd always made an effort to stay home and do things with me each chance he got. He didn't go out or do things with his friends unless he took me along. It wasn't until high school that I truly appreciated how great he was. It was with that in mind that I felt like a terrible daughter since I hadn't paid him a visit in so long.

"Which jail do you need me to bail you out of?" he answered on the second ring.

The laugh that exploded out of me was loud. "Oh, please!"

My dad chuckled on the other end. "I'm just

kidding, baby. How are you?"

Settling onto the couch, I peered at the picture on my side table of the both of us at my high school graduation. "I'm good, Dad. Are you okay?"

"Cool as a cucumber, Kitty. I'm waiting for my next customer to get home and trying not to fall asleep in the meantime. How are the girls?" he asked, knowing I understood that he included Josh with that group.

"They're all good. Nikki is getting married, did you know?" I already knew he probably did. The old man stalked his Facebook account every chance he got, and Zoey was always posting something on there.

"I just got the invitation a few days ago. I made plans to go to the casino with Mike that weekend, but buy her something from the both of us," he said before telling me all about the trip he was taking with his best friend to Louisiana. I told him a little more about Nicole's wedding in Vegas, and then about finishing up my book. We talked easily for a few minutes before he dropped the bomb on me. "No new boyfriend, Kitty?"

I groaned as a response. "Not a boyfriend, just a new friend."

My dad snickered loudly. "Men can't be friends with pretty girls unless they have feelings for them, baby."

"Well this one seems to be an exception. Trust me."

He made a noise like he was thinking before exhaling. "Whatever you say, but if you want me to knock some sense into him—"

"Dad! You wouldn't hurt anyone if I paid you to," I laughed, remembering the times he'd gone out of his way to avoid getting into arguments with people.

"I wouldn't, but I know people!" the silly man answered.

CHAPTER THIRTY-SEVEN

"Girls versus guys."

Nicole let out an unladylike snort. "More like girls versus bitches."

Josh cackled as he tied his bowling shoes. "In that case, I'm on the girls' team."

Tristan turned to look at Calum who sat next to him, smelling his shoes with a face that was a little too curious and not enough disgusted. "You're definitely a bitch, Cal."

"Babe, do you think I'm a bitch?" Calum's deep voice asked Nikki, who was sitting in front of the keyboard typing names away for each of the lanes.

"Baby, I promised you I would never lie to you, so please don't ask me to start today," she said without blinking, her eyes locked on the screen in front of her.

Zoey, who sat right next to me on the lane we'd

designated for the females, laughed and gave me a high-five at Nicole's response. Tristan and Calum sat on the opposite side of the lane and bickering over who was a bigger bitch. "This is going to be fun," she announced with a big smile on her face.

She'd been gone for a little over a week, and I'd missed her pretty face. The night before, Josh and I had gone to pick her up from the airport, before staying over at her apartment to watch the first three Harry Potter movies back to back. Yes, we were an overgrown bunch of geeks who banded together to read all of the books and cried when Dumbledore and Dobby died. I think Josh had a secret crush on one of the characters from the movies, but he wouldn't admit which one.

"Kat and Joshua, you're up first," Nikki said.

"I'm going to kick your fanny, Booger," Josh claimed, going up to the center to retrieve his ball at the same time I did.

"You probably are considering all the experience with balls you have," I snickered with a wink.

The blond snapped his fingers in my face as he brought his dark blue ball up to his chin, preparing to bowl. "You wish you've had as much ball experience as I do."

He bowled a strike on his turn while I only managed to knock down eight pins total. We gave each other a hip bump before returning to our respective seats on opposite ends. About an hour later, we'd moved around the seats a bit. Zoey,

Tristan, and I sat on our original lane, while Nikki sat on Calum's lap between turns, and Josh settled for glaring at the happy couple when he could. We, the females, had won the first game.

As fate would have it, Calum was just as terrible at bowling as Tristan. He kept saying, "I was on a league!" but obviously, he'd been on the same one as Tristan— an imaginary league. Or possibly one with bumpers, was another of my best guesses.

Zoey rested her feet on my lap as Nikki and Calum went up to bowl against each other. "I talked to Ryan this morning," she said with a naughty look in her eye.

"That's cool," I said slowly, raising an eyebrow in her direction. Tristan sat right next to me with his forearm brushing mine, his attention focused on the lane. I mouthed out a "What?" to her, because even though Zoey was pretty random, this was unexpected. She talked to Ryan at least three times a week and had never made an effort to let me know she had spoken to him unless there was gossip. Or, the time she had asked him to prescribe her cream for her hemorrhoids and he flipped out.

She winked at me so dramatically I had to turn my head slightly to make sure Tristan wasn't looking at her. "I didn't know you were going to a wedding with him," she drawled out.

That bitch.

I loved her.

His arm stiffened. It was the smallest fraction of a

movement and barely noticeable. "Yeah, he asked me last weekend when Josh decided to ruin my face." The bruise on my face was more yellow and brown by then rather than purple, blue, and red.

"It was an accident!" he bellowed from the other side.

"Mind your own business!" Zoey waved the nosey turd off. "I'm glad you're going with him instead of that skank he was going to take before. She's such a slut, and you know for me to call someone a slut, she really is one." She sighed dramatically.

It was Tristan and Zoey's turn to bowl, so she held up her index finger asking me to give her a second while she went up and bowled nine before picking up her spare. Tristan, on the other hand, knocked down a total of six. That was the equivalent of a strike by his standards. I couldn't hear what they were saying to one another because their voices were surprisingly low and the music was too loud, but Zoey punched him in the arm on their walk back to their seats.

"Good try." I laughed when I passed by my auburn-haired friend on the way up to the lane as he tugged at my ponytail in response.

"You're going down, bitch," Josh hissed from my right, already prepped and ready with his ball.

After I bowled a strike — thank God — I went back to sit between Zoey and Tristan again. Her smile looked a little crazy and it scared me.

"What dress are you going to wear to the wedding?" she asked like she really cared.

"I don't know."

"Wear that cute blue one, the strapless one that's almost too short. You can show off those legs, tiger." Her voice was even and calm, but the look on her face was a contradiction of alert and amused. Her eyes flickered back and forth between my face and Tristan's. "I told Ry that he needs to think about settling down before all of his friends get married and he's the lonely loser."

Uh. For the record, Zoey couldn't care less about marriage, so her little rant about wanting Ryan to get married was a whole pile of bullshit. When Tristan stiffened next to me, making a noise that sounded like he was clearing his throat, the little vixen gave me a thumbs-up. Oh. My. God.

"I'm gonna go pee. I'll be back." She stood up, wiping imaginary lint off her jeans. "Just bowl for me, KAB." Then, she was off, practically skipping to the restroom.

Tristan decided to turn and look at me then, giving me the opportunity to appreciate the fact that his superb, finely cut jaw was clenched. He didn't say a word as Nikki and Calum sat back down, but he did wave me up to follow him so we could grab our balls to bowl. I was a little faster than him at prepping, so my ball was flying down the lane a few seconds before his.

"You're going to a wedding?" he asked me

casually, while we waited for our balls to come back.

"Yeah, on Saturday," I answered, looking at the machine that returned the balls. I glanced up at him, but his broad frame was facing the lanes while his hands were shoved deep inside his jean pockets.

"Cool," he muttered in a deep voice.

I knew he was leaving on Friday again, because he told me about it a few days before, and that familiar, sickening feeling in my stomach made a mess of my intestines. I had a brief flashback to two days before, when I woke up in the middle of the night to Tristan's form against mine. By the time I got up in the morning, he was already awake and attempting to make French toast. He didn't say anything about the night before, and I sure as hell wasn't going to be the one to point out anything he potentially could have done in his sleep. Why couldn't I be a telepath? Or even have some balls to invite him to spend the night again?

I bowled again for Zoey and waited for Tristan to bowl before I gave him a high-five. Josh was up and talking a whole lot of shit before our turn, and by the time I made it back to the seats, Zoey hadn't made it back. My handsome friend was sitting in his seat with his spine straight and shoulders pushed so far back it looked borderline painful.

The lovely green eyes I was so fond of were looking between my still colorful cheek and eyes. "Want to come over for a while after we finish here? I'll make spaghetti."

Damn him and his mom's spaghetti recipe.

I was such a sucker.

CHAPTER THIRTY-EIGHT

"I haven't been here in years," I said quietly, peering into the huge water world just a few feet away.

Tristan leaned into me, bumping my shoulder against his arm. "I come here with my mom a couple times a year."

We were at the Miami Seaquarium on Thursday. He managed to get off work early and invited me to go with him for fun. It was the first time we'd actually gone anywhere besides the animal shelter, grocery store, and pet store. Not that I minded staying at his house for the most part, because we were both homebodies, but this was a nice change. Still in his work clothes, Tristan was too much for a measly human in his black dress pants, light blue button-up shirt, and rolled up sleeves. Professional Tristan was way too much for my eyes and hormones, and by the sultry looks every woman in the aquarium had shot him, they all agreed with me.

The killer whale and dolphin show had just finished and we were heading to the main reef aquarium to cool down for a bit. I could tell Tristan regretted keeping on his work clothes because the sun was unforgiving and the heat was blistering. The air conditioning felt like a miracle to me and I was wearing half the amount of clothes he was. We paused in front of one of the biggest tanks, taking in the shades of blue that teamed with fish.

"I'm going to the restroom," he whispered into my ear, squeezing my wrist.

I wasn't sure exactly how long I stood there staring at the homes of blue water right ahead of me, but I knew it was awhile when I started to get bored and look around the rest of the aquarium for Tristan. There were only about fifteen other people in this part of the building at the time and none of them were my beautiful friend. The problem was that I didn't have my cell or my purse with me. I'd left my things in the trunk of his car since I didn't think I'd need any of it. I was worried, because I couldn't even call him to check and see if he had bubbly guts, or if maybe he'd fallen and hit his head on the toilet.

Once I located the restrooms, I sat on the bench closest to the doors and waited a solid fifteen minutes. There was an older man walking in the direction of the restroom, so I got up and headed toward him.

"Hi," I said as gently as possible. "I was

wondering if you could do me a big favor?"

Both of his salt and pepper eyebrows went up in response. "Okay."

Oh, God. He probably thought I was a hooker. "I'm a little worried about my friend who was in the bathroom. His name is Tristan. Do you mind seeing if he's still in there?" I spat out as quickly as I could.

The man nodded sharply before ducking into the restroom. Only a couple of minutes later, he came out, shaking his head. "Sorry, ma'am, no one else was in there."

"Oh, okay." I told him as evenly as I possibly could.

Fuck. Fuck. Fuck.

Where was he? I didn't want to risk walking around the Seaquarium looking for him because it might take hours to run into each other. A slight panic clawed its way up my spine, reminding me of the time my dad forgot to pick me up from school right after my mom died, and I got stuck being taken home by my principal. I cried the entire way, feeling alone and abandoned. I didn't think Tristan would just up and leave me, but I had no idea where he could have gone. I didn't move an inch while I waited for him.

Plopping back down onto the bench, I tried to steady the tremor in my hands while trying my best to control my emotions. Nikki's office was only a few blocks away, so I could walk over there to get a ride home, but then I ran the risk of showing up only to have her be gone. I couldn't remember whether or not she had a trial today. *Shit.*

A long figure stopped in front of me, and I looked up, expecting to see green eyes and lightly tanned skin, but the eye color was off, it was a shade of sea-foam green and the skin color was a creamy white. "Do you need some help?" the stranger asked in a gravelly voice.

"I don't know," I replied, taking in the polo shirt he had on with the aquarium's name stitched neatly over a pocket. The man was really good-looking and I mean *really* good-looking. He was almost as hot as Tristan with a straight nose, inky black hair, and full lips. Fuck me. I was worried about being abandoned, but didn't waste any time in checking out the nice employee like the hussy I was. Ha.

The man squatted down so he was almost eye level with me. "I've been watching you for awhile," he said before groaning, pink coloring the cartilage of his ears. "That makes me sound like a stalker, I'm sorry. What I mean to say is that you look lost."

I giggled a little at his words because he did sound like a creep by saying he'd been watching me. Hell, he was a hot creep, so I was mostly okay with it. "I came with my friend and he disappeared."

"Have you tried calling him?"

I pointed at my leggings and lack of pockets. "I left my phone in his car and I don't have his number memorized." Panic laced my words at the end. I knew there wasn't a real reason to freak out, but my body couldn't comprehend it.

"Boyfriend?" he asked slowly with a twitch of his cola-colored eyebrows.

"No," I told him, trying to fight back a smile at his question.

This time the man smiled. "Do you want to wait a little while longer and see if he shows up?"

I had to remind myself that if I left, it would probably be harder to find him. I'd gone on quite a few field trips with my kids and knew the drill well. My mantra floated through my brain: *If you get lost, stay where you are*. Did it count if I was technically not lost, but Tristan might be? I voted yes. Looking at my watch, it was barely three. If Nikki was at work, she normally didn't leave until closer to five, so I was safe to catch a ride, but only as long as long as she was there.

"Yeah, I should probably just wait a few more minutes."

He nodded, gesturing toward a spot on the bench right next to me with his head. "Do you mind if I wait with you?"

"Of course not," I told him as he straightened up, and then sat down. "I'm Katherine." I outstretched my hand in his direction.

"It's nice to meet you," he said, shaking my hand. "I'm Kieran."

"Kieran," I sounded it out. "That's a neat one. Irish?"

He nodded, a big smile coming over his face.

"First generation."

"Nice." I pointed at the stitching on his polo. "Do you work here, or do you just wear that for fun?"

Kieran laughed, and then explained that he was a biologist, which I thought was really cool. Then he asked me what I did, launching us into a conversation about being a teacher and school in general. He'd just turned thirty and loved working at the aquarium. Our conversation flowed effortlessly for short minutes that fell right after another in a domino effect. It was easy to forget that I may have been abandoned by someone I cared about more than he deserved at this point.

"Kat!" a familiar voice exclaimed from the entrance to the exhibit.

I was so focused on Kieran's raspy voice that it took me a second to look up and find Tristan speed walking in my direction as he looked back and forth between Kieran and me. His face was flushed and desperate as he made his way over. "Where were you?" I managed to ask, standing up to face him.

"Walter called me and there was a problem we needed to resolve," he hesitated. "I'm so, so sorry I left you here for so long," he apologized, finally reaching me. He reached up to grasp my shoulder, but his eyes stationed themselves on my new acquaintance. His look was anything but friendly as Kieran stood up as well. Tristan was just an inch taller, I noticed.

I was stuck between introducing them to each

other and just letting the awkward silence continue, but Kieran cleared his throat and faced me instead before smiling gently. "I should be getting back to work, but it was a pleasure meeting you, Katherine." He fished in his pocket for a moment before handing me a business card. "It was nice talking to you... please feel free to e-mail or call me." He winked and my ovaries started screaming. "If you'd like."

I nodded at him in response, watching him take a few steps away before Tristan's steaming presence next to me brought my attention back to him. I felt really irked all of a sudden. I thought it was the fact that he did in fact leave the exhibit without so much as at least telling me *I'll be right back*. I wouldn't have cared if he needed to talk to Walter for whatever porn-related issue he had going on. I felt betrayed, and by the look on his face, I knew he could tell I was a little upset with him.

"I'm sorry, Goldie. I had to run out to my car and it took a lot longer than I expected." He sighed, staring at me with those intense gem colored eyes.

"I thought you left me."

His face took on a pained expression at my words. "I'd never leave you, you should know that."

You should know that. It drove a microscopic stake into my heart. I shrugged in his direction while averting my eyes to the wall behind him. "Okay," slipped out of my mouth, but even I could hear the frustration that tainted my words.

"Goldie," he whispered.

He sighed too loudly and wrapped his arms around me, one over my shoulders and the other across the middle of my back. His warm lips pressed against my temple, making it the first time he'd ever put his lips directly on my skin without the excuse of sleep, and the hairs on the back of my neck prickled in response to his affection. He brushed those full lips against my other temple while tightening his hug. "You're my favorite person in the world, Kat. I could never forget about you."

His words were like a soothing balm to his actions, dulling the emotions that had been wrapped around me before. His words and touches were enough to ease him back into my good graces because I believed him. I felt his affection toward me through his hug and chaste kisses, but the sharp edges of the business card in my hand reminded me of Kieran. I wondered briefly if words and apologetic actions were really enough when it came to this thing with Tristan. At times, I felt like he thought of me as more than a friend or sister, but it fluctuated so much I didn't understand and was not willing to push for an explanation.

I figured if he wanted me, he'd make it known.

Later that night, Tristan was running up the stairs to my apartment, his long legs pumping him up the stairs faster than I imagined he could possibly go. His fist was clenched and his teeth were grinding. The poor sucker needed to pee, and I was taking my sweet-ass time making it up the stairs. "Kat!" he hissed at me.

"I'm coming, I'm coming," I said, walking over to the door and unlocking it.

He pushed passed me and dodged into my bathroom with Matlock trailing after him. He'd been exceptionally sweet the rest of the day after the aquarium incident, taking me to eat at this neat Japanese restaurant before taking us back to his house to play with Yoda a while. Tristan brushed his fingers through my ponytail randomly, put his arm around my shoulder more often, and then kissed my temples a couple more times. Needless to say, I was turned-on beyond belief. I swear he radiated magical sexual energy with his hands and lips. Maybe I was just so interested in him that my desperate body would take any attention it could get and milk it shamelessly.

I wanted him to give me a sign that he felt something for me besides friendship.

I know his actions and looks were more than just platonic. Over the course of my life, I'd had male friends before who were just that — friends — and it was never like this. Never. Tristan was different; I knew that, but I wanted it to be really different. The notion that he was leaving the next day to go fornicate with other girls killed me inside. It killed me because I wanted him to do those things with *me*.

"I may have peed on your toilet seat by accident," his velvet voice stated from the doorway to my bathroom. He stood there in all of his muscular, professional glory and a sheepish face.

I grimaced and tossed one of my pillows at him. "Did you at least clean it off?"

He nodded, holding my pillow between his hands before plopping down on the bed right next to me. "I did, don't worry."

"Yuck," I told him, but honestly, I really didn't care too much. Having shared a bathroom with Josh for a year, I'd become pretty desensitized to the things that could happen when a man peed. Josh used to leave puddles on the floor, and let's just say I was fond of walking around barefoot. I figured that as long as my ass didn't come into direct contact with it then I was fine. A sudden thought popped into my brain, and I felt a little like Zoey as I hopped off the bed and pulled the sliding door to my closet open. She'd be so proud of me and my plan. "Real quick, tell me which dress you think I should wear to the wedding. I can't decide on one."

Silence answered me and I had to bite back a snort. Every time I'd brought up the wedding, which had really only been one other time besides Sunday, Tristan's mouth would lock up like a jail cell. I grabbed the three dresses I had in mind from the closet and laid them out on the bed right next to him. The strapless dress Zoey had brought up the day we went bowling didn't fit anymore and I was relieved by it. Tristan rolled over so he was propped up on his elbow, while his other hand was free to touch the three very different dresses laid out.

One was short, gold, and sparkly with thin straps and a black band of fabric right below where my breasts would be. I thought it was a little on the short side, but maybe not. The other was a sea-foam color that reminded me of Kieran's eyes for a brief moment; it was strapless and a decent length. The third I was definitely not sure about, the midnight blue dress was silky and sleeveless with the material bunching up on one shoulder, leaving the other completely exposed. It was pretty fucking short, and if that wasn't bad enough, I couldn't wear a bra with it. I didn't have huge boobs, but they were still too large for me to successfully pull off going braless.

"Try them on," he suggested. "They might be too short to be appropriate for a wedding."

I nodded and grabbed the dresses to change in the bathroom. I tried on each in order, stepping into the bedroom to show him each time. He simply nodded at the first two, but it was when I wore the dark blue one that I saw his eyes widen. I swear his nostrils flared as I stood in front of him and tugged at the hem. That one was definitely way too short. It barely covered my ass, and the material against my nipples made them pucker up like some of the fish I'd seen earlier in the day.

"Come here," he motioned me forward, keeping his eyes trained on my face and throat. His jaw was clenched, but then he licked his lips when I was right in front of him. If I would have taken another step forward, our knees would've brushed against each other, or I'd have found myself standing in between his legs.

He sat up as his gaze made a hot trail down the path from my nose to my mouth before circulating down to my throat, collarbones, and finally landing on my chest. I was self-conscious, but not, at the same time. A blind man could see how hard my nipples were through the thin silk fabric, and obviously, Tristan's bad eyesight was only limited to small printed words. He started to reach up with both hands, the L shape created by the webbing of his index finger and thumb hovered over the undersides of my breasts for a split second before they suddenly dropped to his lap.

Tristan cleared his throat and shook his head. "Definitely not this one," he said in a husky voice.

My mind reeled at what I thought he was going to do for a moment. It looked like he was going to touch me, and I would've let him a thousand times over, but he didn't. I knew Tristan was all about control. *Control. Control. Control.* That was one of the requirements for being a man in porn. They couldn't be three-minute pump chumps like my first boyfriend in high school. Tristan knew how to control himself, and I kind of hated him for it. As I stripped out of my dress and put on my jeans and shirt from earlier, I made a quiet wish to myself that he'd lose control because I was getting tired of waiting. What did Nicole tell me? I needed to keep living my life.

When I came out of the restroom, Tristan wasn't in my bedroom anymore; instead, he sat on the couch with his new best friend, Matlock. He gave me a tightlipped smile when I sat down next to him. I watched him pet my idiot cat for long moments, stroking his long fur very gently. It was silent, but okay and easy. "You should wear the light blue dress," he blurted out.

"Okay," I replied with a short laugh. "Why that one?"

"It's the longest one." He looked at me, and then had the audacity to wink.

CHAPTER THIRTY-NINE

Ryan Quinn was trying to seduce me.

I was also shamelessly eating up his attention in the same way I would devour a bowl of strawberry ice cream.

His game was on the moment I opened up my door to invite him in. He stood there, all six feet of gloriousness, with dark hair, and cool eyes, while leaning up against the doorframe with a red rose in hand. I wasn't really a roses-type of girl, but I could definitely appreciate the gesture. "Kat, I do believe you might be the most beautiful thing these eyes have ever seen," he cooed, eyeing my sea-foam colored dress appreciatively. "This is for you," he finished, extending the rose toward me.

I rolled my eyes, but blushed profusely, taking the flower from him and waving him in so I could grab my shoes. "Come on in, Romeo."

He was a complete gentleman throughout the service, opening up doors and gently leading me wherever we were heading. Ryan was attentive and sweet, introducing me to all of his friends and touching me every chance he got. We trekked our way across the parking lot to the reception hall where the dinner and dance was taking place. We had just sat down at a table when my phone chimed, alerting me of a text message. I expected it to be Zoey, but of course, it wasn't. 'Magellan' spelled out across the display.

I miss you. How's the wedding?

Was it wrong that I enjoyed the fact that he missed me? I didn't think so. I chanced a look over at Ryan to see him in the middle of a conversation with one of his friends.

Miss you too! Good so far, about to stuff my face :]

Mere seconds later, my phone chimed again.

What time will you be home? I'm having a bad day.

No idea. Maybe midnight? What's wrong?

"Kitty?" Ryan murmured against my ear, effectively pulling me out of my focus.

Slipping my phone back into my purse, I smiled back at him. "Ry?"

"Did I already tell you that you look amazing?" he

asked, gray eyes sparkling in mischief.

I couldn't help but snort. "Yes, you did. Thank you again."

"Carlos! Take a picture of me and my beautiful date!" he said, turning to face the brown-haired man sitting across the table. Ryan tossed his phone to him before slipping his arm over my shoulder.

"Smile," Carlos instructed us.

I slid my seat over just an inch, so our cheeks were practically pressed together before smiling in the direction of his phone. A moment later, Carlos tossed the phone back over to Ryan, who pressed random buttons on the screen until he slipped it back into his pocket. "I hope you're aware that by being my date, you can only dance with me. You may also have to let me kiss you," he said with a straight face, but his cheeks were pulled up tightly in a smile.

"Yes to the dances, and I don't know to the kisses," I told him with a laugh.

Ryan frowned at me in amusement. "I'll win you over."

Sure enough, after a few glasses of bitter wine, which I chugged down, Ryan was freely kissing my cheeks and keeping his arm steadily around my shoulders. He was warm and handsome, focused directly on me despite the fact that half the women in the reception hall had come over to introduce themselves by shoving their tits in his face. When he got up to use the restroom, I pulled my phone out of my purse to see if I had any missed calls or texts. I realized that I did in fact have alerts telling me that I had three new text messages and four new Facebook alerts. I checked my Facebook account first to see that I'd been tagged in a picture, had two people who 'liked' said picture, and one new comment.

The picture was of Ryan and me a couple hours before, the same one that Carlos had taken of us. I had to be a little conceited because it was a really cute picture. Nicole Jonasson and Tristan King 'liked' the picture. Zoey Quinn had commented on it, "*I hope you catch the bouquet. LMAO!*" I couldn't help but laugh my ass off at her comment; Zoey was such an idiot. Of course, I knew she was keeping up her charade for the sake of making Tristan jealous, and I loved it.

Exiting out of the app, I pulled up my messages to see that I had a new one from Zoey and two from Tristan. I opened up Zoey's message first.

I L-O-V-E YOUR DRESS! HOPE YOU LOL-ED MY FB MSG BC I LMAO

In Zoey language, that would mean *I love your dress! Hope you laughed out loud at my Facebook message because I laughed my ass off.*

I texted her back a quick message:

Of course I did. I love you!

Opening up Tristan's texts, I got to the first one that was sent right after my last message to him.

I'll call you. I got fired off two scenes today.

I fucking miss you.

My heart clenched while I read his messages. I

could only imagine how hard his day has been and how it led him to tell me in those words that he missed me. I debated for a moment whether or not to sneak out and give him a call to check up on him, but right then, fingers appeared dancing across my shoulders and arms. Ryan stood next to my chair with an extended hand. "Come dance with me."

I smiled up at him before taking his hand and letting him lead me to the dance floor. His hands immediately went to my waist while I wrapped my arms around his neck. He pulled me in a lot closer than I'd expected.

"Are you having fun?" Ryan asked, looking down at me.

"Yes, thank you for inviting me."

He smiled. "I don't understand why you're still single, Kat."

I shrugged a lonely shoulder at him as I batted my eyelashes, smirking. "Me neither, Ry."

"Is that guy you hang out with gay?" he asked with a laugh, spinning me around abruptly.

"No, he's not gay. We're just friends."

Ryan snickered, pulling me in even closer to him so that we were practically pressing our chests together. "I don't see how any man besides Josh can just be friends with you, beautiful."

"Shut your mouth." I giggled in response. "You sound like my dad."

"I'm dead serious. Your dad knows what he's talking about. Why aren't you together?"

I debated for a moment whether or not to tell Ryan about Tristan's Robby Lingus half, but I didn't. I knew Tristan, not Robby. "I think he's been with a lot of girls," I tried to explain.

His eyebrows went up in understanding. "Most guys nowadays have been, Kat."

I knew what he was saying was the truth. I knew it was also the same reason I had immediately decided that I wasn't against being with Tristan in the future if there was no Robby. I remembered that one of my exes had admitted to me that he'd slept with at least eighty women before me. Did it make me upset? A little. I mean, it was gross to think that he'd willingly been with so many other females before me, and it was also the reason why I always forced him to wrap his peen up. I appreciated his honesty, and for that year we were together, he'd been a nice and attentive boyfriend. Ultimately, we both just wanted different things and split up. Last I heard, he'd gone back to his man-whore ways.

"How many girls have you been with?" I jokingly asked.

Ryan opened and closed his lips in quick succession, frowning for a moment before grinning. "A lot?"

"No," I teased.

He chuckled deep in his throat, leaning forward to plant a kiss on my cheek. "I don't want to tell you. It's a lot."

"Just tell me," I insisted. The curiosity killed me. It

was a well-known fact that Ryan slept around quite a bit, but something inside of me needed to know the vague details.

Ryan sighed while pressing his cheek against the top of my head. He smelled wonderful. "Maybe about... a girl a week for three years... plus more?"

Now, I didn't follow through with my plans to study aeronautical engineering because I sucked at math, but I could easily deduce that Ryan had been with close to two hundred women. Two hundred! *Shit*. I wished I knew how many Tristan had been with, but at the same time, I didn't. I was secretly scared that the number was more than my stomach could handle.

"Please don't tell Zo," he pleaded against my skin. Zoey would eat him alive for sleeping around that much, especially with the amount of shit he'd given her when he found out about her career. He was kind of a hypocrite and he knew it.

I pressed my palm against his chest to push him just a couple inches away. "I won't, I swear."

His handsome face dropped into a sad smile. "I ruined any chance I had of getting you into my bed tonight though, didn't I?" he asked smoothly, kissing my cheek again.

I snorted against him, burying my face into the lapels of his jacket. "It wasn't going to happen even if you didn't tell me."

Ryan stroked the skin on my shoulders softly. "Then you owe me some sugar at least."

Hours later, he was walking me up to my apartment, his smooth hand trailed laps across my shoulder blades. I was a little buzzed from all the wine I'd drank at the wedding, and I knew for a fact that Ryan was sober. He drank a single beer while we ate, and that had been the only thing he had apart from water. It was a little after midnight by the time he was dropping me off, telling me funny stories about things that had happened at the hospital. He was such a nice, goofy guy, just like his beloved sister.

"Want to come in?" I asked while unlocking the front door. I felt comfortable enough asking him inside because I knew he was aware of the fact that nothing would go on between us that could ruin our friendship. He had rubbed his boner against me countless times in the past, so even if we kissed, it wouldn't be any worse than that. To be honest, I really wouldn't mind those pink lips on me. I liked kissing and had missed the feeling you shared when you kissed someone right on the mouth.

He gave me a silly smile almost like he thought I was an idiot. "You know the answer to that... but I should be getting home. I have an early shift tomorrow." He stepped forward, holding my face between his hands. "Thank you for coming with me."

Ryan leaned in, searching my eyes to make sure I was not going to kick him in the balls, before he brushed those thin, light pink lips against mine. He kissed the corners of my mouth and it just felt nice. I kissed him back after the second. His hand trailed up to cup the back of my neck while the other rested on my hip. We kissed more; long, sweet kisses with our mouths closed until my phone started ringing from its spot in my purse. He pulled away, giving me a sheepish smile.

"I'm so sorry," I mumbled, digging into my clutch to silence my phone.

Ryan grinned at me, shrugging. "Don't worry about it. I really should get going."

"Okay," I managed to respond with a sigh.

He leaned into me again and pressed his lips against mine briefly one last time. "Goodnight, beautiful." Ryan smiled and headed back down to his car.

I couldn't help but smile as I went into my apartment and stripped out of my clothes to get ready for bed. Ryan was a good friend in a completely different league than any of my other friends, including Tristan, and I was lucky to have him. There weren't any expectations with him or any hope of heartbreak; he could kiss me as many times as I'd let him and we'd still be fine. I finally crawled into bed with the lingering feeling of warm lips on mine.

CHAPTER FORTY

I felt like the worst friend in the world the next morning when I unlocked my phone to see the missed call in my log.

Shit. I'd completely forgotten that my phone had rung while Ryan and I were outside. It was from Tristan just like he had promised. I glanced at the clock and noticed it was around ten already. Chances were that he was probably up and about. Pressing the screen to call him, I cleared my throat a bit while it rang. After about two rings, a throaty voice coughed on the other end.

"Hello?"

"Hey, Mag, it's Kat. I'm sorry I didn't call you back last night," I apologized.

He coughed once more and yawned long and low. "Hey," he said in a much cheerier voice than I expected. "I was worried about you."

I groaned to myself, feeling really fucking guilty that I didn't call him back. "I'm fine. Ryan had just dropped me off when you called, and then I fell asleep. You okay?"

"Oh." He was silent a moment too long before he sighed this pitiful, drawn out noise that sounded like defeat. "Yeah, I'm okay," he answered, but his voice had lost that cheery edge to it.

"What happened? Why did you get fired?" I swear I almost threw up as I asked him those questions. My heart started beating erratically in my chest at the possibilities as to what could have gotten him fired. I wanted to know, but I didn't. I didn't think I could handle him blurting out that he got fired for reasons I couldn't come up with. What could a guy get fired for in porn? Putting it in a girl's butt instead of her vag? Or maybe blowing his load too quickly? That last thought made me gag.

"One of the directors told me I wasn't fit to perform," he answered steadily.

I choked. Fit to perform? I steeled myself, ready to reassure him with words that could potentially create an awkward situation for us, but I had hopes that our friendship was solid enough to withstand my horny nature. After all, wasn't that what friends did? Picked you up when you're down and helped you kick the person's ass who got you there? "Tristan, you are probably…" I sighed at my words, debating whether or not to continue on my train of thought before giving up. "No, you are the hottest guy I've ever seen in my life. How could they tell you that you weren't fit enough to perform?"

I didn't know what I was expecting him to respond with, but it definitely wasn't the loudest over-the-phone laugh in existence.

"Kat," he gasped for air. "I couldn't get hard," he laughed even louder. "It wasn't that they thought I wasn't attractive enough, but thank you. You just made my day." He cackled obnoxiously.

"Oh," was the only thing I managed to spit out. My entire body flushed fire engine red at my stupidity. *Oh, my God.* Of course that was what he meant. I needed to kick myself in the ass after that. I wanted to ask him why he couldn't do his job, but his laughs were too distracting.

Tristan laughed for a minute longer before controlling himself. "You really think I'm the hottest guy you've ever seen?" he had the nerve to ask.

I groaned and slapped myself on the forehead with my palm. "Shut up."

"Goldie," he said in that silky voice that could seduce every woman on the planet. "Just tell me."

"Maybe," I mumbled out before thinking of a better response to get him to shut up. "Andrew Wood is a close tie. You win because you have better abs." Tristan was a lot more attractive than Andrew Wood; I knew that with every fiber of my being, but still. He didn't need to know that.

This time it was Tristan's turn to groan. "I think you're full of shit."

I couldn't help but laugh at his frustration. "That's the difference between you and me. I know you're full of shit and you just think I am."

"Uh huh," he muttered, but I could hear the amusement in his voice. "I'm coming home tonight. Want me to come pick you up after I get Yoda?"

"Sure, I guess it would be nice to see you," I teased him.

We made plans for him to come get me after he asked me twice more to please confirm whether or not I really believed he was that attractive. Jackass. I got up, showered, and spent the rest of the day hanging out with Matlock on the couch before going grocery shopping. A little after seven, I heard the lock on my door turn and froze. With my heart beating rapidly in my chest, I grabbed the dirty steak knife I had on my plate from lunch earlier and stood up, holding the handle securely in my hand and ready to do something to the intruder. I jumped over the armrest of the couch and gripped the knife tighter.

"Kat?" Tristan's voice called out from the doorway.

"Damn it, Tristan!" I screamed in frustration, grabbing at my chest as if the gesture could steady the thundering rhythm of my heart.

The beautiful auburn-brown hair of my annoyingly perfect friend appeared around the corner of the walkway. He was smiling bigger than I'd ever seen in the past before he frowned, looking from my face down my frame until his eyes landed on the hand that held the knife. "Jesus! Were you planning on stabbing me?" he asked, throwing his hands up in surrender.

I glared at him before dropping my newly acquired weapon onto a side table. "I thought you were breaking in! You almost gave me a heart attack, ass."

"Were you planning on stabbing me, Goldie?" Those warm, green apple eyes twinkled in amusement.

"What do you think? That I was going to kiss my potential attacker to death?" I snickered, trying to calm my breath so my heart could quit racing.

Tristan gave me that crooked smile that made my insides heat up so much I worried they'd melt. "If you were going to kiss me to death, I'd be okay with it."

My stomach bottomed out.

I opened my mouth, but didn't close it.

Did he...?

Did he just say…?

For all I knew, gravity could have ceased to exist and my body could have been floating around the atmosphere.

His nose and high cheekbones flushed the cutest shade of pink I'd ever seen. His eyes darted from me to the wall behind me in quick succession before he sighed and raised a hand to tug at his hair. "Kat." He took a step forward until he was so close I could fully appreciate how much bigger he was than me— a head taller, his shoulders and chest dwarfed my not-so-slender frame.

The mood change easily from our light bantering to something heavy on my skin. I was trembling before his hands touched my face, his palms cupped my jaw, long fingers brushing my hairline. I closed my eyes instinctively, soaking up the sharp jolts of static that seemed to radiate from his hands. "Mag," I said breathlessly.

"I missed you so much," he whispered sweetly against my temple.

His lips brushed lightly across my forehead. I shivered through each vertebrae in my spine. How was it like this with him? How? As nice as Ryan's lips were on mine the night before, I'd take five minutes of this instead of a million of Ryan's kisses. "I missed you, too," I said, eyeing his thick Adam's apple.

He tilted my face up and leaned down toward me at the same time his mouth exhaled warm, peppermint scented breath over my lips. Tristan stayed there for what seemed like a lifetime, just inhaling and exhaling inches from my face. He slid his hands from my cheeks down the column of my neck until they rested on my shoulders. "We should go before Yoda pees in my car," he murmured hoarsely.

A couple of moments passed before I stepped away to grab my purse and shoes in silence. He stood by the walkway to the door with his muscular arms crossed over his broad chest as his jaw clenched again. With my purse under my arm, I slapped his stomach with the back of my hand on the way out. "Let's go."

Tristan locked the door using his key and trailed a few feet behind as we jogged down the stairs and headed to his Audi. Yoda's big, square head stared at us from the front passenger seat with his long tongue dangling out of his mouth. "Yoda!" Tristan hollered at him, swiping at the air like he meant to gesture for the big angel to get back into the backseat. The massive and stubborn puppy stayed where he was until I opened the door and kissed the side of his muzzle twice.

"My boy," I said against his musty coat, giving him a hug that looked more like a headlock.

"Get in the back, Yoda," Tristan instructed him, eyeing the backseat for pee stains. He reversed out of the parking lot as we headed to his house. With only the soft rock radio station playing in the background, we sat together quietly until he cleared his throat. "I just have one more convention I have to go to in three weeks, and after that..."

My skin itched in anticipation. "After that what?"

He glanced at me out of the corner of his eye. "I'm retiring Robby."

I choked on my spit at his declaration.

Retiring Robby?

Tristan glanced at me out of the corner of his eye

while tapping his fingers almost violently against the steering wheel. *Wait...*

I narrowed my eyes in the direction of the one hand clearly in my eyesight. The skin on his knuckles was a flaming red, chafed and split against the smooth pale tone of the rest of his skin. I leaned over the console and hovered my fingertips over the raw flesh. "What the hell happened to your hand?" I asked in a shrill voice.

The green eye in my vision went wide at my question. "Well... you see..." he stuttered.

"Did you get into a fight with a brick wall and lose?" I used the tip of my index finger to brush across the healthy skin of his digits. When he didn't say anything, I sucked in a breath. "What happened?"

"I didn't hit anyone," he answered vaguely, prying his right hand off the steering wheel to rest his palm on my thigh.

A million thoughts rolled through my head as to what could have happened to him, but I didn't want to pry. I knew he would eventually tell me, but whatever it was had to be something embarrassing since he refused to tell me right then. This was the man who told me with a straight face about the time he sharted in his pants. I shoved the thoughts aside and eyed the marred skin on his hand. "Seriously, what happened?"

He coughed and scratched at his face with his short fingernails, apprehension evident on his face. "I punched a wall. Just a regular wall, not a brick one, smartass."

I raised an eyebrow, more to myself than to him. "Why?"

"I was pissed off," he said simply.

I wanted to ask him what he was pissed off about, but I didn't. Instead, I brought his hand up closer to my face to inspect the slender, perfectly boned appendage. "Does it hurt?"

"A little," he said with a wince when I barely grazed his knuckles.

"It looks terrible," I muttered, acknowledging the bruising that circled the wounds. "I'm going to put something on it when we get to your house."

He scoffed, keeping his eyes locked on the road ahead. "Not necessary."

I shrugged a single shoulder before squeezing each one of his fingers with mine. "It's too bad I don't care what you want."

Tristan fisted his hand and closed it around my four longest fingers. He smiled cheekily as his eyes flickered from me to the road. "Did you hear what I said? About quitting?" he asked, in a slightly lower voice than normal.

It didn't seem weird to me at that point that he was bringing up quitting again so quickly. It was easy to forget that this man with a great personality kept to himself so much. "I'm not deaf, Mag. Of course I heard that you're retiring," I managed to spit out, trying to think of exactly how I felt about it. I mean, it was pretty fucking awesome, as long as he didn't start whoring it up— unless he was whoring it up with me. The problem was that I wasn't even sure if he felt anything for me besides friendship. "Why are you quitting? I mean, why all of a sudden?"

We were at a red light by that time, and he turned his head to look at me. His smile was gentle as he answered. "I think it's time."

Time for what? I held up my hand for him to high-five me. "Well, I'm happy if you're happy," I tried to say as evenly as possible because a big part of me was scared of change that could possibly take over my friendship with Magellan. He didn't have a girlfriend because of the porn, so once he wasn't doing it anymore, what would happen? My poor heart couldn't handle being the type of friends we were now and knowing he was getting dirty with random girls for fun. At least with the porn, I knew it was technically a job. A job with a nameless face, no emotion, and no tie.

Eh.

If I hadn't had Zoey in my life for so long, I'd probably feel differently about porn in general. It would be harder to see people in the industry as just *people*. My Zoey, Zoey Quinn, was the goofiest, kindest, and most quirky person I'd ever met, and she was so much more than Zoey Star. What she did when she went to Los Angeles was such a small part of who she was. I knew she couldn't care less about the people she had put her tongue or fingers into. I'm sure she couldn't remember a quarter of the girls' names she'd met along the way. It was for that reason, that knowledge, that my heart and mind could accept Tristan for Tristan King and not just Robby. It also probably helped that I refused to look up his movies, because I'd probably end up crying with a tub of ice cream in my lap. Or, worse, my hummingbird in my hand while I cried my eyes out.

"I think it'll be good for me," he said in a soft voice, peering at me through those thick, dark eyelashes. "We'll have more time to spend together..." he trailed off, squeezing my hand.

My heart fluttered in my chest at his suggestion, but the small — and I mean a very small — logical part of my brain told me not to overthink his words. Things could change in an instant; I knew that from experience. I used to see Robby as a gigantic pain in my ass for making Tristan stay away from relationships, but now I worried that those reins that held him back were actually a blessing in disguise. Fuck! A blessing in disguise? Did I seriously want to just be someone's last choice? Did I want to be his best friend for the rest of my life? Or have him hang out with me only because I was the only idiot who accepted him for who he was?

"That's cool," I tried to tell him, but my voice cracked at the end. "I hope you know that if you would rather hang out with other people, I'm okay with it." My heart broke a little at my words, but I knew I was doing the right thing. If I needed to distance myself so he could keep going with his life, then I'd do it. I didn't want to be anyone's burden or friend out of pity.

Tristan pulled his hand away to tug at the ends of his hair with aggravation radiating from the pores of his skin. He didn't say anything as he kept driving closer and closer to his house. He pulled his car into the garage and quickly jumped out before opening the backdoor to let Yoda out. As soon as I was out of the car, he was already waiting for me and leaning a slim hip against his car. His hand was still gripping at his hair. "Kat... why would you think I'd want to hang out with other people?"

My throat felt constricted all of a sudden, and I looked down at the concrete floor between us. "You could make more friends now that you wouldn't have to lie about Robby," I managed to say.

"Kat," he choked my name out in a gruff purr. "Do you think I've spent all this time with you because I didn't have any other friends? I didn't want anyone in my life because of Robby, because it was complicated, but obviously with you it's different." He sighed and brought up his hand to trace the seam of my shirt. "You're the only person I want to spend time with and nothing will change that, okay?"

I nodded silently, trying to take in his kind words, which only confused me more. What did he really want?

"You matter to me," he said softly, dropping his hand to his side.

CHAPTER FORTY-ONE

"He's quitting?" Zoey asked slowly, her perceptive eyes narrowed in my direction.

I nodded and shrugged, spearing a broccoli stalk with my fork before slipping it into my mouth. The best way to handle a Zoey Inquisition, as I called it, was to be as nonchalant as possible. She was like a shark, except that instead of sensing blood a mile away, she sensed excitement, and then honed in for an attack. "He told me he was retiring Robby."

A thin eyebrow went up, and I knew I was about to be in deep shit with that move. "Did he say anything else after that?"

I ate a few more pieces of broccoli, so I could give myself more time to think about what I wanted to tell her. We had gone to a Tuesday morning hot yoga class and now continued with our routine, which consisted of stuffing our faces. I normally told Zoey everything, but a small part of me was worried about what she would say. She threw herself into whatever she was feeling before she completely thought about the effects. Her method was the direct opposite of mine, considering I had to think and rethink everything. "I told him that if he wanted to hang out with other people, I understood, and he just said he only wants to hang out with me," I repeated as best as I could. "Then, he said I mattered to him."

I swear Zoey's face went red. If this had been a cartoon, there would have been steam coming out of her ears. She squealed and then started wiggling around in her seat. "Oh, my God! Oh, my God!"

My face flushed at her loud squawking. "What?"

"He wants to be with you!" She slapped a hand over her mouth and screamed into it. "Kat! He's quitting for you!"

"That's not the reason," I said with a roll of my eyes. *Don't take her words to heart. Don't take her words to heart,* I repeated to myself.

She slapped her small hands across the table like a maniac, her eyes looking a little rabid. "Um, yes it is!" she tried to argue.

I sighed. *There is no way.* No way.

Right?

"Booger, that guy thinks you hung the moon. I know you don't see it, but I do," she huffed, sliding her plate away from her. "He's totally quitting to be with you, which is the sweetest thing I've ever heard. Seriously. The sweetest thing, and you know I watch a lot of TV."

I groaned and shook my head before shifting my gaze from my friend to the plate below me. I had so many doubts in respects to Tristan that I'd bottled up since he told me about quitting. I thought about his words and behavior recently and they reassured me immensely. He had never lied to me. There was no reason to doubt that he wanted to spend time with me and that nothing would change, but the reasoning behind his decision was what I questioned.

I didn't want to even consider having any hopes that he could have me in mind for anything besides friendship, because I didn't want to get hurt. Who would though? It wasn't that I didn't find myself worthy of his attention, but I also stopped believing in the Tooth Fairy at the age of eight, when I caught my mom sneaking dollar bills under my pillow. I liked to consider myself more of a realist than a dreamer, and Tristan having feelings for me was definitely much more of a dream than a high probability in the real world.

Bright blue fingertips danced across the tabletop, getting closer and closer to me. I chanced a glance at Zoey, who was now sitting on top of her folded legs so she could reach across. Her expression was open and earnest. "Are you worried because he's been with so many people?" she asked softly. I knew this was a sensitive subject for her to consider because of her own past experiences, so I had to tread lightly with my words.

"I don't know, Zo. Maybe? A little? We don't talk about the porn stuff. He rarely brings it up, and you know I'm not going to either. I don't know how many people he's been with, but I don't think I want to know either," I sighed and thought about my words again. "Well, I want to know, but at the same time, I don't."

Zoey nodded, tenting her hands underneath her chin. "I got'cha," she narrowed her eyes a little again. "So, you aren't being stubborn about this because of the other people. What is it then?"

"What if... what if he isn't being, I don't know, genuine? He hasn't even really made it seem like he likes me, anyway, Zo."

"Oh, Mylanta," she moaned way too loudly, causing the people in the table right across from us to turn around and look. "He likes you! Don't be so silly. Who wouldn't like you? I think you need to be the one to take the next step. I was just talking to Ryan yesterday, and he was blabbering about how all of his friends liked you. Even he doesn't understand why you aren't with Tristan."

I wished I were still in elementary school so it would be easy to send him a note asking him if he liked me and to check the box for yes or no.

"What if he doesn't?"

She rolled her eyes. "That isn't going to happen, but if he doesn't, then at least you know to move on, hello." Her eyes went wide in response to something behind me.

"Katherine?" I heard the gravelly voice ask before I saw the figure to my left. Sea-foam colored eyes looked down at me from above a shy smile.

I couldn't help the smile that spread across my face when I finally recognized the strange man. "Hey, Kieran," I said. "This is my best friend, Zoey." I pointed at the way too intrigued female across from me.

Kieran held his hand out in Zoey's direction before exchanging a "Nice to meet you." I, in the meantime, took the opportunity to size up my new acquaintance in a better light than the one at the aquarium. He was just as hot as before, maybe a little more now that I could fully appreciate the fullness of his arms and clear, porcelain skin tone.

He turned his attention back to me with a blush. "I was just grabbing a bite to eat with my friend, and I wanted to come over and say hi," he said.

I smiled at him in response before I felt a swift kick to my shin underneath the table. Zoey winked at me from her side of the table while looking between Kieran and me, mouthing something. "I'm glad you did," I managed to say slowly, while trying to read Zoey's lips.

'Who is he?' she mouthed.

"What a coincidence," he said with a long exhale afterward. He started pulling at some imaginary lint on his shirt. "I was kind of wondering if you'd like to go out to dinner with me?" His face flamed red across his nose.

Another kick a little harder that time landed right on my shin. By some miracle, I managed to swallow the groan that under normal circumstances would have been considered a borderline yell, and instead, diverted my eyes over to give Zoey a forced, saccharine smile. She sat there with a big grin on her face and mouthed, 'Say yes.'

Kieran stood there during our little exchange, tugging on his belt loops as he smiled sweetly. "Or we can do something else if you want," he offered.

He really was too handsome and polite for his own good. If he would've appeared in my life two months before, I would have e-mailed him the hour I got home from the aquarium, but all I could think about was Tristan. But suddenly, his porn-escapades filtered through my brain in a slush. I truly doubted that Tristan had thought about me at all when he was off in Los Angeles, doing what he was doing.

"I'd love to," my mouth responded before my brain had completely comprehended my actions. "I'm free tonight."

CHAPTER FORTY-TWO

It was bad enough that I was nervous to begin with.

The text I got on my way to the movies to meet up with Kieran only served to make my hands sweat more than they had been before. I didn't think it was possible for them to be clammier, but obviously I was wrong.

Are you done with Zoey?

'Magellan' texted me. My stomach rolled in nerves.

He had texted me in the afternoon, asking if I wanted to come over when he was done with work, but Zoey had roped me off to go look at the bridesmaid dresses that Nikki and I had picked out two weekends before. I may have failed to mention that I had a date. I may also have been feeling like shit because a part of me felt like I was cheating on Tristan, which was truly an impossible circumstance.

We aren't dating, was the mantra I kept on repeat in my head. It was the truth; we weren't anything more than friends despite his recent flirting. I was my own woman, I reminded myself.

Which was why it was wrong for my freaking traitorous hands to shake like I was a crack addict. I bit my lip before glancing up at the red light and sighed.

I'm going to the movies and then home :]

I was already driving again when his response came in, so I waited until I was pulling into the movie theater parking lot to read his message. Kieran had offered to pick me up, but I wasn't dumb enough to let him. After all, I didn't really know the guy, and the last thing I needed was some sort of stalker situation in case he turned out to be boring or self-centered. I doubted it. I also doubted I'd mind a hot as fuck stalker, but you could never really know.

Cool. What movie are you and Miss Star watching? =D

My stomach rolled again as I typed the response. I wasn't going to lie to him, and really, I had no reason to hide what I was doing. I was my own woman, damn it.

I'm watching that new comedy with Kieran the aquarium guy.

I waited two minutes for his response before getting impatient and putting my phone on silent. I got out of the car and walked to the entrance of the theater where Kieran's tall, inky-headed form was clearly visible over the scattered people waiting around the box office. He grinned the moment he caught sight of me and walked in my direction. Wearing an emerald green polo, his skin looked even paler than before at the restaurant. His soft, "Katherine," tore me away from my thoughts about his skin color.

In two long strides, he stood in front of me, grinning down. I couldn't help but return his smile while also trying to ignore the fact that his green shirt reminded me of Tristan's eyes. "Hi, Kieran," I said back.

"I bought the tickets already, ready to go in?" he asked, tilting his head in the direction of the doors. I nodded, smiled, and followed after him. He was nice and walked slower so I could keep up before opening the door for me and grazing my shoulder blade with his hand after passing the tickets to the theater employee. He treated me to popcorn, which we decided to share, and individual drinks, because I wasn't about to share a drink with someone I barely knew. I wasn't ruling out swapping saliva via mouth on mouth, but I'd worry about that after the movie.

"Thanks for inviting me," I told him right after we sat down in our seats. We still had about ten minutes before the movie started, I estimated.

Kieran blushed. "I'm glad you came. I wasn't sure if you were interested," he practically whispered.

He was too cute. I almost wanted to wrap him up and put him in my pocket. "I'm sorry I didn't e-mail you or anything, I just had a busy weekend."

"You don't have to explain anything," he replied. "I'd rather you tell me about yourself before the movie starts."

I told him the little things, the unimportant things like what college I went to, what town I grew up in, my lack of siblings, and my affinity for popcorn in five minutes. He managed to squeeze in and tell me that he had three younger sisters, what colleges he went to, and that he too loved popcorn. The previews started mid-sentence, and we both just turned to face forward and watch.

Kieran didn't make a move throughout the entire movie besides patting my arm when I came back from the restroom. Needless to say, I was a little disappointed that he didn't make an effort to at least try to put his arm around my shoulder or something. Even my middle-school boyfriend did the whole yawn, raise an arm, and flop it across my shoulders in the least slick way possible. I smirked obnoxiously every five minutes because I thought the movie was pretty hilarious, and a lot of things reminded me of Tristan. I noticed that Kieran just kind of chuckled quietly when I had tears in my eyes.

"That was the funniest movie I've seen this year," I snorted on our walk out.

He smiled sweetly and nodded. "I thought it was pretty funny, too."

It didn't escape me that he didn't agree with me completely, and not that he should have to, I mean, life is all about difference in opinion, so I just grinned back at him.

"I'll walk you to your car," he said.

"I'm parked over here," I said, pointing in the direction of my car when we made it to the parking lot. "Do you have to work tomorrow?" I asked him, trying to make conversation.

"I do. When do you go back to school?"

I was parked pretty close to the front of the lot, and by the time I opened up my mouth to respond, we were already within ten feet of my car. "I have to go back in two weeks, and then school starts again two weeks after that."

We stood by the driver's seat while I shifted from foot to foot as he tugged on the belt loops of his jeans some more. "I guess this is goodnight then," he said with a shy smile.

He took a step forward at the same time I did, each putting up our arms in opposite directions for a hug. Then I switched my arm positions at the same time he did, so we mirrored each other again. I giggled a little at the awkwardness before we finally met in the middle for a hug. He was warm and hard against me, just the way I liked. "Thanks again," I said against his shirt.

"I had a good time." Kieran pulled back a fraction of an inch before leaning down to plant a kiss on the side of my cheek. "I'll call you," he said.

"Okay. Goodnight," I responded before unlocking my door and slipping into the seat. By the time I had my seatbelt and the car on, he was already walking in another direction.

To say I was a little confused about our date would be an understatement. I figured Kieran was a little shy and that might be the reason why he wasn't more forward, not that it was a bad thing at all, but it wasn't what I was expecting. With the exception of Ryan, every other guy I'd been out with had been pretty passive. I wasn't exactly sure how Kieran felt about our date, but I sure as hell wasn't about to stress about it. I pulled over at Taco Bell on the way home for dinner to-go before I pulled into the same spot I always parked in at my apartment complex. Jogging up the stairs, I caught sight of a long figure wearing a black hoodie sitting against my door.

I froze, clenching the plastic bag in one hand and my purse in the other. I was debating whether or not to grab my pepper spray from my purse when the figure shifted and turned to look in my direction. I recognized Tristan's face beneath the black hood as he hopped up onto his feet a lot more gracefully than a man of his size should be capable of.

"Are you okay?" I asked, taking the remaining steps toward my door.

He didn't say anything as I approached, keeping his steady green gaze on me. I stopped in front of him and looked up to try and read his facial expressions, which I'd like to think I had gotten pretty good at. He exhaled a long breath, continuing his intense glare. My heart thumped wildly against my chest in an off-tempo beat that was impossible to follow. The muscles in his face looked flexed and his jaw more defined.

"What?"

Tristan's hands reached for the bags in my hands to set them on the floor. Unwinding himself back up to his full height, he pulled the hood of his sweatshirt down before sighing deeply. I'd like to think that if I would have been warned beforehand of what his following words were going to be, I would have made sure not to have a bag of *chalupas* between us. His words floated through the air, severing any and every thought from my brain. "I can't stand this anymore. You're all I think about."

CHAPTER FORTY-THREE

I died a hundred times right then.

There would be an obituary in the paper that would say: Katherine Alba Berger, dead at the tender age of twenty-five from the result of a massive heart attack.

Obviously, I didn't die, but my heart did stop beating for all of three seconds. I didn't move. My body, my mouth, and my blood cells ceased to function. I didn't even think any wind blew in those long moments that changed my life forever. At least, it seemed like it was one of those moments that I'd remember the rest of my life. I had a few of those: the day I found out my mom died, when I realized I was never going to be an astronaut, and the day I graduated from college. My mind etched into the fiber of my tissues the longing and pained expression on Tristan's beautiful face after he spoke those words.

His eyes darkened at the same time his brows furrowed. "I don't know what to do." Those emerald orbs searched the surface of my features for something, as I stood there mute. He brought up his left hand to press the back of it against my face. "I miss you all the fucking time," he admitted softly.

I sucked in a breath and let my brain run away with ideas and emotions. Little pieces of reality seemed to settle into the aftermath that his words left. The fragments cemented together, piecing a puzzle that had done nothing but confuse me for long weeks. The reality of Zoey's words just earlier in the day seemed like such a possibility all of a sudden.

My hands went up, aiming for the back of his neck. There they met with soft, thick hair. I used my palms to pull his head down to me without allowing myself to think. Down, down... I pressed my lips against his, my cold ones onto his warmer ones. An electric shock zipped up the length of my spine in response. I kissed his full, upper lip with a peck next. Without a second thought, I kissed that pouty bottom lip with both of mine and pulled away to enjoy the current running through my spine at our touch.

Tristan stood there with his lips slightly parted, his face pale. "Kat," he said breathlessly after a second.

My pulse raced in my veins as I took in the look

on his face, which resembled more of a mask than anything else. He didn't move an inch for a few moments, making me start to doubt the interpretation I'd taken from his words. Of course, he could have been thinking of me all the time, but maybe because he felt guilty? Or, maybe he missed me because we were such good friends? Oh, my God, I was such an asshole. "Tristan, I'm so sorry," I started to say, taking a step backward.

Before I could take another step, he smashed his lips against mine. Smooth, warm, full flesh pressed against me so abruptly I couldn't think straight. I couldn't get passed the idea that Tristan, my Magellan, was using the perfect lips I'd been eyeing for weeks against mine.

He pulled back just an inch with his peppermint breath heavy on my skin as his head shifted so that his lips brushed my ear in the most erotic action of my life. "You need to open that sweet mouth for me."

He'd barely completed his sentence before my lips fell apart, and then Tristan was there. His velvet tongue dipped into me, caressing my own so sensually I could have come in my pants if I were a guy. One mouth slanted against the other, and there was no way I could have known whose did what. I only knew that his tongue stroked mine deeply, and for the lack of a better explanation, it could only be described as fucking awesome. Tristan's hands gripped my waist tightly, fingers digging into the meaty flesh over my hips. I could feel the pressure on my lower back as he pulled me to him.

It was when he started sucking my bottom lip between his that I reached up to grab two handfuls of hair, thinking to myself that his taste was as addictive as caffeine. I moaned against the heat of his mouth when he crushed my breasts against his chest so tightly it kind of hurt. "Kat," he groaned after he stroked his tongue across the corner of my mouth.

"Dang, Kat! Get! That!" a squeaky voice whooped from down the hall.

If Tristan's lips, tongue, and even his saliva weren't practically miraculous, I may have given a shit at being caught by my neighbor. I didn't even bother to step away from him; instead, I just turned my head to look at Christy, my thirty-something neighbor who claimed to have slept with half of the professional athletes in the city. "I would have, if you wouldn't have killed the moment," I laughed, feeling the fingers on my hips loosen their grip.

Christy laughed loudly before unlocking the door to her apartment with a wink. "You get some of that for the both of us, girl!" Fortunately, her dark mop of hair disappeared into the apartment a second later.

I looked up at Tristan, who remained so close our chests pressed together. His cheeks were pulled back into a lazy smirk, but it was his eyes that showed blazing, pure intensity beneath the green. "That wasn't exactly the way I envisioned things happening," he said in a husky voice that managed to affect my uterus.

I blushed and tried to will my brain to think of what to do next since standing in the hallway making out didn't seem like the best idea. "Come inside," I told him, pulling away from his hands to reach for my purse and bag of food.

He grabbed my bags before I did and nodded, smiling and silent. The door was unlocked faster than ever — even the times when I was at the brink of peeing my pants — and we were in my home and on the couch a moment later, sitting next to each other. I was nervous and my lips felt a little chafed from brushing against the scruff of his facial hair. Tristan shifted a few inches over so his muscular thigh pressed against the side of mine, his eyes focused on my face. Rummaging through the bag, I handed him one of the two *chalupas* waiting to be devoured while I opened mine up. "So, Mag, about that out there..."

A breath of air was sucked in harshly. "Please tell me you don't regret it," he whispered at the end of his inhale.

Was he freaking serious? It would have been easy to play it cool and try to make it seem like our game of tonsil hockey a second ago was perfectly normal, but it wasn't. It definitely wasn't normal, and after my up-close and personal encounter with that mouth, it would be pointless and too hard to pretend like there wasn't something there. Something massive, electric, and heavy. This was exactly what Zoey had been trying to tell me to do: make my move.

I leaned into his warm frame and looked up at him from under my eyelashes. "I don't regret it."

Tristan sucked in a ragged breath, shifting his body so that his back nestled into the corner of the couch. His glowing green gaze was steady and wide on me, making my heart rate speed up tenfold. "Would you regret it if I kissed you again?"

I should have told him that we needed to talk about what had just happened, that I deserved to know when he started feeling something for me, when he started missing me the way that he had, but I didn't though. Those perfect lips that millions of women paid to try and replicate were just inches away from my face. I'd tasted those lips, that mouth, that tongue, and I hoped to God I'd be lucid enough to remember to talk to him about everything later. Right then was not the time, and he must have sensed my decision because we both leaned into each other like two impossible magnets meeting out of necessity in the middle.

His lips were on mine. Hot, velvet, and sweet lapped at me with more passion than I could ever comprehend. Tristan sucked my tongue into his mouth, and I moaned in a way that would make Zoey blush. My skin was covered in a feverish rush of blood and the sugary, clean scent that was Tristan. His hands were on my hips, and my hands were trying to rip *chalupas* off our laps because all I wanted right then was to sit on his face. But I'd settle for his lap.

"Fuck," I groaned into the air when he peeled his mouth off me to trail wet kisses across my jawline then neck. "Oh, my...." I stuttered out when his tongue moved to lap against my throat before his lips sucked gently on the sensitive skin there. *Fucking shit. Fucking shit. Fucking shit.* I didn't know what the hell I was doing with my hands at my sides, maybe just opening and closing my fists with each kiss because I was so caught up in him.

Tristan's hands gripped my hips tightly as he pulled me toward him. I wanted to look at the muscles bunching in his forearms, but it was hard enough to remember to breathe when his mouth latched onto various pulse points on my throat. "So good," he mumbled against my skin, so low that I could barely hear him through the rush of blood in my ears.

"Holy..." I whimpered some other unintelligible words as he switched to kiss the other side of my neck. His big hands tugged at my waist again, trying to get me over and closer to his lap. I let him roll me so I shifted onto my knees, leaning over him slightly.

One of his hands brushed over my lower back while the other one kept its steady grip on my waist. He groaned words onto my skin, words I couldn't understand and only partially wanted to. He could have been reciting the alphabet backward for all I knew, or calling me a whore in ten different languages, but when his mouth kept up a trail of open-mouthed kisses across the span of my throat, I heard him groan out my name.

My hands had a mind of their own finally and placed themselves on his broad chest for support as he pecked slow kisses on the corners of my mouth like I had done to him just moments before. Warm breath clouded over my flesh as he pulled away, his fingers kneading my hips.

"Jesus," I whimpered when he left wet kisses across my cheeks.

I could hear him chuckle softly, "I know," in the huskiest voice I'd ever heard in my life.

After a moment of trying to catch my breath, I pulled back just a little to look at his face. His eyes were already locked on mine with such intensity that it felt like he knew the answer to every question in the world. Those long fingered hands slid their way up from my hips, over my ribcage, shoulders, neck, and then face, cupping me gently. That crooked grin spread across his lower face, creating a burst of light that erupted from him. "You are so pretty," he murmured, brushing his thumbs over the apple of each of my cheeks.

I didn't want to say 'thank you' because that seemed too forward, so I smiled at him instead while trying to express through my face how much I enjoyed the mouth-fuck we'd just shared. He beamed at me in return and exhaled loudly all over my face. It didn't escape me that I should have been happy as hell that neither one of us had eaten the Taco Bell beforehand for fear of having terrible breath, but seriously. I totally would have done it again even if he suffered from halitosis, the god-awful breath disease.

Long moments passed between me sitting on my knees while he sat straight up, hunched in my direction before we both relaxed against the back of the sofa, keeping our eyes on each other in silence. I had no idea what I wanted to talk to him about since the only thing I could think of was the fact that I had goose bumps all over me. My stomach was in knots — with my luck a Gordian Knot — trying to accept and come to terms with the last few minutes. It almost didn't feel real. Someone somewhere decided a long time ago that Kat Berger didn't have luck like that, and I'd come to terms with it. The thing was, that this — Tristan and I — felt so real, there was no way it wasn't. The shock that coursed through my veins every time he touched me with his hands or mouth wasn't natural.

"I'm sorry I didn't tell you before," his rough voice murmured over the silence of the apartment. He had his head resting on the back of the couch while keeping his eyes on me, fingertips grazing mine. "I didn't know how to."

"I wish you would have." I smiled at him. "I thought you liked me like a sister."

Tristan snorted just like he had so many times before while solely in my presence. "Not a sister," he said with a laugh. "Definitely not a sister."

I wanted him, I knew that without a doubt in my head, but I didn't want to be just another notch on the bedpost. He thought I was special before today, and I wanted to keep it that way. The only-child gene in me screamed that I wanted to mean something, and I was okay with that. He was going to have to at least try to woo me a bit before the chastity belt came off, especially after all the shit he'd put my poor heart through. Bastard.

There were so many questions I wanted to ask him. I wanted to ask what this meant, because it couldn't be insignificant. I wanted to ask him what he expected after this. How exactly he felt for me. If he quit for me. Why he wasn't buried in me. I wanted to look down and see if he had the boner equivalent of my wet panties. I didn't ask or do any of those things because he scooted over on the couch and slid an arm over my shoulders, pulling me in tightly against his side. Minutes turned into a half hour, and then an hour while we sat there silently. His arm didn't loosen from around me, and I just wiggled deeper into his embrace. Before, it was never like that, occasionally he would put an arm around me randomly or something, but this was so different. It would have been like comparing a full moon to a crescent moon.

We'd figure that out somehow, but not today. I wanted to enjoy the moment. I also wanted to make him squirm just a little.

His mouth was tender against my temple. It

made me forget all of the questions I had and leave them for another day when the moment was less bubbly and warm and when I could feel like I hadn't just won the lottery. "Can I tell you something?"

I laughed against the thick material of his hoodie. How many times had I asked him the same exact thing? "You already know the answer."

He brushed his nose across my earlobe. "I punched the wall because I was pissed off you went out with another guy."

"Oh," was the only thing I could spit out coherently before prying the arm that wasn't around me off the armrest to inspect the tender flesh that he ruined. It was still a bit swollen and scabbed over; honestly, it seemed like a miracle that it wasn't broken. That didn't stop the smile I was sporting, though. "Can I tell you something?"

"Of course."

"You're an idiot for hurting yourself," I told him with a kiss to the veins right by his knuckles. I gave his skin another kiss. "But I'm so glad you're here."

CHAPTER FORTY-FOUR

The next morning, I met up with my two bitches for lunch at the deli closest to Nicole's office. The two forces of nature sat together on one side of the booth, leaving me all alone on the opposite end. I think they did it on purpose in order to interrogate me more effectively, but you could never really be too certain with those two.

"Tell us what happened," Zoey said ominously while looking down at her chicken Caesar salad.

I had to snort, because I didn't understand how she could just know something happened the night before. I hadn't been acting any differently, I thought. "Why do you think I have something to tell you?"

Nikki scoffed before swallowing a bite of turkey sandwich. "You have a stupid smile on your face."

"I really don't think my smiles are stupid." I rolled my eyes as I took a bite out of the roast beef sandwich on my plate.

Zoey and Nikki looked at each other with smirks on their faces, and then nodded in unison like mind-reading twins. "Yeah, you do."

"Tristan came over last night—" I started to tell them before Zoey's high-pitched squeal filled the deli louder than any police siren ever could.

"You slut! You did it with him!" she said way too loudly. The group of businessmen sitting in the booth behind her all turned to look at us with shit-eating grins on their faces.

My face flushed red when the men kept looking over like nosey old biddies until I waved at them, causing them to turn around. "Jesus, I didn't sleep with him, Zo. We just talked. Then made out. Talked some more. Then, we made out again." There was no way in hell I could help the dreamy tone my voice took on as I relived the three times his mouth was glued to mine. I didn't want to think about how he'd gotten so good at using his mouth because that would make me a hypocrite. I wasn't exactly a virgin myself and hadn't been one for some time. Plus, I did kind of kiss Ryan not too long ago. In hindsight, it amused me that there hadn't been any tongue involved then, kind of like I was saving some usage up for Tristan. *Ha.*

"You little slut," Nikki laughed, leaning into Zoey's much smaller frame. "I told you it would happen soon."

"I knew it was going to happen, spank you very

much. I knew it was meant to be when you agreed to go on that date yesterday."

"You went on a date yesterday and didn't tell me?" Nicole hissed.

"Yes, but it doesn't matter; it was with some guy I met at the aquarium." I groaned, taking another bite out of my sandwich to avoid answering any more questions about Kieran.

"He seemed nice," Zoey interjected with glittering eyes. "What did Tristan say?"

I was torn between wanting to tell them and also wanting to keep that special feeling between Tristan and me. It almost felt too personal to put into words. I didn't think they'd laugh at me or anything if I were to tell them that we just sat on the couch for a couple of hours with his arm around me while we shared a few kisses, but it seemed special.

I grinned at my closest friends and shrugged. "He just told me that he thinks of me all the time," I replied as vaguely as possible.

"I knew it," Zoey said in a singsong voice.

Nikki smiled and set down her sandwich. "Now what?"

"We didn't get that far because I didn't want to push. He likes me, I like him, and we're friends." I knew there were things we needed to talk about, but I didn't want to rush the questions I had. It wasn't a matter of life or death, or even a deciding factor on the progress of whatever it was we had together at that point.

Zoey leaned against the leather backing behind her and folded her arms across her tiny chest. "It's just a matter of time before some network makes a television show about us."

Nicole and I both snorted at her idea before raising an eyebrow at each other over the words that were about to spew out of our friend's mouth. "What kind of show would it be?" Nikki asked, taking the bait.

"It's going to be called Porn Wives, hello," she mused loudly. "Nikki is going to be the one married to the really popular porn star. Kat, you're going to be the girlfriend hoping to get engaged soon—"

"Umm, I really don't think—" I started to cut her off.

A small index finger came up to shush me before Zoey kept rolling with her idea. "I'm going to be the single girl looking for a relationship, and then we have Josh, who can be our oddball in the group because he has nothing to do with porn, but we love him anyway."

Nikki looked at me, her hazel eyes were wide with amusement as a big smirk covered her face. "Well, that's settled then. Are you going to start pitching ideas out to networks?"

"On it," she sang the response.

"Hold on, you need to wait until Kat puts out. She can't be in the show if she hasn't at least gotten Tristan's dick in her mouth," Nikki cackled.

One of the men in the table behind us started

choking loudly after Nicole's words. I cringed and wanted to die. With my luck, Zoey would scream out my entire name for the world to know that Katherine Alba Berger hadn't had sex or had a dick in her mouth.

"Oh, yeah," Zoey hissed out with a nod. "Are you gonna put it in your mouth soon?"

"Zo, is the sky blue?" Nicole snorted in a very unladylike manner.

CHAPTER FORTY-FIVE

There were very few things that were easy for me. Things like writing, peeing on myself, snorting, wasting time, and spending time with my loved ones came naturally. On the other hand, there were other things like peeling oranges, reversing, cutting in a straight line, and meeting strangers was both difficult and tedious for me.

Spending time with Tristan—even after our talk the day before changed things— and our friendship-slash-relationship-slash-whatever-the-hell-we-had was still easy as air. When he picked me up the next time I saw him, he gave me that crooked grin that could make a lesbian's panties wet and squeezed the bare skin of my knee.

We talked the same way we always did, but only now, there was no doubt that he was a lot more affectionate. He touched my hair, the expanse of skin on my shoulders, and wrapped an arm around me each chance he got. I ate it all up like a starved animal and did my best to refrain from molesting his bubble butt when he bent over to retrieve the lasagna he made from the oven.

"You were looking at my ass, weren't you?" he asked smugly with his back to me.

I guffawed a little too exaggerated to be believable. "No."

"Tell me the truth," he said, his voice laced with pure smugness.

"Why are you always fishing for compliments?" I asked, trying to steer away from inflating his steady ego.

Tristan looked at me over his shoulder with a playful smirk. "I'd like to know that you appreciate me."

"Oh, my God," I groaned, shifting in the stool that surrounded his kitchen island. "I'm pretty sure I should be the one fishing for compliments, not you, jackass."

"You already know that I think you're the prettiest thing I've ever seen."

Warmth erupted over my cheekbones and ears at his words. Yes, he had told me that I was pretty and cute a few times, but not to that extent. I knew I wasn't unattractive, but I was no Nicole either. "Tristan—"

He turned his entire body to face me, pulling off the manly floral print oven mitts that covered his hands. "I'm serious, Kat." He strode toward me, tossing the mitts onto the counter.

It should be said that Tristan in the kitchen cooking was one of the most attractive things I had ever seen in my life. A big man with lean, perfectly defined muscles that looked to have been carved from marble, towering over the stove would give a chef a heart attack. Tristan taking off oven mitts was way sexier than any man I'd ever seen at a strip club with Josh.

"You don't have to tell me things you think I want to hear," I said to him in a low voice.

Those green eyes rolled before he sighed in exasperation, stopping so close to me that our knees touched. "I won't ever tell you something because I think you want to hear it," that silky voice murmured from above me. "You're perfect." He leaned over and pressed his warm, wet lips against mine. My inner whore kicked in, and I opened my mouth to suck his top lip between mine. He moaned and wrapped an arm around my lower back to tug me forward on the stool so my butt hung on the edge. "You have the best tasting mouth," he whispered when he briefly pulled away from me only to dart his tongue back in.

We took turns exchanging loud groans as the kiss deepened and then lightened over and over again in the most amazing repetitive cycle of all time. His hands clamped onto my hips, keeping me from falling over or scooting forward, because all I really wanted right then was some good grinding action, but he was too far away. Yoda's big head pushed at my leg, bringing us both out of the tongue-induced daze we were in.

Tristan smiled at me in such a seductive way that I didn't know how I restrained myself from grabbing his hand and dragging him upstairs. He pecked me on the corner of the mouth before he patted Yoda on his big, square head and turned back to face the lasagna he had left on top of the stove. "You're going to be the death of me," he sighed loudly.

"Shut up," I said while licking my lips to soak up the moisture he left there.

I got up and took out forks and plates to set on the kitchen island where we usually ate. Filling up two glasses with ice and water, I plopped down and waited for him to finish serving two big slices of lasagna and salad. Tristan slid a plate over as he sat down. He looked at me and then down, before hooking his foot around the supporting piece of metal between the two front legs of the stool under me, pulling me closer to him.

We grinned at each other, but didn't say anything while we ate in silence. Halfway through our serving, Tristan started clearing his throat while looking down at me from under those borderline girlish and insanely long eyelashes. "I was thinking..." he trailed off.

"That's rare," I snorted, only to have him lightly flick my arm in response.

The minute he opened his mouth to respond, my

phone rang obnoxiously loud from the living room. I shot him a look before hopping off the stool and running to answer the call before the caller hung up. Fishing it out of my purse, I made a face at the screen when I read 'Kieran' displayed. I hadn't given much thought to the cute Irishman. Well, when I thought about it, I hadn't given him a single second of my mind since our date.

Pressing the button to answer the call, I glanced in the direction of the kitchen before speaking. "Hello?"

"Hey, it's Kieran," the smooth voice on the other end replied.

"Hi, Kieran, how are you?" I looked toward the open layout of the kitchen to make sure Tristan wasn't eavesdropping even though I was positive he was doing so.

"Good, thank you. I'm sorry I haven't gotten a chance to call you sooner," he said.

I grimaced to myself before sitting on the couch, feeling just the slightest bit guilty. "It's fine."

"Oh, okay," he paused for a moment, allowing me to imagine him blushing on the other end. "I was wondering if you were free anytime soon?"

While my stomach didn't drop at his question, I felt bad. He seemed like such a nice guy, and if the jackass in the kitchen hadn't have gotten his shit together, then I would probably be heading on another date with Kieran. But I wasn't. No square inch of me wanted another date with him now that

Tristan and I seemed to be somewhat on the same page. I didn't want to be a bitch, or string him along just to avoid telling him that I was seeing someone else immediately after we went out.

"Umm," I sighed, wracking my brain for ideas and coming up with nothing. "I'm sorry, Kieran. I had a great time, but I'm trying to work things out with someone I was seeing before you." I was a bitch. A great big, old bitch.

"Well," he chuckled, but I could hear the tension in his voice. "I understand."

Silence ensued for too long.

"This is so awkward. I'm sorry. It was nice meeting you. I think you're a great guy...." Jesus, I was a blabbering mess.

"It was nice meeting you too. Take care," he said.

I made another face at the phone. "You too. Bye," I squeaked out.

Kieran murmured a goodbye in response before we both hung up. I groaned and tossed my phone back into my purse, shaking my head at no one. Slapping the top of my thighs, I stood up and marched into the kitchen to find Tristan sitting on a stool with his arms crossed over his chest. I raised an eyebrow in his direction before sitting next to him. "Yes?" I questioned him.

"If I wasn't so irritated that you went on a date with that guy, I'd probably tell you that that phone call was one of the most awkward conversations I've ever heard in my life," he snickered.

I scoffed, kicking away the thought that he had done so much worse than going on a simple date, which didn't even end with a kiss. "You're nosey."

His eyes widened in amusement. "I don't think you're one to talk, Goldie."

"Oh, leave me alone," I laughed before flicking his earlobe, hoping to steer away from the previous conversation. "What were you telling me before you eavesdropped on my conversation?"

Tristan shifted forward in his seat and smiled. "Do you remember me telling you I have a convention to go to next week?" he asked.

I nodded because I did remember him mentioning that he only had one more engagement before Robby was officially retired. Hallelujah. "Yeah."

"Come with me," he said in a voice that was entirely too insecure to be normal for Tristan.

My eyebrow rose on its own as I took in his suggestion. He wanted me to go with him to a porn convention? "You want me to?" I asked slowly, just to make sure I understood correctly.

"Yes. I only have to be there for an hour to do a signing, and I'm getting my hotel room and flight paid for by my sponsor, so we'd have time to go do things," he said with a waggle of thick, dark eyebrows.

Instantly, I felt terrible. With Nicole's wedding coming up, and the expenses I knew were tied with having to pay for my bridesmaid dress, hotel, food, and travel for her wedding in Vegas, it was swallowing up the money in my savings. I tried not to let the smile on my face show my disappointment, but I'm pretty sure I failed miserably. "I can't, I'm sorry. I'd like to, but I don't have the money with Nikki and Calum's wedding next month," I explained to him honestly.

He frowned and shook his head. "I'll pay for your ticket, Kat. It'll be my treat."

I narrowed my eyes in his direction and shook my head, too. "That's too much, Mag. I can't let you do that."

"Goldie, it's not a big deal at all, I swear. You can thank my grandma later. I want you to come with me. It'll be your early birthday present," he sighed. I caught onto the fact that he mentioned my birthday, and I knew for sure I'd never told him when it was. I figured I'd ask him about it later because all I could focus on was that he was really trying to get me to tag along. "We can go to Disneyland if you want or go to that museum with the tar—"

"The La Brea Tar Pits?" I asked.

Tristan nodded at me slowly, knowing I was falling for his reasoning. I mean, *shit,* the porn had been what made us meet, and I'd have to live with the idea that there were videos of him with other females all over the internet for however long we were friends, or whatever it was that we were. Would it be so wrong of me to at least take advantage of this last trip? I knew my dad would tell me it was too soon to go on a trip with a guy who wasn't exactly my boyfriend and let him pay, but fuck it. The La Brea Tar Pits? Disneyland?

I chose to ignore the fact that I'd be forced to probably look from afar as a bunch of women threw themselves at Robby Lingus one last time.

Plus, I couldn't help but get a little excited that he was inviting me to go somewhere away with him. I think my vag screamed in excitement.

"Make it Universal Studios and I'm in."

CHAPTER FORTY-SIX

Before I knew it, it was Thursday of the following week, and I sat on Tristan's bed, watching him pack to go be Robby Lingus one last time. According to him, for the very last time. I'd been so busy finishing up my book over the course of the last week and helping Nicole choose her wedding dress, that time flew by. My mornings were spent with Zoey at the gym or in yoga class, my afternoons at the apartment writing, and my evenings and nights were a solid mixture of Tristan and my three closest friends.

My relationship, or whatever it technically was, with Tristan made me beyond happy. Friendship with him was easy and seamless to begin with and now with the addition of welcomed touches and kisses, our time together was just that much better. Our words together were the same; it was just our interactions that were different. He never asked for more than my mouth. My mouth on his mouth to be specific, and I kind of liked it a lot.

It made me feel special to know that he wasn't just trying to get into my pants. For someone who hadn't been in a real relationship in maybe six years, I had to be a little wary of his intentions with me. The last two girls he 'dated' weren't exactly girlfriends I liked to think, because you couldn't be in a real relationship with someone if they didn't know your real name, right?

I also wanted him to know in case he didn't already, that I liked him for his personality; I liked his laugh, his snort, his hands, his humor, his stupidity, his love for Yoda, and most days it seemed like the list was endless. I'd never had a boyfriend that I liked for reasons other than enjoying their personalities. One of my boyfriends had been a devout Catholic. Raised in a home with a deacon for a father, I knew from the beginning of our relationship that he was waiting to have sex until marriage. What was funny was that only three months later, he broke up with me because he thought we were getting too serious, and by that I mean he came in his pants twice while we were just making out.

Something told me that if Tristan came while we made out, I would probably like him just as much if not more.

"Am I going to need a bathing suit?" the velvet voice asked me from across the room.

I lay across his bed, belly down with my face cradled between my hands, watching him pack up for our trip the next day. Unlike the last minute mess that was getting ready before me, I had Nicole come over and help me pack the night before. According to her, I wouldn't have chosen the right thing to wear *to get my ice cream sandwich eaten*. To think that she was the most highly educated person I knew.

"Unless you're planning on going to the pool with me naked, then yes," I told him, trying to talk myself out of imagining him naked.

"No bathing suit it is then," he laughed, tossing the black board shorts onto the bed a foot away from me. He rifled through the drawers in the infamous condom dresser and pulled out a handful of T-shirts, making a strange noise deep in his throat with his back still turned to me. "Should I bring earplugs?"

"Why would you need them?"

He snorted and I should have known he was setting me up. "For your snoring, Sleeping Beauty."

"Shut up, jackass. I don't snore," I told him, throwing the board shorts he'd just tossed onto the bed on the floor.

Twinkling green eyes looked at me from over his shoulder, his mouth pulled back into a smirk. "You sound cute, it's fine. I just need to make sure your chainsaw noises won't keep me up all night," he snorted again. A few minutes of comfortable silence later, he spoke. "On a scale of one to ten, how excited are you about going to L.A.?"

"An eleven," I said, petting Yoda's thick coat. The big beast lay right next to me, belly up with his gigantic balls on exhibition. I really was beyond excited to go. I hadn't gone on vacation since Spring Break, when Josh and I went to visit his parents in New York, and it'd been years since the last time I'd gone to California. Pair that in with sharing a room with Tristan, and it was any woman's dream come true. Nikki had suggested I not bring pajamas so I'd have an excuse to sleep in my birthday suit, but yeah, no.

"Me too," he said with a smile before throwing one of the T-shirts at my face. He came over and sat on the bed right next to me. "I used to dread going, but now I'm looking forward to it."

"Why?" I asked, looking at a dark spot on Yoda's coat instead of looking up at my human friend instead. The potential answer to my question made me nervous; there was so much I wanted to know, but also didn't.

Hot fingertips stroked the shell of my ear sensually. "I'm done after this, Goldie. I can quit buying hair dye. I don't have to lie to my parents anymore..." his silky voice trailed off, and my heart clenched just the smallest bit.

I didn't know what I was expecting, what I wanted him to say. Confess his unconditional love for me? Credit me for being the sole purpose he was leaving behind the sexing up of God knows how many women a year? I should be glad, ecstatic even, that he was leaving the porn behind, regardless of the reason, but I could only blame myself and Zoey for building up my expectations. I couldn't be upset with him for being honest with me. The smile on my face was forced, but I hoped he couldn't tell.

"I'm happy that you're happy," I said a little too weakly.

Tristan sighed, exhaling so deeply the warm breath washed over my face. "I've been very happy for the last two weeks."

There was no way that those words weren't genuine and almost enough to make up for the disappointment I'd felt seconds before. "Me too."

"Why's that?" he asked, trailing a long finger over the skin under my ear.

I snorted. Tristan was too much. I swear sometimes I thought he was just as insecure as a teenage girl when it came to certain things, and I sure as hell wasn't going to fall into that. "I bought a new hummingbird," I said in my most even voice.

The mattress right next to me shifted with his weight change until I felt his heat looming over me. "I'd like to meet this hummingbird one day."

Holy Mother.

CHAPTER FORTY-SEVEN

I squirmed in my seat and couldn't help it. At. All. I was also glad that Zo didn't have leather seats. I was moving around so much I'd probably be making farting noises that she would never let me live down. It was kind of a silly worry considering she'd let two rip since I'd gotten into the car. Zoey kept looking at me out of the corner of her eye, trying to be slick.

Unfortunately for her, this was Zoey, and I knew everything about her. She was the size of a roach and made noises that rivaled those of an elephant. She was the antonym to the word inconspicuous. All day I'd been itching in my skin to leave, subconsciously going as far as to wake up a full hour earlier than normal out of excitement for the start of the trip. My bag was zipped and had been sitting by the front door for more than forty-eight hours.

Being that she was the best half-woman half-child

in the world, she was keeping Matlock for me through the weekend and driving me to the airport. Tristan had offered to come pick me up after taking Yoda to his parents' house, but after he told me where his parents lived, it just seemed like a big inconvenient circle of driving to do so.

The smile on her delicate features was deceiving, on anyone else that slanted pull of lips and cheek would seem like a sweet smile, but on this girl, I knew whatever thoughts were rolling through that head were anything but sweet.

Cue the Zoey word vomit.

"Did you bring condoms with you?" her falsetto voice floated through the air.

Jesus Christ. "No, I didn't. Thank you very much."

She nodded, facing forward while changing lanes. "That's fine. We have to get tested all the time and I think Tristan, I mean Robby, always wears a condom—"

I couldn't help the way my neck tensed at the mention of Robby and his dick's doings. Who wants to imagine that the person they have feelings for, the person who likes to snuggle on the couch and gives soft kisses, had also created a career out of having sex with women with monster tits and bleached assholes? Not me. I knew it was only because of my unconditional love for Zoey and my decent amount of self-esteem that I was even able to sit in her car on my way to a weekend of fun and porn conventions.

Zoey sighed so deeply it seemed like she had held

in each breath that she'd taken the entire morning. She turned to look at me for a split second, a soft smile and a wink on her face. "I think it's really cute you two haven't jumped the gun. I mean, I want you to get some sooner than later, but I'm glad you're taking your time, KAB."

"Thanks, Zo," I told her, reaching across the console to pinch the skin on her forearm. "I'm not doing it intentionally; he hasn't pushed, and I haven't either."

The wistful look on her face before she nodded in understanding tugged at me, as she pulled her car over to the curb at the airport drop-off section. I was out of the car and yanking out my small carry-on suitcase from her trunk before she threw her arms around me as she told me to have a good time.

I turned around to find Tristan standing at the massive sliding doors with his duffel bag at his feet, grinning like the idiot he was. He threw up a hand to wave me over, and in no time, we had checked into our flight, dropped off his duffel bag for check-in because of that damned hair dye, and fought over who got to roll my suitcase around since I refused to let him pay money to check it in. "You're such a pain in the ass," I muttered to him once he snatched the handle of my suitcase away from me, starting to drag it down the wide corridor toward our gate.

"Your short legs are kind of a pain in the ass," he snapped back with a snort.

"Three-fourths of the population has shorter legs

than you do, ass. Quit walking so fast!" I huffed, taking quick steps to catch up to him.

He turned to look at me over his wide shoulder and grinned, switching his hold on the handle from his right arm to his left. He held his now empty hand out just a few inches away from his body, but with his fingers extended wide and close to me. I stared at his digits for a few seconds while trying to decide whether or not he was holding it out for me, or not, but those green orbs flickered up to my own. All I could see was some strange emotion that rivaled nerves or maybe indecision staring back at me.

My hand slipped up from its spot on my side over to clasp onto the tips of his fingers. He grinned at me, entwining our fingers together. We walked together silently until we reached the terminal, plopping down on two seats to wait for our flight. "What do you want to do when we get there?" he asked, leaning over the armrest between us to speak directly into my ear.

His beauty was ethereal. He was perfect, with his sharp jaw, straight nose, full lips, and bulging bicep muscles tightening the material of his flannel shirt. I deserved to win an award for managing to focus in his presence. "Let's drive down Hollywood Boulevard." I suggested, trying to talk coherently while his thumb brushed small circles over the webbing of skin between my thumb and index finger.

"Whatever you want, Goldie," he said with a

smirk.

I should have quit being a pussy and told him that he was what I wanted. For that moment. Forever. Whatever. I didn't though, because I was scared. I knew we needed to talk and determine exactly what we were, because I hated the feeling of indecisiveness and freedom between us since there weren't any words that had cemented us together. For all I knew, he might have been into the idea of an open relationship, which would kill me inside, but then I remembered that he admitted having punched the wall out of jealousy, so he couldn't really be into that idea either.

What I wanted to hear were his words. I'd make sure to get that during the weekend if nothing else.

CHAPTER FORTY-EIGHT

"It looks cooler on television," I noted to Tristan, referring to Hollywood Boulevard.

He smiled at me and shrugged, pulling our rental car into a spot at the front of the hotel we were staying at. We had just spent the last two hours driving through Hollywood's shitty traffic, taking in the various buildings and attractions I'd only seen on the tube in the past, and then had dinner at a diner. He'd suggested we pull over to sightsee, but I convinced him it was okay to head straight to the hotel since it was already close to midnight and I was pooped. We got out of the car, and I helped him pull my suitcase out of the trunk.

The plane ride included the lady next to him accidentally spilling her cup of water into his lap. When the old hag leaned over to try and wipe at his crotch with her napkin, I smacked her hand away and made him do it himself. Shit. If I hadn't touched it yet, then I sure as hell wasn't about to let some stranger touch the Promised Land.

Tristan yanked the handle of my suitcase out of my hand and smiled sheepishly while walking quickly through the moving doors of the hotel. "Walk faster, I need to pee," he called out from his place two steps ahead.

He walked toward the front desk, dropped his duffel onto the floor, and settled my rolling suitcase against his thigh while pulling out his wallet to talk to the employee. I stood just a few feet behind him, looking around while he checked us in, taking in the seats and couches in the lobby. Tristan hadn't told me hardly anything about where we were staying, or what exactly we were doing, and I didn't bother asking because he could have said we were staying at some hole in the wall motel with Big Lou working the front desk, vibrating beds, and tube televisions on the dresser for all I cared, and I would have been fine.

"Ready to go up?" his husky voice whispered into my ear, so close to my skin I could feel the moisture from his hot mouth on me even after he pulled away.

I only managed to nod in agreement before I was right next to him on our way to the elevators. He had two keycards in his hand with the duffel pulled over a shoulder like a purse, and his other hand was wrapped around my suitcase handle. "Do we have two different rooms?" I asked him, before I even realized the words were on my lips. I had assumed we were sharing a room.

Green eyes bore into mine while we waited for the doors to open up. "No, we're sharing one," he said, and a thick shiver of anticipation ran through my body. My whole being noticed that he didn't ask me if it was okay that we were sharing one, or even make excuses as to why we weren't in two different rooms. He was just telling me, and I loved it.

I was sure my cheeks turned a shade of pink only found in nature on roses, but I couldn't care less; my smile probably rivaled that of a person in a mental institution. "Okay."

The grin he gave me in return wasn't remotely friendly, I could tell by the look in his eyes, and it made my armpits start to sweat. The elevator doors opened up that instant, breaking me out of the trance I was in as a result of that indecipherable smile. Moments later, he swiped the keycard and pushed the door open to reveal a spacious room with a king-sized bed set against the opposite wall with a big screen television facing it. The hotel was much nicer than any of the budget hotels I'd stayed in the past, so I was happy.

"I'm going to jump in the shower," he said, dropping his bag onto the floor by the television and heading to the door across from the bed, which I could only assume to be the bathroom.

I opened up my suitcase to pull out my pajamas so I could shower once he was done. My skin had this super-gross feeling from the airplane. I realized seconds later that there was a problem— my pajamas were missing. The rest of my clothes were neatly packed away courtesy of Nicole, but the shorts, tank top, and sports bra I had set aside were gone. I don't know why I looked through my suitcase again, as if the items would magically appear if I pulled everything out the second time, but nothing was in there.

My phone was out and pressed against my ear faster than I could physically say, "Nicole," in my worst impression of a growl.

Two rings later, the sultry voice I recognized belonging to my favorite dirty blonde was on the other line. "Hey, asshole, what's up?"

"Did you forget to pack something in my bag?" I whispered into the receiver.

The bitch laughed in response. "Oh, I didn't forget. Trust me, babe."

I groaned into the phone, looking through my suitcase once more. "Damn it, Nikki. Fine, I'll call you later."

A throaty chuckle answered me before she said, "Love you, Kat. Have fun."

I powered off my phone before I heard the dial tone. Fuck. Fuck. Fuck. There weren't any tank tops or sports bras in my bag. This was a disaster. I couldn't sleep with a normal bra on or anything with tight sleeves. Call me claustrophobic or whatever you will, but it was one of the few things I was picky about. Everything in my suitcase was too dressy to sleep in, so I was going to have to resort to asking Tristan to borrow one of his shirts and letting the girls hang out overnight.

"Were you on the phone?" Tristan's voice rasped from the doorway to bathroom.

I looked up and immediately wished I hadn't.

I sucked in a breath so deep I was surprised there was any oxygen left in the room.

He stood leaning against the doorframe with a towel wrapped around his slim hips and nothing else... unless you counted the hundreds of water droplets that were coating the surface of his immaculate body. How the hell was he so ripped? Why didn't he have the courtesy to dry off? Damn. I couldn't remember ever hearing him mention going to exercise at all, and there was no way that body was *that good* as a result of just good genes. If it was, the world and higher beings were totally unfair. My eyes focused in on the deep V-shape of muscles that started high on his hips before disappearing underneath the wrap of white around him.

"Do you work out?" I spit out stupidly.

He laughed deep from within his chest, causing his abs to contract in a way that made them look impossibly better. "Every day before work," he huffed out, grinning.

I nodded, because I didn't trust myself to respond with appropriate words, and stood up quickly, remembering my shower and pajama issue. "Hey, can I borrow a shirt or something to sleep in? I guess I, uh, left my pajamas at home."

He quirked an eyebrow but nodded. "Sure," he turned and dropped to his haunches to look through his bag.

A pair of black boxer briefs flew onto the bed and then a soft, old white T-shirt appeared, being flung in my direction. I wanted to say something about the fact that he'd chosen a white shirt out of all the colored ones he'd brought with him, but I didn't, and settled for a smirk instead. His cheeks and ears blossomed into a light pink color at my expression like he knew I caught onto his bullshit, but he turned back toward his bag immediately while I headed into the bathroom.

The water was hot and relaxing while I washed and shaved away the nasty feeling on me from the plane ride. I slipped on Tristan's shirt to see that it was loose and long enough to cover my ass cheeks. Sure, you could have seen my nipples through the material if you stared, but I'd already gotten undressed in front of him before, so it wasn't a big deal. Right?

After I pulled on my hot pink boy shorts, brushed out my hair and then teeth, I opened the door and walked into the room to find him sprawled underneath the covers of the bed watching television. The room was lit only by a side lamp. His chest was still bare above where the comforter lay pulled up to his pecs.

I smiled at him and walked toward the other side of the bed, slipping under the covers so that a good two feet of mattress separated us. His dark head of hair lulled to the side as he looked at me. "Are you ready to go to bed?"

"Sure," I told him.

He turned off the television and reached over to turn off the lamp on the side table before the darkness engulfed the room. Only the noises we caused shifting under the covers filled the room before his husky voice cleared. "Goodnight, Kat."

"Night," I mumbled out, rolling over so that I faced his side of the bed.

I closed my eyes and immediately envisioned Tristan's sopping wet body against the doorframe again while I fell asleep. It seemed that almost immediately, I was dreaming of Tristan possibly for the first time. He was leaning over me, like he had been the day before when we were talking about the reasons why he quit, but he was whispering dirty things into my ear and grinding against me. I kept calling his name with each dry thrust and even in my dream it felt amazing.

At some point, my mind started to wake up when the rubbing felt a little too real.

Just like at the end of yoga classes, it seemed like every inch of my body slowly awakened, every nerve heightened to the heat and the cold that lapped against it. It started from the cold tips of my toes and slowly ran up my exposed calves and then thighs, which were pressed from behind by muscle, hair, and *oh, my God,* something thick, hard, and long rubbing gently against my bottom. The blanket was kicked to the end of the bed so the cold air of the room washed over me, or technically us, I guessed, but it only caused me to revel in the warmth behind me that much more.

One of his hands was on my hip, already underneath the T-shirt, skimming the skin on my stomach. His mouth was nipping at my earlobe, alternating gentle flicks of tongue against the shell. I moaned, deep and hoarse like a wanton whore. I was still half-asleep as his long fingers circled their way up my flesh until the tips brushed against my chest, causing me to buck against him with a whimper.

Was it wrong to want him this badly? Despite the fact that Nikki and Josh were into casual sex, I was not. Every man I'd been with — the whopping three — had all been boyfriends, and yet, I'd never wanted any of them the way I craved Tristan. Simply put, he was my crack.

"You kept saying my name in your sleep," he groaned into my ear. "Do you have any idea how that makes me feel?"

Shamelessly, I pressed my back into his body, causing him to hiss. "I have an idea," I said, but my throat was thick and still full of sleep, so it sounded raspy.

"It was the hottest fucking thing I've ever heard," he whispered before rolling me onto my back in a flash before his thighs pressed mine apart. It was so dark I couldn't see anything but the faint outline of his large frame hovering over me. Both of his hands were now on my hips, so I could only guess that he was on his knees between my legs.

"I hope this is okay," he murmured, and then gripped the edge of the shirt I had on, tugging it up so that it bunched underneath my chin.

Then I felt cold air brushing my skin before his mouth, with heat that rivaled lava, brushed between my legs. "Holy shit," I panted and arched my back like I was trying to thrust more of myself into his mouth.

Despite the growl in his voice, his mouth was gentle but persistent as he sucked me between his lips. His hands kneaded the skin on my ribs before I felt one hand glide down my side, leaving a trail of heat over my hip bone before cupping me through the material of my underwear. I couldn't think. I couldn't remember my fucking name when he started rubbing those fingers up and down my flesh, pressing deliciously right where I wanted him the most.

I bucked again, whimpering when he moved his mouth away to press against mine in a slant with a deep kiss. Just like his mouth on my breast, his kiss was slow and deliberate before peppering across my chin and down my throat, collarbones, and back down to the tender flesh that missed him. His fingers kept their slow rub up, down, then circling, and doing it all over again. "I'm going to make you come, Kat," he said in the huskiest voice of all time.

"Please," I whined when his fingers tugged my underwear aside. "Please, oh please." I couldn't focus on anything but the parts of my body that were in contact with his. I couldn't think about how we needed to talk. I couldn't do anything but beg.

He chuckled before lapping at the slit between my legs. "Tell me you're mine," he rasped against my skin.

Oh. My. Fuck.

Oh. My. Fuck.

I knew this was totally possessive and territorial. I knew it also wasn't the best time for us to have a talk about what could possibly define us, but fuck me. Who cared?

"Tell me, Kat. Tell me you're only mine."

I cried something that sounded desperate. "I'm yours... only... oh, fuck!" One long finger dipped between my heated flesh, and I cried out again. "I'm only yours, Tristan."

He growled, sounding completely inhuman before sliding another finger in to follow the first. "I'm yours too, you know that?" He raised his head, his warm breath puffing against the sensitive skin on my chest, and I felt my heart constrict. "I only want you," he groaned. Before I could even digest his words, he twisted his wrist and flicked his fingers upward, brushing a spot that made me forget my name. I couldn't breathe as his fingers twirled and brushed against me, making me whimper and cry out. "You're so wet."

Maybe it was his words, but maybe it wasn't. When the heel of his hand started grinding against me, I cried out his name as the most delicious orgasm of my life made my toes curl and my vision literally go black. I'm not sure how long I laid there as a panting mess with my legs wide open and my underwear shoved to the side so my entire lady was out in the air, but it was the warm kisses to the side of my face that brought me back to reality. Tristan brushed his lips against my cheeks, chin, and then kissed my upper and lower lip repeatedly while I calmed down.

"That was…" I mumbled, feeling exhausted and warm again when the covers were pulled up over me. Tristan settled himself right next to me, draping a heavy arm over my bare stomach. His hips were pulled away from me just the slightest bit, but I couldn't forget the monster that had been pressing against my ass just minutes before. "Hey, do you want me to...?"

He chuckled, kissing my temple before resting his head on the same pillow I had mine on. "No, I'll be okay," he said simply. His fingers brushed against my stomach, and I felt him shift just a bit to put his head on top of his folded arm. We were silent for only a minute before he cleared his throat. "Kat? I meant what I said."

I knew we needed to talk, but his words flirted

through my brain. I was his and he said he was mine. The knowledge felt engraved into me already. I knew Tristan, and I was fully aware that he didn't say things just for the heck of it. "I did too."

"Yeah?" he asked in a voice so low I almost didn't hear it.

It shouldn't be so simple, should it? To just commit myself to someone?

I wasn't sure at all, but it felt natural. He bared himself to me, made his move, so didn't he deserve the same?

"Nothing would make me happier."

CHAPTER FORTY-NINE

The next day, I felt like I was living out one of those coffee commercials with the shy smiles that Tristan shot me from across the bed. As soon as I started blinking the sleep away from my eyes, I spied him in his shirtless glory holding up two cups of coffee in those amazing hands that I'd gotten well acquainted with just hours before. The smallest memory of the prior night managed to make me blush as I remembered his lips on my skin. Warm rays of sunshine slipped in through the cracks of the curtain over the window, making it feel even more surreal. I probably looked like a hot mess with dried drool on my face and knots in my hair, but right then, I could not have given less of a shit.

I was in bed with Tristan. My brain lit imaginary fireworks in celebration of the occasion.

"Good morning, Sleeping Beauty," the rich, deep

voice that had purred into my ear last night said. He handed me a cup of coffee over the bed covers and then maneuvered his way over to rest his back against the headboard just a foot away from me. "We need to get going in an hour to make it in time."

I kicked the sheets off my legs, sat up, and smiled in his direction before sipping the coffee he'd handed me. It was just the way I liked it with four sugars and so much cream it made the normally dark liquid milky. Glancing back and forth between my mug and the handsome face just to my right, my brain tried to cope and understand what had happened just a few hours before. The sequence almost seemed dreamlike. Technically, it was something out of my dreams.

Plus, who gets to wake up with this type of perfection between their legs in real life?

I couldn't even get started trying to replay the fact that he didn't ask for me to be his, but rather told me. Sweet baby Jesus, I had never been one for liking possessiveness, but the idea of being Tristan's was just too fucking perfect. I would have settled for a simple, "I think we should date each other exclusively." The dreamy smile on my face must have given me away because I heard him snort.

"What are you thinking?" he asked with a tinge of humor in his voice.

For a moment, I debated whether or not to be coy and pretend like I wasn't thinking about where his fingers had been, but screw it. "Last night," I admitted with a waggle of my eyebrows.

The smile that spread across his face was the most brilliant thing I'd ever seen in my life. Solar panels be damned, Tristan's smile could provide enough electricity to support a small town. "Which part specifically?"

I rolled my eyes at his question and sipped my coffee. "The entire time, doofus."

"I had a lot of fun last night," he chuckled, blushing across his high cheekbones. "Would it be needy of me to say that I'm glad you know how I feel about you?" He looked up at me through those long, dark eyelashes. "What I want from you?"

There was no doubt in my mind that my mouth dropped open at least a fraction of an inch then, but I hoped I recovered quickly enough to not look like a fool. "No, that's not needy at all," I said in a breathless voice. I felt like my heart was in my throat. "I like knowing that you want me in your life as more than just your friend. Until you kissed me last week, I didn't have a solid clue that you looked at me as more than just your buddy Kat."

"I don't think I had a clue for a while that I saw you as more than just my buddy. It was like I woke up one day and realized it," he sighed out the words.

I could appreciate his honesty more than I could ever explain because it made sense to me. He had been so hot and cold with me for weeks that his struggles seemed logical. Part of me liked the fact that he grew into his feelings instead of just admiring some superficial aspect of my outer shell. He liked me for me, and that just felt right.

"I've always liked you," I blurted out. Shit.

His megawatt smile brightened the room again at my response. "You're just..." he sighed, clearly struggling for words.

"Amazing?" I offered with a laugh.

Tristan rolled his eyes then and grinned. "That's not the route I was going, but it'll work too." He set his cup down on the side table and crawled over to me. The rippling of his muscles seduced my eyesight for the first time that morning. Mother fuck. All that was mine? He was mine? The clean and distinct curves of muscle that shaped his entire upper body flexed deliciously so close to me; I had to rein in my inner slut to keep from tracing all that flesh with my tongue. "Goldie?"

"Hmm?" My eyes were still glued to the expanse of peachy skin he had exposed.

His large, calloused hand stroked my cheek with a tenderness I'd never felt before. It was enough to make my sight depart from its current residence on the trail of dark hair that led underneath the cotton of his sweatpants. "I just want you to know that I'm dead serious about what I told you last night, okay? You're all I want, and I don't want anything to make you think otherwise."

I took his words and stitched them onto my heart while we showered separately and got ready to head out for breakfast. Tristan dyed his hair while in the bathroom and came out with his mop of black strands for Robby Lingus' last stint at the porn convention we were heading to. The whole atmosphere between us was different. It was almost like we had this nice, warm bubble wrapped around us that we used to shield us from the pollution we were heading to. He held my hand walking down the elevator, in the car, into the diner for breakfast, and back in the car. His long fingers reassured my shorter ones constantly. The rough and strong tips of his digits grazed the skin on the inside of my wrist and palm in sensual strokes that made me blush.

I didn't want to constantly keep reminding myself that this thing between us was real, but I had to. I was never blessed with the best of luck, so how could I manage to get this sudden oncoming of greatness? Tristan was not just the most attractive man I'd ever seen, but he was smart, funny, and a little loony. Best of all, he understood me. Every time I thought that, I had to be my own cheerleader and remind myself I was attractive, smart, funny, and a little loony too. I couldn't sell myself short either, despite how much the little voice in the back of my head wanted me to.

"Are you ready?" he asked as he parked the rental car in an empty spot. His green eyes were wider than normal as they looked at me for confirmation.

I allowed myself to nod in response while he slipped his reading glasses on. We got out and walked toward the entrance at the side of the convention center. Tristan had our laminates in hand, both of which spelled out 'Performer' on the credentials in nice, big, block letters for the entire world to see. I groaned when the security guard made me put it around my neck before allowing us to go in. As soon as we were through the doors, my hand was wrapped up in a much larger one, reassuringly. I'm not sure what exactly I was expecting, maybe massive orgies going on or at least a few practice blow jobs in front of an audience, but that definitely wasn't happening. A few dozen people walked through the hallways that comprised the backstage area. Some of the women weren't wearing very many clothes, but it wasn't extreme or provocative.

"Not what you were expecting?" Tristan's low voice questioned me just a few inches from my ear.

I shook my head and grinned at him sheepishly. I hated how he had an idea what I was thinking. "Nope. I thought for sure I'd see some butt sex going on."

He choked. A big choke that led him to start coughing so loud a ton of people turned around to see what was happening. His normally perfect, evenly toned face was bright red and his eyes seemed to be bulging out of their sockets. "Do you want to see that?"

I started laughing and squeezed his hand before the man I'd met a couple months before came strolling up to Tristan's red face and my amused one.

His beady eyes darted between our clasped hands like a vulture would zero in on a dead deer, and it was really freaking creepy.

"Tristan," his icy voice cut through my laugh when he stopped right in front of us. His eyes kept bouncing from my hand to his, and then back.

"Walter, you've met Kat," the stud muffin holding my hand said in a voice warm enough to melt through his manager's freezing tone.

The man nodded in the general direction of my face before looking back at our joined hands. "Hi," he said simply, and then cleared his throat. "Is there something I should know?"

I felt Tristan tense up before I saw the muscles in his shoulders and arms go rigid. "What makes you think there's something you need to know?"

Eyes stayed on the hands.

"I've been your manager for a long time now, *Robby*," he emphasized the name with the squint of his left eye. "Is she the reason why you're quitting?"

Normally, the top of my head just barely grazed over the highest point of Tristan's shoulders, but after the words slipped out of his manager's mouth, I lost another inch when his shoulders went tense. I looked at the dark eyes in front of me and then up at Tristan's smooth jawline, eating up the intensity of their conversation and looks. I knew Tristan had already told him his plans on retiring Robby, but I wasn't sure if he'd given him a reason, not that he really needed to. "We can talk about this later,

Walter. In private." Tristan's voice was tight and ready to snap in half.

"I'd rather us talk about this now. You've already brought her here."

Under normal circumstances, I would have said something back to Walter, because fuck if I was ever going to let some douchebag talk about me like I wasn't there. On the other hand, Tristan getting riled up seemed to rile up my panties, so I talked myself out of saying anything.

When his fingers started unraveling themselves from mine, I may have mildly started to panic because I thought for one split second that he was denouncing us in front of his manager at the first sign of struggle. I was wrong, and I should have known it. His heavy band of flesh slipped over my shoulders and pulled me close to his side, his palm cupping my shoulder.

"She," Tristan snarled in a voice I didn't think he was capable of emitting, "is the reason why I'm quitting, and you get paid for what I do. I'm here getting paid and so are you, so I'd hope you remember that," he spat. "We had a good run, but it's over." Green eyes glared with a fury I'd never witnessed on anyone besides Nicole. "What number booth am I going to?"

With that, Walter barked out a number I couldn't bother to remember, and then turned on his heel to walk away.

Tristan didn't move; instead, he just squeezed my

shoulder once before tugging on the end of my ponytail.

I stood frozen watching the slim figure retreat like a dog with his tail between his legs. I was literally dumbstruck. I was torn between being in awe at what just went down and being really turned on by the fact that he defended not just me but himself.

I tugged at his sleeve so he could slouch down enough for me to speak into his ear. "You are so fucking lucky I threw away my True Love Waits ring when I was seventeen."

His pale cheeks and ears flushed red at my comment. He grinned and then frowned, like he wasn't sure exactly how to react. Tristan opened his mouth and let out the oddest giggle I'd ever heard in my life. A man giggle?

"Cat got your tongue, Mag?" I teased him with one of my signature, unladylike snorts.

He smiled so mischievously it kind of scared me. When he nodded in response, instead of opting for words, and then started pulling on my arm to lead me toward the double doors on the opposite side of the room, I got a little worried. He slung an arm around my shoulders on our way, pulling me in real close to his solid frame. I felt the warm breath on my ear before he whispered, "You're going to have my tongue later, my little gold digger."

I fucking tripped.

What I tripped on, I had no idea. It might have

been the air for all I knew, but my foot caught onto something, and I was suddenly on a one-way trip heading toward the floor. To make matters worse, I had the dumbest look on my face, after all, what other face could I possibly have when the hottest man I'd ever known just finished telling me that I was going to have his tongue? His tongue! I didn't know where, but just the way in which he said it was shudder-inducing. Or in my case, trip-inducing. Tristan could've stuck his tongue in the crook of my elbow or armpit, and it'd be the hottest thing in the universe.

His large hands caught me around the waist before I face-planted. "Whoa there," he laughed, pulling me upright to stand.

I let out a laugh that sounded like a donkey braying and grinned at him. A small group of people were standing off to the side, looking in my direction with smirks on their faces. I held back from flipping them off and flicked my wrist in the sharpest movement, hoping my asshole wave made up for my lack of an obscene gesture. "Assholes," I muttered to myself before looking back up at my savior.

Tristan turned in the direction we had just walked in with his forehead furrowed. "What did you trip on?" he indicated with his head in the direction of the floor we'd just covered.

"Shut up," I groaned, slightly humiliated.

"Seriously, what did you trip over?" he insisted, laughing really loudly. Green eyes glittered in amusement at my flustered face.

"Don't you have somewhere to be, Robby Lingus?"

He smirked after composing himself. His hand wrapped around my forearm before squeezing. "Yes, but don't change the subject." We started walking side by side toward the doors again. He leaned closer to me. "You liked what you heard, didn't you?"

I'm sure my face flushed a color only seen on fire trucks, and possibly lobsters, but I couldn't help the snort that slipped out of my nose again. With a sharp push, Tristan had one of the doors opened that led out to the main convention hall. He strode up next to me after I passed through the opened door, careful to keep a short distance between us. I knew that standing next to him or holding his hand was out of the question because he was now in full-blown Robby mode, but that didn't mean I couldn't remind him that he brought me here with him and would leave with me in a little over an hour.

Over my shower that morning, I decided I needed to get my shit together and support him through this. I tried to mentally prepare myself for what could potentially happen while at the convention. Some gonorrhea-infected fans might try to kiss him or grab his bubble butt. Women with loose, flapping vaginal lips that were capable of clapping would try to hug him and whisper suggestive things in his ears. I was going to try my best and be okay with it. It was just an act. I mean, actors had to kiss other women on sets, right? Tristan was technically an actor, but in his case, his dick was the main attraction.

Ugh. I wanted to cry.

As I looked up at him, biting my lip to keep from sobbing out to the Holy Spirit that matched people together, I caught him looking down at me with the sweetest smile on his face. His beautiful, clear eyes were guileless, and he looked so damn at ease right then that all my insecurities went away. That smile was mine. It wasn't for anyone else; it was meant for me and caused by me.

Plus, didn't he just tell Walter that he quit for me? Me? Little ole Kat Berger who laughed like a man? I wanted to jump up and down then do the running man in joy. Tristan didn't say things just for the sake of using his vocal chords, so I knew it was true. I wanted to ask him about it, but figured right then was not the right moment for that conversation.

Maybe later when he was using his tongue. *Ha!*

A really ingenious idea formed in my head. I tugged at the sleeve of Tristan's V-neck T-shirt again. He leaned down, and I brushed my bottom lip lightly against the shell of his ear. "I think you should meet my tongue later," I said in a throaty voice.

I heard him gulp from his spot next to me.

I wasn't really sure where exactly I was getting these brave words from, maybe Nikki was channeling a bit of herself into me for moral support. Maybe she wasn't. I knew I wanted Tristan to think of me while he was stuck signing autographs for other women who found him just as attractive as I did. It might have been a little insecure of me to desire that, but I wasn't going to worry about what it meant.

We walked through the first row of booths in silence with quick side-glances at each other and sly smirks. I couldn't find it in me to pay attention to the booths and businesses we walked by because my main focus was Tristan's pink face. He kept pushing his eyeglasses up his nose even when they weren't shifting in the slightest. Evidently, he knew where we were going or had an idea of the way the booths were set up, because in no time, we were approaching a booth that had the same large picture of Robby Lingus I'd seen just a couple months ago when we met.

My stomach churned painfully at the raw sexuality and masculinity that the picture exuded. The big E-sized tits belonging to the topless woman in the picture with Robby seemed to mock me from thirty feet away. The flat slope of her stomach and definition in her abs cracked jokes about my plain, flat stomach as I made it closer. His hands seemed larger and more possessive in the poster this time around than they had the last and only time I'd seen it before. Why did looking at that poster, even though I knew it was old, hurt so damn much?

Tristan turned to me and placed a warm, sweet kiss on the hollow behind my ear. "I'd do this all over again a hundred times as long as I met you in the end."

He took off before the words were completely out of his mouth, leaving me a trail of verbal breadcrumbs in his wake. To say that I was stunned would be an understatement. Where did he get this from? This Tristan, who up until two weeks ago just clenched his jaw when he overhead me talk about hanging out with other men. This Tristan, who even then maybe didn't comprehend that he felt something for me besides those feelings that all friends have with each other.

I valued his bravery and newfound openness more than I valued just about anything. When and where did this man grow some balls?

I followed after him, keeping to the plan we'd decided on in the car. He'd suggested that I walk around until he was done, or just hang out and watch if I wanted to, an idea he wasn't completely crazy about. I decided to hang around for a while until the urge to puke all over his fans got too overwhelming. Or until I began to get homicidal and started looking for the first spork I could find to inflict bodily damage, whichever came first.

The line in front and around the booth where his naughty poster was perched was at least twenty people deep. Apparently, Robby had fans who were as different as the dogs you'd find in a shelter. Fucking bitches. Each woman had the same expression on her face: slack-jawed and bug-eyed. It looked like they thought he was the second coming or something. He was going to be some kind of coming later, and it wasn't going to be the same way in which the kind they were referring to was spelled.

I forced myself to take a deep breath and parked myself at the booth across from Robby's so I could keep an eye on my temporarily dark-haired boyfriend. Boyfriend? Was that what he was? It was the wrong moment to deliberate what kind of wording could be used to describe the sex god across the walkway. He was already sitting down behind a table, signing away pictures or whatever the women were handing him. Possibly naked pictures of themselves, ugh.

The booth I was at had a large cross hanging from the curtain behind it and three pretty blondes smiled sweetly at me. They had pink shirts on with 'I Love Jesus' written across the front. "Hi!" one of them greeted me the moment she caught me glancing at the cross.

"Hi," I responded, trying to smile just as warmly in return.

"I'm Bambi, and these are my soul sisters, Lady and Jasmine," she said, and immediately I frowned more at myself than at her. "Do you know Jesus?"

I stuttered, torn between trying to understand why one of them would choose Lady as her nickname and wondering why she was asking me if I knew someone who died two millennia ago. "Yes?" I responded, unsure of whether that was the right answer or not.

"Great!" she said enthusiastically, shoving a pamphlet into my hands that had 'Jesus Loves Everyone' across the front cover.

"Thanks," I said and gripped the handout close to me, turning around to chance a look at Tristan.

He was hunched over as he scribbled something for a woman who looked a lot like Zoey's mom and handed it back over to her. He smiled at the woman, moving his lips to say whatever Robby Lingus would say, and then with only his eyes, he looked at me before smiling just as sweetly as he had minutes before.

Two women with platinum blonde hair cut off my view after only a millisecond when they stopped directly in front of me. I tried to move over to look around them before I heard them.

"Doesn't he look like that guy who works with my dad?" one of them asked in a whisper.

"Oh, my God, that does look just like him! He just has like, dark hair." The woman talking then gasped. "It can't be him! Can it?"

"What's his name? Travis? Teddy?"

Oh, snap.

CHAPTER FIFTY

I stood there frozen like an icicle. The two girls walked off with a shrug after trying to guess Tristan's name. Maybe I should have said something. Maybe I should have done something to keep their minds off trying to determine whether or not he looked familiar, but I didn't. I let them walk off while I absorbed their suspicions. I didn't want to risk bringing myself to their attention only to have them remember me in the future. I didn't have glasses and dyed hair to hide behind when I went back to Miami. While I didn't consider myself to be distinguishable or recognizable, I couldn't run the risk that they'd remember my face and connect the dots if they ever saw me with Tristan back home. Realistically, there was always a chance that Tristan's double life could have been discovered at some point. I mean, he'd been in the industry for so many years and had fans, for goodness' sake.

The timing just seemed so off though.

Today was his last day, damn it.

Real life didn't allow things to happen when you expected them or needed them to. Wrong moments, worst timings, and dealing with tough situations were a natural part of life, but I still felt horrible. I knew this would stress him out. I knew he was going to worry about the potential outcome of someone possibly recognizing him. While the girls didn't get his name right, there was no doubt they were on the right track.

I looked over at the dark-haired man sitting behind the table and caught him looking right at me, probably recognizing the worried look on my face. His brow furrowed when I mouthed "Later" to him, and then he was busy signing some other artifact the next woman in line handed over. I was stuck. I knew I needed to tell him about what I overheard, but the selfish half of me was debating whether to do it as soon as possible, or if I should wait until the weekend was over to lay it on him. If I told him soon, it could possibly ruin our weekend because he'd stress. If I waited, then I'd feel like a liar and an asshole for keeping something important from him.

I was a terrible liar to begin with.

I'm not sure how much longer I stayed there. It was more than likely just a handful of minutes, but I was in my own little world while thinking more and more about the blondes who could ruin my weekend and my favorite person's career. Once I snapped out of it, I caught Tristan stealing glances at me through those dark frames a couple of times with a crease in his forehead. He knew me well enough to be aware that something was bothering me, and I didn't want to distract him from these last minutes as Robby.

With a small wave, I walked away from the booth, looking at people and objects that littered the tables and aisles, but not paying attention to anything in detail. It all seemed like a blur. I smiled at people when they smiled at me, but a second later, his or her face was already forgotten. My nerves were wrapped neatly around my thoughts in a distracting way.

It wasn't until my third lap of the room that I realized people were probably smiling at me so much because of the big lettering on my credential that said 'Performer.' Shit.

I felt like a robot while I walked around devoid of emotion. The porn convention wasn't like the one in Miami with Nicole. Back there I was worried I would see someone I knew. Here I was so far away from the people I knew and grew up with that I couldn't care less to be discreet.

I saw a familiar looking Maya standing by a booth and thought about my Nicole back home. If I would have been in a settled mood, I might have taken a picture of her just to piss off one of my dearest friends, but I didn't.

After passing what felt like the thousandth booth,

I looked at my watch and realized it was almost eleven and Tristan, or Robby, would be done in no time. Somehow, I managed to loop around to where he was at without getting lost, to find that there were only two women left in line. I stopped at the booth to the right of his and took in the massive, tattooed man who stood there with his arms crossed. There were rows and rows of DVDs packed neatly together on the table with sections that said Anal, Man on Man, Threesomes, Teen, Big Asses, Big Tits, and other words that narrowed down races for you.

"Can I help you with anything?" the deep voice asked.

I looked at his dark eyes, taking in the piercing on his eyebrow, and shrugged, smiling. I felt like such a pervert for stopping at the one booth that sold pornos. For a split second, I wondered if there were any Robby videos for sale. "Nah, I'm just looking."

He smiled, flashing big, pearly teeth at me. "I have a wide variety that's not up, so feel free to let me know if you do think of anything. I got some transexual and bestiality, too," he said, like it was the most natural thing in the world for him to mention.

What the fuck? Was he just teasing me? I didn't think I looked like someone who would be into animal action, but then again, what exactly did those types of people look like? I'd heard of grannies looking at porn, as disturbing as that seemed to me.

"Uh," I grimaced, shaking my head. "Okay… thanks?" I responded with a squeaky voice.

It was when he laughed in response to my facial expression that I saw the DVD propped up to his left. The familiar looking brown-haired man on the cover instantly reminded me of how long it had been since I'd seen him. Had it been months already? I used to think he was perfect, but now, even though there was no denying he was an attractive, older man, my girly parts just didn't respond the way they used to. Either way....

"How much for one video?" I asked the big guy before even realizing the words were coming out of my mouth.

He flashed me a sly smirk. "Which one?" I pointed at the video I wanted and he narrowed those dark eyes in my direction. "For you, baby, five bucks. You're the first person to make me laugh today."

The five-dollar bill was out of my pocket before he even got the chance to finish answering me. He slipped the DVD into a small, dark bag at the same time I felt a hand grasp my shoulder. I knew it was Tristan before I even turned my head to look at him. The expression on his face was one of confusion as he looked between the big man and the small bag he was handing me. "You ready?" he asked me in that soft voice I loved.

I nodded and grasped the bag out of the air. "Bye!" I told the man with a grin.

"Bye," he answered with another deep laugh as Tristan frowned and put an arm around my shoulders.

"How did it go?" I asked him as soon as we were a few feet away from the booth. It didn't escape me that his arm was wrapped tighter around my shoulder than ever before. His steps were slow and steady to let me keep up with his naturally longer stride.

"Good," he said simply, looking down at my bag. "I just need to wash my hair out, and then we can head over to the museum."

"Okay."

In no time, we had trailed around the booths and were flashing our laminates at security guards to let us go to the back where we had come from. He dropped his arm from around my shoulder and wrapped his hand around mine, entwining those long, slender fingers through my own. The smile he gave me was the same one from before, all sugar, sweet, and happy. Tristan pulled me in the direction of a large family bathroom that was off to the side. There were more people in the back area than there had been before, which wasn't all too surprising since it was later in the morning by that point.

"Hey, Robby!" a voice from the other side of the area belted out.

He stopped and his muscles tensed. Green eyes bore into mine like they were trying to convey some sort of message telepathically before he snapped his gaze over to where the female had called out to him. I felt my stomach do a free fall. It reminded me a lot of the time I went sky diving with Zoey and Josh; the longest thirteen seconds of my life were when I did that tandem jump with a much older man strapped to my back, and it seemed like we were rushing through open air for hours while my intestines floated freely. Dread filled the empty space that my stomach left as I looked in the same direction as well.

There was a pretty redhead, obviously a fake ginger by the hint of dark roots that were growing in, sauntering over to where we stood. He let out a shaky breath followed by a groan when I guessed he recognized the female. "Hey," he muttered in a less–than-enthusiastic tone.

"How you been, handsome?" she asked, approaching him. Her light gaze hadn't moved in my direction at all, but my eyes were glued to the bouncing monstrosities that her bright pink shirt covered.

"Good. You?" Tristan replied, squeezing my hand.

"Fabulous. I haven't seen you," the way she said the last word made me want to vomit because I caught her eyes wandering to his crotch, "in a very long time."

"Yeah," was his only response while squeezing my hand tighter.

Was it too much to ask for him to be an asshole and blow her off? Was I being a bitch for wanting him to tell her to fuck off and put on a bra for baby Jesus' sake? If I wanted to look at tits and nipples, I'd look at my own. I wanted him to acknowledge the fact that I was standing right next to him, holding his damn hand while another female ogled him. Another female he had probably been with at some point, hopefully a very long time ago. Ugh. I wasn't sure if the burning sensation in my center was heartburn or what, but I was really craving some Tums right then.

"We should totally talk to our managers and see if we can work together again soon," the redheaded slut practically moaned.

Tristan just nodded, but I could see the clench in his jaw. "Umm..."

I'm not sure where it came from, but I reached over and pinched him in the ribs with my free hand. Unfortunately, since he practically had no body fat on his torso, it probably wasn't as effective as I'd hoped, but he flinched just a little in response. The redhead at that point turned to look at me, and then at our hands exactly like Walter had done an hour before. My stomach churned and my armpits immediately started sweating in response to her cold stare. Why did it feel like everyone was teaming up against us today?

"I didn't see you were here with someone," the girl said in a flat voice, talking to Tristan but looking at me.

"I've been standing right here," I said with a smirk. I'd let him have his moment before with Walter, but I sure as hell wasn't going to let some tramp try to belittle me.

Her eyes narrowed as she placed her hands on

her hips. "Okay." She looked back and forth between Tristan, me, and our hands once more before rolling her eyes. "I'll talk to you later then, Robby. Don't forget to talk to your manager." She cast another long glance in my direction, then turned on her heel and walked back to where she'd come from.

My adrenaline was already pumping from when I'd thought I was going to have to tell this bitch off, so I felt a little frustrated that Tristan didn't bother to change the topic or tell her he'd quit when he had the chance. With my luck, my face was already red in a blend of anger and frustration at the situation.

His gaze was on me as he bit that full bottom lip of his. "What's wrong?"

I pointed at the restroom we'd been heading toward before the redheaded interruption and pulled my hand out of his. "Nothing," I told him, pushing open the heavy door of the room.

"Kat," he said from the same spot he'd been in before. "Are you mad at me?"

I wanted to flick him in the forehead, but all I did was ignore his question. "Didn't you want to wash your hair before we go to the museum?"

He shook his head and gestured in the direction of the exit doors. "I changed my mind. Let's go to the hotel and do it there." His eyes focused on my face. "We have time."

I shrugged and started walking to where we'd entered the building from, careful to keep my hands close to my sides. I knew there was a chance I was being a bitch, but I didn't care.

"Kat," Tristan hissed from behind me, taking two long strides to catch up to me. "Kat."

"Let's go, I just want to hurry up and go to the museum." Okay, so maybe I was kind of being a child and a bitch, but my emotions were swirling inside of me so fiercely I couldn't control them. I was pissed and, frankly, a whole lot of jealous, but I didn't want to make a scene in front of people. I pushed open one of the glass doors that led outside and at least held it open long enough for Tristan to follow me out.

"Kat!" he called out as I speed walked ahead of him, going toward the rental car. He grabbed my bicep and pulled me around to face him, his eyes were wide and pleading. "Why are you mad?"

I couldn't look him in the eye, so I settled for shrugging instead, like that was an appropriate answer. My feelings were hurt, and I was jealous at the stupid, pretty woman who had been with him and was trying to be with him again.

"Are you jealous, sweetheart?" he asked me so quietly I almost didn't hear him. His free hand came up under my chin to tilt my head up. "Kat."

"I'm being stupid," I muttered, not looking up at him even though my face was up.

"Maybe a little." He chuckled, warm breath fanning my face.

I glared at him then, which I realized too late was exactly what he wanted. "You're an asshole."

His smile was sad and sweet like he understood why my anger was directed at him. "I'm sorry you're jealous." His thumb brushed the length of bone that comprised my jaw. "I'm sorry I didn't tell her I quit, but I didn't want to talk to her any longer and have to explain that I wasn't in the industry anymore." He brushed the patch of skin right next to my ear. "I couldn't remember her name to save my life, if that makes you feel any better."

"Just a wee bit," I admitted with a sigh. It did, in fact, make sense to me that he didn't want to talk to her any longer, and I did feel better that he couldn't remember her name. He knew me, and that was more than I could say about every other female who had come into his life. It almost completely made me forget that he'd slept with her. Almost. "I'm sorry for being like that."

"It's okay. I'm sure the next time I see that Ryan guy, I'll probably act the same way, if not worse." He grinned, and then kissed my forehead.

I snorted, pulling away. "I only kissed him, Mag," I taunted him, walking backward.

His face went blank before he walked toward me, plump lip between his teeth again. "I didn't know you'd even done that." He clenched his teeth and, I swear, ground them together.

His words struck a chord with my memory, reminding me of the incident earlier with the two women. I knew I needed to tell him right then, but I really didn't want to upset our weekend because I was a selfish bitch. "Speaking of things you don't know, hurry up and get in the car because I need to tell you what happened."

Minutes later, we were in the car heading to the hotel and Tristan was silent. I told him everything that happened, not that it was much, and apologized for not saying anything to them. He agreed it wouldn't have been a good idea for me to bring attention to myself in case they ever saw me again. His silence, while he contemplated the effects this could have, made me feel terrible. He'd been so happy to quit, and now this was going to loom over his head. It was the worst anticipation ever.

When we were getting really close to the hotel, he let out a shaky sigh. "I don't think I have anything to worry about. My boss thinks his daughter is pretty much a nun, and I really don't think she'd tell her dad she thinks his employee is in porn," he said. "Imagine that conversation."

Well, when he put it like that, it made a lot of sense. I know there was no way in hell I'd ever tell my dad that someone he knew did porn. That would probably be the worst conversation of my life. I'd have to explain why and how I knew. Yeah, no thanks. While I still wasn't assured she wouldn't say anything, I figured it was pointless to make him think otherwise and just have him stress.

"Either way, they can't fire me without good reason," he snickered, pulling into a spot in the parking lot. "I know my law."

I rolled my eyes and got out of the car, following him through the lot and into the hotel. He put a hand on my shoulder and led me upstairs, unlocking the door to our hotel room and gently pushing me in before him. He went straight into the bathroom while I plopped on the edge of the bed and kicked my shoes off. The water to the shower turned on for a few minutes while I relaxed on the sheets, content to just look out the window. The door to the bathroom was open, and when I heard the water turn off, I swallowed hard.

"Tristan?" I yelled loud enough for him to hear me.

"Yes?" he responded just as loudly.

"You told your manager that you quit because of me," I stated.

Silence.

"That's not what you told me before," I kept going, swallowing hard again.

Heartbeats later, his well-defined frame, clad in only boxer briefs, appeared in the doorway. Wet hair askew, he lifted a hand to scratch across the flesh of his chest. "I told both of you the truth."

Pushing my ass further back on the bed, I frowned. "Both of us?"

Those legs with thick, muscular thighs stalked toward me. God, his legs were so long, and even though they were kind of hairy, I really liked it. He was a man, a perfect fucking man. He leaned over me, using a flat palm to push me against the bed. "It's both," he said in a husky voice, caging me in on both sides with an arm. Those green eyes laser beamed right into me, all heated masculinity, even when he dropped to his elbows bringing that delicious body just a couple inches away from my heaving one. "You're the main reason though."

"Oh," I squeaked out before he pressed his warm lips against mine.

Long minutes of slanted mouths, rough tongues, and my hands buried in his soft, wet hair passed by. Fuck, I couldn't get enough of him. He was moaning into me, kissing the corners of my lips, flicking on my earlobe, then licking and sucking at the skin of my neck in quick succession. I arched against him, wanting to feel the heat that was radiating from his body directly on mine. He looked at me through heavy-lidded eyes, sensing the movement of my lower body. Tristan raised himself up further away from me so he was on his hands.

I made a noise that was a strange warp of a whimper and groan as he got on his knees and started unbuttoning my jeans. He didn't ask for permission when he started tugging them down my hips, and finally tossed them behind his back onto the floor, or hell, for all I cared. Luckily, I'd come prepared with some of my cutest black lace panties. When he rumbled deep in his chest at seeing them, I felt fucking awesome.

"Jesus," he grunted. Big hands spread my legs apart, and even though I should probably have been a little self-conscious, I wasn't in the least bit. I looked at Tristan, who bit his lip and looking at my underwear like they were his last feast, before raking my gaze down and seeing it.

The smooth, pinkish head peeped out from above the black band of his boxer briefs.

Holy Mother of Christ.

The outline of him in those poor briefs was the hottest thing I'd ever seen in my life. I could see the general impression of the beast in his underwear, and then, I whimpered.

In no time at all, Tristan lowered his face between my thighs and kissed the soft skin on the sides. "Kat," he said in a low growl. "I want you to watch me."

I propped myself up on my elbows to look at him.

He dipped his mouth between my legs, licking me right where I wanted him to, through the material of my underwear. I swear the world felt like it shifted when my hips bucked up. His warm, rough tongue lapped at me, first right at my favorite spot, before languidly in long strokes. Then he sucked that special spot with pursed lips, and I couldn't fucking think. I couldn't move. His eyes stayed locked on mine as he moved his head up, and then pulled my panties down my legs so slowly I thought I'd turn twenty-six before he was done.

As soon as I was naked from the waist down, I yanked my shirt over my head and tossed it on the floor while he watched, slowly resuming his position back where he'd been.

"You're so pretty, Kat," he murmured, stroking my thighs with his calloused thumbs. He whispered something then about tasting me, but I couldn't hear very well because angels were rejoicing in my ears.

With quick but unhurried flicks, he tasted me while I moaned and groaned, pushing my body closer to his mouth. His hands gripped my thighs, keeping them opened as I bucked. If I could think straight, I would have laughed at myself for rhyming, but I didn't think I could even recite my ABCs if I would have been paid a million dollars to do so.

"You're delicious," he cooed against my wet flesh.

"Tristan," I panted, arching my back as he passed over me with his tongue one more time. "Oh, fuck! Tristan!"

He groaned louder than I did as I climaxed for what felt like forever. My eyes were pinched tight as wave after wonderful wave clenched my insides. When I was finally able to open my eyes, I found him right where he'd been moments before, smiling smugly. He got up on his knees and scooted over to lay down next to me with his hand gripping my ribcage.

"You're amazing," I panted.

"Amazing enough to throw away that stupid Andrew Wood DVD you bought?" he asked with a raised eyebrow, smiling coyly.

I nodded and licked my lips, making a show of

looking down at the pink head that was still peeping out from his boxers. It was fucking on. "Definitely," I took a deep breath and got up onto an elbow. "Remember me telling you about my tongue earlier?"

For me to say that I was good at oral sex, or that I liked giving blow jobs, would make me feel and sound like a tramp.

With that in mind, I would gladly admit to the fact that I was one.

For Tristan.

He grinned in response to my question, this sly, distracted smile as he was more focused on my breasts than face. Despite the fact that my only child tendencies made me unable to share things in life with most people, the hot-as-shit man lying on the bed was not just any person. He'd already proven to me that he was anything but selfish.

I yanked down the elastic band of his boxer briefs before he had a chance to make the slightest peep in protest, and gasped. His pink cock slapped against his stomach angrily. That moment was what I imagined the discovery of the meaning of life would be like: all encompassing, time-stopping, and brilliant. The word *little* had no room in my vocabulary when I was with him naked. I mean I shouldn't have been surprised that every aspect of him was nothing less than perfect and beautiful. This was Tristan. There was no part of him that wasn't immaculate, besides two crooked toes that had been broken and not put back into place.

Unfortunately, I'd seen some nasty dicks in my life, both in person and onscreen. Peens that couldn't spell proportionate if they tried; thin, short and thick, crooked, super veiny—there were a million varieties that could constitute my interpretation of an ugly penis.

This one...

Would it be too forward for me to immediately put his balls in my mouth? Even his nicely trimmed sack was plump and virile looking.

I said a silent prayer to whatever Holy Spirit was watching over me that, while Tristan was far better endowed than any other man I'd ever been with, he was not Calum Burro. But my poor vag knew it was in a world of trouble already by his length and girth.

A warm hand cupped my chin, bringing my focus back to that chiseled jaw I was enraptured with. Dark green eyes gazed at me from across the mere feet that separated us. "What are you doing?" he asked in a hoarse voice.

"What I want," I told him, my voice sounding way huskier than normal as I pulled his boxers down his long legs and tossed them onto the floor.

He sucked in a breath and brushed his thumb across my lower lip, while staring at me through heavy eyes. "Fuck, Kat," he murmured when I slipped my tongue out to lick the pad of his finger.

In a second, his thumb was delving into my mouth by the corner, and I was sucking it in. His hips twitched, making his long cock bob in the air. I may have drooled just a little at the sight. The next thing I knew, I was sitting back on my knees and licking him with all the experience I had gained as a kid when I was obsessed with lollipops. I sucked him down as far as I could over and over again, gagging every so often and not giving half a shit when it happened.

Tristan panted. He moaned. He groaned. His hips bucked with a lack of control I'd never seen from him. Those eyes stayed on my mouth and my tugging hand constantly as his left hand gripped the comforter.

"Fuck... oh, shit..." he grunted out. "Baby, you're so... fuck... oh, my fuck... good at...come here..." His free right hand beckoned me to him.

Not wanting to break our contact, I kept my right hand wrapped around his length. I slipped over him, stroking and tugging at his wet, hard flesh until I was on his right side, hovering over his face.

Vibrant eyes gazed up at me before his hand wrapped around the back of my head and pulled my mouth down to his lips, kissing me so deeply I completely forgot what my hand was supposed to be doing. His hot tongue stroked mine, over and over again while I tightened my grip around his base and pumped faster.

"Why are you so... *oh*....? I'm gonna fucking..." he cried out, bucking those slim hips in the air in time with my hand.

"In my mouth?" I whispered against his ear.

His eyes flickered over to mine for the briefest moment in time before he yelled, "Fuck!" His cock erupted, his body straining beneath mine.

Muscular arms dropped to the sides, resembling a frozen snow angel. His broad chest heaved as he calmed down and my pumping slowed as I tried to ease him out of his orgasm. I smiled, kissed his bottom lip, and jumped off the bed to wash my hands, and then grab a towel to wipe off his splattered abs.

When I got back into the room, he was in the same position he'd been in before I left, but as I approached the bed I found that he was grinning with his eyes closed. I cleaned off the ridges of his abs and dropped the hand towel on the floor.

I couldn't help but glance at his semi-boner in the process. Even half flaccid it was impressive.

"Stop looking at me," he muttered, opening one green eye.

I snorted, thinking that he, the now retired porn star, wanted me to stop looking at his peen. He wrapped an arm around my shoulders and pulled me down to lay next to him. His warm lips kissed my hair, temple, and cheek. When he scooted down to nuzzle my neck, his hot breath made me break out in goose bumps.

"I knew it," he whispered and mouthed against my skin. "So much better with you."

My insides melted a little.

CHAPTER FIFTY-ONE

"A little lower."

"Right there?"

"Oooh, oh yeah, right there."

"You're so—"

"Oh, shit, just a little more."

"You want more?"

"Yes."

"Kat—"

"That feels so good."

Tristan chuckled as the joint of his thumb made a detour from my shoulder to dig into my ribcage, making me suck in a breath. He nuzzled his nose against the shell of my ear while his large hand continued massaging the aloe vera gel onto my sunburnt shoulders. "You sound like such a dirty girl," he whispered, trying not to let the other hundred passengers on the flight overhear us.

"Shut up," I giggled, tearing my eyes away from the dark night out the window to look at the beautiful man over my shoulder.

His full mouth was pressed into a large smile highlighting the pink shading that covered the slope of his nose and cheekbones. He looked down and squirted more gel into his hand before spreading the cool substance all over the exposed skin of my shoulders and tops of my arms. Yesterday, after the Epic Suck-Off, as I was calling it, we'd gone to the Page Museum and then driven down to Malibu's Escondido Beach, where I opted not to put any sunblock on. Hence, the reason why I was currently suffering. I was, in fact, an idiot.

Warm breath blew steadily on the shoulder closest to Tristan before he slipped the travel-sized tube of gel into my purse. "I told you to put on sunscreen, but *nooo*," he mocked in a whiney voice, trying to imitate me. "*I'm fine. I don't burn,*" he kept going, batting his long eyelashes with a pinched face.

Asshole.

I glared at him as best as I could and stayed hunched over. My forearms rested on my knees while I waited for my skin to fully absorb the aloe vera. "I'm fine," I said with a roll of my eyes.

It had been fine besides the fact that I wouldn't let him sleep anywhere close to me the night before, because my skin felt like it was on fire. Tristan woke me up at the ass crack of dawn to make it to Universal Studios before the park opened. I had to borrow one of his T-shirts so the material was loose on me and covered almost as much skin as a long-sleeved shirt would. He laughed, of course. I looked ridiculous, but I shrugged it off and shoved him when he started smirking at me with those green eyes dancing across the front of the shirt. I felt a little bad, because I knew he'd spent an arm and a leg on our tickets, food passes, and random trinkets.

My favorite of the random crap he'd bought at the gift shops and booths was a picture of us on the Jurassic Park ride. My hands were just barely in the air and a huge grin was plastered on my face, while Tristan had his hands firmly wrapped around the security bar in front of us, teeth clenched in a horrified grimace, and eyes on me. He claimed his stomach started hurting halfway through the ride. *Sure*. We'd barely had enough time to make it back to the hotel, shower, and get to the airport in time for our flight.

His calloused index finger made a hot trail across the forearm closest to him, before continuing its path upward over the tops of my arms to brush the strap of my new Universal tank top. "I'm glad you came with me this weekend, Goldie," he stated.

I winked at him, because the weekend had been a ton of fun minus the porn slut and the two girls. "Me too, thanks for inviting me." I paused and let my insides swell. “Thank you for everything.”

He smiled, this sweet crooked thing that made my heart stutter in its cage of bones. One of his hands reached up to pinch my earlobe between two fingers. "I had a lot of fun," he said. "Even though you squealed like a little girl on each ride."

I scoffed and shook my head, knowing he was out of his mind. "I'm pretty sure that was you squealing like a pig on each ride, Mister I-Have-An-Upset-Tummy. Pansy."

"I think you may have hit your head a little hard." He grinned.

"You're lucky I didn't hit you in the head on Saturday after the convention," I muttered before I realized what I said. It was the truth. I just didn't want to bring up what had happened that day because I knew he was stressed enough about the girls thinking he looked familiar.

He sighed, weariness filling the emerald color in his eyes. "I'm sorry, Kat. I know it's hard to be with me because of Robby..."

My heart clenched at his words. I felt like a total bitch, because he felt bad for who he had been and what he'd done in the past. I knew Tristan for all his jokes and sweetness was tenderhearted. For years, he had put a block to prevent others from getting into his heart, and he'd let *me* into his life. If I were to reject him, to make him feel bad for his past, I knew it would hurt him deeply. Fortunately for him — well, for us really — as much as the porn and Robby Lingus bothered me, I couldn't hold it against him. We'd all done stupid things in our past that we weren't exactly proud of.

Like the video I knew I needed to tell him about at some point.

Fucking shit.

"Hey, don't worry about it." I gave him a gentle smile. "It's a little weird, but we'll figure it out."

He pinched my earlobe again. "It's done now at least. You didn't get too upset that day, right?"

The reminder of what happened Saturday tugged at my nerves. I had never been the jealous type, but over the last day and a half, when I'd catch an attractive female looking at Tristan, I'd wonder if he had been with her at some point and couldn't remember doing it. My skin itched. I genuinely had no interest in knowing exactly how many people he had been with before me, not that I technically counted because he hadn't fermented my flower yet. I wasn't naïve enough to believe that he was anywhere near my single digit number, but the acceptance of his past still ate away at me just a little.

Each time I'd even slightly drift off into that train of thought, he would pinch my side, pull my hair, or kiss me. The more time we spent together, the more it became clear to me that he knew my moods. Not even my last longtime boyfriend knew half as much about me as Magellan did. I knew I was overreacting by making those assumptions, but I forgot about them as soon as he started picking on me.

"I was a little," I admitted, keeping my peripheral view on the finger resting on my shoulder. "I'm fine though."

Tristan rolled his eyes and leaned closer to me, pink lips just inches away from my own. "You can ask me anything, Kat." The rough pad of his finger traced a line from my shoulder across to my throat, slowly. "I'll always tell you the truth."

His words wrapped me up in warmth, and I couldn't help the small smile that came across my face. There were very few people in my life who I trusted and readily believed, and this man was one of them. He cared for me, he was honest with me, and he understood me. Tristan was my easiest friendship. I had no reason to doubt him, and I hoped I never would.

I shrugged a pink shoulder in his direction. "I know."

The full lips that were inches away from mine brushed the skin on my shoulder lightly. His voice was much lower than normal. "Stay with me tonight?"

I snorted and fought the urge to slap my palm across his forehead and sound too enthusiastic about saying yes. I had to go to school the next day for a faculty meeting, but it would totally be worth it. "Sure, Mag."

His gaze swept across my chest and shoulders, up my neck, and finally landed on my face. Heavy, hooded eyes looked at me in a way that made me breakout in goose bumps. "Good, I'm not picking up Yoda from my mom's until tomorrow since we're getting home so late."

Hours later, I found myself pulling my suitcase along the path to Tristan's back door. His broad shoulders led the way before he unlocked the back door and turned off the alarm. When we got off the plane a little less than an hour before, the clock showed that our flight landed a few minutes shy of midnight, so by then, it was close to one. I walked in after him, adjusting my eyes against the bright light of the kitchen while I followed him through the house and up the stairs.

"The house seems so empty without Yoda," I told him, walking into his room where he was standing with his back to me. I'd become so used to having the big monster following me around and darting around my legs that I missed his presence. Even the bed looked empty without his meaty body draped across it. My nerves suddenly made my stomach hurt. We'd slept together a few times already, but this felt different. Intimate.

"I know, it isn't the same without him here," Tristan agreed, looking right at me.

I knew we both needed to wake up early, so I opened up my suitcase to grab my toiletry bag and makeshift pajamas. I felt really strange standing inside his bathroom, brushing my teeth in his sink while he did things in his bedroom. I felt weird, but not in a bad way. I think it was just difficult for me to wrap my head around him inviting me to spend the night with him after we'd already spent two other nights together. Most guys would have wanted to get life back to normal, right?

"You don't mind if I use your shower? I feel gross," I called out to him, already pulling my tank top over my head as carefully as possible so the material didn't scratch my heated skin.

"You don't have to ask!" he hollered back from his bedroom.

Not knowing whether to leave the door open or not, I kicked it partially closed before turning on the water and peeling off the rest of my clothes. I hopped in and let the lukewarm water run over me, wincing at the feel of it on my sunburned skin. Using his soap, I lathered up and chanced a glance, while I was shaving my legs, to peer through the foggy stall door. Tristan stood on the other side of the glass, resting his behind against the sink counter with one arm gripping the edge of the sink while he brushed his teeth. His gaze was locked on me.

I didn't say anything as I rinsed off, and by the time I looked up again, he was out of the bathroom.

Once I was dressed in the first T-shirt he'd let me borrow and a clean pair of underwear, I found him on top of the sheets in sleep pants and a T-shirt with his long legs crossed at the ankles. He had a book open on his lap before he saw me and set it on his nightstand while grabbing something off it in exchange.

"You aren't going to shower?" I asked, climbing onto the other side of the bed slowly, but keeping an eye on him while he drank in my chest through the nearly translucent white of his shirt.

He shook his head as he licked his bottom lip. "No." He patted the bed in front of him. "Come here so I can put more aloe gel on you."

Well, okay then.

I crawled over as quickly as I could and plopped down just to the left. He surprised me by swinging his lower body around so that I sat between his legs. Warm hands snuck underneath my shirt to squeeze my waist, before he grabbed the bottom hem of the shirt I had on and pulled it up and over my head completely. "Umm..." I managed to stutter out, bringing my hands up to cover my exposed boobs.

"The shirt was in the way," he said in a hoarse breath as if it was a logical explanation.

Two hands swept over my shoulders and arms. They brushed the back of my neck gently, and then made another pass over me again. It was when his tongue lapped at my earlobe and the skin right underneath it that I tensed up like a virgin would if they'd encountered Calum's abnormality in the flesh.

"Did you know," he breathed on my neck before kissing it with a wet, open mouth, "that I want you more," he bit me gently on the throat, "than I've ever wanted anyone before?" He nipped at my neck one more time, holding each side of my ribs in his hands. "So much more, Kat. So fucking much more."

I arched and then curved my spine the opposite way, feeling like I was going to explode inside my skin from his lips and hands. Fuck. How would it feel when it wasn't just his hands on me? "Oh."

His big hands went around me, cupping my own, which were holding my breasts together. "Why do you feel so good?" His voice was thick against my skin. I leaned back to feel his cotton-clad chest against my back.

I pulled my hands away so his palms could cup my chest. His rough hands squeezed and kneaded my flesh lightly. "Tristan, please," I begged for what I didn't know.

He groaned and brushed his thumbs over each of my nipples once. I saw him grab for the shirt he'd just peeled off and tugged it down over my head, leading my arms through the sleeve openings. "Not tonight, you have that burn and we both need to wake up early," he said, but I could sense a tinge of disappointment in his voice.

I grunted and snapped my head around to look at his face. "Seriously?"

He just grinned and pulled the covers over to slide underneath them. "Dead. Come on." He held up the covers right next to him so that I could slip underneath them too. "It's only because I care about you that I don't have you pinned underneath me."

I scowled at him and slid deeper into the sheets. I knew I probably wouldn't enjoy getting down and dirty with him since my shoulders ached, but I thought that was beyond the point. What a fucking tease. "You suck."

He flicked the lights off before settling in close

enough to brush his fingertips against mine. I had just started dozing off when I felt his fingers tighten in mine. "Thank you," he whispered.

I wondered what exactly he was thankful for.

CHAPTER FIFTY-TWO

A week passed in the blink of an eye.

My sunburn went from a seven on the pain scale down to a two during that time period. My quick recovery was mostly in thanks to Tristan and Zoey dousing me in aloe vera gel each chance they got. By the end of the week, my back had begun peeling, and I had to resort to whacking Tristan's hands away from my shoulders when he tried to peel off the dead skin.

I stayed over at his house one other time during that week at his insistence. I woke up after he returned from the gym, just before he made it back into the shower. It wasn't a coincidence that I woke up in time to see him peeling off his sweaty workout clothes. I learned after my first morning that he made it back home right at six-thirty in the morning. My alarm was set to five minutes before then, which allowed me a chance to hit the snooze button once, before I got to witness the best strip show on Earth. I had to fight the urge to throw dollar bills at his smoking hot body the first morning I saw him all wet, sweaty, and perfect.

I wanted to be wet and sweaty with him, but he somehow managed to keep us fully clothed and only engaging in mouth-to-mouth activities. After a particularly fun evening on his couch, where my shirt ended up on the floor while I straddled his lap and his hands gripped my ass, I had to go home and pull out one of my favorite Andrew Wood DVDs. My beloved hummingbird came out to play as well. Half of me was beyond disappointed that he had such a tight rein on his control, somehow managing to stop us when we started getting a little too intense.

The other half of me, the one that wasn't a whore who craved Tristan's cock on an hourly basis, got excited about the fact that he was taking his time with us. I'd been worried in the past that I would be meaningless to him, that being with me would be just like being with any other female, porn or no porn. Was it wrong that I wanted to be special? I didn't think so. Everything he did when we were together cemented the idea that I was important to him. I couldn't expect anything less from him though, even as strictly friends he'd always treated me much better than any other man in my life, besides Josh.

The week before school started, I was in my

classroom setting up my walls when my cell's alert went off. Digging into my drawer for my purse, I pulled out my phone to see Magellan's name across the front.

Which number is your classroom?

I typed out my response in a second. **10B. Why?**

:) Was the only response I got a minute later.

I shrugged and left my phone on the desk while I finished grabbing the poster I'd been hanging on the wall when the text came in. I'd just turned around to tape it to the bland cream wall when the door to the classroom opened.

"Stop!" the deep voice that I'd grown too fond of called out.

"Jesus!" I squeaked, spinning around on my heel to face the source of the voice. "You scared the shit out of me. What are you doing here?" I asked Tristan, dropping the poster and roll of tape onto my desk.

He grinned at me before shuffling three cylinder-shaped containers under his arm onto the closest desk to the door. In his dress pants and button-down shirt, he strode two long steps over to me and wrapped his arms around my upper back before squeezing me to him. "I came to see my favorite teacher," he chuckled. "Ms. West, the kindergarten teacher."

I laughed and ducked my head instinctively for the spot right underneath his chin where I could breathe in his clean scent, and then wrapped my arms around his ribs. "Oh, you came to see Ms.

West? I'll make sure to tell her girlfriend you came by," I said against the dark blue material of his shirt. Ana West was the only employee at Tucker who recognized Zoey off the bat the first time she came to visit me. Apparently, her girlfriend was also very familiar with Zoey's work. Needless to say, they were big fans.

"I guess that's why she told me we can't see each other anymore, damn it," he muttered, squeezing me tightly against him one more time before pulling away. Green eyes raked over my jeans and cardigan quickly before he leaned forward to plant a warm, lingering kiss on my lips.

I made some kind of weird moaning noise when he kissed my bottom lip. "You should visit me more often."

"I will." Tristan pulled away smiling and pointed at the boxes he'd brought in. "I took too long eating, and then trying to find your room so I can only stay a few minutes, but I brought you something. Or things, I guess."

He handed me one of the large cardboard cylinders that was lying on the desk. I didn't say anything as I tore off the tape at the top, and then used my fingernails to pull off the end. Flipping the container over, a rolled up poster slipped out, and I unfolded it to see a large poster of Albert Einstein and a quirky quote beneath his picture.

I turned to look at him, grinning because I loved the poster and Albert Einstein. "Mag—"

Another container was thrust into my hands before I kept going. "Open up all of them, and then you can tell me thank you," he grinned.

I pulled the top off the second one and flipped it so that another poster slipped out. The second one was of Rosie the Riveter, who was flexing her guns in the picture with "We Can Do It!" displayed across the top. My body sucked in a deep breath of its own, feeling slightly overwhelmed at his thoughtfulness.

"One more," his velvet voice said, pushing another into my hands before he squeezed my shoulder in passing.

Opening up the last package, I pulled out a poster of three sharpened pencils facing up with one upside down, words about individuality dotted across the bottom.

My heart did this weird kind of thing where it felt like it expanded and tightened, sucking the air out of my lungs. To say I felt overwhelmed would be an understatement. I'd been extremely fortunate in my life to have such amazing parents, then three friends later in life who filled my life with love, and now this dorky, beautiful man who bought me posters for my classroom. Posters. For. My. Classroom. The gesture tugged at my insides and my head.

In a split second, I'd dropped the poster onto the desk, and in a move I didn't think I was capable of, jumped up and onto Tristan before wrapping my legs around his slim waist. He took a step back to brace himself since he wasn't expecting me to do that and grabbed my thighs to hoist me up evenly. "Jesus, Goldie," he chuckled, gripping my thighs tightly.

"Thank you so much," I whispered into his ear, because the moment felt so personal and so close to my heart that I didn't want to risk sharing it with anyone else. I pressed my lips against his cheeks, while raking my fingers through his soft hair. "Thank you so, so much."

I saw his dreamy eyes flutter to a close while I scratched at his scalp, and then kissed his thick eyebrows and nose. "Kat," he murmured.

I thought my heart was going to explode into a million pieces while I absorbed his actions and his perfect face. I almost couldn't believe that this was real life. He smiled with his eyes closed, shifting his arm to slide underneath my ass while the other wrapped in a slant across my back to grip my shoulder. My chest was pressed against his in this new position and I sucked in another breath. I closed my eyes and pressed my forehead against his smooth one.

Was this real?

This had to be. It just had to.

Warm lips pressed against my top and then my bottom lip, sucking each gently. His hot breath washed over my face, and my chest ached again. "I'm glad you liked them," he said just as quietly as I did before.

"Thank you, Mag," I said, opening up my eyes to look into his. The corners of them were crinkled with his smile that made my heart clench. "I love them."

After he left, I stayed in my classroom hanging up my new posters and thinking about Tristan more than I had ever done before— and that was saying something considering I thought about him pretty much all day. It seemed like every other thought in my head revolved around him, but there was something after this last short and sweet visit that made these thoughts different. I felt different. Better. There were some teachers here who had gotten flowers from their boyfriends or husbands, some even got balloons, but there was something about the thought he put into specially ordering me things to decorate my classroom that seemed so much better than that.

I had never felt this way with anyone else in my life before. I knew that. I knew I loved hanging out with him. I knew I loved it when he teased me. I knew I loved his mouth. I loved his kind heart.

I thought, and then I thought some more.

CHAPTER FIFTY-THREE

That night, I went over to his house for dinner. I'd tried to figure out why the intensity between us felt so altered all of a sudden. We had only technically been together for three weeks, but we'd been friends for a multiplied version of that time. I'd cared for him for months, even before he was really my friend. I mean, who else would go and take care of a sick person they barely knew? I liked him as a person and for his hot-ass body from the moment I met him. Besides Nicole and Zoey, who I had clung to like a trapped insect on a spider's web, there had never been anyone I'd taken to so easily, and yet, he and what we had was completely different.

"This is so good, Mag," I moaned, slurping my noodles. "I think I love your mom."

He nodded, shoveling another forkful of fettucine into his mouth. "I need to take you over to see them," he garbled.

I couldn't help but smile at the idea that he wanted me to go meet his beloved mother. It would be a lie if I said I didn't like knowing how much he valued the relationship he had with his parents, but especially with his mom. Maybe it was because I lost my mom so young, but knowing that he was close to his made me more grateful for the time I'd gotten to spend with mine. I couldn't help but appreciate my dad that much more. "I'd like that," I told him.

His smile was cheeky and sweet. "She's been harassing me for the last week to bring you over. If I don't do it soon, she's going to show up here randomly."

Polishing off the last portion of my food, I wiped my mouth and watched Tristan eat as non-creepily as I could.

He slapped his palm across the countertop unexpectedly like he remembered something important all of a sudden. "Goldie, I want to see the pictures from Universal Studios," he said with a mouthful of fettucine alfredo. He'd already reminded me about wanting to see the pictures at least three other times, but I kept forgetting to bring my computer over.

I nodded at him and hopped off the stool. "I brought my laptop. Let me go grab it," I said, walking into the living room to grab my computer from its spot on his coffee table and nudging a passed-out Yoda with my foot.

Tristan was putting our plates into the sink when I came back in and set the computer on the kitchen island before unlocking it and then opening up my iPhoto. He came and sat down on the stool next to mine. Instead of scooting his seat closer to mine, he grabbed the sides of my stool and started pulling it closer to him before I slapped him on the chest with the back of my hand and stood up.

"I'll wash the dishes while you look at them," I said with my back to him. "I've already seen them."

"Deal." He shrugged. Tristan tilted the screen in his direction to start clicking through the twenty or so pictures we'd taken with my digital camera. I'd completely forgotten that I brought it with me on the trip until the last day, like a moron.

I'd just started scrubbing the large pot when I heard him laugh. I turned to look at him over my shoulder and found him smiling at the screen. "What?"

"You looked like such a hobo in my shirt," he answered, smiling at the screen while his fingers kept clicking through pictures. "Like a cute, little hobo."

I snorted as unladylike as possible and turned back. "Whatever."

I heard him chuckle a few more times in the next few minutes, but it was when a few minutes turned into even more minutes that I glanced over my shoulder again to see him staring at the screen intently.

Then I heard it.

I heard a moan that I hadn't heard in years. Four and a half years to be exact.

The plate I'd been washing slipped from my hands and clattered into the ceramic sink, my guts felt the world tilt on its axis.

It felt like time slowed down considerably as I turned around completely to look at him, every muscle in my body tensing up and freezing. His eyes were locked on the screen and his jaw was loose.

"Tristan," I called out to him as I slapped my hands onto my jeans to rub off the soap, not even bothering to rinse them off.

I was going to puke. Oh, my God. I was going to puke or pass out, and then, hopefully, I would have amnesia and not remember that this happened.

His eyes darted to mine as another low and completely overdone moan filtered through the speakers of my computer. "Is that you?" His voice was low and raspy, flicking his eyes back and forth from me to the screen.

I gulped and walked over to stand behind him, hating myself for keeping that stupid video on my computer. Why the hell didn't I ever delete it? My neck ached with the pressure of my tensing.

"Yes," I squeaked out, looking at a topless, younger version of myself on the computer. Zoey's own topless form scooted on her knees over her old bed, back when she lived in her tiny studio apartment. It all seemed so surreal watching hands in long and short hair, mouth on mouth, stroking hands against exposed chests. It lasted all of five minutes, but it seemed like it was half my life played out before my eyes.

I found my mouth opening on its own volition as soon as the video ended abruptly. Tristan was looking down at the keyboard with his eyes clenched and his hand gripping his thigh. "I thought you said you never did porn," he whispered.

"I didn't. I mean, I haven't." I heard the trembling, uneven tone of my voice. It was the same sound I made before I cried. "I told you Zo wanted to get into the industry. She tried going to some of those screenings that they have for new women, but no one ever called her back," I started to explain. "So, she thought that doing a homemade video and sending it to different places would work better. She didn't have a boyfriend, and I mean Zoey wasn't going to have sex with a random stranger back then. She even asked Josh if he could do her a favor, and they kind of tried," I had to giggle a little at the memory of Josh and Zoey trying to kiss. It was probably the most visually awkward experience of my life. I'd laughed my ass off watching them fumble through just putting their lips together.

"It didn't work out, obviously. So, then she asked Nikki to do it, and she refused to because she was already in law school at the time." *Don't throw up.* "Nik has this birthmark on her shoulder blade that everyone can recognize, so it wouldn't have worked, you know. She wasn't brave enough to risk it. Zoey asked me if I could do it for her." My throat felt so dry, I had to swallow. Tristan was still looking down, but his free hand was now pulling at his hair. "I love Zoey, and I knew how badly she wanted it. I couldn't tell her no. I didn't want to do it. I *really* didn't want to do it, but I love her. How could I tell her no?" I rambled. "I couldn't. She'd do anything for me, and I'd do anything for her."

My eyes stayed on his frozen frame. I knew I didn't do anything wrong and that he had no right to be upset if he was, but still. "It was so fucking weird and, luckily, neither one of us wanted to ruin our friendship by doing anything too uncomfortable so we agreed just to keep our underwear on and our hands above our waists. It took a couple of weeks afterward for us to get back to normal, but Zo got what she wanted, so I can't regret it, Mag. I'd give you my left lung if you needed it," I added, hoping to let him know that he was just as special to me as Zoey was.

My mouth kept spewing out words on its own. "It isn't on the internet or anything. Only the people she sent it to have seen it and—"

Two hands were on my waist, tugging me forward to press me against his solid chest. He was clinging to me, pressing his mouth against mine so forcefully I thought my lips would bruise. When his tongue delved into my mouth and kissed me with more passion than I'd encountered in my life, I wrapped my arms around his neck. Kissing him and kissing him more, my mouth slanted so I could suck the tip of his tongue. Tristan was breathing hard through his nose, wrapping his arms so tightly around me that there wasn't an inch of space between our chests.

He tore his mouth away and gasped as his eyes locked on mine. I couldn't help but pant as I tried to understand the look he was giving me. I'd thought when he saw the video that maybe he was upset or had gotten all possessive over me, but this look was different. Completely different. It made my heart tighten fiercely just like it had earlier. His hands shook on my skin. "Kat," he murmured, inches from my lips. "You are the sweetest, kindest, and most selfless person I've ever met. You know how many people in the world would do that for someone? Not. Enough."

His hand grazed up my spine to land on the back of my neck, pressing the pads of his fingers into my skin. His face leaned into mine, his forehead pressed against my own, and his hot, panting breath scorched the surface of my lips. His free hand went to grab mine and placed it over the left side of his chest, right over his heart. "Goldie, I love you," he breathed, kissing my cheek softly.

His words, his hand on me, and his breath over my mouth ingrained themselves into my memory at that point forever. That moment exploded within me, and I knew I stopped breathing, thinking I could stop what just happened and relive it over and over again. Tristan loved me? I couldn't, Jesus, I couldn't think of anything.

He stroked my cheek with his fingertips, talking to me with his lips just an inch away from mine. "I love you," he repeated in a low voice. "So much."

I wasn't sure what exactly happened in the seconds after that, but it was almost like I unleashed some kind of beast that lay dormant within me. His words and his love ignited me from the inside out, and my mouth, my hands, and my legs were wrapped up in him. It was gentle but crazed as I leaned into him, sucking his bottom lip between my own as I touched him everywhere I could reach over his shirt. Tristan loved me. I thought angels were singing in heaven for me, sensing the deep emotions that ran through me at the knowledge. I could feel him hardening as I shifted closer to him, taking as much of his mouth and tongue as possible.

I whimpered his name against his ear when his lips made a slippery slope to suck on my neck. *Oh, fuck me.* I loved that. "Please."

He nodded against my throat, knowing better than I did what I was asking from him. His hands slid down my back and toward my thighs, pulling them closed around his hips so I could wrap my legs around him, before he grabbed my ass in two handfuls and pulled me even tighter against him. He stood and walk through his house while I pressed my closed mouth into the slight stubble that covered his neck and cheeks, kissing and licking his jaw like it was going to be the last time I ever got to touch it.

Tristan loved me, and that knowledge was amazing.

"Fuck, Kat," he moaned, stopping for a moment to capture my mouth in his before he pulled away. His breathing got a little uneven as he walked us upstairs and finally into his bedroom.

The bed pressed against my back when he leaned forward and dropped me onto it. He unbuttoned and peeled off my jeans slowly. I eyed his face the entire time, taking in how calm he looked in comparison to the way I felt. I thought I was going to combust as his hands pulled off my socks and then trailed up the backs of my calves and legs at a snail's pace. His eyes were looking at the path he made, only stopping at the plain cotton underwear I'd worn that day. He looked up at me then and smiled. "You're absolutely perfect."

Long minutes passed as he took his time unbuttoning my shirt and slipping it off my shoulders, then pulling my underwear down my legs, kissing and nipping at my thighs while he did it before finally ending when he unhooked my bra with shaky fingers and nuzzled my chest. I wanted to take off his clothes like he had done to me, but he was off the bed and standing at the foot while he pulled off his shirt, and then unzipped his pants, pulling them down along with his boxer briefs.

I forgot to breathe when I saw him standing there

completely naked and bobbing in the air. This man just told me he loved me. How was it possible? I took in every muscle on his body, finely cut and defined in the darkened room, and I took a deep breath, reminding myself that the last thing I needed was to pass out. He stood there watching me for the longest moment of my life, and I caught his tongue sweeping out of his mouth to lick his bottom lip before he put one knee on the bed and then another.

Hands squeezed my shins, knees, hips, and then rested on the edges of my ribs to graze the outer mounds of my breasts. He was silent as he laid his body over mine, holding himself up on one forearm while his other hand circled each of my breasts before heading down to the juncture of my legs. Tristan kissed me slowly before returning my same whimper when his middle and ring finger brushed over my lower lips. Before I could even think about his fingers grazing me, they were plunging, stroking me and seeing for themselves just how excited I was.

"Fuck..." I moaned, moving my mouth to the side of his when he curled his fingers.

Then, he was out, making a quick circle-shaped tour of where I throbbed and sucking my nipple into his hot mouth. "Can I have you?" he asked against the skin of my breast, green eyes up and alert.

"Always," I stuttered, not even thinking about what I was saying. I felt him start to lift himself off me, knowing he was going for a condom in his dresser. I grabbed his wrist and pulled him to me. He knew I was on birth control after having seen me take it in the mornings, and I knew he'd never had sex with anyone without protection before. Any logical thinking woman would have let him grab the condom and slip it on, but I didn't want that with him. I'd made such a stink in my head about wanting to be different for him, and I knew I could do my share and make it different for him, too.

Tristan knew what I was trying to tell him by stopping him from getting off the bed and going for his stash because he smiled and nodded, stretching his long body out over mine. I could feel his well-endowed organ slide between my legs, the shaft grazing my skin when he thrust, as his hands caressed me, and his lips sucked and licked my breasts. My hands went into his hair and my hips bucked up, enjoying the feel of him pressing against me with each slippery stroke between my thighs.

With a shift of his hips, his hands grabbed mine from their spot on the back of his head and settled them on the mattress above me, as he slowly eased his way into me, entwining our fingers together. I arched my back, trying to get used to the feel of him filling me inch by inch.

"Goddammit," he groaned, tilting his hips forward a bit more so that he sheathed himself inside of me completely. I gasped, partly because he was big and partly because I couldn't believe he fit. "Oh, my fucking lord," he grunted, squeezing each of my hands. "You feel so good, baby."

Holy shit, I'd never been happier I wasn't a guy, because I probably would have blown my load in response to his groans and words if I had a dick.

I'm not sure how long he stayed completely still inside of me before he started thrusting, shallow, slow strokes. He cursed things I didn't understand between pressing his mouth against mine. I wrapped my legs around his waist, digging my heels into the muscle right below his ass, which let him sink even deeper in me. All I could think about was the way his hips felt against me, the way his mouth kissed me just right, the way his fingers clenched around mine when he kept our hands above my head even when he started speeding up his strokes and making them so much fucking deeper.

"Oh... my... shit... *shit...*" I started moaning when he pulled himself up to his knees and started pushing in and out of me steadily, my hips meeting his each time. My skin started to pearl over with sweat as I tried to keep up with his thrusts and tried not to solely think about how fucking good it felt each time his thick tip brushed and pressed into a spot in me that made my toes curl.

I'd thought I'd had good sex in the past, but this couldn't compare to anything before. It wasn't one thing or another that made me feel amazing; it wasn't just his erection that stretched me, it wasn't the way his sweaty body slid against me, or the way his mouth worked mine sweetly and then more erotically than anything. I could feel it in my bones how different this was with him because of him.

Hips became frantic, hands squeezed each other's in time, and I felt that sweet ache right in me when he started grinding down on me with each upward stroke. My legs tightened around him, and even though my shoulders were sore from my hand position over my head for so long, I tensed up, gasping and whimpering. "Tristan... oh!"

He was watching me, rubbing me with the short, coarse hair that covered the base of him on each stroke. Then, I just burst, covering a scream of "Tristan!" by pressing my mouth against his shoulder, clenching through the most amazing orgasm of all orgasms.

He grunted as I came, thrusting into me hard and deep a couple more times before tensing up from his neck through his thighs. Tristan trembled, covering my cheek with his clenched teeth as he came, spilling in me, saying something I couldn't begin to understand. His thighs twitched against mine as he shifted himself to lay his cheek on my chest. With one leg between mine, he dragged the comforter that had ended up hanging off the edge of the bed and pulled it over us. We lay there, catching our breath, and I stroked his damp back from shoulder blade to right above his perfect ass.

"That was..." I let out a huge exhale because no word seemed to be fitting for a description. "Amazing?"

I felt his chest shake on top of mine as he

chuckled. "Really, really amazing." Warm lips pressed against my chest. "I didn't know it could be like that," he said softly.

That same pressure in my chest from earlier made my heart feel huge. "Me either."

I wasn't sure when we fell asleep in a mess of sweaty, warm, and heavy bodies, but we did. I woke up some time later out of the blue to find that I was still on my back with Tristan's arm and leg thrown over me. I looked at the side of his face, noticing how much more beautiful and handsome he was in his sleep. He was perfect. His full lips, his face, but it was more than that. He was the sweetest person I'd ever met when he wasn't being a jackass, but if I was honest with myself, I liked it when he was a teasing jackass. A lot.

No one I'd ever met made me feel a fraction of what he did. No one. I doubted I'd ever meet anyone who could even be half the man and friend he was to me.

Then it hit me. The thing I felt in me, that tightening sensation wasn't pain. I loved this dork. This man who loved his dog, his mom, and me.

We were so caught up in each other after he told me that he loved me that I didn't say anything back, and I felt like a complete bitch.

So, I shook his arm, hard. He grumbled over me, blinking slowly and opening and closing his mouth like a goldfish. Those sleepy, green eyes made their way to my face. "What's wrong?" he mumbled.

Maybe it was a little dramatic, but maybe it wasn't, because now I was bursting with this feeling in my body that I couldn't completely understand, but I recognized. All those tears I'd shed while he was gone filming, and that guilt I felt the two times when I went out with other men— it was all for the same reason. I'd been in love with him. I *was* in love with him. I pressed the tip of my index finger against his nose and leaned my head toward his. "I've loved you way longer than you've loved me."

CHAPTER FIFTY-FOUR

Good luck and I have never been on the same page. Most of the time, I didn't even think we were in the same book.

I kept expecting the other shoe to drop, or whatever the saying was, and that something terrible would happen that broke me out of the state that I was in. Emotionally, I was in absolute happiness or what I would consider to be Hawaii. Easygoing, carefree joy.

So, when my period started the day after Tristan found out about the video with Zoey, and then told me he loved me— I wasn't surprised. I braced myself for worse, like my apartment burning down, cracking a tooth, or getting a yeast infection. Any of those would have been more along the lines of what I would have expected. I may have screamed in frustration, because I was so fucking ready to pull down his boxer briefs the first chance I got, but oh, well. We'd only gotten a few minutes together before I was leaving his house and trying to make it back home to grab clothes and make it to work in time.

After work, I met up with Zoey at the yoga studio we frequented. Since I had to go back to the real world and start working again, we'd gone to our fall and spring routine, which consisted of a nighttime hot yoga class and dinner afterward once a week. As soon as she spotted me walking into the studio, she screeched.

"You slut! You did it!" she announced to a, thankfully, empty yoga studio.

I looked down, trying to see what in the hell could have given away the fact that I'd slept with Tristan the night before, but I didn't think my bloated stomach would have been a giveaway. Frowning, I put my index finger to my lips to get her to be quiet. "Tell the whole world, Zo," I hissed, rolling my eyes.

She did this thing that looked like a bunny hop, bouncing forward off two feet twice. "Oh. Mah. Gawd," she squealed. Her small hands went up to cup my face and pinch my cheeks. "You're walking funny," she giggled.

"I'm walking funny because I'm on my period, and I'm cramping, damn it," I muttered.

"Or because an extra-large sausage stuffed your bun last night," the little bitch howled.

I threw a hand over my face before dropping my

bag and mat onto the floor. "Oh, Jesus Christ, keep it down. My dad is going to freaking hear you."

Zoey laughed even louder, enjoying my embarrassment a little too much. I had to blame it on her hanging out with Nicole more often without me. "How was it?" she asked.

Pulling away from her, I set my yoga mat and bottles of water down alongside hers and huffed. "None of your business," I teased. She knew damn well I would end up telling her something. Only seconds later, from my spot bent over, I looked up at her excited almond shaped eyes and couldn't help but waggle my eyebrows suggestively. "Fucking awesome."

"Oh, mah gawd. Oh, mah gawd," she panted, plopping onto her ass. Zoey rolled onto her back and kicked her feet in the air, reminding me of Yoda when he lay in the same position. "That is like, the sickest thing I've heard all month."

I flinched at her words. I think even my colon flinched. Then, I burst out laughing. Did she just....? "Zo, please, please, please, I'm begging you, please don't ever use 'sickest' again. Ever."

"I thought it was making a comeback," she explained, frowning.

I snorted and pinched my nose to keep from doing it again. "No, it's not. Maybe if you did wakeboarding or— never mind. Please, just don't do it."

She let out a frustrated sigh before pulling her

legs close to her chest. "Fine," she consented like a small, chastised child would. Only she was my small, sweet Zoey.

"He saw the video," I whispered into her ear, trying to distract her from her mopey face.

She sat up faster than lightning, straightening her back. "No way," she hissed, eyeing the women who were filtering into the room.

Zoey had always known how apprehensive I was about the video, before and especially after it was done. Although the people she sent it to had no legal right to post it without her consent, there had always been a worry in the back of my brain that someday some asshole would try. Luckily, no one had up until then. Years later, we'd talked about whether or not I would ever tell someone I was in a relationship with about what we'd done, but I never planned on it. Until Tristan. Only Tristan, if anyone, would understand why I did it. Either way, that wasn't public knowledge I'd pass on to any man entering my life. I knew people were vengeful, and there was no way in hell I'd risk some pissed off boyfriend sending the video to my dad.

"Yes, way," I told her, sitting down onto my own mat.

"What did he say?" It made me laugh that Zoey tried to whisper, but really just managed to lower the pitch of her voice.

I shrugged and pulled my feet together to stretch. For a split second I debated whether or not to tell her the three best words I'd ever heard from his mouth, but I couldn't keep that from her. I had a feeling she'd been praying for me at night, or at least crossing her fingers frequently. "He told me he loved me," I said in the quietest voice I could manage.

Zoey opened up her mouth wide, and then slapped her palm over it. Whether she was screaming or squealing, I don't know, but her face turned bright pink. She got up onto her knees and threw herself against me, tackling me onto the floor. "Kat," she whispered into my ear. "That's amazing." Kissing my hair before scampering off, she added, "You deserve all the happiness in the world."

"Thanks, Zo," I said with a smile. She really was the best girl in the world.

The teacher came in a moment later, setting up her mat as close as she could in front of the mirrors, talking in hushed tones. At some point, while we were in downward dog, I heard Zoey making a low whistling noise from next to me. Turning my head slightly, I saw her bright eyes on mine.

She whispered to me, "We need to do this more often."

I mouthed back a "Why?" It was bad enough I came once or twice a week with her.

Zoey winked at me before rolling her body into upward dog. "The camera adds ten pounds." I must have given her a quizzical look because she shook her head. "For Porn Wives."

Oh, lord.

CHAPTER FIFTY-FIVE

"What do you want for your birthday?" Tristan's warm breath washed over the cartilage of my ear.

We sat on the couch next to each other with his arm looped over my shoulders, fingers tracing the valley of my collarbone. My eyes narrowed on their own while I tried to figure out if this was a trick or not. "You already got me a birthday present," I reminded him.

While some people may not like to celebrate their birthdays, I was not one of them. I liked my birthday. I like birthday cake and balloons, and doing whatever the hell I wanted because it was my day. Only this year, like last, I had to work on it. It could have been worse though. I reminded myself that it was early enough in the school year to where my students still didn't know me well and, therefore, wouldn't give me much hell. Yet.

His straight nose wrinkled as he made a face. "That wasn't your birthday present."

"Uh, you told me taking me with you to California was my birthday present."

"That was my grandma's birthday present to you," he clarified with a roll of green eyes. "I used her money. It doesn't count."

There were two things wrong with what he was telling me. I had never met either of his grandmas, which would merit a present, and I never would. I could remember him explaining to me that one of them left him some money in her will. By some money, I meant a lot of money. It was the same money he used to buy his house and car. The lucky asshole. The only thing I got from my grandma when she died was a collection of creepy dolls. "That does too count."

"Kat," he muttered in a low tone. "Just tell me what you want."

I couldn't help but sigh, thinking. I knew how stubborn he was, and I knew he wouldn't let it go, so I thought more. Then it hit me. Sliding my hand over my lap and then slowly letting it glide to where I could grip the thick muscle in his thigh, I squeezed. "I know what I want."

The perfect profile of his face was visible when he stiffened, staring forward. "What is it?"

"You," I said with a squeeze. "In." Another squeeze accompanied my words and I heard him suck in a breath, waiting for me to finish. For me to tell him what he wanted to hear. "An apron. I want you to make me a cupcake."

A loud whoosh expelled from his lungs, followed by glaring in my direction. "You're cruel, and that's not something I can buy you."

I tried to give him the most innocent smile in the world, but it probably came out looking like I was constipated. "I don't know what you're talking about, and you never said I needed to tell you what to buy me."

He seemed to think about what I said for a minute too long, and I had to wonder what was going through his pretty head. "I'm not good with my hands—" he started to say before the noise that erupted out of my throat stopped him.

"Liar," I choked out, remembering the night he woke me up in Los Angeles with those hands. "You are good with your hands."

Tristan threw his head back and laughed, snorting at the end, and it made my heart clench a little. "You're right, I am good with my hands."

"Asshole," I muttered, elbowing him in the ribs. I pretty much asked for that answer, but still. We both knew *how* he was so good with his hands. "Prick."

"Aww, Kat," he groaned, realizing he'd aggravated me. "I just meant that I'm not good at building stuff. I'm not creative at all."

I started to nod before he was even done with his sentence. As soon as he said he wasn't good at building things, I had to agree. We tried to put together an elevated feeder for Yoda and that didn't work out so well. The glare he gave me in response to my acknowledgement of his weakness only made me laugh. "What? It's true!"

"I could build something if I wanted to," he said indignantly, tightening the hold around my shoulders.

"You're right, you can," I agreed with him, trying my best to keep a straight face. "I'll buy you some Legos or Building Blocks for you to get started."

His face was a mask of cool and collected as he eyed my face blankly. But I knew him, I could see there was something building under his eyes, something close to amusement and teasing. It felt like minutes of silence passed between our words. "You need me to go get your emergency panties from your car again?"

CHAPTER FIFTY-SIX

As my wonderful luck would also have it, my cycle lasted three days longer than it should have. I wanted to send Mother Nature a big two-finger salute in thanks for being a cock-blocker.

The week leading up to my birthday was spent doing lesson plans on the couch with Tristan, while trying to forget that I'd seen the beast in his pants, and trying to avoid reminding myself that I was turning twenty-six. I could remember being twelve and thinking that eighteen was practically half a century away. Once I finally turned eighteen, I thought it would take forever to turn twenty-one. Somehow, right after I turned eighteen the next seven years went by in a blur. It was exciting, but scary because I wondered how fast the next twenty-five years of my life would pass.

There was also something about twenty-six

getting closer and closer to thirty that made me think of my mom much more often than I was accustomed to. It didn't help that I was on my period because everything reminded me of her and practically screamed out that I was right around the corner in my own life from when she'd lost hers.

Could I imagine dying just a few short years from now? No, I couldn't. I had to remind myself each time my thoughts would go in that stray vector that I could easily die today, or tomorrow, six months from now, eight years from now, or hell, seventy years from now. I knew my mom wouldn't have wanted me to live my life counting down to my death. I knew I wouldn't want anyone I loved to live life expecting to die.

If anything, all the time I spend with Tristan made life feel a little more precious to me. Life was short.

With that in mind, I was in a great mood when Nicole called at four-thirty in the morning to wish me a happy birthday. Under normal circumstances, I probably would have called her a slut-ass-whore or something along those lines, but I didn't. The rest of my early morning was spent answering calls like Josh's, his being a rendition of *feliz cumpleaños* in an atrocious Spanish accent. Tristan called me at some point between Josh and Zoey's calls to wish me a happy birthday and assure me we'd see each other after work. I spent my day wishing the school day would go by a little faster so I could get out of there to make it home and celebrate my one special day of the year. I'd made plans to go have dinner with Tristan and my dad, then bowling with my bitches.

Dad. Tristan. Dinner. Together. Shoot me now.

It wasn't that I thought my dad was going to threaten Tristan or anything, but because I knew my dad was going to tease the hell out of me. I'd only brought one of my boyfriends around him in my life and that was The Virgin, or as my dad started calling him in the months after we broke up— the Virgin Mary. Needless to say, my dad knew the moment I opened up my mouth that I was his daughter without a doubt. He'd told me once, after I had backed into his work truck for the second time within a month, that the "dumbass gene" ran rampant in the Berger family. Nicole claimed his statement explained a lot.

I was dressed and ready for Mag when he called to tell me he was pulling into my apartment complex. Jogging down the stairs as quickly as I could in heels, I found the long, lean frame of a man stepping out of his car by the time I hit the landing.

Jesus Christ. He was wearing a suit for once, a dark gray ensemble that looked tailored to fit his wide shoulders, full arms, slim hips, and muscular thighs. How the hell did he go through the day without getting slipped a Rohypnol by every woman he came in contact with?

He was looking down, his hands shoved deep into the pockets of his charcoal slacks while he walked toward me. At the sounds of my heels clicking against the pavement, his eyes came up and widened. He stopped. Tristan turned to look behind him, back at me, behind him again, and then back at me. He brought the heels of his hands up to cover both of his eyes, groaning. "Am I dreaming?"

"What?" I asked him, stopping just a few feet away from where he stood.

"Is this a dream?"

I couldn't help but snort, tucking my clutch between my arm and ribs. He looked so cute standing there, lips pursed, hands over his eyes like a little kid. "No. Why?"

His fingers moved, twisting in the air while he ground his palms into his eye sockets. "You're wearing that goddamn dress. This has to be a nightmare," he muttered more to himself. "A fucking nightmare."

Instinctively, my hands went to tug at the hem of what I was wearing. It was the same blue dress I'd tried on in front of him a month before for the wedding, the same one he'd told me was too short. "I thought I looked nice..." I trailed off, trying to keep my voice steady. I swear, if he told me I looked bad, I'd nut-punch him.

He chuckled, a deep, throaty, cynical sounding thing while dropping his hands from his face. His eyes opened slowly. "Kat, Kat, Kat," my name was hissed from lips like a snake's prayer. "What am I going to do with you?" he asked with a shake of his head. Large hands reached out to grip my waist, bringing me close to his warm body. He leaned down before brushing his bottom lip against the cartilage of my ear. "You're my control's worst goddamn nightmare. How do you expect me to survive the night seeing you in this?"

Oh. My. Shit.

I felt his hands drift down my sides, over my hips, and to the bottom of my dress. Cool fingertips danced underneath the fabric, stroking my thighs, and I was really fucking glad I'd shaved before dressing. "I thought I was going to burn in hell when you tried this on for the wedding," he admitted. His fingers grazed the backs of my thighs before pressing into my flesh. I couldn't help but remember the way he'd looked at me when I'd put it on, the way his hands hovered over me, and his heavy-lidded eyes.

"Does that mean you like it?" I asked stupidly, absorbing the heat from his body.

"Do I like it?" he snickered quietly to himself. Green eyes peered down at mine mischievously. Tristan chuckled again, raking his fingernails gently over the top of my thighs. "I like it enough not to care whether you're still on your period or not."

CHAPTER FIFTY-SEVEN

It all started with Facebook.

There were plenty of things I could blame Facebook for. One would be the spreading of 'planking.' The second would be that it gave me a reason to dislike pretty much every person on my friends list. The third would be the outing of Josh's sexual preferences; he decided to post it in his profile instead of calling his family to let them know he was — literally —*pitching* for the other team. For a second, I thought I would also be able to blame it for a possible heart attack.

What started off as a good first dinner with my dad and Tristan spiraled into a mess of nerves in a matter of seconds. The first minutes of dinner were tense, as Frank Berger spared no expense in sizing up my companion, my friend, my Tristan. His dark eyes had been dancing back and forth between the arm

Tristan had thrown over me and the long fingers that were caressing my upper arm. I felt more like a teenager than an independent adult with the way my dad was looking. I sipped my glass of water, waiting for him to say something. Anything. It wasn't until Tristan got up to go to the bathroom that he finally leaned forward.

"So, Kitty, when did you and the movie star start dating?" my dad asked casually.

My nose became a fucking fountain. The water that had been going down the back of my throat made a detour to shoot out of my nostrils, leaving a burning pain at the bridge.

What. The. Fuck!

I coughed and gasped, passing the water from my system while he chuckled. "You hiding a squirt gun in your nose?" he teased me with a grin.

Pinching my nostrils together, I coughed a couple of times and glared at the man sitting across the table. It felt like my heart was going to burst out of my chest. "He's not a movie star, Dad. Why would you think that?"

"I checked his Facebook page," he explained with a shrug of his shoulders. The expression on his face reminded me of Nicole's when she thought I said something stupid.

"Why are you stalking his page?" I asked, looking in the direction of the door that led to the bathrooms to make sure Tristan wasn't walking back.

"A person's profile says a lot about them," I swear

to God he rolled his eyes at me. My forty-five-year-old father rolled his eyes at me. "I just needed to make sure you weren't dating some eyeliner-wearing drill bit, Kitty."

My brain only locked onto one thing he said. "What the heck is a drill bit?"

His hairy upper lip twitched in confusion at the same time one of his thick, dark eyebrows arched. "Isn't that the saying nowadays?"

I frowned, trying to figure out what in the world he was talking about before I realized it and laughed out loud. "You mean a tool?"

Frank slapped the table, making his silverware shake. "That's it! A tool! I just wanted to make sure my baby wasn't dating a tool. You see, my friend's daughter was dating a guy who wears eyeliner and thinks that tank tops are appropriate everyday clothing, and there is no way in hell my girl is going to get knocked up by that kind of *tool*." He had the nerve to wink at the correct use of his last word.

"Oh, my God, Dad." I wanted to die of shame. Die. Dissolve. Explode. Whatever.

He snickered with wide, dark eyes. "What? It's true!" The deja vu when he happened to repeat things that I was prone to saying was almost too much. Jesus, I really was my father's daughter. I might as well accept the fact that I'd grow up to be a male version of Frank Berger with boobs, embarrassing my kids every chance I got. "His friend is always 'checking him in' in Los Angeles, so I searched his name, but nothing came up. I was just curious."

My stomach dropped at how close he came to figuring out that something was going on. I'd call him nosey, but I was pretty positive I'd done the same thing when Nikki had dated her last boyfriend. "I'm pretty sure stalking is against the law." I could see the mess of reddish-brown hair appear by the restroom doors, getting closer and closer by the second. "He's a law student, *One Hour Photo*. He isn't in any movies."

My dad winced at the mention. He'd made me sit through the movie with him years back and had been terrified to take his pictures to get developed since then. The chances of some employee becoming obsessed with him through his fishing pictures seemed pretty slim, but whatever. "He's a good-looking guy, don't blame me for assuming he was an actor."

"Who's a good-looking guy?" Tristan's deep voice asked as he pulled his chair out to sit down.

"You are." I laughed when my dad made a face at my answer.

Tristan's cheekbones went pink and he smiled, looking at the man sitting across from me. "Thank you." He hesitated for a split second. "Your beard is... nice."

Then it was my dad's turn to get a little red in the face. "Thank you?" he said, making it sound more like a question than a comment. "Your hair is nice?"

A hand went up to tug at auburn-colored hair instinctively. "Thanks, uh, I like your jacket," Tristan responded.

"Thank you?"

Silence.

My dad was looking up at the ceiling while Tristan inspected the clean, white tablecloth. *Well, this is awkward.* "Should I get you two a room together or something?"

Brown and green eyes snapped to meet mine, both in what I would like to consider a mix of amusement and annoyance. "No," they barked out simultaneously.

"I mean, I can leave if you two want some alone time," I snorted out before the feel of a warm palm cupping the inside of my leg stopped me cold.

My dad smirked, not noticing the movement of Tristan's hand and shook his head. "I swear, I think your mom dropped you as a child. Repeatedly, more than likely. It would make a lot of sense."

"I'm going with repeatedly," Tristan, the traitor, chipped in. "Your skull took most of the impact, I'd say."

Frank nodded in agreement. "Definitely."

I had a feeling I wasn't exactly going to like where this bromance was going.

CHAPTER FIFTY-EIGHT

"Your ass is getting old, Booger," Josh cackled from his spot next to me while we waited for Zoey to bowl her frame. We had finished our game and were now patiently waiting for everyone else.

Nikki popped her big sandy-colored head between the two of us, using her Goliath-like stature to throw an arm over Josh's shoulder and smirk in my direction. "Yeah, bitch, I'm going to start buying you stock in Depends."

"You two," I said with a mouthful of popcorn Tristan bought while we waited for our lane to open up, "are older than I am, so shut the hell up."

Nicole, being the absolute lady that she was, shot me the finger without any pretense of trying to be discreet despite the families in lanes close by. "Call me old, and I'm going to start giving you birthday licks again," she threatened me with a wink.

My ass immediately clenched in fear, remembering the horror that was birthday licks courtesy of Nicole Jonasson. I think I would rather let Tristan meet my back entrance sans lube before I'd willingly let Nikki slap my ass. Okay, maybe not. "Please don't," I begged her shamelessly. I'd rather taint my honor than have my ass marred by her brutal, manly hands. Those hands had taken several Krav Maga classes and could beat my ass. They could probably actually beat just about anyone's ass, really.

The bitch giggled, slapping the top of my thigh lightly. "Just kidding, I'll spare you today since you chose me on your team. I didn't want to be paired up with the two worst bowlers in existence." She eyed the two ex-porn stars across the lane, who were busy talking to each other with really animated facial gestures as they pointed at the lane while also looking like complete goofballs.

Josh and I both nodded in agreement, because seriously, Calum and Tristan were awful. Those two deserved to have their own YouTube channel dedicated to their lack of skills. Two hot guys who sucked at bowling? Bowling, which required them to bend over? Hell. Yes. I think Josh enjoyed watching them more than Nikki and I did.

We'd been at the bowling alley for two hours by then. My dad had left the restaurant to head back to his hotel immediately after we'd eaten, so he could get a good night's rest before his drive the next day.

After Tristan and Frank's verbal make-out session, they'd banded together to make fun of me for the remainder of dinner. Honestly, I enjoyed them getting their bromance on even if I was the butt of the jokes. The last thing my dad said to Tristan before we got into the car to head to the bowling alley was, "What kind of shampoo do you use?" It was a freaking miracle I didn't pee on myself from how hard I laughed.

Minutes after we left, a deep frown creased Tristan's face while his eyes locked onto my bare thighs. "Wait a second, how are you going to bowl in that dress?"

I couldn't help but snort. "Zoey is bringing me leggings and socks, silly. You thought I was going to let everyone see my butt cheeks?"

"Maybe." He laughed, the same throaty way that made my heart flutter. His right hand inched across the middle console to grasp my knee gently. "I want to see your butt cheeks later," he warned.

A pinch to my bare arm brought me out of my Tristan-driven memory and made me focus on the gray eyes dancing in my line of vision. Zoey was smiling as sweat coated her forehead, talking so quietly only I could hear her over the blaring music. "Are you having a good birthday, K?"

"A great one," I told her honestly. Having dinner with two of the three men in my life that I cared for the most, and then just hanging out with my friends, was perfect.

"What did the wannabe *Big Lebowski* over there give you?" she giggled.

I looked over at Tristan, who was going up for his last turn. His nice, tight ass clenched beneath the charcoal color of his dress pants. "Nothing. Our trip was supposed to be my present, so I'm not really expecting anything." I kept my eyes locked on that big, round butt bending over to throw a ball right into the gutter.

Zoey snickered, flicking me right on the nipple through the thin material of my dress. "I bet you want that snausage wrapped in a pretty pink bow, eh?"

Yelping, I flicked her back where her own nub would be, knowing it was rare that she wore a bra to cover her tiny titties. Zoey winced before smacking my hand away from her.

"You little slut, that hurt." I laughed even though my poor nipple was throbbing.

Josh leaned into me, grinning. "Want me to do the other one? Even it up and all?"

"You guys should be rubbing my feet or something since it's my birthday, not flicking my nips." I covered my boobs with my hands so that neither one of them could get another flick in. I wouldn't hold it past them to do it.

"Oh, quit your crying. We already gave you your birthday presents, so just suck it up," Josh whined. They'd given me my gifts when we'd first started bowling by way of shoving boxes onto my lap. Zoey had bought me the new straightening iron I'd been eyeing for months. Nikki and Calum gave me two Andrew Wood DVDs, much to Tristan's groan of disapproval, before giving me new running shoes. And Josh bestowed upon me enough new underwear to save me from doing laundry for a month. Later on, the cheeky bastard had pulled me aside and said I was going to need cute underwear for "daily stuffings."

The screen above the lanes started blinking, signaling that our time was up. A collective groan worked its way throughout our small group; shoes were kicked off and purses were grabbed while we filed out. Tristan helped me grab my boxes and put them into his car to head back to his house while I got hugs and kisses from my three closest friends and Calum.

"Are you tired, Goldie?" his asked on the drive.

"Just a little bit."

He reached across the car to squeeze my thigh over the black leggings I had on. "We're almost home," he assured me.

What felt like seconds later, he was pulling into the garage, and then silently carrying my presents inside. I followed him in, making a beeline to let Yoda out of his crate so the big lug could go out to the backyard. "Come on, Yoda," I called out after a couple of minutes. I could see him smelling the poop he'd just taken in the corner of the yard.

"He can stay out there for a little while," hot

breath purred against my ear.

A shudder crawled up my spine, across my shoulders, and through my entire nervous system. Tristan's large palms rested on my shoulders then slid down my biceps. He tugged me backward into the house, kicking the door closed with the toe of his shoe before pulling my back tightly against his hard chest. Fingertips brushed my hair to the side as lips and warm kisses dotted the curve of my neck and shoulder.

Tristan brushed his mouth higher across my neck, light caresses against the column while his hands wrapped around my wrists. "Happy Birthday," he said into my skin.

I nodded slightly, not knowing how else to respond. It must have been enough of a response because his mouth started a downward trek across the muscle that led to the knot of blue cloth keeping my dress on. His tongue licked across the skin surrounding the material before he let go of one of my hands, bringing his free one up to pull the material to the side and over my shoulder, leaving me bare. His mouth continued its lazy mapping of my exposed flesh from shoulder to shoulder, his free hand holding my hip while the other hand stayed wrapped around my wrist.

"Come on," he murmured all husky and thick against my earlobe.

I couldn't think straight as I followed him up the stairs, holding onto him by hooking my index fingers into his belt loops. He knew I was off my period after I'd whispered it into his ear at the restaurant when my dad went to the restroom. His response had been to choke on his drink of water. The next thing I knew, we were in his bedroom, and he was pushing me onto the edge of the bed, kneeling right in front of me with a clenched jaw. His hands landed on my ankles, creating a path over my legging-covered calves, the bend in my knee, and then ending their journey by slipping into the confined space between my dress and thighs. Higher and higher he went until I felt his fingertips curl into the band while his mouth latched onto mine. The kiss was soft and sweet, a molding of his full lips individually sucking on each of mine.

This man lit me up from the inside out, scorching me with slow kisses on the corners of my mouth, burning something deeper into me than any tattoo ever could. He marked me with an open mouth, wet sucks against the column of my neck that made me whimper. Those long fingers started pulling at the band of my tights and underwear, urging me to lift my hips as he pulled them slowly down my legs, never breaking our mouths' contact.

Then, any control I had became nonexistent. Big hands wrapped around the angle of my knees to spread them before pulling me to teeter off the edge of the bed. His hot mouth nipped at my inner thighs, biting gently on a one-way course to the juncture of my thighs. I think Tristan moaned louder than I did when his hands tugged the hem of my dress up and over my ass so that the silky material bunched around my hips.

"Goddamnit, Kat," he groaned before pressing those sweet, plump lips and raspy, long tongue against the center of my body.

I think I might have sounded like a dog with rabies, planting my arms behind me to hold me up while I sat there on the edge of the mattress. One of my legs was thrown over his shoulder roughly, and the other was being held captive by a hand, keeping me spread wide. "Fuck," was the steady chant that slipped out of my mouth while his tongue lapped at me over and over again.

Second after second, he sucked and delved, pulling away for just a brief moment. "I could do this to you all day," he said against my thigh before biting it. "My sweet girl."

"Oh, my holy... mother..." Who the fuck says that? The beautiful man between my legs buried his mouth against me again, and the curses coming out of my mouth were anything but sweet. His nose brushed my sensitive flesh, his slight stubble scraping my skin in the most pleasant torture.

Tristan was just as persistent as I was turned on, coaxing me through my orgasm a second later with the flick of his tongue against my nerves. When he sat back on his heels, moisture tinting the corners of his mouth and chin, I lost it. I was off the bed and kneeling in front of him with my hands deep in his hair, kissing him like he was everything in life that mattered, tasting myself on him. I couldn't think then to analyze that notion because it wasn't worth any thought. He was everything to me, and I knew that on a molecular level. I craved him more than anything in the world, and it went deeper than his skin. It was his smile, his laugh, the stitching of his personality, and the fibers that made him up, that I loved.

His hands reached for my bare ass, cupping and kneading the flesh so erotically I thought I'd die, and I couldn't comprehend anything again. It was his mouth that pulled away first, but I couldn't think before he was dipping his head toward my chest and sucking on my hard nipple through the thin material covering it. "I've wanted to do that since the first time I saw you wearing it," he muttered before smothering the neglected peak with his hot mouth.

"I said to myself, 'Tristan, this is your friend,'" he continued. "'Your Kat with perfect, round tits, and hard nipples.'" He moved his mouth again, lapping at the wet material. "I almost touched you, you know that? But I thought it would ruin us."

Oh, my shit.

Heat spread across my shoulders and chest, listening to his low voice say those things to me. I remembered everything. His hands were up and just inches from me, teasing me with their movements, but he remained in control unfortunately. Letting out some kind of twisted moan, I arched my back to get him closer, almost like I was offering myself to him. "Nothing is ruined," I somehow managed to pant out.

The hands on my ass squeezed, pulling me flush against him, and then he was standing and bringing me along with him onto the bed. In a flash, my dress was up and over my head, tossed onto the floor in a mess of blue silk and wet stains. Tristan leaned over me with his mouth on my chest and hands stroking all the skin within reach.

I was coherent enough to start yanking his shirt out of his pants, undoing his belt, unzipping his slacks, and then finally shoving them down his hips along with his boxer briefs. I sensed him kicking them down his legs, but I was too busy trying to get his shirt unbuttoned, practically ripping it off his shoulders along with his undershirt. I touched the smooth expanse of his chest. Hard muscle quivered under my hands as I glided over the ridges of his abs and pecs, smoothing the coarse sprinkling of hairs under his belly button with my thumbs. It was impossible to miss the long, pink cock bobbing in the air begging for my attention.

"You're so pretty," I mumbled without thinking.

I heard him chuckle while he shifted on the bed, brushing his hands over my shoulders, and then down the side of my ribs to grip my hips. "You're the prettiest thing," he said directly into my ear.

Looking up, I saw that he was kneeling on the bed, legs spread wide and in a perfect ninety-degree angle. I couldn't think of anything as he pulled me to him, pressing my chest against his in a meeting of taut and soft. Tristan kissed me, slanting his mouth against mine, while that magical tongue now delved deep into me, searching for something. He loosened his grip and slid his hands down to cup the back of my thighs, and then I was up, hovering over the tip of his cock and balancing precariously in his grip while he sat back onto his calves.

Slowly, he lowered me onto him, until I stretched around his length and girth so he was fully sheathed in me. We both groaned, moaned, and I was pretty sure I whimpered out some kind of nonsense. Wrapping my legs around his waist, I couldn't help but take in the feeling of him deep in me, his chest pressed against mine, his hands strategically placed where my ass and thighs met. His face nuzzled my own. "I love you," he said in his rich voice.

"I love you, too," I said in a tone that was anything but even and calm.

I cherished the silence as he rolled his hips up and into me, holding me in his hands and using his strength to move my heat over his. There was something about this, something that was just as good, if not better than, the only other time he'd been in me. It sang through my veins, didn't let me think about how long this was going to last, or what I was going to do the next day, or even my own fucking name. All I was then was this. His.

Up and down, he thrust and stroked that thick,

long cock in me. I could feel every inch of him. He returned each of my moans, whispering things under his breath.

"The best," he bucked.

"So wet," he murmured, sucking on my neck.

"Amazing," his voice strained out.

It was slow and perfect when he started grinding his hips into me, rubbing me just the right way with the blunt tip of his cock and the rub of his skin on my wet and charged flesh. I came, moaning and crying out against his neck, my climax washing over me and him so tightly and intense that he grunted the entire time. He was covered in sweat, shaking in exhaustion from holding me up for so long.

Tristan wrapped an arm around the middle of my back and shifted his way closer to the massive headboard, still buried in me, laying me down so close to it that my hair brushed the wood. His hands were gone, gripping the top of the headboard with his immaculate upper body stretched above me. The slow strokes turned hard and fast, flicking into me with a roll so perfected that it almost made me think about things that I shouldn't. I couldn't help but look at him while he pushed in and out of me. His green eyes were closed briefly, and then suddenly he spent half the time looking me right in the eye, and the other half at the slippery, wet place where we were joined.

"So good," I cried out, placing one hand between my skull and the headboard when he started rocking me into it. I grabbed his ass with my other hand, like I was trying to urge him into me deeper.

"Fuck, fuck, fuck!" Tristan grunted. He let go of the headboard before lowering his body over mine and pressed his forehead against my own while he thrust faster. His hot breath washed over me as his strokes turned frantic, and then, he tensed and screamed, burying himself to the hilt one last time with trembling muscles.

It took us forever to stop gasping for air with his heavy body draped over mine. I could feel him inside me, throbbing gently.

"That was so good," my mouth heaved out.

He nodded against my shoulder. "That doesn't even begin to cover it."

Later, once we'd both caught our breath, he reached over to his nightstand and opened the drawer to pull out a slim, long box. Rolling us onto our sides, he handed it to me. "I didn't make you a cupcake, but I hope you like it."

Pulling the lid off of the plain, white box, a necklace with a small pendant lay nestled on the velvet inside. It was a crescent moon made out of a row of opals and another row of what looked like small diamonds with a single opal crafted between the curves of the moon. A thin, silver watch chain was slipped through the pendant, and I couldn't help but bite my lip and open my mouth to tell him that it was too much.

"Before you tell me I shouldn't have, I didn't buy

it, okay? It was my grandma's, and it's really old. I saw it a while ago when I was helping my mom sort through her belongings and it reminded me of you, Goldie." His voice lowered before he kissed my collarbone. "You're like my moon. Pretty pointless according to other people, but without you, the world is pretty much over. I wouldn't have any stability, there wouldn't be any cool things like tides; if you broke into a million pieces, you'd kill everything on the planet," he tried to say it with a straight face but he couldn't.

Snorting, I sucked in a harsh breath, looking at my gift. I wanted to cry and he knew it because he kissed my nose and each of my eyebrows tenderly. "I love it, Mag. Thank you so much."

"You're welcome."

I didn't want to ruin the moment, but this felt larger than anything. He'd given me something of his family's, and even though it was proof of a love greater than I could understand, the tiny nugget of curiosity that had always nibbled away at me needed to be answered. "Tristan? Can I ask you something?" He groaned something out that sounded like a bear's growl. "Why did you start talking to me?"

He was quiet, only breathing loudly through his nose. "At the convention?"

"Yeah."

"I don't know," he said in a low voice. A kiss planted itself on the crook of my neck. "You were digging in your butt, and then you were so goofy— I don't know. You made me laugh." He was quiet, but I could sense he was still deliberating with an answer. "I guess I wanted to understand this pretty girl who could make me laugh."

I wormed a hand through his sweat soaked hair, raking my fingers over his scalp. "I'm glad you think I'm funny."

"Kat," he murmured against my ear, taking the box from my hands and placing it on the bed behind him. Tristan moved his hips and hardening cock in me, slowly. "I'll never get tired of laughing at you."

CHAPTER FIFTY-NINE

"I'm gonna cry."

"Be quiet."

He hiccuped. "I'm not kidding. I'm gonna cry."

"Josh, shut up."

"This is a big day," his voice trembled, eyeing Nikki as she made her way down the aisle.

"For Nicole," I whispered into his ear.

"For all of us," he hissed back.

I couldn't disagree with him there.

I'd spent the night with my three best friends, leaving Tristan alone in the room we were sharing during our stay. Since Nikki had opted not to have a bachelorette party, we'd deemed the night our own to say our goodbyes to the single life of Nicole Jonasson, She-Who-Hath-Slept-With-Gay-and-Straight-Men-Alike. Zoey had claimed the night before when we huddled in her room that she felt like she was getting married, too. I was nervous and excited, and Josh was just an emotional wreck. Even though it was always Nikki who took care of us emotionally and physically, I likened the feeling to having my own child getting married and starting her own life. I knew it was part of growing up and all, but it was still bittersweet.

It seemed like the last two weeks leading up to Nikki and Calum's wedding had passed in a flash. It was my birthday, and then in no time, we were flying out of Miami to Vegas for the wedding. Now, we were standing in a garden while our resident badass and her dimpled, donkey-sized love waited to exchange rings and promise each other forever.

When I'd first found out that they'd decided to get married in a garden in Las Vegas, I'd laughed. If they wanted to get married in a garden, I could have hooked them up with Tristan's pretty stellar backyard. Later on, he had explained to me that Calum had been pleading his case to have the ceremony done by an Elvis impersonator or on the Treasure Island ship. Nikki wanted to do it in Las Vegas just because. So, they compromised on a garden not too far from the Strip after extensive debating. Mag and I laughed and agreed we'd totally do either the Elvis impersonator or the ship before the garden wedding, but to each his own.

Zoey was the first one to burst into tears during the ceremony; she dropped her bouquet of flowers on the floor and covered her face with her hands. She murmured something that sounded strangely like, "So beautiful," but with Zoey you could never know. She could have been referring to Calum's sister sitting in the front row.

Josh was next, sobbing through the second half and earning a middle finger from Nikki in the covert way of an eyebrow scratch.

I was the only one who didn't burst into tears. Looking at my closest friend and seeing the elation on her face, and then catching the same emotion reflected in her soon-to-be husband's eyes made me so happy. It wasn't until the very end when they were exchanging rings that one fat teardrop escaped, leading a short and suicidal life halfway down my cheek before I caught it. Looking up then, I spotted Tristan's green eyes on me, a small smile crossing his face.

He stood directly to the right of Calum since he was the best man, but each time I'd look up to see what he was doing, I found him staring in my direction. Over the course of the last three days, we had only seen each other on the flight since we had seats next to each other. In the days prior to that, I saw him every other day. Half of our time together was spent naked, which was absolutely fucking wonderful if those words alone were enough to describe it.

I tried to push the memory out of my brain when Zoey's shoulders started twitching with tears again right before the end.

"You may now kiss the bride," signaled for Calum's loud family to burst into cheers.

After what I considered to be the Clash of the Tongues in the form of Calum and Nicole's mouths meeting for the first time as a married entity, we all screamed in joy. Tristan caught my wrist as we followed the newlyweds down the aisle, making our way to the small reception hall across the compound. He wrapped a heavy arm over my shoulders, pulling me in close to his side. His hand hung over my collarbone, lazily brushing his fingertips across the fine chain of the necklace he'd given me for my birthday.

"I think you're one of the most beautiful things I've ever seen," he said as we walked.

I snickered and tilted my head to look him in the eye. It was a testament to my love that I didn't nut-punch him right then. "I'm pretty sure you should only tell someone that they *are* the most beautiful thing you've ever seen. One *of* the most isn't exactly a compliment."

He squeezed me tight, laughing. "The only other person just as beautiful as you is—," he let the words hang in the air. "My mom," the asshole had the nerve to snort. "This girl I used to like on those Spanish soaps is my number three."

I couldn't help but laugh in response to his admission. "You're lucky it's your mom, jackass," I said, elbowing him in the ribs. "I'll give you your number three since I'm sure she was probably the first girl you jerked off to."

"She was!" Tristan was laughing hysterically, pulling me tighter and tighter against him with each heave of his chest. "So many times, you have no idea."

"Oh, lord." I shook my head, imagining a young Tristan sitting in front of his television wanking off.

His laughs died down as we walked into the reception hall, stopping right at the entrance. His pretty face was flushed from amusement. "If I had to choose between saving your life or hers, I would choose you."

"Oh, thank you so much, Mag." I slapped his chest with the back of my hand, rolling my eyes at the same time. "Such an honor."

He grinned in amusement, stooping his head low so that we were eye to eye. "I love you so much, you know that?" He kissed my lips chastely. "I'll always choose you."

"Oh, yeah?" I asked him in a teasing voice, nuzzling my forehead to the smooth edge of his jaw.

"Yeah." He snickered, pressing his dry lips to mine. "You're the best thing in my life."

Josh walked past us right then, fanning his eyes and letting out an exasperated sigh. "Get a room."

Pressing up onto the tips of my toes, I kissed the man in front of me one more time, mouths closed and warm on each other. Despite how much I enjoyed having his tongue battling mine, there was something so intimate and sweet about the slow, sensual kisses with our tongues in their respective mouths, that made my toes curl. It was gentle and loving, just like Tristan. "We should go inside before they come embarrass us," I warned him, pulling away to tug on his hand.

He nodded, following behind me with a sly smile.

The next two hours went by in hyper speed. There was a toast by Zoey, in which she drunkenly blurted out, "To Calum and Nicole Burro." Three-fourths of the audience, including Calum's family, were well aware of everything, so it wasn't a big deal, but the others who didn't know just looked on in confusion and chalked it up to Zoey blabbering because she was wasted.

Tristan followed up with another toast, thankfully a sober one. "As many of you know, Calum and I have been friends almost our entire lives. We met in second grade when he tried to save me from getting beaten up for my lunch money by a fifth grader, but instead, he got both of us beat up. We spent the next four years getting our asses kicked because neither one of us seemed to take into consideration that if only one of us got beaten up, the other could still buy lunch to share. After Calum started getting a lot bigger in middle school and I wasn't, he made sure no one picked on me. He could've left me to fend for myself, but he didn't. As we've gotten older, but not necessarily much wiser, we've kept that mentality between the two of us. Our friendship turned into something different, and Cal became the brother I never had. Wherever one of us went, the other one followed, and now, I'm glad he's found someone else in his life to watch over and protect. Someone a lot better looking than I am, who can talk him out of doing stupid stuff instead of egging him on." It was then that I stopped paying attention because he started wiping at his eyes, smiling in the direction of his best friend.

Was it wrong that I wanted to mount him when he was in tears? Maybe, but I was so zoned out and focused on his facial expressions that I couldn't absorb the rest of his speech. I didn't even know he was done until he'd taken his seat next to me afterward.

"You are so sweet," I leaned into his ear, whispering. Sliding my hand across my lap and onto his, I squeezed the firm muscles of his thigh. "You should cry tears of joy more often."

Tristan laughed, the smooth sound ringing in my ears while he put his hand over mine. "What my Kitty wants, my Kitty gets," he teased with my dad's nickname for me. Immediately after meeting Frank, he'd added that name to his repertoire. Annoying, but typical.

I rolled my eyes and bumped my shoulder against his.

The remainder of the reception was spent between the dance floor and the table where the cake was. Josh and I did everything from the running man to the sprinkler around Nicole in her beautiful cream wedding dress. The bitch knew better than to even think about putting on a white dress. I think she had a fear of getting struck by lightning if she did it, since God knew there wasn't any part of that girl that could have been considered even marginally virginal. Tristan stayed seated, moving between the tables Calum's family sat at and ours on the occasion that I sat down to take a quick water break between songs.

"Having fun?" he asked, coming up to me while I sat at the table for a moment.

I nodded and smiled because I was having a really good time. I was with the people I loved the most, besides my dad of course, and it was impossible to not soak in the abundance of joy and excitement that Nikki and Calum were radiating. "Are you?"

"Oh, yeah, I'm having a blast sitting over there watching Cal's cousins drool over you." He chuckled.

I turned around to look in the direction where Calum's loud-ass family was sitting and pretended to squint. "Was it the cute ones?"

Tristan laughed and pinched my ass. "Yeah, they're just your type. One is hitting forty, and the other one is close to your dad's age."

"Shut up." I snorted, turning back to face him.

He grinned down at me for a moment before wrapping his arms around me, pulling me into him. I took a long and deep inhale against his chest, taking in the faint smell of his cologne. His nose brushed against the top of my hair, which was now a sweaty and, more than likely, stinky mess. "You smell like oranges and salt."

"Salt has a smell?"

His answer was interrupted by the sudden stop in the music through the hall. Calum and Nikki stood in the middle of the floor, looking all too eager to get out of there and braid each other's privates together. "We're leaving!" Nicole announced, making her way toward the table where her dad and aunts sat. I pulled away from Tristan, squeezed his wrist, and then made my way over to Zoey and Josh who were waiting patiently to say their goodbyes to Nikki.

Zoey looped her arm through mine, resting her head on my shoulder. "I'm so happy that it makes me sad," she admitted.

Josh looked over at me from his spot on the other side of Zoey with wide eyes. We were both all too familiar with the random, senseless shit that came out of her mouth when she drank. Trading smirks with each other, we waited another two minutes before Nikki made her way to us while hiking up her dress. Nicole Jonasson, the Ballbuster of Miami, was glassy-eyed and beaming. It was kind of scary, like the calm before the storm, but I pushed the thought out of my head.

"I'll call you guys as soon as I get back," she told us. They were leaving on a red-eye to Hawaii for their honeymoon.

We all nodded in synchronization, maybe doubting the strength in our voices as a whole, but I'd never know for sure. "Have fun. I love you, Nik," I broke the silence, extending my arms out so the giant of a woman could give me a hug. She squeezed me so tight my boobs hurt, and repeated my words to me.

I took in her face and that of Zoey and Josh while they said bye in their own ways. Calum stood back, talking to Tristan, and smiling like he'd won the lottery or something. Our tight little circle had expanded and warped into a larger one so quickly it kind of took my breath away, but I knew it was life.

I knew better than anyone that life was unexpected and fast, and that you couldn't plan for anything. I mean, everything really did happen for a reason, even if it didn't make any sense. How different would our lives have been if Nikki hadn't gotten those passes to the AFA's porn convention all those months ago? We'd probably still be sitting on her couch talking about Calum's gigantic dick and going out all the time. Happy, but not to our fullest potential.

Five minutes later, the newlyweds were gone and we all stood outside trying to catch cabs back to our hotels. Tristan and I rode along with Tweedledee and Tweedledum after they changed out of their clothes, wishing them a goodnight while they headed out of the lobby to hit up a club nearby while we walked back to the hotel room with our fingers loosely linked. He smiled at me really goofily when we made our way in, and then again when he followed me into the bathroom after I told him I was going to shower.

He peeled his clothes off faster than I did, turning on the water and slipping in while I was still trying to undress, but really, I was too busy swallowing up the smooth lines of his body. Once I'd taken off the strapless, plum bridesmaid dress and underwear, I got into the large shower with him. There should be something said about Tristan all wet. He was already the most handsome man I'd ever seen fully clothed, but naked? There was no comparison for good looks when he had water dripping from every inch of his creamy skin.

He moved over to let me wash my hair, stroking the tips of his fingers across my neck while I lathered it, and then trailing them down my spine when I rinsed the shampoo off. He washed my back for me with just the palms of his hands and some of the liquid soap the hotel provided. I washed his back for him after he'd done mine, but I dipped my fingers to press into the tight curve of his ass when I got the chance.

"I'm going to start charging you."

"For what?"

"For touching my ass all the time."

My head fell back when I laughed in response. "Oh, please."

He smiled at me, those perfect white teeth coming

out to say hi. "I'll meet you out there after you finish."

My shower was over a minute later, but he was already slipping out of the bathroom, so I took my time drying off and brushing my teeth before putting on my underwear and sports bra to sleep. I found him sprawled on top of the covers, long legs wide while flipping through channels using the remote. He winked at me and patted the spot right next to him. I climbed on, wobbling over the mattress until I could snuggle against his side.

I didn't say anything while he kept changing the channels until suddenly, a silhouette of a girl riding a guy popped up on the large, flat screen television. The sound of moans filtered through the speakers.

"Well, this is awkward." I snickered, trying my best not to think about Robby Lingus, but it was impossible. Just two months before, Tristan had been — yeah, I definitely didn't want to think about it.

"Sorry," he apologized discreetly, which only made me feel like shit. I knew what I was getting into. I'd known who he was. What he did. I couldn't change it, but I also really shouldn't hold it against him.

"It's fine," I said, reaching over to place my palm on the inside of his thigh.

Tristan placed his hand over mine, squeezing it. "You know you're the best, right?"

"Nah, you are."

He shifted back on the bed so that his back was

resting on the headboard. "I am, but you are too," he chuckled. "Come here." He patted the hand resting on his thigh, trying to get me to sit on his lap. I made a big show about getting up and straddling him, tucking my legs under me with my butt on the middle of his thighs. Those large hands that I loved cupped my cheeks and brought my face so close to his I could smell the toothpaste on his breath.

"I missed you," he said, taking my bottom lip between his, "the last few days." Then he took my top lip, sucking it lightly.

I shivered, pushing my chest against his, feeling him hard and insistent against my stomach. "I missed you, too," I croaked out when he started kissing my cheeks and jaw.

"Did you like the wedding?" he asked me, earning a gurgling noise of response when he started sucking on the thin skin of my neck.

His long index fingers dipped into the material of my bra, pulling it down just an inch to reveal the tops of my breasts. "Yeah, why?"

"Just wondering," he said, planting a warm kiss on the exposed skin. He tugged down, revealing more skin. "I have something important to ask you."

"Shoot," I gritted out when he kissed me right below where he had a moment before.

Tristan slipped his hands around my lower back and tugged me forward on his lap just the right way so that I could feel him hard beneath me. "Would you have chosen the Elvis or the ship if it were your wedding?"

Another stupid noise came out of my throat when he lifted his hips up just slightly. I really wanted to focus, but I couldn't. "What?"

"Elvis?" He tugged down at the material even more, enough so that the deep pink of my nipples showed. "Or the ship?"

I gasped when he kissed and then dragged his tongue across the edge of my bra. "Um, Elvis."

He stopped for just a brief second, and then bucked his hips up once more, his green eyes looking into mine. "Good answer."

His words and question nibbled at me, my subconscious having just enough reasoning to wonder why he would ask me that. Maybe I knew, but I didn't choose to think about it then, instead allowing myself to just feel his warm body under me and in front of me. He nuzzled my neck for the briefest moment, and I had to thank whatever god was listening right then for bringing this man into my life. He sure as fuck wasn't perfect, but at the same time, he was.

What other man would care enough about my feelings the way he did? He was always telling me that he loved me and being sweet, while I returned the gesture afterward. Just like when I'd been dealing with keeping my emotions closed off from him to avoid attaching myself, which obviously hadn't worked very well at all. I realized I was still guarding my words with him, still hesitating with really letting him know that everything he felt about me, I reciprocated even if I wasn't as bold as he was. He'd left me no doubt that he loved me and wanted to be with me, but I was still cautious.

"Mag?" I choked out, trying to think of my words. "I have an, *oh*," he passed his tongue over me again, "important question, too."

"Hmm?" he murmured, not breaking contact with my chest.

"It's not a question, actually." I sucked in a breath. He'd let go of one side of my bra only to tug down the other so roughly I heard some of the stitching snap. He stopped though, looking up at me through long, dark eyelashes. "I just wanted to tell you…" I couldn't help but smile, feeling a little insecure. "Don't laugh, okay?"

He nodded a slight bit, probably worried about what I'd blurt out, but I knew it wasn't bad. I knew it was the truth even in the marrow of my bones.

"You'll always be my favorite person in the world. Always."

EPILOGUE

In the distant… but not too distant future

"Marry me."

It looked like her ears perked up at my words; her whole body tensed up and I thought she stopped breathing.

We were lying on the grass in the backyard. Yoda's two-hundred-and-twenty-pound body was belly-up next to me with Kat on my other side.

"What... uh, what did you just say?" Her voice was high and squeaky.

"Marry me," I repeated, rolling onto my side to look at her.

Kat was on her back with her mouth wide open, her hair a mess of tangles around her head. Those dark brown eyes I'd gotten used to waking up to every morning were darting from me to a tree behind my head. She flushed pink and coughed.

"Are you asking me? Or telling me?" she croaked.

"I'm telling you. Marry me."

She rolled to her side, propping her head up on her elbow. Her face was still pink, but this time her eyes were a little glazed over. "I don't think that's the way it works."

I shrugged in response, smiling so much I knew my face would start hurting soon.

"I don't even get a please or anything?" she asked, trying her best not to smile, but like typical Kat, she couldn't help it.

"Goldie, marry me. Please," I told her gently.

She threw her head back and laughed, her pretty face going from pink to red. "Try again!"

I snorted loudly at her response. There was no doubt that I loved her. Who the hell else would ever make me redo my half-assed proposal?

"Katherine Berger?" I said, lowering my voice.

She batted her eyelashes at me, grinning. "Yes, Tristan King?" she said in an equally low voice that changed in pitch when she started giggling.

"I think I've loved you from the moment you called me a pussy," I said, earning a howl of laughter from Kat. She had tears in her eyes, but I wasn't sure if it was from laughing or from what I was telling her. "You mean more to me than all of my collectible Star Wars figurines times a billion—"

"Only a billion?"

I rolled over, tucking my knees under me so that I could sit up on them. Clasping her face between my hands, I lowered my head while still chuckling. "Times infinity, my sweet little gold digger."

Kat was breathing hard, her warm eyes wide and shiny, but she smiled wickedly. "Go on."

"I love you so much," I told her, kissing the tip of her nose. "Marry me." I kissed her again, pulling away far enough so I could see her face clearly when she responded. I dug blindly into my front pocket to pull out the ring I'd been carrying around for weeks. "Please?"

She scrambled up to her knees faster than I could have ever imagined, not even looking at the ring I was holding out toward her, when she tackled me. I grunted from the impact knocking the wind out of me, but all I could focus on was the look on her face. She was smiling hard, wiping away the tears from her face when she kissed me. Pulling her lips back just a centimeter, she breathed out her answer, "Yes. I will."

ABOUT THE AUTHOR

Mariana Zapata lives in a small town in Colorado with her ball and chain and their two terrors, their Great Danes. When she isn't busy writing, rewriting, or reading, you can usually find her doing something outside.

 @marianazapata_

 marianazapatawrites

www.marianazapata.com

marianazapata@live.com

Made in the USA
Monee, IL
11 October 2021